POOL OF RADIANCE

Again Shal focused her thoughts, staring into the brilliant swirls of blue inside the globe, trying to envision her mentor. In a moment, she saw him.

She sucked in her breath. How could a man have changed so in a matter of days? Ranthor's robes were torn to shreds. His hair was unkempt and wild-looking. And his eyes . . . his eyes were haunted-looking, as if he had seen sights no mortal eye should see.

"Shal, listen carefully. There is little time. I have risked everything to send this message to you. Despite our efforts, the beasts have somehow infiltrated the tower. My old friend is dead . . . murdered. I must warn you to beware of the dragon of bronze. I have done all that I can to diminish its awesome power, but it still thrives. Shal, you must—"

"Ranthor! Look out!" Shal screamed wildly, but her words obviously didn't penetrate through the crystal. A dark figure loomed behind her teacher, and before Shal could do or say any more, it began to slash savagely at him with a long black dagger. . . .

FANTASY ADVENTURE

Pool of Radiance

James M. Ward and Jane Cooper Hong

Cover Art by
CLYDE CALDWELL

TSR, Inc.

POOL OF RADIANCE

Distributed to the book trade in the United States by Random House, Inc. and in Canada by Random House of Canada, Ltd.

Distributed in the United Kingdom by TSR UK Ltd.

Distributed to the toy and hobby trade by regional distributors.

FORGOTTEN REALMS, PRODUCTS OF YOUR IMAGINATION, AD&D, and the TSR logo are trademarks owned by TSR, Inc.

First Printing, November 1989
Printed in the United States of America.
Library of Congress Catalog Card Number: 88-51726

9 8 7 6 5 4 3 2 1

ISBN: 0-88038-735-1

TSR, Inc.
P.O. Box 756
Lake Geneva,
WI 53147 U.S.A.

TSR Ltd.
120 Church End, Cherry Hinton
Cambridge CB1 3LB
United Kingdom

To Dad and Aleta.

—J.C.H.

To my mother. Thanks, Mom, for making me take that typing class. You were right and I was wrong.

—J.M.W.

❦ 1 ❦

Look Into the Crystal

Shal had spent days scouring the markets and traders' shops of Eveningstar and Arabel, the two towns nearest to the keep of her master, the Great Ranthor of Cormyr. The object of her search was a rare Wa herb, which her teacher refused to find for her. When she finally located the component he claimed made "a superlative dust for incendiary spells," she returned to his keep, where she read and reread the Burning Hands spell and tried for several days to master it. By the fourth day, Shal's hands were the only things blazing after repeated attempts to cast the spell.

"Drat!" she cried, hurling her spellbook and herbal components down in disgust, convinced that it was time for her to move on to another profession. Before her eyes, the handful of herbal dust puffed into a sensational blue cloud, and a vision of Ranthor, her teacher, appeared, besieged by a horde of vicious-looking orcs. The pig-faced creatures were armed with murderous weapons, and they were surging toward Ranthor in a wide band, leaving him no avenue of escape.

Blood and drool dripped from their grotesque mouths. Shal could feel herself being caught up in the vision, could smell the orcs' filthy bodies as they pressed closer, jabbing their jagged swords and knives at Ranthor . . . at her. She backed away, but the wall that kept her from backing farther also seemed to stop Ranthor. Fear gripped her like a torturous clamp, making every muscle in her body rigid, unresponsive. Sweat streamed down her face, her back, and her breasts. She could no longer control her own breathing, and she knew she was going to die.

At that moment, Ranthor cast the Burning Hands spell. White-hot jets of flame burst from each of his fingertips, blasting the entire horde of orcs high into the air, incinerating each of the creatures they touched. The handful of orcs that landed on the ground alive proceeded to claw, pull, and scramble away from the wizard as fast as they could go, leaving the smoldering bodies of their companions behind them.

"Nice spell, Burning Hands," said Ranthor with a chuckle. "Comes in handy sometimes."

The blue cloud vanished, and Shal saw the discarded components arranged neatly on top of her spellbook. . . .

That had happened more than three weeks ago, and she had mastered the Burning Hands spell the next day. With that one vision, Ranthor had managed to renew her interest, not only in a spell she had given up on, but also in spell-casting in general. Without a single harsh word, he had provided the insight that allowed her to identify which gesture she was performing incorrectly. Ranthor always seemed to have some way to keep her enthusiastic about magic. With subtle encouragement, he could get her dreaming of moving mountains or defeating the numerous monsters that threatened the people of their sparsely populated region.

Whenever she felt discouraged, her old master would remind her of her great promise. Whenever she grew tired of the rigors of memorizing spells or performing the dozens of routine tasks that made up her day, she would receive a magical message from him, reminding her that promise means nothing without diligence.

At the moment, Shal stood on the grounds of Ranthor's keep, struggling with a Weather Control spell he had encouraged her to try once she had mastered the Burning Hands spell. She faced the wind, just as Ranthor had instructed, and tried to visualize it. Her mind pictured the wind as pale, violet-white wisps of cloudlike material, and she imagined herself collecting the wisps within the exaggerated reach of her gesturing hands and molding them into a flat sheet so thin and so swift-moving that it could slice her enemies in two. Next she envisioned a solid wall of force that would push back her opponents. Then a churning funnel cloud that would suck them into its whirling vortex. Finally she intoned the words to the spell, taking care to match the inflection indicated in the runes she had so painstakingly memorized.

Unfortunately, each time she tried the spell, the results were the same. There was no wall of force . . . not even a good strong gust. There was no cyclone . . . not even a tiny dust devil. There was just a faint *whoosh*, and instantly the wind would pass by and out of her reach.

Tired and discouraged, Shal left the wind to its own devices and went inside the tower. She wished Ranthor were present to give her some of his usual valuable advice and support—some clue, anything. She wished, plain and simple, that he was back from his mission so she could stop worrying about him.

The day after Shal had mastered the Burning Hands spell, the same day Ranthor had suggested she try her hand at Weather Control, her master had departed. Shal had been in Ranthor's spell-casting chamber working on a Lightning spell. She knew she wasn't ready yet to attempt the spell outside. She wanted merely to create one little bolt that would arc between the conductor she had positioned on the crux of Ranthor's casting stand and the copper spike she'd fastened to a nearby shelf of components.

She meditated for a moment to help her mind focus, then traced and retraced with her eyes the path that she wanted the lightning to follow. Finally she lifted her hands and spoke, with all the intensity she could muster, the words of the spell. A crystal orb on a nearby shelf of components began to blaze red, growing steadily. With the final word of the spell still on her tongue, Shal screamed for Ranthor, and immediately the lightning began to pulse about the room, rattling the jars of magical components and sending several crashing to the floor. Her aging master rushed into the chamber as fast as his rheumatism-ridden legs could carry him. In one hand, he held a wand, its tip glowing with a molten fire, and in the other, he held a small bag of sparkling dust, no doubt some powerful weapon he had grabbed to use against whatever horror he found in the spell-casting area.

When he entered the room, he found Shal braced against the wall, an expression of stark terror on her face, pointing at the glowing crystal. He took one look and began to laugh, first a light, whispering snicker, then a full belly laugh. "Shal, my student of three years, do you not yet know that wizards use orbs to contact each other? That is simply my old friend Denlor calling me," Ranthor explained, pointing at the crystal. He breathed a single arcane syllable, and the orb rose into the air and began to float toward Shal. Despite her teacher's amusement, Shal could feel the hairs rise on the back of her neck as the glowing orb drifted closer.

"Pick it up, Shal." Ranthor removed the bronze cone from the center of the three-legged casting stand and pointed at the crux where the three legs met and crossed. "Pick it up," he repeated when she hesitated. "Put it here."

Shal expected nothing less than for her fingers to sizzle the moment they made contact with the blazing crystal ball. She reached out gingerly, turning her head aside so she wouldn't have to watch as her flesh melded to its fiery surface. Much to Shal's surprise, the ball was cold to the touch—icy, in fact—and when she did touch it, she felt her body suddenly awash in fear of a different sort. So chilling was the ball's aura that Shal nearly dropped it before she could place it in the ebony stand.

"Watch, and I'll show you how this is done," said Ranthor, his voice still sounding with a hint of laughter. "Not that you should be playing with crystal balls on your own any time soon, you understand . . ."

He waved his hands over the globe with practiced deliberation, then stepped back with a pleased look on his face as the ball floated to a secure position just a hand's height above the casting stand. "Concentration is the key here, young lady. Concentration, and not letting the crystal ball touch anything before you're completely finished with it.

"Look into the crystal with me. Concentrate. Picture a wizard . . . much like myself, but shorter, stockier, and dressed in red."

Shal closed her eyes to concentrate.

"No! You must look into the crystal. The crystal will project the image, but it needs your help."

Opening her eyes until they were mere slits, Shal stared into the swirling, iridescent red blaze of the globe. Wizard, she thought. Like Ranthor but shorter. She leaned closer. Yes! There was something there—the outline of a robe, the image of a man. . . . Finally it came into clear focus. The man in the globe was obviously a wizard, but he looked nothing like Ranthor. Even with his crippling rheumatism, Ranthor had a commanding presence. His gestures, his meticulously pressed blue robes—everything about him bespoke style. The man in the globe, however, was rumpled, disheveled-looking. He obviously cared little about his appearance. Nonetheless, his smile was warm, and Shal could feel an unusual bond of loyalty flowing between this mage, Denlor, and her master.

"Ranthor, my trusted friend! You must know how glad I am to have reached you."

Shal stared, wide-eyed. Denlor wasn't speaking. Instead, she was somehow *experiencing* his thoughts—the words, as if spoken aloud, and much more than that. She could feel his exhaustion . . . and his panic.

"I would not have called on you, Ranthor, if my need were not great. Every vile beast ever belched up from the Pit is clamoring at the gate to my keep in Phlan. The protective magicks emanating from my tower are steadily weakening. I need your help, old friend. I can't hold out much longer, and there is much more at stake than just my aging bones."

Denlor's desperation washed over Shal. She could hear the sound that had echoed in the mage's brain day after day for untold nights—the din of a thousand unspeakable beasts growling, snarling, slavering, clawing at the walls that kept him and his tower from destruction. Denlor thought of his waning defenses, magical and otherwise, and as he did, his thoughts were Shal's thoughts. She gasped as she realized that she now knew the location of every trap in Denlor's keep, the arcane words that would open or seal every door in his tower, and she sensed the vulnerability of what had once been an impenetrable magical fortress.

"Ranthor, please . . . please help me!" Denlor pleaded imploringly.

Suddenly the image within the globe faded into a swirl of red, and then the sphere returned to its original icy crystal white and nestled gently back into the crux of the ebony tripod.

Shal let out her breath and turned to her master.

"My dear Shal, I'm so sorry," Ranthor began sincerely. "That wasn't any way to introduce you to crystal balls. Please understand that they can bear good news as well as bad. But this time, I'm afraid, the news is bad indeed. I must go immediately to the aid of my friend. I charge you to keep up with your magical studies and watch after this place until I return."

Shal never even had a chance to respond as Ranthor flew from one room to the next with a flurry of gestures, words, and instructions that left her dizzy. Just as she finally recovered the presence of mind to ask if there was anything she could do to help, the mage whisked into his private spell-casting chamber, the door closed with a definitive thud, and she was left standing outside, alone. More than an hour passed before Ranthor emerged, but when he did, Shal was still standing exactly where he had left her.

He paused and faced his apprentice, holding out a yellow, rolled parchment. "Keep this scroll, Shal. Open it only if you have reason to believe I will not return. I must go now to Denlor, to Phlan. May the gods be with you—and with me." Ranthor had whispered a magical command, then vanished into the smoky blue haze of his Teleport spell. . . .

That was the last Shal had seen or heard from her teacher. She knew she wasn't likely to make progress on her Weather Control spells or any other kind of magic until she received some word of reassurance from Ranthor. In the meantime, she realized, there was a tower full of chores that beckoned—wonderful, mindless activities that would serve as distraction from her anxious thoughts.

She decided to tackle a task she had been putting off for days—dusting the countless shelves of magical components in Ranthor's storeroom. A wizard's components, she knew from her training, were almost as important as his spellbooks. Someone had to keep them all in order, and once a wizard reached a certain level, that someone was almost invariably an apprentice.

As Shal entered the storeroom and faced its row after row of shelving, she sighed and began musing to herself. She sometimes wondered why anyone would ever want to become a wizard's apprentice. It seemed a never-ending stream of menial chores and discouraging hours of practice. Somehow she couldn't picture Ranthor ever stumbling over a word, as she frequently did, when he cast a spell. Shal smiled grimly as she tried to imagine Ranthor stooping down to dust shelves. He·must have found some way to bypass the apprentice stage and progress straight to wizard, she thought wryly.

Shal stared at the rows of shelving stretched out before her. It would take hours. The dust hadn't been at all selective about which shelves or components to cover. The fine film of gray powder coated everything, and the spiders had been having a heyday. Shal stood staring for several more seconds, then grabbed a rag and plunged ruefully ahead into the maze of shelving.

As Shal reached the end of a long row of shelves, she wiped her brow and paused, turning to glance at herself in the large viewing mirror that Ranthor used to practice his gestures. Her shoulder-length hair, though matted with perspiration at the ends, was vibrant and silky and shimmered auburn red even in the dull light from the handful of lamps that lit her master's huge laboratory. Her skin was clear and as smooth as polished ivory, and her nose and cheeks were fine and delicate. She couldn't help but know she was attractive—just tall enough to set off her perfectly sculpted petite frame, and just saucy enough in her mannerisms to attract the attention of almost any man she took a fancy to.

From her studies under Ranthor, Shal had learned of the damage that certain powerful magic could do to the caster's skin, hair, and overall vigor. She had discussed the subject with Ranthor on several occasions, expressing some of her fears. Ranthor had chided her for her vanity, but he also reminded her that beauty and magic were not mutually exclusive. "There are times," he had said, "when you *must* use strong magic. There are other times when you can avoid it. But you must never get caught up in your fear of the physical consequences of spell-casting. It will hinder your ability to excel at your chosen profession."

Nonetheless, Shal had still persisted in asking Ranthor about the effects of different spells. She knew that the Burning Hands spell was not one she wanted to use often. The Weather Control spells were not so bad—and, of course, they'd never hurt her at all if she didn't figure out how they worked! She turned her attention back to the dusty shelves, wishing she knew a spell that would make the chore a little less tedious.

She thought about Ranthor, trying once more to picture him as an apprentice dusting shelves. As she did, a thought came to her. Of course! she reasoned. Why didn't I think of it before? Ranthor would never pick up every vial and pouch. He'd use the very first cantrip he ever taught me! And here I thought I was going to be here till dusk!

She turned back to the row where she had left off, located a bit of elk horn dust in her pouch, and sprinkled it on the shelf. Then she whispered three arcane words and shouted, *"Rasal!"* Instantly the vials and components on the rack before her rose several inches from the shelves. As they hung there suspended, she quickly dusted the four tiers in a fraction of the time it would have taken her otherwise.

"Ah, yes, there are advantages to magic," Shal said jubilantly. She moved on to the next rack of shelves and the next, repeating the same cantrip. After cleaning three more racks, she decided to try her hand at doing two at a time.

She concentrated a moment longer this time before incanting the words of the cantrip. To her delight, all of the items on both racks floated from the shelves. As before, she reached out with her dusting cloth, but this time, one of the magical items, a large crystal sphere, began to glow a bright blue. Shal leaped back, startled out of her wits. Instantly all of the components came crashing down with a terrifying clatter—except for the sphere. The sphere proceeded to glow ever brighter, its indigo light blazing like a hot flame, searing Shal's wide-open eyes with its brilliance.

Instinctively she called out to Ranthor for help. But, of course, Ranthor wasn't there. She realized, once she recovered from her initial start, that the glowing blue orb that hung before her was probably carrying a message from Ranthor. After all, blue was his favorite color, and there hadn't been any word from him since he'd left.

Quickly Shal picked up the sphere, whisked it into the next chamber, and placed it on the casting stand. Ranthor's words came back to her: "*Concentration is the key here . . . Concentration, and not letting the ball touch anything before you're completely finished with it.*"

But how had Ranthor raised the crystal to just the right distance above the casting stand? Shal didn't know. Surely her master hadn't used anything as mundane as the Raise Objects cantrip she had been practicing moments ago. . . . It couldn't hurt to try, though, Shal thought. Slowly she waved her hands over the glowing ball as she had seen Ranthor do. Then, concentrating hard, she spoke the words of the cantrip. Moving so slowly that Shal could hardly detect it, the globe rose to a perfect hand's height above the casting stand, just as it had for Ranthor! Again she focused her thoughts, staring into the brilliant swirls of blue, trying to envision her mentor. In a moment, she saw him.

She sucked in her breath. How could a man have changed so in a matter of days? Ranthor's robes were torn to shreds. His hair was unkempt and wild-looking. And his eyes . . . his eyes were haunted-looking, as if he had seen sights no mortal eye should see.

"Shal, listen carefully. There is little time. I have risked everything to send this message to you. Despite our efforts, the beasts have somehow infiltrated the tower. My old friend is dead . . . murdered. I must warn you to beware of the dragon of bronze. I have done all that I can to diminish its awesome power, but it still thrives. Shal, you must—"

"Ranthor! Look out!" Shal screamed wildly, but her words obviously didn't penetrate through the crystal. A dark figure loomed behind her teacher, and before Shal could do or say any more, it began to slash savagely at him with a long black dagger. She could see no face, no features, only that the arm lashing out with the dagger was adorned with a bizarre snake's-head armlet.

"Sha—!" Ranthor's scream ended in a grotesque gurgle, and the crystal ball burst into shards and splinters.

Shal's muscles went limp and she dropped to the floor. "My god! Oh, my god! Ranthor . . ."

Tears formed in her eyes, and she stared absently at her arms. Blood was welling up in a dozen places where fragments of crystal had embedded themselves in her flesh. Shal watched numbly as droplets of blood became engorged and then burst and trickled down her arms. She reached up and touched her face, brushing gently at more splinters lodged there.

"Damn it, Ranthor! Why didn't you teach me more so I could warn you or cast a spell and save you? You should've taught me some way to help you! Damn! You can't leave me like this! Please . . . come back!" In rapid succession, numbness turned to anger, anger to rage, rage to disbelief, and disbelief to depression. Sobs racked Shal's small frame as she continued to sit, clutching her knees to her chest.

"*Keep this scroll, Shal.*"

Shal bolted to a standing position. The voice was her master's, and she had heard it as clearly as if he were standing beside her. Could he still be communicating with her through the crystal? No, the crystal was no more.

"Open it only if you have reason to believe I will not return. . . ."

It was Ranthor's voice once again, and this time Shal realized that he was not speaking to her himself. She remembered him telling her about Magic Mouth spells, which enabled wizards to leave messages in their own voices. What she was hearing, she knew, was from a spell he must have cast before he left. Something she had done, or something that happened, had triggered the voice.

Shal plucked the remaining fragments of crystal from her skin and clothing and hurried to her study area. Her master was no longer with her, but she could still observe his wishes.

There, on her study table where she had left it, was the scroll, a blue aura shimmering around it. Her hand trembled violently as she reached for the scroll. She didn't want to read it, knowing that to do so was to admit that Ranthor was dead. Finally she clenched her teeth and picked up the carefully tied piece of parchment. As Shal unfastened the silk tie, the blue aura dispersed. She knew that if someone else had tried to open the scroll, his hand would have burned to cinders when he violated the magical seal. She placed one of her spellbooks on the top of the unfurled scroll and one at the bottom and sat down to read it.

Ranthor's script was bold and fluid. He had always chided Shal for her sloppy penmanship, and as she recognized for the first time the full beauty of Ranthor's writing, Shal vowed that she would work to improve her own.

My dearest Apprentice, Shal Bal of Cormyr,

I cannot know the exact circumstances that bring you to read this, only that, somehow, I have been taken from you and from the Realms we walked together as teacher and student. You can do nothing for me, except to follow my instructions one last time.

Go now to my personal chambers. The door will open at your bidding when you speak, with the full authority of magical command that I have taught you, the word "Halcyon."

Use wisely the magical legacy and treasures you find within those walls. I know you can surpass me and become a great spell-caster—if that is your most sincere desire.

You have my eternal love. May the gods be with you.

Ranthor

Shal sat for a moment, dazed, staring at the letter. She read it through again, then cried aloud, "I don't want your treasures, Ranthor! What kind of a ghoul do you think I am?" She was about to crumple the scroll and throw it across the room, when the center of the parchment began to smoke. A pale yellow flame licked up, burning an ever-widening circle in the paper. Shal quickly grabbed her spellbooks from the desk before they, too, were caught in the magical blaze. The fire stopped as suddenly as it had begun, leaving no damage whatsoever to her desk and not even a trace of the scroll Shal had just read.

Shal wanted to scream out, but the words from the scroll prompted her to action: "*Go now to my personal chambers. . . .*" Shal swallowed hard, raised herself to her feet, and walked purposefully to the door of Ranthor's quarters. Straightening her shoulders, she held her head high and cried, "*Halcyon!*" The great oak doors swung open at her command, and she walked in, her eyes wide, knowing that this room contained her master's most cherished personal items and that he was entrusting all he had left therein to her.

She definitely did not expect, however, the stamping, snorting bluish-white stallion that stood proudly in the center of the room. "*A magical steed for a magical journey.*" Shal was startled once again by the sound of Ranthor's voice, no doubt the product of another spell cast before he left for Phlan. "*Trust his warnings and you won't go wrong. I summoned this steed, my trusted familiar, when I was your age. Cerulean has served me well, and so he will serve you.*"

Shal had seen Ranthor riding the big white horse, but it had never occurred to her that the animal was anything other than just a horse. Shal had talked with Ranthor about familiars, intelligent animal companions many mages relied on for character judgments, a word of advice, or a second set of eyes during times of danger. Ranthor had said Shal would know when it was her time to summon a familiar, that the desire for trustworthy companionship grows stronger as a mage becomes more engrossed in his or her craft. At the time, Shal had taken that as one of Ranthor's many gentle nudges to work harder at her magic.

Shal gingerly held her hand out toward the obviously high-strung horse, then sighed in relief as he relaxed, whuffled quietly, and nuzzled her hand. Next Cerulean nudged Shal's shoulder and walked toward the back of the room. Shal followed him to a huge onyx table. Running her hands over its shiny black surface, she stared in awe at the array of magical items spread before her. She recognized two potions of healing that she had helped

Ranthor collect ingredients for and the Wand of Wonder she had often seen in her master's hand. There were also a small square of shimmering indigo velvet, a ring, and a straight rosewood staff that stood taller than Shal.

"I wish I could be here in person to guide you, Shal, but you must learn your craft by yourself." Ranthor's voice, as preserved by his spell, was soft and gentle. She could sense his regret. *"The items assembled before you are functional and powerful. They will aid you until you mature in your own spell-casting ability. The potions, of course, you already know how to use. The Wand of Wonder is simply pointed at a target in a time of need, while you express the need in the tongue of the arcane. But I must caution you: Do not use the wand unless you have no alternative. Its effects are always wondrous, as the name implies, but they are random, which can sometimes be dangerous. The Cloth of Many Pockets I have filled with everything you might need for a journey."*

"Everything I might need? In this?" Shal lifted the small square of velvet and unfolded it—again and again and again. Soon the blue cloth was spread over the entire table. Dozens of pockets covered its surface.

"Simply tell the cloth what you need. As long as it's one of the things on the list you'll find in the top right corner pocket, you'll find it simply by reaching your hand into any one of the pockets. Try it. Say 'Feed for my horse,' and reach into any pocket." Ranthor's voice paused.

Shal felt as if she were being watched. " 'Feed for my horse,' " she said self-consciously. Even after being told what would happen, Shal could hardly believe it when she reached into a pocket and removed a sack of oats and a feed bag. The cloth was an incredible resource, worth many thousands of gold pieces on the open market.

"Now pick up the staff." The voice was again Ranthor's, but this time it seemed to be coming from the other side of the room. He must have left yet another message pre-

served with a spell. Some day, Shal vowed, she would learn the spell Ranthor had used to communicate his final wishes. The voice went on: "*This is the Staff of Power. Look carefully, and you will see many runes etched along its length.*"

Shal hefted the staff, admiring its workmanship. It was much lighter than it appeared, and it was perfectly balanced, a splendid weapon even if it had no magic. The lower portion of the staff was polished to a smooth finish and tapered to an end just blunt and thick enough to support the weight of someone using it for a walking staff, but sharp enough to use as a weapon if need be. The rest of the staff, from a point about a foot off the ground to the large, perfectly smooth wooden ball that capped its end, was ringed with the carved figures of each of the benevolent gods of the Realms. As Ranthor had noted, the surfaces between the carvings were covered with ornately etched runes.

Ranthor's voice continued its explanation. "*The runes are now just so much poetry, but speak the same word you used to open my chamber door and the staff will be covered with the magical script I have taught you to decipher. Study these writings. They are the command words you will need to make this tremendous weapon serve you. I received the staff from a wizard friend who has passed from this plain, so unfortunately there is no way of knowing how many magical charges it retains. Therefore, do not squander its power. Keep the Staff of Power in the Cloth of Many Pockets until you are forced to use it. I advise you not to use the staff in front of strangers unless you plan on killing them, or you are willing to trust them with your life. Many a young mage has lost his life as a result of displaying such power to newfound friends.*"

Shal felt a chill pass through her body. She had never had reason to kill anyone. Somehow, though, as she heard Ranthor's voice speaking of killing, she felt a deep rage rising up inside her. What moments ago had been senseless anger directed at herself, at Ranthor, and at the world at large was growing into a directed fury against whoever, or whatever, had taken Ranthor from her. Nothing she could do would bring her master back, but she vowed to avenge him. She owed Ranthor that and more.

The voice continued. *"I have one more thing to show you, Shal. Pick up the ring and place it on the middle finger of your right hand. Say nothing and do nothing further until I have finished."*

Shal was startled by a sudden sternness in Ranthor's voice. She placed the ring on her finger, marveling at its perfection and the way it fit—almost as if it had been made for her hand.

"You now wear on your hand a Ring of Three Wishes. You have studied wishing lore, so I'm sure you understand how great a force you have at your disposal. Use it only at times of greatest need. And one more caution. Don't even think of wishing me back."

Her master had read her mind, even in death.

"Though the ring is powerful enough to accomplish even that, I am now where fate and the gods would have me. I lived many years and am fully prepared for what awaits me in death. You must now use the ring and all else I have given you for your own good."

Shal bit her lip. She could feel the tears starting to well up again.

"Weep not for me." Ranthor's voice was now directly in front of her. She could almost imagine his warm hand grasping her shoulder. *"My life was full, especially these last three years that you were with me. May yours be as much and more. Farewell, Shal Bal of Cormyr."*

Shal knew that she had heard her master's voice for the last time. She thought back to how she had come to

JAMES M. WARD AND JANE COOPER HONG

study under the great wizard. Her family—her father, her mother, and brothers—were all sell-swords. Shal was quite small and slightly built, to the point that wielding even a short sword was difficult for her, not to mention trudging the countryside decked out in pounds of chain mail and other battle gear. There had never been any magic-users in their family, and her parents had no reason to suspect that their daughter should have any talent in that area, but when Shal turned sixteen, they heard of the proclamations announcing that the great Ranthor of Cormyr was interviewing for an apprentice, and they sent Shal.

She had watched transfixed as a young man before her had caused a cloth to ignite by speaking a word. A young woman had made a pitcher rise into the air and pour a drink for the wizard. Shal had felt foolish and inept. She couldn't even perform a simple shell trick, let alone true magic. Her parents had admonished her, "Be honest and promise diligence at your studies," and that is what she had done. When Ranthor asked her what magic she had studied, she wanted to run away and hide, but she'd said with all the courage she could muster, "None, sir." When he asked her what purse her parents had brought to pay for her education, she wanted to bolt from his presence. They had sent nothing with her. She stammered a response. "It—it was billed as—as an apprenticeship. They—I thought my labor would pay."

"And it will," Ranthor had said simply. It was not until much later that Shal learned that most apprentice mages pay enormous sums for their educations, especially when they study under a wizard of Ranthor's stature. She also learned, as she came to know other young apprentices, that many youthful mages were veritable slaves to their masters, yet Ranthor never expected more of her than the performance of routine chores—and above all, diligence at her studies.

Shal stared down at the onyx table, her eyes taking in the many things Ranthor had left her. Suddenly Cerulean nudged her shoulder with his muzzle. He pushed the sack of oats to the floor and quickly began to rifle the bag. "Poor thing. I suppose even magic steeds have to eat." She poured some oats into the feed bag and held it out to the horse. Instead of eating greedily as Shal thought he would, the horse pressed his head hard against her back and pushed her toward the doorway.

"Oats aren't good enough for you, or are you just being friendly in some odd way?" Shal asked, amused at the animal's gesture.

Naturally I like oats, but I don't really need them. After all, I am magical, you know.

The mental communication from the horse took Shal completely by surprise. The last thing she had expected was a response. She'd lived around magic for three years and had seen many unusual things. In the back of her mind, she even knew that familiars communicated somehow with their masters, but she had never experienced the mental barrage of telepathy—or taken part in a conversation, telepathic or otherwise—with a horse. She found it more than a little unnerving.

It's you who needs to eat. You're planning to go to Phlan, aren't you?

Shal looked at Cerulean quizzically. As if mental communication wasn't jarring enough, he "thought" with the pronounced accent of someone from the Eastern Realms. Shal responded aloud. "I've been thinking about it. Do you read minds, too?"

No, but I'm far from stupid, and I'm not afraid to express my ideas. The horse raised its head a little with that thought. *I just assume that you will be wanting to dispatch whoever or whatever killed our master.*

"*Our* master? I'd rather you didn't phrase it exactly that way. It makes me sound like I'm a horse."

My apologies. How about if I call you Mistress from now on?

"Fine. So, what do you do when I'm not riding you?"

Sometimes our mas—uh, Ranthor—would make me climb in one of the pockets of that cloth. Cerulean angled his head in the direction of the table, where the indigo cloth still lay spread out. *I don't much care for that, actually. It's dark in there—pitch black, in fact. As long as there's plenty of room, I prefer to just vanish and walk around.*

"Really?" Shal asked. "And what if there's not plenty of room?"

Then I just wait outside—you know, invisible. As long as no one runs into me, it works out fine. But we can discuss all that en route to the kitchen. You really should eat, Mistress. And then we need to make travel plans for our trip to Phlan.

Shal shook her head. She didn't know what startled her more—the fact that the horse could communicate or that its communication was so decisive. She wondered for a moment how Ranthor had interacted with Cerulean. Whenever Shal had suggested that Ranthor had been working too hard and should eat, he would all but shoo her away. She couldn't imagine Ranthor taking instructions from a horse. She looked wistfully toward the last place from which she had heard Ranthor's voice. Although she expected no answer, she still asked the question: "Ranthor, you said this horse served you well. You didn't say it had rather firm opinions about being left in the dark, or that it stood around outside waiting for someone to run into it. Where's my 'magic steed' instruction booklet, Ranthor? Aren't you the one who thought of everything?"

Well, if you're going to be that way about it. . . . Cerulean's eyes assumed a hurt look, and he stomped out of the room and vanished.

"Cerulean, come back here!" Shal called out to the thin air, feeling rather foolish. "I just haven't got the hang of this yet."

You mean you'll eat?

"Yes, I'll eat. I'll meet you in the kitchen." Shal walked down the corridor, fully expecting at any moment to bump into an invisible horse, but when she reached the kitchen, Cerulean was already there. He was quite visible again.

Shal cut herself two pieces of goat's cheese and bread and poured herself half a flagon of mineral water. She took a bite of the sandwich and then raised the flagon in her right hand and held it up toward Cerulean. "To Ranthor, to magical horses, and to magical journeys! May the gods be with us, Cerulean!"

Cerulean nodded his head and whinnied softly. *To Ranthor and the past. To you, Mistress, and to the future.*

Shal finished her simple dinner with an apple, which she shared with Cerulean. After tidying up, she packed, putting everything she thought she could use in the Cloth of Many Pockets and adding a few more things in Cerulean's saddlebags. Then she went through the entire keep, magically sealing doorways, rooms, and passages with the command words Ranthor had taught her. Spells of protection had been one of Ranthor's specialties, and Shal knew as she stood at the outer gate of the keep that nothing short of a god could enter before she returned.

"Not bad for an apprentice—right, Cerulean?" The big stallion laid its head on her shoulder and looked back at the keep. After a last brief moment of remembering, Shal turned, mounted Cerulean, and resolved to make Ranthor proud of her on this, her first true adventure. "To Phlan, big fellow. Let's go!"

Cerulean galloped like no horse Shal had ever ridden. The movements of the stallion's huge body were so fluid that Shal almost felt as if she were flying. She rode for miles at an incredible pace, and Cerulean never tired.

Shal took advantage of the smooth ride to study her new magical tools and learn the command words written on the Staff of Power. Before she knew it, the sun was setting. "Well done, Cerulean! Let's stop and rest."

Shal started to go about the motions of setting up camp as she'd seen her brothers do when she was younger. She kept her riding gloves on to protect her hands as she gathered wood and kindling. There was no need to struggle with flint and steel to start the fire, either. Instead, she used a simple cantrip Ranthor had taught her. As the fire began to blaze, Shal stood back and proudly admired her handiwork. She unrolled her bedding and was about to heat a piece of jerky for dinner when Cerulean began to snort and stamp. "Is something wrong?" Shal whispered, wondering if she was about to encounter intruders.

Aren't you going to take care of the beast that brought you? Do you think I want to carry these saddlebags all night? Or chew on this hunk of metal in my dreams?

"Oh, I'm sorry!" Immediately Shal began to remove the offending tack. Unstrapping Cerulean's bridle and removing his bit was easy. Undoing the stiff saddle harness wasn't even too taxing. But when Shal started to lift the saddle and packs off Cerulean's back, she almost buckled under the weight.

"Oof! This is heavy! I wish I were stronger!" And with her last words, she let out a gasp.

The magic of the Ring of Three Wishes worked instantly. Shal could feel herself growing larger, stronger. The saddle became like a feather in her hands. Her once perfectly fitted riding gear bound her flesh so tightly that the seams split. She flung the saddle to the ground with a force her petite body had never been capable of and watched in horror as her delicate hands and slender arms grew into what she perceived as huge, brawny appendages. She watched her feet, calves, and thighs expand in a similar fashion, and she could feel a sheath of muscled flesh building on her once trim stomach.

"No!" she screamed. "No!" She knew enough about wishing lore to know that she had made the cardinal mistake of wishers. She had wished carelessly. "Look at me! I'm a monster! I'm huge!" she cried. Shal fell to her knees, terrified and disgusted by what she had done. She knew the change was permanent unless she used another wish.

Cerulean tried desperately to break into her thoughts. Her terror and revulsion registered on his brain like a stabbing knife. The image projected by Shal was of a grotesque parody of a human female, distorted almost beyond recognition by musculature and sinews. The reality was quite different. Cerulean could perceive human beauty. He certainly had a sense of what Ranthor found attractive in women. Shal had indeed changed as a result of the wish; she was considerably larger than she had been. But the basic beauty of her features and the proportion of her figure had not changed. If she was unattractive, it was only to someone who could not find beauty in a large woman. Her appearance was marred only by the ripped, ill-fitting clothing that still managed to hold a few parts of her expanded figure captive.

But Shal was oblivious to Cerulean's mental shouts. She stared at the big calves that protruded from where her ankles had been, and at her forearms, where they tested the limits of the wrist cuffs. She could only imagine what her face must look like.

Her immediate thought was to wish herself back to her former size. But as much as she wanted to make that wish, she shook her head resolutely. No, Ranthor had entrusted his entire magical legacy to her. It was not to be wasted. Shal's one goal was to make him proud. She had made a gross mistake, and she must live with it. The ring's magic must be preserved for her quest to avenge her master's murder.

"What a fool I am! I can't even trust myself with a simple ring!" she chastised herself. Shal reached for the ring to pull it off, but her hands had grown much larger than before and the ring wouldn't budge. "Damn! Instead of wishing to be strong, I could at least have wished that me and my belongings were in Phlan—"

"No!" Shal screamed as she felt the ring's magic working once more. Before she could even blink, she found herself kneeling on the planks of a long wooden dock, facing the twilight silhouette of a city she had never seen but knew without a doubt was Phlan. Her bedroll, her saddle, and Cerulean were beside her. The horror of her stupidity bludgeoned her like a battle-axe, and she fell prostrate on the dock and wept, beating her fists against the planks with each rage-filled sob.

Passersby gawked at the huge but comely woman and her seemingly shrunken leather clothing, but none moved closer or offered assistance. They could see a great war-horse standing protectively by the woman's side, and if that wasn't enough, the big woman was rattling the two-inch-thick boards of the dock with every blow of her massive fists. If the woman wanted to cry in public, there were few if any who would question her or try to stop her.

♣ 2 ♣

The Test

Two wagons bumped and jolted their way along the deeply rutted road. "Yo! Tarl!" Brother Donal called down from the head wagon. "Can you interrupt your hammer-throwing long enough to lead the horses up out of these ruts?"

"No problem, Brother Donal," answered Tarl. The young cleric hurried ahead of the first wagon to retrieve the war hammer he had just launched at an unfortunate sapling, and then he jogged back to the lead draft horse. Tarl pulled gently but firmly on the horse's bridle, guiding the animal to the side of the narrow roadway where the path was a little smoother. The horses pulling the second wagon followed suit, stepping into line behind the first. Tarl continued to walk just ahead of the front wagon, knowing that they would soon reach the point where they must leave the pass through the foothills of the Dragonspine Mountains and follow the legendary Stojanow River south into Phlan.

Brother Anton, who had been riding beside Brother Donal, jumped down to join Tarl. "Your practice is comin' along well. Unless my eyes deceive me, you haven't missed your mark in a dozen throws."

An unabashed grin broke out on Tarl's face, and he muttered an embarrassed thank-you as the giant of a man reached his side. Like Tarl and the other ten men journeying together to Phlan, Anton was a warrior cleric in a sect that worshiped Tyr, the Even-Handed, God of

Justice and War. Anton's weapon of choice was the throwing hammer. He could split a good-sized tree—or a good-sized man—with one well-aimed throw.

"Now, don't go gettin' puffed up from a word o' praise," said Anton sternly. "What I was wantin' to tell you is that you're doin' just fine with that toy hammer of yours. Fact is, you don't even have to think about it anymore." The big man mimicked a limp-wristed throw—"Whoosh, thunk, bull's-eye . . . every throw. It's time now for you to learn to put your back into it, lad. Get yourself a real hammer and start practicin' a man's throw."

Anton reached under his tunic and pulled from his belt a hammer that was easily twice the size of Tarl's.

Tarl shook his head from side to side. "But that's a smith's hammer. It's for fixing armor, not fighting."

Anton stiff-armed Tarl to the ground. "Foolish whelp! Do ya think I don't know what kind of hammer this is? Do ya think you'll always have your choice of weapons in a fight?" Anton held the hammer down to Tarl, and when Tarl grabbed hold, Anton jerked him to his feet with an effortless tug. "You'd better get used to usin' anything ya can get your hands on as a weapon—I don't care if it's a smith's hammer or a hunk o' wood. Now, start throwin'. Start shatterin' a bit of this countryside instead o' just dentin' it."

Tarl stared dumbly at the hammer for a moment, feeling its weight and its awkward balance as he shifted it in his hand.

"One more thing, Tarl. I want you to make every fifth throw lyin' on either your back or your belly. Many's the time I had to take an enemy down after bein' decked myself," Anton said with a grimace of recollection.

Tarl seriously doubted that the huge Anton had ever been knocked down in battle, but his stinging backside was an effective reminder that he was in no position to argue the point. Besides, Tarl had no business even thinking about arguing with a senior brother in the order, and anyhow, he knew Anton was right. Tarl shifted the heavy hammer back and forth in his hand several times, then raised it and stepped into his first throw. The big hammer spiraled crookedly through the air and fell to the ground a good six feet short of the tree Tarl was aiming at. Tarl jogged past the lead wagon to where the hammer had landed. Anton fell in step alongside the head wagon and left Tarl to his throwing.

It had been nearly two years since Tarl's eighteenth birthday, when he had taken his clerical vows in the Order of Tyr. He had been traveling with these eleven brothers in the faith for only eight weeks, but he believed he had learned more in that short time than he had in his previous twenty-two months at the temple in Vaasa.

Even on the road, Tarl continued to be tutored in his studies and devotionals, and the combat training was more intensive than anything to which he had previously been exposed. Brother Donal had drilled Tarl in techniques for guarding the flanks and rear when fighting with allies. Brother Sontag had taught him the use of the ball and chain, a grisly weapon almost as dangerous to use in practice as in battle. Tarl had received a nasty blow to the head in the middle of one of his own practice swings that left him with the utmost respect for Brother Sontag and his chosen weapon, and a headache as well. Even before today's instruction, Brother Anton had worked with Tarl for many days, in his usual gruff but effective manner, drilling him on the use of the shield as both a defensive and offensive weapon.

Tarl was anxious to test his new skills in battle, and he knew his chance would come before long. He and the eleven brothers with whom he was traveling had been charged with delivering the sacred Hammer of Tyr to the newly built temple in Phlan. None of the men had ever been to Phlan before, but they had learned something of the port city's history before setting out on their mission.

As Tarl understood it, some fifty years ago, Phlan had been completely leveled by marauding dragons. Evil creatures of all description had subsequently moved into the ruins, and it had been only in the last few years that people had regained control of a portion of the city and brought back to it some semblance of civilization. However, most of Phlan was still inhabited by chaotic, evil creatures, and the Stojanow River, which had once been the city's lifeblood, had been mysteriously turned to a vile, stinking channel of acidic poisons.

The Temple of Tyr was the first temple to be erected in the city since its fall. The revered Hammer of Tyr would provide symbolic strength to the occupants of the temple, and would be wielded by the temple's head cleric when the warrior clerics were ready to assist Phlan's residents in the reclamation of even more of the city's lost territory. Tarl and his companions were to add their strength to the existing forces of the new temple.

The thought of real action stirred something in Tarl. He yearned to earn a name for himself as a great warrior of Tyr, a powerful cleric serving the cause of good in the Realms. Tarl already had gained the respect of his teachers for his exceptional clerical abilities. But his healing powers were a gift from Tyr, not a skill he had developed through sweat and dedication. He wanted to prove his devotion to his god and the order by succeeding in battle, the true vocation of the Tyrian clerics.

As Tarl continued to practice, he envisioned all manner of foes. He took dead aim at tree-ogres, stone-orcs, and stump-kobolds. Unfortunately, the monsters seemed to be winning. Tarl focused his concentration on his next throw—aim, step, close, swing . . . and release. The smith's hammer whirred as it spun end-over-end and smashed with a resounding *clunk* into the small boulder Tarl had targeted. It was Tarl's third hit since he had started practicing with the awkward hammer, but the first two had only reached their mark; this one split it in two. Had the rock been a hobgoblin, its head would have been split wide open.

"One enemy dies, Tarl, but another waits! Quick, behind ya!" Anton's voice carried over the rumble of the wagons. Knowing Anton's intent, Tarl grabbed the hammer, dropped to the ground, rolled, and threw the weapon at a white pine nearly twenty paces from where he lay. The hammer thunked into the tree's trunk just an inch from the ground.

"By Tyr, he'll be hoppin' for a day or two! Ya did some powerful damage to his foot, lad!" Anton laughed as he approached Tarl.

"Even when ya throw from the ground—no, especially when ya throw from the ground—ya still need all the momentum your body can give ya. Channel your energy so the full strength of your torso is packed behind your throw. That way your arm snaps forward with the force of a released spring, and your hammer does the damage ya need it to." Anton took the smith's hammer from Tarl and dropped to the ground to demonstrate. The big man moved with a speed and ease that belied his giant stature. True to his instructions, his arm snapped like a spring, sending the hammer forward with a force Tarl hadn't realized even Anton could manage from his back. When the hammer thwacked into a nearby tree, the entire length of the trunk split, as if it had been struck by an axe.

It took all his concentration, but many tries later, Tarl felt the tightly wound tension and powerful release of the snap that Brother Anton had spoken of. Tarl's throw missed its mark by several inches, but he knew he would never forget the technique, the feel of power in that throw. He also knew that he had been lacking that energy even when he had thrown from a standing position. He continued his practice with renewed enthusiasm all through the afternoon and into the evening, feeling a growing sense of pride and accomplishment as his hammer thrummed through the air with newfound speed and energy.

Though he was no giant like Anton, Tarl was tall—easily six feet—and strong. Nevertheless, by the time the brothers stopped for the night, Tarl's arms, shoulders, and back ached from the repeated use of previously underworked muscles. When Brother Sontag sent him for water in the morning, Tarl could barely hoist the yoke to his shoulders. At Anton's suggestion, Tarl heated a poultice and spread it between his shoulder blades. Anton instructed the young cleric to lie down on his bedroll, and he massaged the tarlike substance into Tarl's back and shoulder blades with his huge hands. The medication from the poultice quickly spread a penetrating, rejuvenating warmth through his aching muscles.

"You've made the mistake of all young men," Brother Sontag said, sitting down beside Tarl and Anton. Sontag was the eldest of the clerics in the group and, as such, its leader. He often had a word of advice for Tarl or even some of the other brothers. "You let a single success possess you. For a day, the hammer was your master. When you go back and practice again, you will be the master."

"You said the same thing about the ball and chain, Brother Sontag. Do all weapons punish us before we gain mastery over them?"

"Yes, Tarl, they do—and because you understand that, I believe you are ready for the Test of the Sword."

Anton's face paled noticeably. "Tarl's just a pup—barely twenty, if I can count. What's the rush, Brother Sontag?"

Sontag waved a hand toward Anton to silence him. "How many weapons have you mastered, Tarl?" Brother

Sontag stared directly into the youth's eyes as he asked the question.

Tarl thought for a moment. He knew of the Test of the Sword—that it was the final challenge he must face before becoming a full-fledged cleric in the Order of Tyr—but the nature of the test was a secret. For all he knew, Sontag's question could even be part of the test. Tarl sat up, squared his shoulders, and returned the elderly cleric's piercing gaze. "I can better my use of any weapon, Brother Sontag, but you yourself have told me I have mastered the ball and chain and that I will master the hammer. I believe, then, by my feelings, that I can also say I have mastered the shield."

"And the sword, Tarl? Have you mastered the sword?" Sontag prompted.

Tarl laughed nervously. "Of course not. The clerics of Tyr don't carry swords. There's no one here who can teach—"

"Wrong, Tarl. You knew that was wrong before you even spoke the words. Didn't you wield a sword before you took your vows?"

"Sure, I used a sword," Tarl answered self-consciously, aware that Brothers Donal, Adrian, Seriff, and the rest had gathered round to listen.

"And did you master it?" Sontag asked, his wizened eyes glittering.

"I—I guess I was pretty good. Of course, I didn't have the kind of intensive training I've received from all of you with the other weapons." Tarl was no longer looking at Brother Sontag. He felt that somehow everything he said was wrong. During the months since he'd taken his vows, he had asked more than once why clerics of Tyr couldn't use swords. Each time the response had been silence or a gruff "You'll know soon enough." Swords were wonderful weapons, certainly easier to wield than any of the weapons favored by the clerics of Tyr. Tarl was deeply committed to Tyr and the order, but he had always assumed that the clerics' refusal to use swords was some quirk of fanaticism of the type that seems to infiltrate almost any religious order.

"We all wielded swords before we joined the order, Tarl. There are men among us who could teach you proficiency with a sword, if you wanted to learn."

"I do want to learn, Brother Sontag. Swords are fine weapons. It's a shame the warriors of Tyr don't learn to use them." Tarl's heart pounded with both enthusiasm and trepidation as he launched into the argument he had rehearsed mentally a dozen times. "A man with a sword can easily disarm a man with a ball and chain, numchucks, or a throwing hammer, just by the proper timing of his thrust. And a kill with a sword is clean. There's no need for bludgeoning—"

Brother Sontag waved his hand at Tarl as he had at Anton a few moments earlier, then stood and walked toward the lead wagon. The clerics that were gathered round parted to let him pass. None spoke or moved to his aid, even as he returned with a large leather bag that was obviously very heavy. "Can I help you with that?" asked Tarl, dropping the poultice as he stood and held out a hand toward Sontag.

"No." It was Anton who answered the question. "It's Brother Sontag's job. He's the oldest among us."

"What's his job?" asked Tarl. He dropped his hand to his side and backed up several steps, feeling once again that he could say nothing right.

"To administer the test," said Anton. "When a cleric of Tyr can't give the test anymore, he retires."

Sontag untied the bag and pulled out a long silver cord. "Stand still," he said to Tarl coldly. The old cleric placed one end of the cord on the ground several feet from Tarl and then proceeded to lay it in a perfect circle around the young cleric.

Tarl felt a chill run up his spine as Sontag closed the circle. He felt trapped, though he knew that was ridiculous. He could step over the cord at any time. Or could he? For some reason, he couldn't, but he didn't know why. "Isn't anyone going to tell me what's expected of me?"

"You can ask all the questions you want once the test begins," Anton said.

Sontag pulled two swords from the bag, a long sword and a short sword, and placed them at the edge of the circle. He did the same with two more, a broadsword and a two-handed sword, and then with two more, one a jousting sword and the other a fencing sword. They were all fine weapons of the highest quality. Tarl felt compelled to touch and lift each one. When he was through, he stepped back to the center of the circle.

All the clerics except Sontag formed a circle around the cord, then faced Tarl and stepped back three paces. Tarl watched, curiously, as they rolled up their sleeves and leggings. Was this being done to intimidate him? Tarl wondered, noting the many gruesome battle scars that marred the skin of each man.

Brother Sontag picked up his ball and chain and stood within the circle of men but still outside the cord. "Choose your weapon, Tarl," said the old cleric. "You must kill me before you leave that circle—unless you pass the test."

"I—I don't want to kill you!" Tarl shouted, his voice breaking. Sontag slammed the ball inside the circle a scant two inches from Tarl's feet. "Choose your weapon or die in the circle!"

Tarl leaped back and made a move to jump over the cord. Sontag swung again, hard and low. The chain wrapped around Tarl's leg, and Sontag jerked back hard. Tarl slammed down on his left side, jamming his elbow on the rocky ground. Pain such as he had never known surged through his body, and Tarl cursed Tyr and all the other gods as he struggled to free his leg from the chain before Sontag could jerk it again. Tarl grappled for the pile of swords, then rose and turned on Sontag in fury as he got a firm grip on the broadsword.

"I'll kill you!" Tarl screamed. The sword felt natural in his hand. He lunged forward and lashed out at Sontag, rage and pain guiding his movements. He felt the sword bite deep into the flesh just beneath Sontag's breastplate. Sontag faltered for a moment, and Tarl tried once more to break out of the circle, but Sontag clipped him across his left shoulder with the ball, and Tarl fell hard inside the bounds of the cord. Hot jets of pain pulsed from his shoulder through the rest of his body, and he jumped up and lashed out wildly at Sontag. He lunged repeatedly, each time following the point of the sword with his body. Again and again Sontag dodged Tarl's thrusts or deftly deflected them aside with his weapon.

Furious, Tarl reached back to exchange his weapon for the long sword, but for some reason he couldn't shake the broadsword from his hand. "What is this!?" Tarl shrieked. "Why can't I change weapons?" Terrified that Sontag would take advantage of his awkward position, Tarl jerked the broadsword back into place in front of him.

But Sontag was not rushing toward him. Instead, he stood at the edge of the circle, blood seeping through the folds of his tunic, but at the ready nonetheless.

"The choice ya made was final, Tarl," Anton's voice boomed from behind him. "That broadsword is your weapon of choice for the test."

"I chose nothing!" Tarl yelled in response. "Look at Brother Sontag! I didn't want harm to come to him, but did I have a choice? I can't even leave this bloody circle without killing him. What's that supposed to prove?"

"Ya did have a choice, Tarl. Ya didn't have to hurt him. The point—"

"What kind of choice was that, Brother Anton? That I could let him kill me? That I could 'die in the circle' as he said?" Tarl was shifting his weight from one foot to the other. The sword felt alive in his hand. He wanted to lash out at Sontag again and again, to stab, to hurt him as he was hurt, to relieve the tension building inside himself. His every muscle was tensed, and he was ready to spring on the old man at any moment.

"One question at a time, lad," Anton said quietly. "You'll die in the circle only if ya don't pass the test. You'll die at Brother Sontag's hands only if ya try to leave the circle without passin' the test."

Tarl tipped his head back slightly and let his shoulders drop. "I'll die in the circle only if I don't pass the test? I'll die at Brother Sontag's hands only if I try to leave the circle without passing the test? What's that supposed to mean? And you, Anton—why are you the only one talking to me?"

"When you asked me what was expected of ya, you were choosin' me as your tutor for the test. The others are answerin' the questions ya haven't asked yet with their bared arms an' legs."

Keeping a wary eye on Brother Sontag, Tarl glanced around at the men surrounding him. As before, he noted their many scars, but this time he saw one thing more— that each man, including Anton, bore one scar that stood out from the rest—a scar with a silver cast to it.

"As my tutor, you'll answer any question?"

"Aye, as long as you can't answer it yourself."

"I think I know, Brother Anton, what I need to do to pass the test, but I'm not sure I understand. Why don't the clerics of Tyr use swords?"

"Before the test, Brother Sontag was askin' about the weapons you'd mastered . . . When can ya say you've mastered a weapon?"

Tarl thought for a moment, then answered Anton.

"When you are confident in the technique required to use a weapon, you've mastered it. That doesn't mean you can't improve on your technique, just that you know it. But what—"

"And are ya master of the sword?" Anton prompted.

Again Tarl reflected. He could thrust, jab, stab, slice, parry. What more techniques could be applied with a sword? And yet somehow he didn't feel the same control he felt with the hammer or the ball and chain. He shook his head. "No, but I don't understand why not."

"What did you feel when you dug that blade into your teacher and fellow brother?"

The answer made Tarl sick. He looked down at the sword in his hand and then over at Brother Sontag. The older brother was standing stoically, his hand pinned to his side in an attempt to stanch the flow of blood. Tarl had come to love Sontag despite his occasional gruffness. Sontag had counseled Tarl through many of the tougher stages of his studies. And now this brother and friend was wounded, perhaps even dying, at Tarl's own hand.

Tarl looked again at the sword. It was a weapon like any other, but it was also unlike any other. The man who wielded it was driven by it. His movements were no longer completely of his own choosing. And Tarl knew the answer to the test: No one masters a sword. The sword masters the man, and a cleric of Tyr serves no master but Tyr. But knowing the answer alone would not save him from confinement to the circle. He must do what he knew each of his brothers had done to complete the test. "The sword is not my master!" shouted Tarl, and he swung the blade of the broadsword down on his thigh. Blood pulsed from the gash, and Tarl screamed out in agony to right his own wrong. "Help . . . help Brother Sontag!" Tarl's last memory was of the brothers who had been standing silent around the circle rushing to Brother Sontag's side.

*   *   *   *   *

Tarl awoke to Brother Anton's voice, bellowing, "Are ya goin' to sleep till we get to Phlan, lad? Wake up! Don't go supposin' that just because you're a full-fledged cleric now there's no chores important enough for ya!"

"By the gods, I hurt all over!" Pain pounded through Tarl's body, from his jammed elbow to the self-inflicted wound on his thigh. Every bump of the wagon sent fresh, white-hot spasms coursing through his body.

"Now, that's gratitude! I spend the night a-patchin' and a-prayin', and you complain as though ya ain't been healed."

"No disrespect intended, Brother Anton, but if this is healed, I'm glad Tyr spared me from the hours since the test!"

Brother Sontag's head appeared between the edge of the wagon and the curtain that shielded Tarl's cot from the sun. Tarl struggled to a sitting position and tried to speak, to apologize, but Sontag raised a hand to silence him. "That'll be enough bellyaching, Brother Tarl. Look at me—three times your age, and with a wound that would down a horse. Do you see me complaining? Brother Donal just spotted the poison river that leads south into Phlan. Can't afford to have a strong young cleric like you in bed when we run up against the riffraff that's rumored to inhabit this area."

For two years, Tarl had been studying and training for the chance to serve Tyr in battle, to contribute to the establishment and expansion of a new temple. He was the only one in the group without actual battle experience. This finally was his chance to prove himself to the men who had taught him so much. Tarl threw back the bedding, stood up, and vaulted over the side of the wagon with all the exuberance of his age . . . and crumpled helplessly to the ground. Yesterday's agony returned in full force as the self-inflicted wound on his leg reopened from the impact.

"You'll be limpin' for a lifetime if ya keep that up!" yelled Anton, and he leaped over the side of the wagon after Tarl. Anton tied a strip of cloth tight above the wound to stop the bleeding, while Brother Sontag spoke the words of a clerical spell and held his hands against Tarl's leg. Tarl could feel the exchange of energy as Sontag's powerful healing went to work. He watched as the tissue on either side of the gash on his leg fused slowly together. Flesh melded with flesh, covering exposed muscle, and finally the skin closed over the tissue. Tarl's eyes gleamed with wonder as he realized there was no more pain. There was a scar, though, and Tarl saw that it shone a dull silver, just like those he had seen on his brothers. Sontag removed the tourniquet, stood up, and held a hand out to Tarl.

Tarl clasped Brother Sontag's hand between both of his own and exclaimed, "Thank you, Brother Sontag! May I one day share your skills!"

"Your healing skills already rival that of most clerics. You will soon be my equal at healing. For now, though, go dress yourself for battle."

"Don't be forgettin' your hammer, either, Brother Tarl," said Anton.

"Brother Tarl." The words sounded better than ever. These men truly were his brothers now.

* * * * *

The Stojanow River was an eyesore. Its color was an unnatural greenish black, and not a scrap of vegetation stood along its banks. Even trees a hundred paces and more from the river struggled for survival, their leaves withered and unhealthy-looking. Worse than the river's appearance, though, was its smell. Tarl had shoveled chicken manure from the coops at the temple in Vaasa and never been so offended by smell. The acrid odor from the Stojanow burned the nostrils and lungs, and the stench of rot and decay made him want to wretch. Tarl could tell he was not the only one disturbed by the corrupted river. The horses were stamping and whinnying and threatening to bolt. Without even exchanging words, Brothers Adrian and Seriff, who were driving the wagons, turned the horses and led the party as far as they could get from the river without losing sight of it.

The going was rough but uneventful. The battles they had anticipated never came, even after several days of traveling south following the river. It was dusk of the fifth night since Tarl took the test when they spotted a high wooden fence that they took to be a part of the City of Phlan's fortifications. In the distance, behind the fence, they could just see the pinnacles of the towers that made up the main fortress of the city. Determined to make their way into Phlan and to the temple within the city walls, they pushed their way through the rotting boards of the wooden fence. Just as the last man in the party came through the fence, a deafening clang broke out.

Anton, who was one of the first inside the walls, inadvertently stepped on and turned a large flat stone—a gravestone—and as he did, he realized that the tall grasses hid dozens more. "By the gods, there be death inside these walls!" shouted Anton. A bony hand reached up from the ground near Anton's leg. "Get back to the grave from whence ya came!" he shouted. With a swing of his hammer, he shattered the bony hand, and immediately the skeleton burst, screaming, from the ground, its frame guarded by a shield covered with earth and worms. The sickening shriek of the undead was even worse than the clanging. Anton slammed his heavy hammer down on the skeleton's shield full force, and the disc crashed from its hand. With another swing, Anton sent the bony frame of the undead creature splintering in a hundred directions.

More armed skeleton warriors erupted from the ground in front of the party. "The hammer!" shouted Brother Donal. "Protect it at any cost!" He shoved the sacred Hammer of Tyr at Tarl as the warrior clerics moved quickly to form a protective line in front of the youngest of their group.

"The horses!" Tarl's shout of warning was too late. Skeletal arms were reaching up from the ground and slashing the underbellies of the terrified creatures. The animals' death shrieks were hideous, but there was no chance to mourn for the horses as the skeleton warriors attacked with a vengeance. Swords clanked against shields and metal shattered bone as the clerics pressed forward. The sight of dozens of undead soldiers made every man's blood run cold, but the brittle warriors stood no chance against the heavy hammers and ball and chains favored by the clerics of Tyr.

In a matter of minutes, the area was littered with bone fragments, but no man had a chance to catch his breath. Dozens more skeletons appeared, and grotesque zombies burst from the ground, their half-rotted bodies covered with maggots and dirt. Brother Sontag challenged the zombies with his holy symbol. "In the name of Tyr, begone!" A ray of pure white light shot from the holy symbol to the chest of the first of the lumbering creatures. The zombie's rotting flesh began to smoke, then to bubble. Maggots, inflated from the intense heat, burst with the sound of popping corn. Like a cube of ice held over a fire, the zombie melted, layer by layer, until nothing was left but a puddle of slime.

The other clerics quickly raised their holy symbols against the zombies that followed. For each holy symbol, at least one zombie was turned to slime, but in their place followed even more zombies, along with some of the most frightful creatures of legend—wraiths, the ghostly mists that kill. Tarl could no longer quell his own terror. Shimmering clouds, gruesomely magnified images of giants, ogres, and other terrors closed in all around the clerics. By the dozens they came, from every corner of the graveyard. "Back, you spawn of evil!" shouted Brother Sontag, still wielding his holy symbol. "Press on, brothers! We must flee this place!"

The Hammer of Tyr clenched tightly in his hand, Tarl plunged forward. The other clerics followed, holding their holy symbols high, but the wraiths were undaunted. Tarl heard a hideous scream behind him. He recognized the voice as Brother Seriff's. The next scream was Brother Donal's. More followed in rapid succession.

Anton and Sontag ran on either side of Tarl, their shields held up at their sides. The ethereal hand of a wraith reached through Brother Sontag's shield as though it were air and clawed at his face. Sontag didn't have a chance to scream. Before he could finish his next step, he dropped to the ground, a withered husk. Tarl spun belatedly to the aid of the elder brother who had initiated him into the Brotherhood. Three wraiths floated over the body, their slime-green eyes bulging in the excitement of the kill.

"Abominations! Get away from him!" Tarl screamed. The Hammer of Tyr burned hot in his hand, and he threw it with all the fury pent up inside him. The sacred weapon blazed a brilliant blue as it spun toward the misty visages. Tarl watched in awe as three wraiths exploded the moment the glowing hammer passed through their bodies. He realized at the same instant he saw the hammer's power unleashed that he had just discarded the holy object he was sworn to protect. "No!" he shouted, furious at his own stupidity. But before he could do anything, the hammer was sailing end-over-end toward him. Somehow it had reversed directions like a boomerang and was headed back straight toward his waiting hand. Without conscious effort on his part, the handle pressed into Tarl's palm as though someone had slapped it into place.

Instantly the hammer blazed with an even greater radiance, bathing Anton, Tarl, and the three other remaining clerics in its holy aura. The skeletons and zombies were held at bay by the light. They shielded their faces with their bony arms. It was as if the eyes in their empty sockets were being blinded by the blue-white glare. The undead giants and ogres screamed in agony as they were touched by the light, and as one they turned and ran in fear. But the light from the mystical implement of Tyr didn't stop the oncoming wraiths—or the creatures that followed.

"Back the way we come!" Anton shouted. "Run as you've never run before!" Anton shoved Tarl in front of him and wasted no time following. The big man was as fleet as any as he leaped over graves and slammed skeletons, splashing holy water on the bodies of the dead as he ran. "Bless . . . ya, brothers!" he gasped.

Tarl threw the Hammer of Tyr repeatedly as he ran. Wraiths exploded, and cries of the undead were everywhere. The other brothers continued to use their clerical powers—turning the undead with their holy symbols, throwing holy water, and muttering prayers to Tyr as they ran. Their powers were strong and undoubtedly would have been enough to save them under other circumstances, but the sheer numbers of undead made it impossible for the clerics to protect themselves completely. Tarl heard the screams of two more of his brothers, and then a third. Only Anton ran beside him now.

"Give usss the hammer." Tarl pulled up short, and so did Anton, as they faced a line of six ghostly creatures, their distorted, taloned hands outstretched. "Give ussss the hammer," they said once more.

Anton grimly assessed the situation. "They're specters, lad, and a vampire leader."

Tarl was overwhelmed by revulsion, rage, and unadulterated terror. Left by himself, he felt he would die of fright, but the Hammer of Tyr became a living extension of Tarl's innate strength. Blue beams erupted from the hammer, blasting the remaining wraiths into cool white bits of fog. As more beams followed, the six specters were driven back.

"Well dooonnnne, lad!" A deep, evil-sounding voice echoed all around Tarl. Where the specters had stood only a moment ago, a handsome, white-robed man now floated in the air. His deep-red eyes shone, and his gaze seemed to burn into Tarl's soul.

"No, Tarl! Don't meet his gaze!" shouted Anton. "Get back, ya wretched vampire, ya spawn from the Abyss! As Tyr is my god, leave us alone!"

The robed figure seemed to flinch at Anton's words, but then he stiffened and floated closer, smiling evilly. His deep voice echoed again throughout the graveyard. "Yooour puny god has no hooold over me!"

"Blasphemer! My god will swallow your unholy flesh and vomit you back to the Pit where ya belong!" Anton held out his holy symbol and quickly recited prayers to Tyr for turning the undead.

Tarl clutched his own holy symbol in one hand and the Hammer of Tyr in the other, but the creature's glowing red eyes showed no fear. Even as the specters cowered back, the vampire floated closer. If it weren't for the grisly fangs revealed when he smiled, the vampire would appear almost friendly. Tarl took a step forward, no longer afraid but drawn to the handsome figure.

"No!" Anton shouted, and Tarl felt the man's huge paw clamp down firmly on his shoulder. Anton jerked Tarl back behind him and hurriedly incanted another clerical spell. "Let the flames o' Tyr strike ya dead!" he shouted at the creature, and he threw a handful of sulfur toward it.

With a *whoosh*, a torrential column of blue flame shot

down from the sky and bathed the robed figure in white-hot fire. It screamed in agony, and its robes disintegrated as it fell to the earth in flames. Naked, the vampire was revealed as a creature of nightmares. Its translucent skin was stretched taut over its bones. Its coloring remained a ghostly white, except where the flames had blasted patches of skin from the bones, leaving black, charred holes. There was no sign whatsoever of blood.

Then the creature rose and threw back its head in a laugh that forced Tarl to imagine the unholy depths of the Abyss. It was a horrid, hollow sound that Tarl would never forget. "Deeeear brother," the vampire growled, "yooooour spell was powerful, but yooooou wished the wroooong thing. Yoooou can't strike dead what is already dead!" Once more the creature laughed.

"Run, brother!" Anton whispered. "I'll keep this abomination at bay till you can flee with the hammer!"

Tarl wanted nothing more than to flee, but he wasn't about to leave his only remaining brother in the faith. "I'm with you, Brother Anton, and so is Tyr and the power of the hammer!"

"Then, by the gods, we'll beat this bastard!" Anton swung his arm, shouted an arcane syllable, and released a blue symbol from his hand.

Thwack! The blue character, the holy symbol of Tyr, rocketed through the air and embedded itself in the forehead of the vampire.

"Aaaaghhh!" The creature dropped to its knees as the character sizzled and burned deep into its ghostly white skin. Still kneeling, the vampire lifted its head and cursed. "Nooooow I trade yooooou word for word, doooog of Tyr!" The creature spit the word "*Gnarlep!*" at Anton. A black shape flew from its bloodless white lips and seared itself into Anton's forehead.

Tarl gasped as he saw Anton bellow in agony and clasp both hands to his forehead. The big man clawed at the black mark with all his strength, but the unholy symbol was already burning its way deep into his flesh. He let out another agonized bellow and dropped to the ground, flailing and writhing like a madman.

"Stop it!" Tarl shrieked at the vampire. "Whatever you're doing, stop! Leave him alone! What do I have to do before you'll leave him alone?"

"What dooo I want?" the vampire asked caustically. "A dooozennn hoooly mennnn enter my graveyard carrying that wretched hammer that wakes the undead and leaves noooone of my minions at peace, and you ask what I want?" The vampire fought to stand. "I want that blasphemous weapon—nooooow—or yooooour friend diessss!" With a twist of his bony hand, the vampire threw Anton into even greater throes of pain.

"Stop! Leave him alone!"

"The hammer, oooor he diessss! Give me the hammer, and I'll provide yooooou and him with safe transpoooort from this place." The vampire raised his hand toward Anton and held it up threateningly.

Tarl hurled the hammer directly at the creature, but the vampire flung itself to one side, and the hammer flew by harmlessly. The creature gestured madly, and before the hammer could return to Tarl's hand, it was caught and held in red webbing that suddenly appeared in the air. The look of fear that had entered the vampire's eyes a moment ago changed to a gleam of pleasure. "Thank yoooou, boooy," the monster hissed.

Tarl dropped down beside Anton. The big man was still writhing in pain. He spoke only one word that could be understood—"No!" Tarl could imagine what Anton intended to say: "No, Tarl! Don't throw the hammer! Don't listen to him!" But it was too late. Tarl had lost the Hammer of Tyr, and now he would surely die with his friend.

"Now get away from me! Leave me be!" the vampire shrieked. There was no pleasure in its voice anymore, only pain. "Where will yooooou gooo? Tell me, and be gooone!"

Tarl didn't understand why the creature would give him and Anton leave, but he wasn't waiting around to find out. "To Civilized Phlan. To the Temple of Tyr," he replied quickly.

Suddenly a huge puff of deep crimson smoke surrounded Tarl and Anton. For a moment, all Tarl could see was red. He could see neither the vampire nor Anton, nor indeed even his own hands. The roar of an unfathomable wind churned and swirled all around him, but he could feel nothing. It was as if his body were protected by layer upon layer of soft, impenetrable cloth.

When the red cloud finally cleared, he was sitting beside Anton in front of a gate to what was obviously the new temple of Tyr.

"Brothers!" Tarl cried from the gate. "Brothers of Tyr, help us!"

Tarl could see men moving in the twilight. Two approached, carrying lanterns, and when they saw the condition of their two fellow brothers, they called for more help. It took four men to carry Anton to a bed within the confines of the temple. For hours they worked on his feverish body, hardly exchanging words with each other or with Tarl as they tried to ease the pain of their fallen brother. When finally they had done all they could, an elder of the order who resembled Brother Sontag rested his hand on Tarl's shoulder and led him to a room crowded with tables. "Sit," said the old man. "Talk, and I'll get you some food. I can see from your eyes, and from the condition of your brother, that there must be much to tell." The elder brother left and returned shortly with stew and bread and bitter ale, then sat down beside Tarl.

Tarl ate absently. His body craved the food, but he had no energy to think about it. He had lost everything this day—ten of his brothers, the sacred object they had entrusted him with, and, he feared, Anton. After a night of spell-casting and laying on of hands and applying poultices, the brothers had succeeded only in easing Anton's pain enough so that he could lie in some semblance of peace. But there was no spark in the man, no sign of understanding, and only a dim glimmer of recognition for Tarl when he was nearby. He had not spoken a word since they left the graveyard.

Again the old man prompted Tarl to speak. Tarl reached out and clutched the brother's hand. "Twelve men started this journey, brother . . ."

"Tern. Brother Tern. And you are called . . . ?"

"Tarl . . . Those same men trained me and initiated me into the Brotherhood of Tyr. . . ." Tarl quickly related the story of their journey from Vaasa and their first sight of the Stojanow River.

"Here, we call it the Barren River," Brother Tern interspersed. "No life can survive in its poison waters."

Tarl nodded and continued. He told of the skeletons and zombies and wraiths, and of the horrible, screaming deaths of his brothers. But he did not mention the graveyard, nor did he tell of the vampire. He referred to the ruins of Phlan and expressed his belief that the Hammer of Tyr, with its tremendous power for good, must have awakened and infuriated all the undead of the city simply by its proximity. What evil had left its mark on Anton's forehead, he did not know. He vowed to find out.

When he told the cleric that the Hammer of Tyr was missing somewhere in the ruins, he could see the older man's pain. The clerics of Phlan had counted desperately on the hammer's strength and power as they finished their temple and went out in numbers to face the very creatures Tarl was describing.

Aloud, Tarl vowed to help the brothers of Phlan in their search for the missing hammer as soon as he could clear his mind through mourning and meditation. Silently, Tarl vowed that he would spend his days building his knowledge, skills, power, and experience until he could, himself, regain the sacred hammer from the vampire and exact vengeance for his friends. The lies to Brother Tern were so much bile in Tarl's mouth, but he knew that the responsibility for the loss of the hammer was his, and he was determined to set things right by himself.

The old cleric was sympathetic to Tarl's plans. He believed he had convinced the young man to rest within the confines of the temple for at least a day and then seek out a private place, perhaps in the woodlands north of the city, to fulfill his need to pray and recuperate from the horrors he had witnessed.

When Tarl was finished with his meal and Brother Tern had departed, he went to Anton. Every cleric in the temple had laid hands on Anton, accomplishing almost nothing, but Tarl could not help but try again himself. His hand reached out toward Anton's forehead, but it recoiled when his fingers made contact with the gelid skin. Where the black word had buried itself in Anton's flesh, the cold was so intense that it burned. Tarl forced himself to press his hands onto his brother's forehead, then began to pray. He could feel the healing powers of Tyr strong within his hands, but he felt no exchange of damaged energy for whole as he usually did in healing. When there wasn't even a glimmer of warmth or recognition from Anton after Tarl had spent several hours with him, Tarl rolled out his bedding on a cot and lay down beside his teacher and friend.

❧ 3 ❧

The Night Begins

There would be no peace tonight, Ren thought, eyeing the crowd in the tavern. The homey pub was filled with people—soldiers, thieves, adventurers, even a magic-user or two—most of them newcomers to Phlan, here no doubt in response to the town council's offer of money and treasure for each uncivilized section of the city cleared of danger. Most of the strangers were ready to make voluntary expeditions in exchange for promised rewards, but recently the town council had even begun to send convicted criminals on expeditions outside the walls of Civilized Phlan, in lieu of jail terms. As Ren examined the crowd, he thought for the thousandth time how strange it was that they all looked so young—much too young to be facing the monsters that controlled the ruins of the old city.

Ren never thought of himself as old, though he felt he'd aged a lifetime in the last year, but he wasn't wet behind the ears like the roomful of youngsters around him. He'd stolen the best from the best. He'd killed monsters by the dozens, and men in even greater numbers. And he had loved—god, how he had loved! He knew that no one in the packed room could have experienced a love like his. He closed his eyes and thought of Tempest. Her hair was the flaming sienna red of bur oak leaves in autumn. She was a tall woman, with a striking full figure. She could move with the grace and silence of a cat or the provocative bawdiness of a street wench. When the two of them had prowled the streets and rooftops together, she had always worn black leathers. The thought of her, buxom and strong, working her way over the rooftops with ease, stopping to tease him with a glance or a motion of her hands, made Ren's blood stir. . . .

"Have you fallen asleep standing up, man?" Sot's angry voice bellowed from behind the bar. "There's tables to clean and orders to take! Move yourself with some alacrity inside my pub, or you'll be moving yourself even faster to the doorway."

Ren shook his head. "Sorry," he muttered, and he began working the tables again. There was comfort in the mind-numbing dullness of the job. He could think—or not think—as he chose, and continue his work. He brought four flagons of ale to one table, five bowls of Sot's renowned pork and cabbage soup to another, two glasses of wine to yet another. He mopped the floor where a pig of a youth had spilled a pitcher of gravy, and he cleared three tables so a band of young fighters could sit and slurp beer till they dropped.

He'd been working for Sot for nearly three weeks now, the most recent of a baker's dozen of odd jobs he'd held as he traveled aimlessly since leaving Waterdeep. It had been more than a year since he'd practiced thieving, the trade he'd taken up when he met Tempest, more than a year since the bastard assassins had killed her over some goods he and she had stolen from a member of the assassins' guild. They hadn't known when they lifted the gems and daggers that their mark was the head of the guild—not that they would have left him alone had they recognized him, but Ren knew now that if he had it to do over again, he would gladly have returned even the precious ioun stones and anything else in his possession to have kept Tempest from harm.

He still awakened night after night with the vision of her standing there, screaming a silent scream as a dagger

lodged deep in her left breast. The wound would probably have killed her anyhow, but the assassins had treated
the knife with a madman's poison that had left her body
twitching and flopping on the floor of their bedroom until Ren was forced to put her out of her misery. Oh, he'd
killed the three who murdered his beloved, killed them
while they were still in his home, but they were mere
hirelings for the head of the guild, who was the one really responsible for Tempest's murder. He still had a price
out on Ren's head for the return of the daggers and ioun
stones, which were still in his possession. But Ren didn't
care. The bastard would get the ioun stones from Ren
when he fought him in the Abyss, but not before.

Ren delivered another order of food and booted a
drunken troublemaker out the door. To the people around
him, he was merely a bigger-than-average barkeep, a
large fellow with matted, gnarled hair and a rumpled tunic. That was just the impression Ren wanted to give. He
had no desire to confront any assassins until he could confront the one who'd ordered Tempest's murder.

"Hey, big fella!" came a call from the bar. "Unless I miss
my guess, you've got some muscles under those skunk
coverings. What do you say you use some of that brawn
of yours to bring us some food and a couple more
pitchers?" The speaker was one of three women fighters
who'd been in the pub together since early afternoon.
The three had a catcall or a teasing invitation for almost
every man who walked in the door, but they'd also given
the boot to more than one of the men who'd made his
way to the ladies' table, hoping for a little friendly action.

"No problem, ladies," said Ren, an amiable grin spreading across his face. The three were impressive. Each was
dressed in fine quality chain mail that had seen plenty of
use, and all three were bristling with swords, daggers,
and throwing axes . . . also well used. The smallest of the
three, a willowy brunette, and the tallest, a big muscular

blonde, appeared to take their cues from the third woman, whose salt-and-pepper hair made her appear older. A man might be attracted to any of the three, but to Ren, who had been all but oblivious to women for a full year, all three seemed remarkably attractive, and even more so for their forwardness.

Ren slipped behind the bar and addressed his boss. "Sot, we've got a food and ale order from *that* table again," said Ren, gesturing with a nod of his head. "Would you fill two of those pewter pitchers for me?"

The rotund old innkeeper looked at Ren curiously. The heavy pewter wares at which Ren was pointing were generally reserved for highborn lords or ladies, who occasionally found their way into Phlan's busiest but not necessarily fanciest inn. Something in Ren's expression left no room for argument, however, so the innkeeper obliged. Ren's eyes sparkled with mischief, and he felt a certain warmth inside of him. He had kept to himself for too long. It was past time to blow off a little steam. He backed through the swinging door into the kitchen and barked at the cook. "Food, friend, and lots of it—on those big metal platters, if you please. Oh, and haul out three of those heavy metal trenchers to serve it in."

"What're ye thinkin' of, laddie?" the grease-covered cook asked as he spotted the gleam in Ren's eyes.

"Keep an eye out the door after you serve it up and you'll soon see!" Ren replied lightly. The cook was a temperamental man, as feisty as he was short, and Sot tolerated him only because his tasty food was the inn's main draw. Ship captains and traveling merchants alike made a point of visiting the Laughing Goblin Inn when they were in Phlan. Fortunately, Ren had managed to stay on the cook's good side, and he wasn't afraid to ask the man a favor if he knew he could offer a snatch of entertainment in return.

Ren pulled a giant war shield from behind the pantry

shelves, a souvenir from a fighter who had tried to leave without paying his bill. A large man, with the skills of a ranger and a thief, Ren had a knack for "convincing" people to pay their bills. In fact, there hadn't been many who couldn't afford to pay since he'd started working for the inn, and that fact kept Sot more than happy. Ren gripped the shield firmly, then easily ripped the leather handles from it. Then he laid the cook's big oak cutting board on top of it, followed by a linen cloth over the board. "Now help me load this thing with food, and grab those two tankards I just brought in."

"Ya big galoot, ya don't think you're gonna lift that mass of metal an' grub by yerself, do ya?"

"I most certainly am," said Ren.

"Ha!" the cook blurted out after adding the pitchers from the bar to the tray. "I'll part with a silver if that don't weigh more than me."

"I hope it does," said Ren, smiling enigmatically. "Now, open the door for me, please."

Ren dragged the shield off the counter and balanced it on his right hand. The cook gasped as he got an indication for the first time of Ren's strength. There were few men as tall as Ren. The cook was sure by the way Ren had to duck under the doorway every time he came into the kitchen that he must be nearly six and a half feet tall. But he had never realized what kind of brawn the big man hid under his sloppy tunic. As Ren hoisted the huge war shield and the many pounds of metal on top of it, his muscles bulged till the loose-fitting tunic pulled tight around his arm, shoulder, and back. He used his left hand to balance the big tray as he stepped out into the crowded inn. The cook followed Ren to the door, shaking his head and reminding himself that he never wanted to get in a fight with this quiet man.

No one in the main hall thought anything of Ren bringing in the tray. None could see all the metal on top. He moved easily through the crowd, stopping at the table where the three fighters were sitting. The big blonde who'd given the order was the first to notice him.

She smiled coyly as he approached and began to tease him about his tardiness. "It's about time you brought our food. I was beginning to think I'd have to go on a town-council expedition to find you and our grub. The delay could affect your tip, big fellow."

The brunette slapped the shoulder of the speaker. "Jensena, I know the tip you have in mind, but he's so smelly, it'd take you a week to get clean." All three laughed at the jest. Ren merely cocked his head and raised his eyebrows slightly.

The leader of the three, the woman with the salt-and-pepper hair, glanced at Ren over the rim of her cup. "I expect he could bathe in a hurry if he thought it would get him anywhere. Not only that, I'd wager he could teach you both a thing or two. After all, he's nothing but a tavern tart." They all broke into peals of laughter. Ren knew he must act quickly or he'd miss his opportunity.

"Wager away, ma'am. I wager your bill for the night against an equal sum that you ladies can't even do ten minutes' worth of the work that I do."

Throughout the course of the afternoon, the three had racked up a good-sized bill. They answered together without hesitation: "You're on!"

From his post at the doorway, the cook smiled, knowing what was coming next. That Ren was a bold rascal. He'd have to hand him that.

"Here," said Ren, holding the tray forward. "Just see if you can carry this tray and everything on it from here to the bar without dropping it. That should be no problem for any of you ladies—assuming, of course, that you're sober."

Ren eased the tray down onto the table. Even people at the other end of the bar could hear the groan of the wood as the table bowed under the weight of the huge shield. The three women were now able to see the full metal pitchers of ale, the pewter tableware, platters, and trenchers, and food enough to feed an army. They also spotted the heavy war shield.

The brunette, Gwen, recognized the trick Ren had played on them. Purse-lipped, she started rummaging through a pouch on her belt, looking for some coins to pay the bill and the bet. But her friends weren't so easily daunted.

"Jensena, you're the strongest. Give it a try," said the older warrior.

Jensena was the biggest of the three, with brawn that would put most men to shame. She tossed her blond braid to the side and flexed her muscles. She had no qualms about showing off her strength, but eyeing the great metal tray, she wondered how even a man the size of the barkeep could have hefted it with one hand. She wasn't at all sure she could raise it even with two, much less carry it from their table to the bar. Nonetheless, she moved to a position beside the platter and stretched her arms and shoulder blades to pull the kinks out. As she did, her well-oiled chain mail rippled across her chest and shoulders, displaying her muscular flesh. Then, straining with everything she had, she slowly began to raise the platter with both hands. The two pitchers started to tip, but Ren reached out in a flash to steady them.

Ren could feel the tension in the air. Virtually all eyes were on him and the three women. His little jest could quickly turn sour on him. These were strangers to the town, proud strangers. He could tell they didn't like the fact that they had been duped by a tavern worker, and Ren was certain there were many other customers who would side with them in a brawl. Even Sot and the cook stood ready with cudgels lest a fight should break out.

"Enough for now, ladies," Ren said. "I wouldn't want you to let this perfectly good food and ale go to waste. Eat, drink, have a good time. We can settle our wager later." With a brief bow, Ren left the table and resumed his duties. The tension level dropped immediately, and soon it was as noisy as ever as the guests in the pub renewed their conversations where they had left off.

When he was sure all was calm once more, Ren returned to the table where the women were still sitting. He moved close to the table and smiled warmly. "I didn't mean to offend you," he said quietly. "I really just wanted to get your attention."

"The joke was on us, and a good one, at that," said the older-looking of the warriors. She discreetly pushed a sack of coins she had out on the table toward Ren. "I'm Salen, the leader of this small band. The dark-haired bladeswoman is Gwen, and the one who tried to lift the tray is Jensena."

"My pleasure, ladies—Gwen, Salen, Jensena. My friends call me Ren. I'd prefer that you call me the same."

"So, Ren, are you brave enough to wager us for that gold one more time—in a contest of our choosing?" asked Salen.

"Miss, I doubt there's a man alive could take all of you on and survive."

The corners of Salen's mouth turned up in a smile. "I expect you're right."

Ren picked up the sack of coins and tossed them to the innkeeper, who had been watching Ren since he returned to the table. Sot set his big cudgel down with deliberation on the bar. He was obviously annoyed that Ren had risked a night's business for a prank, but when he opened the purse and saw the large amount of gold inside, he grinned and winked his approval to Ren. "Have an ale and see what they have in mind!" shouted Sot, and he pushed a tankard down the bar toward Ren.

"What kind of contest were you thinking of?" Ren asked as he grabbed the tankard and turned back to face the three warriors.

"Your muscles, however well hidden under that baggy shirt, won't help you in a dagger toss," said Salen coyly.

"No, I suppose they wouldn't," said Ren, "but I should warn you—I've thrown a knife or two. Are you sure you're still game?"

The other two, who hadn't looked up from their food since Ren had come to the table, burst into laughter. "This time you've met your match, big fella," Jensena said, pointing her fork toward Salen. "I've never seen Salen beaten yet, and I've watched her throw almost as many times as I've been in battle."

The three finished a few more bites of food and then stood up and carried their tankards over to the small table beside the inn's well-used wooden target. The great round slab had been taken from a gigantic pine that had seen hundreds of years of life. Concentric growth circles were etched into its surface, making a perfect target.

Salen removed a leather box from her backpack. She lifted the cover of the box to reveal two pairs of daggers, one glistening black, the other white.

"Lovely weapons," said Ren. "May I?" He waited for Salen to nod before picking up each dagger in turn to test its balance. The blades were made for throwing into live targets, but they were perfect for the game as well. Each blue-steel blade was wider near its point than it was at its base. The onyx and crystal handles were slim and capped with gold ends that offset the weight of the wide blades. In the hands of a skilled thrower, any one of the daggers could easily slice through flesh and bone. Ren had no doubt they had been used for just that purpose.

"Go ahead, try a throw," urged Salen.

Ren needed no coaxing. After a year's absence from thieving, rangering, or any other kind of action, he was more than ready to heft a balanced weapon in his hand. Even though he had chosen a seemingly aimless existence until such time as he was ready to hunt down the person responsible for Tempest's death, Ren was generally a man of action. Passivity was not in his makeup. Somehow these three lighthearted women, with their wagers and laughter, had awakened a part of Ren's nature he had kept buried for too long. He picked up the onyx-handled pair of daggers and released each in turn with a fluid twist of his torso and flick of his wrist. Both blades thunked solidly into the line that bordered the center circle of the target.

"Not bad," said Salen, taking up the crystal-handled pair. "I enjoy a challenge." Her movements were deft and experienced. The blades landed within the border of the center circle, hardly a hairbreadth apart.

There are probably a hundred ways to play the game of daggers, and Ren and Salen started by haggling over the rules. Before beginning in earnest, they each made several more tosses till each player thought he had the measure of the other.

Ren hadn't felt so good in months. He'd forgotten how a good blade felt in his hand, the splendid feeling of control when his body did exactly as he wanted it to. For the first time since Tempest died, he found himself scanning the room, sizing up the people. His rangering skills enabled him to tell at a glance if a foe was formidable. His thieving skills allowed him to estimate the possible takes available in the room. Salen was good, but the contest was yet to begin, and Ren was feeling great.

As Salen removed the blades from the round wooden slab, Gwen came up close to Ren and touched him lightly on the arm. "You're good," she said, "and you're no eyesore, either." She ran a finger teasingly close to the opening of his tunic, and turned her body till she was directly alongside him. He could feel his heart speed up as she tossed her rich dark hair back and her body brushed his side. Her thick, brown hair smelled like a summer meadow, and he could feel his head reel as sensations he had ignored for twelve long months rose now, unbidden. "You know, if you didn't smell so bad, I could see us getting together."

Before he could respond, Gwen whisked away from him and returned to the table where Jensena was now sitting, awaiting the start of the match.

"It's getting hot in here," said Ren, turning back to face Salen.

"I'm sure you think it is," she said with a knowing glimmer in her eyes. "What do you say we get started in earnest?" Ren nodded, and she returned his two black daggers and made her first toss of the contest. One thunked into the outer edge of the center circle, and the other landed in the border between the center and the second ring.

She's tough, Ren thought, but not tough enough. In one motion, Ren slid both blades into throwing position, one in each hand, and flicked them both toward the target with only a fraction of a second between throws. He watched in horror as the two blades parted as they neared the target and slammed into the board several inches wide of center! He stalked to the board and jerked out the two black-handled blades. They looked right; they even felt right—until he pulled out the crystal-handled daggers and felt the difference in balance, and then he knew he had been duped. These ladies were clever. The difference between the blades he had started with and the ones they had substituted was as subtle as the exchange had been. It was a perfect response to his stacked-platter prank, but he would not be duped.

He returned to the throwing mark, shaking his head. "Salen, you're throwing with a vengeance. On the other hand, I appear to be losing my touch. I'm afraid if we make too many more tosses, I'll only be humiliated. What do you say we make one last throw for the money and call it quits?"

"That's all right by me," she said quickly, her hands shooting out for the white daggers. She carefully took her stance, tossed, and planted both of her daggers in the center of the circle. The quivering blades were barely over an inch apart. She stood back proudly, her eyes on Ren's big hands and the black-handled blades he was holding.

"I'm sure you won't mind if I use my own daggers for this final throw," Ren said matter-of-factly. In a blur of motion, before she had a chance to respond, he had dropped the substitute daggers and pulled his own ebony killing blades from his boot tops. Without a moment's hesitation, he threw his daggers with full force at the pine target. They slammed into the board, lodged up to their hilts, perfectly positioned at the center of the board, directly between Salen's blades.

The three fighters glanced nervously at each other and at the quivering hilts of the ebony blades. Ren walked to the board and removed Salen's daggers and his own as if he were pulling them from warm tallow.

As he returned to the three, Salen tossed him a sack of silver. Then the three of them headed for the door of the inn without saying a word. "Maybe another time," said Ren softly as he watched them go. He hadn't meant to insult the three female warriors or chase them away. They were as competitive as he, and it had been too long since he'd faced a good challenge. He realized that he had thoroughly enjoyed himself.

He sheathed his daggers and returned to the bar. "There's tables to be wiped," said Sot in a near whisper, awe apparent in both his voice and his look.

"No problem," said Ren amiably. It was the beginning of the best night he'd had in a long time.

❧ 4 ❧

Fists and Friends

The sun was setting on a cloudless sky over the city of Phlan. As with every evening in Phlan, a double shift of watchmen and soldiers readied themselves for whatever dangers the night might bring. Darkness was the time favored by the many monster tribes living in the ruins of Old Phlan, which surrounded the new walled portion of the city that its builders called "Civilized Phlan." Orcs roamed the slums immediately adjacent to the new city. Goblins and hobgoblins wandered the neighboring Kuto's Well and Podol Plaza areas. It was said that fire and hill giants ruled at Stojanow Gate and Valjevo Castle, landmarks that could be seen from the walls of the merchants' quarter. Rumor had it that even these monsters were afraid of the undead that were starting to rise in greater and greater numbers from Valhingen Graveyard, which was a mere five miles from the city's shipping docks.

It was on one of the city's wide piers that Tarl was walking when he spotted the figure of a woman, lying belly down, hammering on the dock so hard that she was actually causing the heavy wooden planks to rattle with each blow of her fists. Beside her stood a great horse. As Tarl moved closer, he could hear that the woman was crying. His curiosity piqued, he edged closer still.

The horse raised its head as Tarl approached, but it made no movement or sound. The woman remained oblivious to his presence. Tarl could see now that blood was caking to the sides of her hands, where they were worn raw from hammering against the nails and wood splinters on the dock planking. Compelled by his faith, Tarl squatted down and grabbed the woman's large hands in his own. "Please, lady, you must stop. Enough is enough." Had the woman struggled against his grip, he probably could not have stopped her from pulling her hands loose and resuming pounding the dock, but she turned her head toward him and left her hands extended, as if perhaps her energies were spent. Tarl could feel the power of a healing spell flowing through his own body and into hers as he muttered a prayer to Tyr. Slowly the caked blood loosened and sloughed off. New skin formed, pink and pale, to seal the broken blood vessels. More new skin formed to cover the tender wound. Soon her torn hands became smooth again.

Though Tarl's clerical skills did not approach those of Sontag, he was blessed with great innate power. He had used his healing abilities before, and had always found healing a very special exchange. The process inevitably involved sharing something extremely deep and personal with the receiver. Healing this woman was no different, except that he felt as though she also had shared something deep and personal with him. He squeezed her strong hands in his own and then pulled the woman gently to a sitting position. He stared into her eyes, and even in the dim twilight, he could see that they were a captivating green. The highlights of her long, full hair shimmered red in the flickering light of the torches that lined the docks. He glanced down, aware that he was staring, and that is when he realized that her leather garments were ridiculously tight, stretched over her tall frame in such a way that they awkwardly revealed much of her impressively ample body.

Tarl cleared his throat and started to speak. His voice cracked as he introduced himself. "I am . . . Tarl Desanea, a cleric of the warrior god, Tyr. I am . . . at your service. . . ."

"Thank you," said the woman quietly.

Still holding her hands, Tarl pulled the young woman up to her feet. He swallowed hard as he realized that she was nearly a fist's height taller than he and impressively fit. His face reddened as he noticed that a patch of material above her left breast had torn loose, revealing more woman than he had ever seen in his twenty years. He stepped back toward the horse, releasing his grip on her hands. "Uh, do you have a . . . blanket . . . or something?"

The big horse stamped and snorted, and Tarl flushed once more.

"Yes, of course," said the woman, quickly pulling the panel up to cover herself as she realized the reason for the cleric's embarrassment. She then turned to the horse. "Easy, Cerulean. I think we can trust this man." She pointed toward a bedroll lashed securely to the horse's back.

Tarl untied the bedroll, rolled a blanket from it, and moved close to drape it around the woman's broad shoulders. As he did, he noticed her warm, perfumed scent, and as he stepped back, he prayed a silent thank-you to Tyr for not demanding abstinence from his clerics.

"I'm sorry. It seems I've forgotten my manners," said the woman, turning demurely to face Tarl again. "I'm Shal . . . Shal Bal of Cormyr. I am a mage, formerly an apprentice to the great Ranthor."

Tarl found himself staring again. He had never before seen a mage so long on physical prowess. Most, he assumed, found their way into the mentally taxing profession because they did not have the physical strength for other jobs, and once they became practicing magicusers, they damaged their bodies even further by repeatedly performing physically taxing magicks. This woman called Shal could be mistaken for a smith, or even a warrior. With practice, Tarl thought, she could probably wield a hammer as well as he, or perhaps even Anton.

As Tarl stood appraising Shal, she was doing likewise. The young cleric's white hair did not match his youthful face. His steel-gray eyes were wise, and yet innocent at the same time. She had no real reason to trust him. She knew only what he had told her—that he was a warrior cleric of Tyr—but she had felt a strange bond from the minute he took her hands in his and healed her. She recalled, too, that Ranthor had always spoken highly of Tyrian clerics. He'd referred to them as "just" and "men you can trust at your back," words he didn't use lightly.

"Uh, Tarl," Shal began awkwardly. "Do you know this town? Is there some place I could go to purchase some new leathers?"

"Of course . . . forgive me." He looked tentatively at the horse. "Can we both ride that animal? I mean, I assume you do, but will he let me ride, too?"

"What do you say, Cerulean?" asked Shal, reaching for the saddle.

If I have my say, I'd say either one of you is quite heavy enough.

Shal hadn't really expected an answer, and as before, the horse's mental communication took her by surprise. She was by no means used to the idea of the familiar sending messages directly to her brain.

"So what do you want me to do—ride while he walks?" she answered in annoyance.

Tarl looked at her quizzically. "What did you say?"

"Nothing. I was just answe—uh, talking to the horse." She might have to explain about Cerulean to him sometime, she thought, but not now. She let Tarl cinch the saddle and help her up into it, then reached down and gave him a hand.

Oof! Double oats tonight, Mistress, especially after you made me do all that running for nothing.

Shal attempted a mental *Shut up,* but she could only guess that Cerulean had "heard" her when he snorted and bolted into a trot before he had even gotten off the docks and onto shore.

"Whoa, Cerulean! We'll hold it to a walk for now," Shal directed.

The horse obliged, but Shal couldn't help but wonder if he was intentionally adding an extra jar to his previously smooth gait.

Tarl had only been in the city of Phlan for two days himself, but the brothers from the temple had been free with advice about the merchants in town, and he had done some exploring himself as he tried to learn more about the beasts and undead creatures living outside the walls of Civilized Phlan.

He directed Shal to a seamstress, a pleasant woman who had mended Tarl's robes for him just the day before. When Shal let the blanket drop from her shoulders, the seamstress had to fight to keep from gawking. She couldn't recall another woman she'd ever done a fitting for with a physique like Shal's, and she certainly couldn't remember anyone with such ridiculously fitted clothes. "Wha—what can I do for ya?" she finally spluttered.

Shal winced as she saw what she took to be the woman's reaction to her size. Shal had been painfully aware, when she first stood next to Tarl, of how tall she had become, but his stares had seemed to be warm, even vaguely admiring. This woman was looking at her as if she were a freak. Shal almost wanted to break down and cry again, but she fought to keep her voice firm. "I need some clothes for the night—anything will do—and I'd like to pick up a full set of tailored leathers just as soon as you can have them ready."

The woman looked at the rack of clothing behind her and shook her head slowly. There wasn't a stitch of women's clothing in her shop that would fit the woman standing in front of her. But then she had a sudden thought and went quickly to the back room. In a few moments she returned with a full set of leathers and leather armor. "I can't fit you up very pretty, miss, but I do have this," she said, holding out the outfit at arm's length. "It was made for a man—a good-sized man. He was going to pay me for it when he finished a mission to Sokol Keep. I should've suspected he'd never come back. He was too adventurous for his own good. . . ." Her voice trailed off, and Shal sensed that the woman must have cared for the man.

"Are—are you sure you want me to have these?" asked Shal.

"Sure I'm sure," she said softly. "Besides, customers your size are few and far between." The woman saw Shal bite her lip and quickly blurted, "No offense intended, miss. I'll need to alter this some before you wear it. I mean, you're tall and all, but you've got a trim waistline, and there'll be . . . other adjustments to make. Isn't that right, young man?" she said, turning to Tarl.

Tarl hadn't taken his eyes off Shal since she had removed the blanket. Now his face burned red, and he grinned sheepishly. "Yes, ma'am. I'm sure you'll need to make some adjustments."

"Fine lotta help you are!" scolded the woman, and she shooed Tarl out into the street, with an admonishment not to come back until she pulled the curtains open again.

The leather tunic and leggings were the softest things Shal had ever felt against her skin. She brushed one sleeve admiringly, and the seamstress cooed proudly, "Genuine chimera leather. It don't come cheap, but it'll last you a lifetime if you treat it right. Now, you stand still, and I'll mark the places that need altering. I'll be able to send you home with these tonight, if you've got eight silvers and a couple of hours."

"I guess I have both and not much choice, regardless." Shal watched the woman as she whisked about her. She was as slender as a praying mantis, and not a muscle marred her silky skin. *Just hours ago, my figure was like that,* Shal thought. *Now I'm nothing but a giant, some kind of freak. I even tower over Tarl, and he must be over six feet tall. . . .*

"So, is that cleric your beau?" asked the seamstress nonchalantly, interrupting Shal's thoughts.

"No. Uh . . . he's a friend . . . an acquaintance, really."

"His eyes weren't sayin' acquaintance, miss, if you don't mind my sayin' so."

"We just met. He . . . he healed me. I'd injured my hands, and my clothes were ruined. . . ."

"You aren't exaggerating there. They look as though you burst out of 'em. I'll never understand how they coulda fit in the first place."

Shal didn't know what to say, or indeed whether it was worth explaining to this stranger or not, but she wanted to justify herself, to explain to somebody that she hadn't always looked like this. She told the woman part of her story, leaving out the part about how foolish she had been but explaining how she was magically changed to her current size.

The seamstress looked at her with genuine pity. *It's sad enough a woman has to worry about her looks from the day she's born,* she thought. *This one's prettier than most, but she still feels she has to tell stories to explain her appearance.* The seamstress tried to be reassuring. "I haven't seen many women your size in this part of the Realms, miss, but you don't need to apologize about your appearance to anyone. You look healthy as a horse, and you've got a nice face and beautiful hair. Why, you should've seen the look that young cleric was givin' you. There's many a woman who goes through a lifetime without being at the receivin' end of a look like that!"

Shal only felt worse, sensing that the woman's words were prompted by pity. She was certain Tarl's look was either that of a young, rather inexperienced man who'd never seen nearly so much of a woman exposed, or perhaps that of a warrior cleric admiring a person of equal brawn. At any rate, she really didn't want to think about it, so she stood quietly through most of the remainder of the fitting. It wasn't until the seamstress began sewing that she decided to find out if the woman knew anything about Denlor's tower. The seamstress knew of it. She said she'd heard that the old mage had managed to hold on to new territory gained in the northeast corner of Civilized Phlan for several months before finally succumbing to the onslaughts of the creatures attacking from the outside. Shal shivered at the way the local woman said "outside," as if she were pronouncing a curse or speaking of the Abyss itself.

The seamstress finished taking in the last tuck and handed her the tunic and pants to try on. When she had slipped the incredibly soft leather on, the woman helped her lace the leggings and girdle. "Very impressive, if I do say so myself, miss. The black looks good on you. Do you want to comb those tresses of yours and then take a look in the mirror in back?"

"I—I'll comb my hair; it must look awful. But I think I'll pass on the mirror. I trust your judgment." Shal shuddered at the thought of seeing her reflection. She'd seen the size of the pieces the seamstress worked with, and tucks or no, they were huge. Regardless of how the clothing might look on her, though, it felt wonderful. As soon as Shal finished brushing and combing her thick, long hair, she paid the seamstress the eight silvers she had asked for, plus a generous tip.

The moment the woman pulled open the curtains to the shop, Tarl entered. He was frankly stunned by what he saw. Shal's freshly combed red hair shone like highly polished rosewood against the deep black leather velour of the tunic. The green in her eyes blazed in the bright light of the seamstress's lanterns. Most of all, Shal's full figure was accented in devastating accuracy by the seamstress's careful tailoring.

"Pull your jaw up, boy," said the woman sternly. "You'd think you'd never seen a woman before."

"You look . . . great, Shal," Tarl said, faltering.

Great? Shal shook her head imperceptibly. She couldn't possibly look great, but she did have to admit that she felt a little less awkward with the new clothes on. Certainly her legs and arms didn't seem so conspicuously out of proportion now that she wore garments that were the right size. It helped, too, that the new leathers didn't bind her so tightly that she felt like an overstuffed sausage. "Thank you," Shal said absently, and she turned to leave.

Tarl followed her out like an adoring puppy. "Shal, I'd be honored if you'd allow me to help you find a place where you can stay tonight. Maybe we could have dinner together, if you feel up to it. I'd really like a chance to talk some more."

"I'd like that, too," said Shal. "But I could use a little time alone. I've lost something . . . some things . . . very dear to me recently, and I'm really not myself."

Tarl helped Shal mount Cerulean. "I know what you mean, Shal. I've lost something important to me, too. I think that may be why I felt such a special bond with you right from the start." Tarl mounted the horse behind her and wrapped his arms around her firm waist as they began to ride toward the center of town. He had yet to get a room for himself—he'd spent the previous night at the temple, and would probably do the same tonight—but he'd been told that the Laughing Goblin Inn offered safe, if a bit overpriced, lodging. He remembered the general direction but wasn't familiar enough with the town yet to know the most direct route to the inn. When they finally arrived and left Cerulean in the stable, Tarl had the distinctly odd feeling that the horse was annoyed with him.

The common room of the inn was already crowded. It took some time to locate the innkeeper, but fortunately there were vacancies. The prices Sot charged kept the inn from getting too full. "I'll show ya up to your room myself, miss," said Sot to the big woman. "Your dinner's included in the price," he added.

"For what you're charging the lady, you should throw in meals for a week, but we thank you nonetheless," Tarl said wryly.

Looking to Tarl and without missing a beat, Sot said, "It'll be another silver if you're planning on staying with her."

Tarl coughed. "I won't be, thank you. I'll see her to her room, though."

* * * * *

As Sot left the two of them, Tarl remained in the doorway. "Shal, take as long as you need. I'll be down in the common room waiting whenever you decide to come down."

"Thanks for all your help, Tarl. I won't be too long."

Tarl closed the door, and Shal stared straight ahead. Hanging on the inside of the doorway was a full-length mirror. She clasped her hand to her mouth and stifled a sob. Standing before Shal was a creature that frightened her more than any of the monsters rumored to lurk outside the city. She knew she had changed. Every time she looked anywhere, she was aware that her perspective was that of a considerably taller person. She had been able to see hands and arms, feet and legs, that belonged to a different person. Now that she saw her full reflection, she fully comprehended the fact that every inch of her body had grown proportionally. Even the fine black leathers didn't conceal the fact that she was bigger, considerably bigger, than she had ever imagined she could be.

Shal had always taken pride in her slim, supple arms and legs. She was proud, too, of her small feet, delicate fingers, and fine facial features. An almost completely changed woman returned her stare in the mirror. She was relieved to see that her body parts were not distorted, initially one of her big fears. The essence of her features, the intangible something that made her recognizable as herself, was still present, but she looked as if she'd gone through a major post-adolescent growth spurt and gotten incredibly serious about physical fitness. Shal tipped her head back and sighed. There were no more tears left in her. She had chided herself for her foolishness. She had mourned the loss of her petite body. She now faced the new Shal Bal. She didn't like it, but this was the Shal who would avenge Ranthor's death, and this was the Shal she would face until . . . until she died, for all she knew.

She backed away from the mirror till her legs brushed the bed. The big bed groaned as she lay down, mentally exhausted. She did her best to ignore it, lying still and breathing slow, easy breaths, the cleansing breaths Ranthor had taught her to quiet her mind and spirit. Each time she inhaled, she focused on pulling the loose ends of a particular fear from her extremities, and as she exhaled, she purged the fear from her body. By the time she went downstairs, her anxieties were gone. She was not happy to be living in her new body, but she was at peace. From the landing, she scanned the crowded common room until she spotted Tarl's silver-white hair.

When Shal reached Tarl's table, his face lit up. It crossed her mind that she was fortunate to have found a companion like Tarl. Within moments after she sat down, the two were talking about recent events in their lives. Shal's conversation meandered from present to past and back again. She described the events leading up to Ranthor's death. She told Tarl stories of the special things her teacher had done for her, and talked about how it felt to be carrying on without him. Embarrassed, she related the story of her squandered wishes and the little she knew about Denlor's tower.

Tarl, in turn, described the horrors he had faced in the graveyard. For some reason, he disclosed to Shal even more than he had told to Brother Tern. He described in detail the horror of the horses' screams and the screams of his brothers. He told about the vampire, with its bloodless skin and bone-chilling deep voice. He omitted only the exact way in which the hammer was lost, since he considered its recovery his personal quest. Perhaps he would tell Shal about it in time, but for now he had said enough.

"I'm sorry to bore you with my story," Tarl concluded. "The deaths of my friends weigh heavily on me, but I still can't believe I'm telling all this to you."

At a loss for words, Shal sat quietly for several minutes, lost in thought. "What makes me feel so bad," she said finally, "is that I let you heal me and help me find clothes and a place to stay without ever even considering that you might have your own problems."

"Enough said, my friend. Let's eat." Tarl clapped his hands to get the attention of the big blond man who was working the tables.

"We'll take chowder and biscuits . . . oh, and wine for the two of us," said Tarl after consulting with Shal. "Is there anything else you'd recommend?"

The big tavern worker didn't respond. Instead, he stood staring, slack-jawed, at Shal. Tarl cleared his throat to capture his attention again.

"Yes, sir . . . ma'am. Would you repeat that?"

Tarl repeated his order and his query.

"Well, we have some quail eggs that the cook does a terrific job on. They'd go well with your chowder." The tavern worker's intense blue eyes never left Shal as he spoke, and Tarl noticed that she was turning red under the big man's scrutiny.

"Is there something going on here that I'm not aware of? Do you two know each other?" asked Tarl, irritated by the attention the man was paying to Shal, not to mention the obvious discomfort he was causing her.

"No, sir," said the tavern worker, and he bowed hurriedly and left the table. Tarl noted that the man did not move like a typical tavern worker. Despite the fact that he stood a hand taller than Tarl and had brawn that rivaled Anton's, the big man made his way through the crowd with the grace of a warrior, or perhaps even a thief.

In minutes, he returned with a tray full of food, which he spread out on the table one dish at a time. Again, his full attention was focused on Shal.

"Are you always in the habit of staring at the inn's guests?" Tarl asked, catching the tavern worker's sleeve to get his attention.

"Was I staring?" The waiter paused, and his face flushed a deep red. He realized that was exactly what he had been doing. "Please accept my apologies. It's just that you . . . you remind me of someone. I really am sorry."

"Hey, you!" came a shout from a nearby table. "What happened to our food?"

"Yeah, what does a guy have to do to get some service in this joint?" called another voice.

Ren was oblivious. "Allow me to introduce myself. I'm called Ren . . . Ren o' the Blade." Ren shook Tarl's hand and then Shal's. He consciously looked down at the floor to avoid staring again. The woman could have passed for Tempest's twin. Seeing her was eerie, like seeing a ghost, but overwhelming at the same time. The woman shared all the traits that had originally attracted him to Tempest—her firm figure, her captivating eyes, her flowing red hair. And if anything, she was even prettier. Her facial features were fine for a woman her size, and the green of her eyes was even more intense than Tempest's had been.

One of the men who had called from a nearby table, a warrior with a sword and a long dagger at his belt, was approaching Ren from behind. "Hey, you there!" The man's words were slow and slurred, but Ren understood nonetheless. "Ya big galoot! We got food comin', and we're sick o' waitin' for you."

"I'd like to speak with you again later if I have a chance," Ren said to Tarl and Shal, then turned to face the warrior. "Excuse me." He turned and ushered the drunk back to his table. "I'll have your food in a minute," Ren said as he sat the man down firmly. "Now, if you'll all pardon me," he added, bowing as he left the warrior and his companions.

Shal watched Ren work his way back through the crowd, then she turned back to Tarl. "First that seamstress, and now this guy. Every time I start to feel as if I can cope with the change in my appearance, someone looks at me as if I were a freak."

"He said you remind him of someone. I'm sure that's why he was staring," Tarl assured her. "He didn't seem to be trying to be rude or unmannerly. In fact, he went out of his way to be polite and took a big chance of offending that warrior and his comrades."

"That's for sure. I hope he doesn't turn his back on those fellows tonight." Shal took her first spoonful of the chowder and realized after having a second that she was famished. Tarl did likewise, and the two forgot about conversation and began to eat heartily.

When Ren finally brought out the beef pies and refills

of the pitchers of ale ordered by the table of fighters, they complained bluntly about his service. Under ordinary circumstances, Ren probably would have apologized and tried to do something to make amends, but on this night, he wasn't even paying attention. Instead, he was staring once again at Shal. He set the plates down on one end of the table, making no attempt to match orders. And when he started pouring the ale, he accidentally overfilled one of the cups, sloshing ale in the laps of the customer.

"What do you think you're doing, you clumsy oaf?" the warrior blurted angrily.

"I'm awfully sorry. Here," said Ren, handing the man a bar rag. "I've got to find out her name," he muttered, as if to himself.

Ren turned on his heels and strode to the table where Shal and Tarl remained seated. Behind him, the fighters were sputtering angrily, but Ren neither saw nor heard them. He was staring down again at the woman who so startlingly resembled his lost love. "May I know your name?"

Shal didn't answer. Instead, she pointed behind him. Ren didn't react, but Tarl did. From the corner of his eye he had been watching Ren ever since he first approached the warriors. When Ren spilled the ale and walked away, Tarl knew there was going to be trouble. "Dagger!" shouted Tarl, and he rushed past Ren and tackled the approaching fighter.

Ren spun around to confront the three other men who had been sitting at the table. Normally Ren would have tried to maneuver in such a way that he only had to face one man at a time, but he didn't want any of these rabble getting anywhere close to the woman behind him. He spread his bearlike arms as wide as they would go and plowed forward, taking all three men to the floor with him.

Sot heard the noise of the fight before he saw what was happening. "Not *another* fight!" he muttered to no one in particular. "Used to be a scuffle in a tavern was no big deal, but now the town council sends the Watch Guards out to break it up. A guy can lose customers that way." He grabbed his club and leaped over the bar. Unfortunately, he landed hard on the foot of a customer who was making his way toward the center of the action. Sot learned the hard way that it is almost impossible to apologize with a cudgel in your hand, and in moments the entire inn had joined the fray.

Shal watched as Tarl expertly administered a chop to the neck of the man with the dagger and sent him reeling. Quickly he followed up to finish the job, while Ren was wrestling with two of the warriors he had knocked to the floor. The third was up and was about to kick Ren in the spleen, but Shal leaped into the action and pushed him hard from behind, screaming, "Leave him alone!" The man fell full belly onto a table of food and immediately began to be pummeled by several people who had been calmly attempting to eat despite the fracas.

"Hey! What do you know?" said Shal, looking down at her hands. "Being strong has some advantages after all!"

"You all right, Shal?" asked Tarl, pausing after fending off still another brawler with a well-placed kick.

"So the name is Shal, is it?" Ren shouted as he pushed one of the warriors toward a boisterous knot of fighters that had formed near the center of the room. "Do you have any relatives in Waterdeep?"

"No," called Shal above the din. "Why do you ask?"

At this point, five fighters advanced toward the trio. Two well-armed women rushed toward Tarl like charging bulls, and two good-sized men began to pummel Ren with their fists. The fifth fighter planted himself squarely in front of Shal and began to wind up for a punch to her midsection. Shal had never been in a fistfight before. Instinctively she threw her arms up to protect her face and tensed every muscle in her body. His blow to her firm stomach didn't even phase her. Slack-jawed, the man looked up at Shal, his face turning green. She looked down at him, formed a fist just like her attacker's but larger, and slammed a hard uppercut into the man's chin. He staggered back and crashed to the floor well beyond where her first victim had landed.

Meanwhile, Ren and Tarl had dispatched their attackers just in time to see the results of Shal's punch. "Whoa there, girl!" Tarl called out, panting. "You should be protecting us!" Tarl stole a moment to glance at Ren, and Shal and the two men broke into smiles and turned as one to face whatever riffraff might still be of a mind to tackle them, but there were no takers. Most of the crowd were occupied with brawls of their own. The few people who'd been paying attention were frozen by the remarkable prowess of the three fighters, who fought as if they'd been battling together for years.

"We'd better get out of here," grunted Ren to his new companions. "The Watch Guard will be here any minute. They sentence people for brawling now in 'Civilized' Phlan."

Quickly the three worked their way to the inn's big double doors and pushed through. Before they even had a chance to step into the street, they were blocked by seven members of the Watch Guard. The guards wasted no time expertly slipping the loops of their man-catchers around the necks of the three. The strange implements were basically nothing more than nooses on long poles, designed to keep captives a safe distance from their captors. A quick jerk of the torturous implements by the guards sent the three to their knees, choking, effectively eliminating any thoughts of resistance. Another practiced jerk, and they were standing again.

"Take them before the council," instructed the group's

leader. "We'll get the rest of this rabble cleaned up in short order."

"Even man-catchers have their weaknesses," Tarl whispered to Ren.

Ren shook his head. "Don't try anything, friend. The sentence for fighting here is mild compared to the one for resisting the Watch Guard. It isn't worth it."

"You've got that right," one of the guards said as he prodded them along. "Now, shut up and get a move on. The night's council representative is waiting for you."

* * * * *

Porphyrys Cadorna loved night council duty. As Tenth Councilman, he seldom had a chance to demonstrate his wisdom; there were always nine others whose views superseded his. But during night duty, he was judge and jury for whatever citizens were dragged into the council chambers. Cadorna dreamed of the advancements he would earn as the wisdom of his judgments became known to the rest of the council and the voting representatives of Phlan. Naturally he would make certain that his decisions were widely known.

Porphyrys was the last living member of the noble Cadornas, a family respected for its wealth and power until the time of the Dragon Run. The Cadorna Textile House was among many businesses and landmarks destroyed by the onslaught of dragons that leveled Phlan fifty years ago, and its ruins remained just outside the civilized portion of the city, under the control of the darker forces of Phlan. When his last uncle was on his deathbed, Porphyrys vowed, for reasons of honor and reasons of his own, to return the name of his family to prominence. His personal goal was nothing less than to rule Phlan, no matter what the cost. Porphyrys was a patient man—he had worked his way through the ranks of the assembly and finally attained the position of Tenth Councilman—but he had been a long time waiting, and now he was ready to take any steps necessary to get what he wanted.

Cadorna stretched his long legs. Yes, making the council, even the tenth seat, was definitely a step in the right direction. With the council supervising every facet of the city's life, there was hardly anything he wasn't able to get his hands into. A man on the council was a veritable king.

And the man in the first seat *is* king, thought Cadorna, or at least as close to king as one could get in Phlan. He moved around the table and sat in the First Councilman's chair. Yes, this feels more like it, he thought, wriggling down in the plush seat to make himself more comfortable. His thoughts were interrupted by a knock on the door. Quickly getting up, Cadorna hurried back to the tenth chair. "Come in!" he shouted, a little louder than necessary.

"Your dinner, Councilman," the attendant announced. "Also, the mage, Gensor, is here and wishes to speak with you about one of the parties whose case you will be reviewing in the next session."

"Send him in."

Gensor worked for the city, checking and setting up magical seals, scanning prisoners for magical items, and sometimes providing interpretations of supernatural events. In addition to his official duties, he also worked privately, on an assignment basis, for Cadorna. Cadorna found Gensor's insight useful, but nevertheless always felt uneasy around the mage. It was said that magic-users could read men's minds.

The black-robed mage entered the chambers and found Cadorna sitting down before a plateful of mutton and potatoes the attendant had just brought in. Gensor always marveled at Cadorna's appetite. Nearly every time he came to see the man, he seemed to be sitting down for a meal or a snack, yet somehow he remained as lean as a lizard.

Almost anyone who spent any time with Cadorna, including Gensor, could not help but be aware that the man had a busy social and political agenda, and while Gensor didn't care for Cadorna on a personal basis, he knew he was a man to watch.

"What is it, Gensor?" demanded Cadorna. "Can't you see I'm busy?"

Gensor smiled, deciding to assume that Cadorna was joking. "I thought it necessary to speak with you. An unusual trio is coming before you for judgment during your next session. There's a tavern worker from the Laughing Goblin, a woman new to town, and a cleric of Tyr."

"So? Come to the point, will you, man?"

Gensor interpreted the councilman's impatience as posturing, something at which he excelled. Consequently, he took his time with the explanation. "I thought you should know that the tavern worker radiates a powerful but isolated magic."

"What do you mean 'isolated'?" Cadorna set down his fork and leaned toward Gensor.

"I mean it comes from his boots and must be the boots themselves or something he carrying in them. I'm sure he's no magic-user."

"So he's carrying a magical item," Gensor stated. "That doesn't seem particularly unusual."

"As I said, whatever it is, it's very powerful. But at any rate, I wasn't finished. The woman radiates magic like a beacon in the night. I have no way of knowing what items or power she has, but I've never received a stronger reading from my spell. The cleric is just what he seems. He has no magical devices on his person, save his holy symbol." Gensor could almost see Cadorna's mind at work. He was tempted to use a spell to detect the man's thoughts but decided not to. He rather enjoyed watching Cadorna as his mind worked.

"There is one other thing I wanted to mention. Apart

from their magic, the three probably make up the most physically powerful trio I have ever seen. I think, under the circumstances, you may find these three useful."

"Thank you, Gensor," Porphyrys Cadorna said thoughtfully. "Well done. You may go now." He watched as the mage left, and then he allowed himself the pleasure of gloating over the possibilities. Technically, he should reserve judgment on a group such as this for the First Councilman and the Eighth—the first because of the magic attested to by the mage, and the latter because he was a Tyrian cleric and therefore presided over matters concerning the temple of Tyr.

On the other hand, Cadorna mused, Gensor was right to point these three out to me. They certainly could do me some good. Some kind of a test is in order, and I think I know just what it should be. If they can survive the dangers of Sokol Keep, they may be worthy of some other tasks I have in mind. . . .

Cadorna savored the last bite of mutton. The cook had finally gotten the seasonings and cooking time right. Now, if he could only work on the potatoes . . . the sauce they had simmered in had boiled away to nothing, and the potatoes were dry and overdone.

When the attendant came in to pick up the dishes, Cadorna suggested he tell the cook to start learning more quickly if he didn't want to be replaced.

"Yes, Honorable Tenth Councilman." The attendant quickly wiped off the table and turned to leave with Cadorna's dirty dishes.

"Wait, boy. How many cases for review this session?" asked Cadorna.

"Two, I believe, sir. The watch warden would know for sure."

"Obviously he would know, but he's not here, is he? It wouldn't hurt for you to pay attention to such details, would it?" Cadorna snapped. "In any case, remind the watch warden that I like to have spectators present. Have him admit any who are waiting and drum up a few more if he has to. I'll be ready to start the next session in fifteen minutes."

The attendant bowed awkwardly, taking care not to drop the dishes, and then took his leave. Cadorna used the time to check his attire. He firmly believed that intimidation was critical to passing judgments, and that a person was always more intimidating when he looked his best. Finally Cadorna lifted his sleeve to check his poison dagger. It was held in place by a gold armlet, an heirloom that featured the Cadorna family crest, a snake with its tail coiled around a weaver's shuttle. The dagger was loose and at the ready. Cadorna also believed that a man in his position could never be too careful.

When Cadorna finally entered the hearing room, he was pleased to see that it was almost full. Crowds always made cases more interesting, and he felt his growing reputation deserved maximum exposure. The next case, according to the watch warden, involved two feuding groups of clerics. Each band held that the other was stealing its worshipers, but Cadorna was only half listening. Instead, he was watching the three the mage had spoken about.

The tavern worker was a huge man, dressed in a loose tunic. With his knotted hair and baggy clothing, he appeared at first glance to be nothing more than a giant dullard, but Cadorna could see from his forearms, the breadth of his shoulders, and his posture that the man was incredibly well muscled. The woman was almost as tall as the tavern worker, and she looked strong enough and fit enough to take on almost any man. Cadorna shivered. He was himself quite tall, but he hated big men, and he had no use for large women. He preferred women who were petite and meek. The cleric of Tyr was a handsome, well-built man, obviously powerful, but nothing like the big tavern worker. His face was that of a young man, yet his hair was silvery white, the color of a much older man's. Cadorna stared intently at each of them, hoping to detect something of their magic, but he had no such ability.

He straightened in his chair. If he was going to use these three to his best advantage, he must make a good impression on them. He directed his attention to the cleric who was testifying. "What was that you just said, Canon? I'm sorry, I didn't catch your name."

"Dessel, your honor. Canon Dessel. Honorable Councilman Cadorna," the cleric pleaded, "these fights between our two faiths must come to a stop. No one profits from such bickering."

"Yes, I quite agree, and I believe I have just the remedy." Cadorna had heard just enough of the case to have an idea. He stood up and swept his arm from one party to the other, in a grandiose gesture. He'd seen the First Councilman make the same motion before, and he was very taken with the effect. "A cleric from each temple will be dispatched immediately to spend thirty days helping heal the brave watchmen who suffer injury while guarding the walls of the city. For every report of disputes between the two temples that reaches the council, another cleric from each temple will be assigned to thirty days of healing service. In this manner, each side will be encouraged to put aside petty bickering or have little time for the maintenance of its own temple. Of course, in the meantime, you will both be serving the needs of our city."

The crowd began murmuring. For a moment, Cadorna worried that he may have gone too far in his judgment. Then he saw the tentative nods of agreement and smiles on people's faces. Several clerics from each of the temples actually walked, albeit reluctantly, to the center of the room and shook hands! Cadorna beamed with pride at the sound logic of his decree.

"The Tenth Councilman has spoken," the watch warden declared. He ushered the canons of both temples away and then returned to announce the principals in the next case. "Shal Bal of Cormyr, Tarl Desanea of Vaasa, and Ren o' the Blade of Waterdeep will stand before this session of the council to be judged in the matter of disorderly conduct and brawling within the city limits of Civilized Phlan."

Porphyrys Cadorna gazed down from his place on the dais in the most condescending and accusatory manner he could muster. "This is the council chamber of the city of Phlan," said Cadorna in his most official-sounding voice. "You have been brought here by the Watch Guard for wrongdoing in our fair city. Rest assured that I will hear out what you have to say and carefully review the nature of your case before passing judgment."

Ren was barely aware of what Cadorna was saying. He was busy making a mental note of the full names and home grounds of his two newfound companions. He was still wrestling with the idea that Shal might be somehow related to Tempest. Related or no, he was stunned by her looks and more than a little taken with her candid, bright-eyed manner. Likewise, Ren had been impressed by Shal's cleric friend, Tarl. Tarl hadn't had any reason to jump into the midst of that fight. In fact, he could probably have sought sanctuary at his temple instead of facing judgment.

For Shal, everything about the night had seemed strange and artificial, like a play she was watching from the wings but which she could begin acting in at any time. When the guards first caught her in their wretched nooses, Shal had been terrified. She had seriously considered pulling out the Staff of Power to learn exactly what it could do. It was the relative calm of Tarl and Ren that had kept her from doing something foolish. Neither of them had seemed particularly concerned about being captured. She also felt reassured by the councilman's manner. She was impressed by the fairness of the decision he had imposed upon the clerics, and he had promised fairness in reviewing their case. Whatever the sentence, she hoped it wouldn't take long to fulfill. She had hoped to travel to Denlor's tower the next day, after a good night's rest. This could hold her up considerably.

Tarl had himself observed the clerics of Sune and Tempus arguing in the streets over converts and then watched with interest as they brought their argument before the night council. He, too, was impressed with Cadorna's judgment because of its twofold prospect for good—helping the temples, while at the same time helping the city. Somehow, though, the wisdom and fairness of the decision didn't ring true with his gut intuition about Cadorna. Tarl had seldom gone wrong trusting his first impressions of people. He was as comfortable with Shal and Ren as if he had known them all his life, but he had no such sense of comfort in the presence of Cadorna. He was conscious of the man's posturing, something common to political leaders, and there was something else that made him feel very cool toward the man, but he couldn't quite put his finger on it.

"So, you three have been picked up for brawling at the Laughing Goblin Inn. How do you plead?" intoned Cadorna.

"Guilty, Councilman," said Ren, holding his head high. He reasoned that if their sentence were too severe, he could always use his lockpicking skills to escape. The worst sentence meted out in Phlan was being thrown over the city walls at night, but that possibility seemed remote, considering the relatively minor nature of their offense. They would undoubtedly be held in a cell for at least a little while before anything so drastic happened, and Ren could get them out.

"Guilty, Councilman," Tarl said. The cleric knew that the high cleric of the temple of Tyr held a position on the council. Tarl expected that he could appeal to him for leniency for himself and his two friends if need be.

"Guilty—that is, if brawling means defending yourself and trying to get away from a fight you didn't start, Councilman," Shal said.

This brought smiles to more than a few faces in the crowded room, including that of the presiding councilman. "Yes, well . . . Ah, be that as it may . . ." Cadorna was startled by the temerity of the woman and the confidence of the two men. He began to hope that these three would become the first to survive his test.

"The council's main function is not punishment in the customary sense, but rather giving lawbreakers such as yourselves incentive for serving the community. We provide them with missions allowing them to challenge and attempt to overcome the evil that lurks in the ruins around the civilized portion of the city. For your sentence, the three of you will undertake such a mission. Thorn Island, which is located south of Civilized Phlan, across the bay, has for too long been avoided by the good merchants of Phlan. There are purported to be monsters inhabiting Sokol Keep, the fortress that occupies much of the island's surface, and these monsters are said to make sailing in the proximity of the island all but impossible. You are charged with the task of discovering the secret of the darkness that makes Sokol Keep and Thorn Island uninhabitable. Bring back any information that may be of benefit to us in recovering the island. If you are successful in this venture, you will not only have fulfilled the terms of your sentence, but you will also be rewarded by the council. For now, you are released on your own recognizance." Cadorna signaled to the watch warden.

"The Tenth Councilman has spoken. Next case," the

watch warden declared, and he ushered the three companions out of the council chambers.

As the three made their way back to the Laughing Goblin, they spoke nervously of what the morning would bring. They also exchanged tales of their battle experience—or lack of it—and Tarl and Shal told Ren much of what they had told each other about their activities during the last few days. By the time they reached the inn, they were laughing like old friends. After shaking hands with Shal and Tarl and taking a last longing glance at Shal, Ren parted to go to his room in the loft above the stables. Tarl saw Shal to her room and then returned to the Temple of Tyr, where he accepted the hospitality of his brothers in the faith for what little remained of the night.

❧ 5 ❧

Sokol Keep

None of the three slept well. Shal had come to Phlan for one reason only—to avenge the death of her mentor—and so far, she had not even gotten to Denlor's tower. Shal hadn't planned on being sent on any mission for the town council.

Tarl, too, was anxious. When Tarl checked on Anton that night, the big man voiced two words, but they were "no" and "die," and his glazed eyes looked haunted. Tarl couldn't help but think his friend was even nearer to death. Tarl's only hope for quieting his feelings of guilt and helplessness was to take the time he needed to prepare mentally and spiritually for his return to the graveyard to regain the hammer. He had not counted on being required to "recover" Thorn Island, but he would make the best use he could out of the town council mission.

Ren, on the other hand, was actually excited about the expedition to Thorn Island. For the first time in a year, he had a clear goal in mind—an assigned goal, granted, but a goal nonetheless. And he would be among interesting company besides.

Tarl awoke before dawn and spent time preparing his armor in quiet meditation, as was the custom of his faith, contemplating the rightness of his motivations, and focusing on the need to display bravery and skill to the honor of Tyr. The ritual of his meditation was broken more than once by the memory of the screams of his brethren at the hands of the undead, the image of the vampire mocking him, the humiliation of giving up the sacred Hammer of Tyr, and the nightmare of Anton's flesh sizzling at the impact of the unholy symbol from the Abyss.

Tarl shook his head to clear it of such thoughts and said a final prayer to Tyr, thanking him for providing companionship as he sought to hone his skills until he would be ready to make his return to the stronghold of the vampire and demand the return of the hammer.

As the sun cleared the rooftop of the temple and its light touched the back of his neck, Tarl felt invigorated. Surely it was a sign that his god had renewed his clerical powers. He stood and stretched, relishing the feel of his freshly oiled chain mail adjusting itself to his form. Picking up his backpack, shield, and war hammer, he whispered the word "Ready" and set off to find his friends—and his destiny.

* * * * *

Ren, too, was observing a ritual—that of a ranger-turned-thief. First he checked the sharpness of the two jewel-handled daggers in his boots, bittersweet reminders of Tempest. She had given him the daggers as a gift some years ago, and he had later had two ioun stones from the take for which she was killed concealed inside their jeweled hilts. Ren thought of the daggers as Right and Left, in keeping with his usual straightforward line of thinking. As always, the blades were keen enough to split a baby's hair. Ren went on to inspect his lockpicks, fire flask, hinge oil, climbing hooks, and door wedges. All seemed to be in perfect order. His nine throwing daggers and his two short swords, on the other hand, were dull and required sharpening. As a ranger, roaming the woodlands, Ren had preferred the longbow and long sword to short swords, but since he had turned to thieving in the streets of Waterdeep with Tempest, he preferred weapons that brought him up close and personal.

After checking his other basic supplies, Ren pulled out the small amber-inlaid chest he had carried with him from Waterdeep. He brushed a layer of dust from its surface and chided himself for not taking better care of the container that held the most important tool of his trade. After disarming the three traps designed to keep intruders from the box, Ren lifted the cover.

A sensation akin to an electrical charge coursed up Ren's spine as he touched the enchanted gauntlets. "It's been far too long since we were together," Ren whispered. Carefully he pulled on the jet-black gloves. As they warmed to the temperature of his skin, their color and texture changed to match his tanned skin perfectly. He held his hands up admiringly. No one would ever know he was wearing gloves. He fitted his favorite lockpick into the palm of his right glove, and it disappeared into the perfectly camouflaged surface. Then he tucked a pouch of sneezing powder under the right glove. Where there should have been a bulge, there was only his wrist. The magical gloves not only protected his hands, but more than that, they also added a measure of speed and dexterity to his movements.

Ren joined his hands together, cracked his knuckles, and then reached for his black leather armor. He smiled wistfully as he lifted the durable featherweight vest. He could remember the day Tempest had stolen it for him— and how she'd taken it off him that same night. After checking the fastenings, Ren slipped into the armor. He caught sight of his reflection on the polished surface of a copper planter, and he let out a low whistle. It had been a long time since he looked that good. "This one's for you, Tempest," he said softly. "And when this is done, I'll get that bastard who killed you. . . ."

With everything in place, he was ready for the final step in his ritual. He stood with his feet wide apart and began the first moves in a slow and complicated set of exercises. Shal Bal would have recognized them as a wizard's trance relaxation routine. Tarl would have called it a Dan muscle stimulation. Ren simply called it the last thing he had to do.

* * * * *

Like Tarl, Shal had been up since before dawn, memorizing spells she thought she might need. The last she struggled with was one Ranthor had taught her in recent months, which was called Web of Entrapment. Dipping into the Cloth of Many Pockets, Shal easily found the necessary components for the spell. She smiled, aware once again of how well her master had provided for her. "I hope to make you proud, Ranthor," she whispered softly.

She donned the fine leathers she had bought yesterday and her cloak, as well. "This mission isn't what I had in mind, but it will be an adventure," Shal said aloud, talking half to herself, half to the spirit of her mentor. "My first adventure into the 'real' world. I don't suppose you packed 'adventure equipment' into this cloth, did you, Ranthor?" She repeated the words and then reached inside the cloth. Amazing! she thought as she pulled out item after item—a pair of daggers, a rod with a perpetual light at the tip, an odd belt with a seemingly unending array of sheaths and pouches, a leather purse filled with an assortment of common spell components, and a small bag of flour.

"Flour? I can guess what everything else is for, but why the flour?"

Shal reached into the final pocket and found a tiny scroll. She unfurled it and discovered a note written in Ranthor's fluid script: *The flour is there to reveal what is invisible. You should have known that, Apprentice.*

"My teacher, you truly knew me too well. I wish you could meet my two new friends," she sighed.

Shal took a deep breath and paused for a last moment to prepare mentally for the test she must pass before making her way to Denlor's tower. She wondered if perhaps Tarl and Ren might help her when—if—they returned from Sokol Keep.

She found perfect stowing places for her spell components, rods, daggers, and magical cloth on the oddly designed belt. Shal held the belt up wistfully before buckling it, aware that it might have gone around her former self twice. Now, she needed to use the last buckle hole. When she'd pulled it snug, she marveled at the fact that it was virtually weightless once it was secured. Finally she practiced drawing the Staff of Power from the magical cloth. The six-foot-tall staff looked more than a little odd coming out of the small square of indigo cloth, but it came easily to her hand every time she asked for it. She almost laughed at the thought of employing the staff or any of her magical items on real enemies. "Yes, Ranthor, this is me, Shal—the same Shal who was afraid of a Burning Hands spell."

* * * * *

Ren was already in the common room, talking with Sot, when Shal came downstairs. He bit his lip when he saw the way she'd pulled her hair back. A large copper clip lifted her auburn hair off her face, accenting her high, flushed cheekbones, without even beginning to tame the wild red tresses that raged down her back. It was not a style Tempest had ever used, but it was stunning, and it made Ren see Shal for the first time as having a beauty unique to her and not tied up in his memories. "Good morning, Shal. You look wonderful!"

Shal blushed and smiled. "Good morning!" Shal stopped and stood stock still at the bottom of the stairs, staring at Ren. The self-described ranger-thief, whose body had been hidden yesterday in a mangy, baggy tunic and pants held up by a drawstring, was now dressed from head to foot in body-fitting black, oiled leather. His physique was impressive, not at all that of the dumpy barkeep Shal had conversed with the day before. Whereas yesterday Ren's blond hair had been matted to his head, today it shone a honey gold, cascading smoothly to his shoulders. His blue eyes glimmered, their deep color intensified by the brilliant blue of the gemstones set in the shoulder pads of his black armor. Shal noticed, too, that concealed cleverly on his person was a veritable armory. Strategically stowed for quick access were knives, daggers, two short swords, and several devices Shal couldn't attempt to name. "I—I hardly recognize you," she managed to say.

"Me neither," echoed Sot, eyeing the big man. "Ain't he a sight, though. I guess I'll have to be puttin' up a sign for some new help around here." His expression changed suddenly as he realized how his words might be interpreted. "Not because you won't be coming back from the island, of course. I just mean that I . . . I can see you've got more important things to do with yourself than waiting on tables."

Ren smiled and pulled out a stool for Shal from behind the bar.

Shal smiled, too, touched by Sot's obvious concern for Ren. Then she shivered suddenly. It was possible, perhaps even likely, that they would be killed. She hadn't realized that she had been avoiding the thought. She let out a slow breath and turned her mind to more immediate concerns. "Is Tarl here yet?" she asked as she started to sit down.

"Yeah. He just went out for a minute to check on your horse," Sot replied.

Shal slapped one hand up to her mouth. "Cerulean! Excuse me . . . I should be seeing to my own horse. I'll be back in a minute."

Before Shal even reached the stable, the familiar was bombarding her with snide remarks. *Oh, sure, off on an adventure, and you're going to leave me cooling my heels in this pig sty. No, worse—you'd forgotten you even had a familiar, a faithful magical steed prepared to serve you regardless of the risk. . . .*

"Cerulean, I'm sorry. I've been so wrapped up in things that I didn't even think to tell you about the trip I must make. I promise to have the innkeeper tend to you while I'm gone," Shal said as she approached the huge horse's stall.

Unnoticed by Shal, Tarl had entered the stable with a sack of corn fodder to spread in the horse's trough. "Good morning, Shal," he said, looking at her rather strangely. "Apologizing to your horse now, eh? I gathered yesterday that you were pretty chummy with him, but—"

"But he's not a horse—" Shal began.

I'm not? Cerulean's telepathic message interrupted Shal's thought.

"I mean, he is a horse, but he's more than that. . . . Oh, I don't know what I mean! Could you . . . could you excuse us for a minute, Tarl?"

Tarl looked oddly at Shal once again and shrugged. Then he turned and headed slowly for the door, muttering all the while. "No problem, whatever, Shal. I don't rate even so much as a 'Good morning,' but the horse gets a moment in private with you. That's just fine," he said, obviously a little confused.

As soon as Tarl closed the door, Shal turned to face her familiar. "You can't come, Cerulean," she insisted. "We're taking a boat. We'll probably have to scale walls. There's no place to—"

No place to put me? Have you forgotten your legacy from Ranthor already? Not that I like being put in that thing, mind you. As I said before, it's awfully dark in there. But if I'm not with you, I can't possibly warn you of any danger, can I?

Shal threw up her hands. So much for feeling on top of things. How forgetful could she be? She pulled the Cloth of Many Pockets from her belt and held it out toward Cerulean. "So how do we go about this? For some reason I seem to have trouble picturing a great big horse like you jumping into one of these tiny little pockets."

Just stand back and watch!

Shal opened the stall gate and backed up against the stable wall, holding out the small piece of cloth. To her horror, the giant horse began to paw the ground, then charged toward her, its ears flat against its head and its nostrils flaring. Just as she was certain she would be smashed against the wall, Cerulean reared, dived, and poured like so much liquid into one of the pockets in the cloth.

I hate doing that. I hope you can see why now. The familiar's mental communication was muffled slightly by the cloth.

You hate it! I'm amazed Ranthor didn't die of a heart attack long ago! I hope your entrances into the outside world are a bit less dramatic. By the way, can you get out of there if I don't summon you?"

You would *have to ask that. Indeed I can—as long as you don't tell me I can't.*

Shal looked down at the indigo cloth as she tucked it back into place inside her belt. She was about to reply again when she realized how foolish she must look— would look—if anyone were watching her, so she decided to try her hand at telepathy. *I won't tell you you can't, but rest assured that if I find you in my lap at some awkward moment, you'll be back in the dark until further notice. Understand?*

Quite clear, Mistress.

And don't sneer when you say that word! Shal knew

her telepathic thought hit home when the familiar, for once, didn't try to have the last word.

*　*　*　*　*

Tarl and Ren were just sitting down to breakfast with Sot when Shal came back. "Save any for me?" she asked, her appetite sparked as she entered to the smell of hot biscuits and porridge.

Sot looked on with a bemused smile as Tarl and Ren stumbled over each other to pull out a stool for Shal, but the young mage didn't even notice. She was too worried about how to seat her much-enlarged frame down gracefully on the quaint stool. She wondered as she watched Tarl and Ren resume their seats how men could always sit down without looking awkward, no matter how big they were.

Tarl poured her a cup of milk and offered her the biscuits.

Ren leaned forward and began to speak eagerly. "Sot here says he had a grandfather who was doing guard duty at Sokol Keep during the time of the Dragon Run."

Sot interrupted. "He was a guard there at the time, but he wasn't on duty when the dragons struck. Otherwise, he never coulda given this to my dad." So saying, Sot pulled a heavy bronze medallion out from beneath his shirt.

Tarl sucked in his breath as he saw the bronze piece. Quickly he plunked down the bowl of porridge he was handing to Shal, nearly spilling it, and extended his hand out toward Sot. "May I see that, please?"

"Sure." Sot lifted the thick chain up over his head and handed the medallion across the table to Tarl.

"Do you know what this medallion is?" Tarl asked excitedly, running his fingers over its embossed surface and examining the inscriptions on either side of it.

Sot shook his head. "Why, no . . . I never did find out

❦ 102 ❦

what that symbol on it stood for. It's just somethin' I've held on to since I was a kid 'cause my dad told me it was from my granddad."

"It's a special holy symbol of Tyr, the god I serve." Tarl pulled out his own holy symbol and held the two up next to each other for comparison. The icon depicted on the front of each—a war hammer topped by a scale—was identical, but the runes were different. "Your grandfather must have been a cleric of Tyr. But he was in a sect that I've only heard about. They were said to have been very devout in their faith."

"All I know is that my father always said Granddad was a guard at Sokol Keep. I guess I'd heard that there'd been a temple at the keep, but I never knew my grandfather was connected with it." Sot pointed at the medallion. "Would that medal be of any use to you, seein' as how you're a cleric and all?"

Tarl's heart leaped. "Absolutely! The power of my god flows through such holy symbols. They help protect the wearer."

"Well, seein' as how you're the ones going off to a place that's supposed to be overrun by ghosts an' spirits, why don't you take it? You can give it back to me if you—*when* you come back." As he spoke, Sot reached out and folded Tarl's hand over the medallion.

"Thank you most heartily!" Tarl said sincerely. "I'll put this to good use."

"Now, don't be gettin' mushy on me, young fella. You've got devils to face, and the town guards'll be throwin' you to 'em if you don't get a move on. You'd all best be goin' before they have to come for you." Sot shooed the three out the door and called out to wish them luck as they started down the street.

Driven by nervous energy, the three quickly made their way to the city's docks. The shoreline was crowded with vendors selling wares from incoming shipments, and the docks were lined with boats and small ships. The water of the Moonsea and the southeastern edge of the Bay of Phlan was a brilliant tourmaline blue. To the east, the waters of the Stojanow belched into the bay, spreading their putrid stench into the bright, clear water.

No one had to tell the three where Thorn Island was. It was easily visible from the shore, and they could see why merchants sailed wide to avoid it. A dark shadow hung over the small, bleak island. It was as if, as they turned their heads to scan the horizon, someone dropped a translucent black scarf over their faces just as the island came into view. Almost as ominous were the charred walls of Sokol Keep itself, which jutted up, gray and desolate-looking, from the low slate cliffs that made up the island's shoreline.

"That councilman did say something about a reward in this for us if we bring back information that helps them to recover the island, didn't he?" Ren asked.

"Personally, if we ever return from that place, the only reward I want is to serve Tyr," said Tarl looking out at the blot of desolation defiling the bay.

Shal stared at the fortress with a mixture of fear and curiosity. "My master told me about such places—places enveloped in such darkness that they appear shadowed even in bright sunlight. He said it was almost always a sign that there were undead existing in torment."

Tarl blanched at the word "undead." He would rather face an army of orcs than another specter or wraith . . . or vampire. "Shal, I want you to wear this." Tarl held out the medallion he had received from Sot. "I have my own holy symbol. I can probably protect Ren for a little while if we face any undead, but I don't have the skills to keep them away from both of you. I don't know how good you are at your magic, but with a holy symbol of Tyr protecting you, you should be even safer."

Shal removed the chain from Tarl's hand and looped it

loosely around her neck. "Thank you, Tarl," she said softly.

"C'mon, you two," urged Ren. "If we're not prepared for the worst now, we never will be." Ren's eyes scanned the docks, searching for a boat for hire. He didn't expect to find anyone who would take them to Thorn Island. If they knew the destination, there might be precious few who'd be willing to even let them rent a boat. In fact, Ren fully expected that they might have to buy a boat outright.

Ten inquiries and an hour later, Ren finally found a crusty old boatman willing to part with a decrepit rowboat. "You'll get your five silvers deposit returned when I get my boat back," he cackled. The gnarly old man threw his head back and laughed hard. "But I won't expect to be seein' it ag'in till I get to the Abyss!" he called, laughing even harder.

As they started toward the boat to load their gear, a trumpet sounded behind them. They turned to see the trumpeter and a town crier, awaiting the approach of Porphyrys Cadorna on a speckled horse with a great feather plume attached to its bridle.

"Hear ye, hear ye!" the crier called loudly. "All stand and await the approach of the honorable Porphyrys Cadorna, Tenth Councilman of the City of Phlan." The herald stood at attention while vendors, shoppers, and boatsmen milled about curiously.

Cadorna reined his mount to a stop immediately in front of Shal, Ren, and Tarl. He waved his hand over the three and let out a low whistle. The big inkeep, in particular, looked striking in his fitted armor, and together the three looked formidable. "I am impressed indeed," said Cadorna, casting his eyes over the group. "Perhaps, unlike your unfortunate predecessors, you will be the first group worthy of the council's trust. You are charged, as was explained to you last evening, with the task of discovering the secret surrounding the darkness that makes Sokol Keep and Thorn Island uninhabitable."

Ren stifled a caustic reply. He knew that "worthy of the council's trust" could be translated "who might come back alive," but there was nothing to be gained by challenging the man. At least they weren't being tossed over the wall of the city at night, which was widely rumored to be the fate of some criminals. "I don't suppose you'd care to foot the bill for the boat, would you, Your Honor?"

"If you bring it back, I'll buy it from you . . . for an excellent price," said Cadorna with a grin. "Which reminds me . . . it has come to my attention that the Lord of the Ruins himself has somehow gotten wind of your impending venture. I suspect he'll send some of the rabble from beyond the wall to harass you—orcs, goblins, kobolds perhaps. Surely nothing the three of you can't handle."

"The Lord of the Ruins?" Shal asked, wondering if her companions knew whom Cadorna was referring to.

Ren started to reply, but Cadorna quickly cut him off. "The hordes of monsters that plague our fair city are obviously controlled by someone or something, or they surely would have killed each other by now. Occasionally hobgoblins, orcs, or other humanoids we capture make mention of their leader, the 'Lord of the Ruins.' From all accounts, his power is awesome. Naturally he fights every effort of the council to regain sections of Old Phlan."

Cadorna paused, as if expecting some sort of response. When there was none, he plunged ahead. "Of course, I'm sure the Lord of the Ruins would have no way of anticipating a party of three such as yourselves."

"Thank you, Councilman," said Shal, comforted by his apparent confidence in them. "However, what we've heard of Sokol Keep"—she pointed to the island—"and what we've seen are hardly encouraging."

Cadorna's face formed its most sincerely sympathetic expression. "I'd be lying if I told you there was nothing to fear on Thorn Island. In the months since I've sat on the council, four parties have undertaken this mission, and none has . . . ah . . . been successful. But I sincerely believe that your chances for success are greater than those of the parties who have preceded you. I am, of course, here to see that you fulfill your sentence, but I am also here to wish you a safe and fruitful mission."

Shal and Tarl bowed in the manner customary when taking leave of an official. Ren simply turned on his heels, stepped down into the boat, and snugged it up close to the mooring so the other two could board more easily.

* * * * *

Cadorna remained to watch as they rowed out into the bay. They just might be the ones I've been waiting for, he thought. I've waited too long for the chance to recover the dignity and position of the Cadorna family . . . and the fortune that is rightfully mine. If they succeed, it'll be an ideal situation. They'll receive a reward and recognition from the council. Phlan will prosper because shipping will increase greatly. I'll be rewarded and will gain power within the council. And the Lord of the Ruins will be grateful because I tried to warn him! Cadorna shuddered at the indignities he had to bear to communicate with the Lord of the Ruins—sending messages through slime-bellied hobgoblins—but he grinned from ear to ear when he thought of the rewards. In exchange for passing on the simple message that a small, ill-matched party of three was headed for Sokol Keep on a reclamation mission, a highly promising meeting had been arranged between Cadorna and a certain sensual, doe-eyed woman, who just happened to be the daughter of the head councilman from Thentia. Still, Cadorna couldn't wait for the day when the Lord of the Ruins would be forced to send messengers to him, instead of the other way around.

* * * * *

Shal was watching Ren row when they entered the dark veil that shadowed the island. She immediately felt her breath constrict, almost as if someone had pushed hard against her lungs. She thought at first that it could be her own fear finally getting the best of her, but a glance at the others told her that they felt it, too.

Tarl leaned forward in the boat and held up his holy symbol. "Bless me with the strength of your faith, Tyr. Grant us power over the darkness that reigns over this place."

Whether coincidence or not, Shal immediately felt a loosening of her breathing. "Your god serves you well, friend."

"I just hope that's a sign that you're the right man to have along on this trip," said Ren, taking a deep breath.

Tarl didn't respond. His prayer had been a reaction to his own terror. The pressure on his lungs had been a vivid reminder of the powerlessness he had felt that day in the graveyard. The undead seemed to have the power to suck a person's very life energies, making breathing, even the beating of the heart, things that couldn't be taken for granted. Tarl couldn't help feeling contempt for himself for not being able to help Anton or his other brothers when they needed him. He spoke once more, silently this time, to his god. *My prayer was born out of fear for myself, but you responded nonetheless. Let this day enhance my faith and add a measure to my experience so I can better serve you and return to you and your servants what is rightfully yours.*

Tarl lifted his head and pointed. "Over there, Ren. There's a break in the rocks."

"Not much of an opening," said Shal, eyeing the small

opening to which Tarl was pointing. "Are you sure you can get through there, Ren?"

"I'm about as handy in a boat as either of you are, which isn't saying much," Ren replied. "But I'll jump out and pull the boat to shore if I have to."

Shal laughed nervously. Ever since breakfast this morning, she had been stealing glances at Ren when she didn't think he was looking. She hadn't missed the fact that his ruddy complexion had grown paler as they drew closer to their destination. "I'd use a Navigation spell if I only had one," she said. "But since I don't, you'd better pull on those oars if you don't want us to smash into those rocks."

Ren managed to maneuver the boat between the two rocks unscathed, and in a few minutes they had beached the ancient rowboat on a sandy segment of shoreline.

"So we're here. Now what?" asked Shal, looking anxiously toward the low, sheer cliffs that made the island a natural fortress.

"There's a stone stairway over there," said Tarl, pointing down the shoreline.

"Why don't we just knock and see if anybody's home?" Ren offered.

"Save the sarcasm," Shal scolded. "Do you have another idea?"

Ren reached into his pack and pulled out one of his favorite thieving tools. "Simple but effective," he said, holding up a three-clawed hook with a long, coiled rope to it. "I'd vote for following the shoreline a couple thousand feet and then making our way up somewhere where it's secluded."

"Agreed," said Tarl, realizing that Ren's suggestion made good sense. Why announce their presence to whoever—or whatever—waited up there?

The air was uncannily still as they made their way along the shoreline at the base of the cliff. As they went, they spotted wreckage from several small sailing craft. Rotting remains of bodies dead for weeks, perhaps months, lay in grotesque attitudes amidst the debris.

"They may have run aground in storms. I've heard the island is practically invisible at night." Ren paused and pointed up toward the cliff. "Looks like there's a break in the stone face up there. This looks like as good a place as any." He began to twirl the rope above his head in ever-lengthening circles. "One, two, three . . ." he counted softly, and then he released the grapnel into the air. It arched up over the lip of the cliff and landed with a muffled clink. Ren pulled the rope taut and then tested his full body weight against it. The rope held firmly in place.

"After you," he said, bowing quickly to Tarl and Shal.

"I—I'll never be able to climb that," Shal said, staring up at the cliff's face. "Maybe I could use a Jump spell or even a Spider Climb, but I don't have the arm strength to climb that rope."

"You don't have the arm strength?" Tarl reached out and circled his hands around Shal's muscular upper arm. "If you can't climb this rope, we'd better turn around and take our chances with Cadorna, because Ren and I will never make it either." Tarl regretted his words even before he finished speaking them.

Shal was looking down with distaste at the circumference of her arm where Tarl's hands had touched it. "Thanks, Tarl. Perhaps for my next stunt you could have me arm-wrestle a dragon!" she snapped. "The only trouble is, these tree trunks growing out of my body aren't mine!" Shal shook her arms in a violent shudder, as if by shaking them they might fall off and be replaced by the slender, petite arms that had once been hers.

Shal clenched her fists and faced the rope. She had seen her two companions looking on with what she was sure must be pity, and she berated herself for her own vanity. "There'll be no more pity on my account, you two.

Yes, you're right. With these arms, I can climb this stupid rope!" She grabbed hold of it and began hoisting herself up, arm over arm. Her movements were smooth and effortless, and before she reached the top, she was actually marveling at the ease of her own movement.

Ren stood dumbfounded at the bottom of the cliff, anchoring the rope, his face a mask of confusion. Tarl's face bore the same expression of bafflement.

"D'you suppose we should follow that woman?" Ren asked, gazing up at Shal.

Tarl didn't answer. Instead, he started up the rope. Ren followed, and soon the three squatted together atop the cliff, facing the charred walls of the ancient fortress of Sokol Keep.

The blackened walls were encrusted with sea salts. Molds, weeds, tall grasses, and saplings were doing their best to infiltrate the stone wall, growing profusely from large cracks in the coarse blocks. Beyond the tall grasses, at the end of the keep farthest from where the three stood, they could see the top of the stairway Tarl had sighted from below. No one waited at the top. A wide pathway led from the stairs to the keep's dilapidated wooden gates.

"If it weren't for the dark veil that hovers over this place, it would almost be pleasant," Shal said quietly. "It seems so quiet, so peaceful."

"The aura of evil is strong here," Tarl whispered back. "Can't you feel it? I don't think we're going to fool whatever inhabits this place by trying to come in the back door."

"Maybe not," whispered Ren, "but I still think we should take our time and have a good look at the grounds before going in."

"No," said Shal. "Tarl's right. If there are undead here, we aren't going to surprise them no matter which way we come from."

Ren glanced at Shal, surprised by her forcefulness. "Okay, lady. Whatever you say." Striding right up to the front door went against every thieving bone in Ren's body, but he could feel a rush of excitement as he pulled out one of his short swords and prepared to lead the way. "Stay behind me, on either side," he whispered to the others. "Move with the grass, not against it. Try not to leave a trail. Like this," he said, parting the grass gently with his extended sword and stepping lightly so as not to make a sound.

Ren passed through the tall grass with the ease and silence of a leaf floating to earth. Shal and Tarl did their best to imitate his stealthy movements, but despite their efforts, the grass made a distinct rustling sound with their passing. Suddenly, without warning, Ren came to an abrupt stop. Ten feet in front of him, a skeleton hand was pushing its way up through the ground. Clods of earth flew up in all directions as a skeleton warrior burst from the ground and began to walk toward them. Dirt and fungus clung inside its eye sockets and to the remnants of its leather armor. Sow bugs, beetles, and grubs scurried to the ground by the hundreds as the skeleton strode forward, and maggots streamed from the creature's open mouth.

Tarl shook off his own panic and charged in front of Ren, holding out his holy symbol. "Die, creature! Rest! Do us no harm!" The skeleton came to a halt, reached forward one last time, and collapsed to the ground.

Ren walked up to the remains of the skeleton warrior and started peeling off its decayed armor.

Shal stifled a gasp. "By the gods, Ren, what are you doing?"

"Looking for loot. What do you think?"

"You can't rob the dead!" Tarl exclaimed vehemently. "It's—it's sacrilege!"

"It certainly can't do any more harm than stealing from

someone who's alive. What's he going to do with any-thing, anyway?" Ren asked, continuing to rummage through the creature's remains. He found nothing under the armor, but then he noticed that one of the skeleton's bony hands was clasped tight shut. Forcing it open, Ren removed a heavy bronze chain.

"Nice work, Brother Tarl. I think you just killed a friendly messenger. Take a look at this." Ren held up the chain. An embossed medallion hung from it.

Tarl looked on in horror. Ren was right. The warrior had tried to offer them a medal of Tyr to wear inside the keep. Tarl let out a slow breath as he examined it. It was identical to the medallion Sot had given him, and it showed no sign of corrosion despite the years it must have spent in the ground. Tarl had let his fear get in the way of his faith.

He held the medallion skyward. "Great Tyr, the Even-Handed, God of Justice, once again you have demon-strated your presence with us. Forgive me for not recognizing your messenger."

Tarl held the medallion out to Ren. "This is for you. I guess you didn't need to steal it after all. He meant for you to have it."

* * * * *

The wooden gates of the keep had fared poorly against the elements. Tarl had only to push, and the big doors swung open, revealing a large courtyard lined by the charred remnants of several buildings. In the center of the keep, reasonably unscathed by dragon fire, was an airy building filled with tables, probably the mess hall. To the right were the blackened shells of what appeared to have been the stable and blacksmith's shops. The tallest building in the keep, and the only one built of stone, obvi-ously the temple, stood in the far left corner of the court-yard, intact except for what must have been a wooden bell tower at the top. The wooden buildings in front of it had suffered extensive fire damage.

Here and there in the courtyard, the tall, unkempt grasses grew very thick, as if the blood and flesh of the men who had stood to face the dragons had nourished it. Tarl knew that the men living inside Sokol Keep must have died much as his brothers had in the graveyard—screaming in terror and without adequate defenses, pained beyond imagining by their own suffering and their inability to prevent what followed. No wonder a dark shadow hung over this place!

"Something's been here—something alive," Ren said softly. "And not long ago. See the way that grass is matted down over there on the left? There's also a lingering smell that doesn't fit this place. You remember what Cadorna said about the Lord of the Ruins sending troops to meet us? We need to watch our step."

The three had gone no more than fifteen feet into the courtyard when clods of grass and earth started flying up everywhere. Screams and moans erupted all around them as dozens of skeleton warriors burst from the ground. More emerged from the buildings and ruins of the keep. All walked deliberately toward Ren and Tarl and Shal, their weapons raised. Ren pulled out his two short swords and planted himself in front of Shal. "We've got to get out of here—now!"

"No!" said Tarl firmly. "These are warrior clerics who serve my god. Hold up your medallions."

Bony arms stretched out toward Shal from every side. Her body seemed to go cold, refusing to function normally. Her breath came in constricted gasps, as it had in the boat, but this time the pressure was even heavier. She had to fight merely to breathe, and she struggled even harder to regain control of her arms and hands so she could lift up the medallion.

Ren was shaking his head violently. "They can see the

medallion on my chest, and it's not stopping them! I'm getting me and Shal the hell out of here!"

Ren pushed the nearest of the skeletons back with one short sword. When a second skeleton started to wrap its bony hand around Shal's arm, he raised the other sword and brought it down swiftly, chopping the creature's hand off.

"Behind you!" Shal shouted. A large skeletal warrior, Ren's equal in height, was directly behind him, about to swing at Ren with a rusty long sword.

Ren spun and met the swing with both short swords, but when he tried to push the creature back, he momentarily lost his balance when he stepped in one of the holes from which the vile monsters had emerged. Instantly another skeleton burst partway out of the earth and grabbed Ren's legs from behind in its icy grip. Ren fell hard, but the skeleton did not release its grip. Instead, the bony fingers closed tighter and tighter, till Ren thought they would surely sever his legs.

Two more skeletal warriors had grabbed Shal, one by the right arm and one by the left. They were pulling in opposite directions.

Tarl was oblivious to Shal's predicament. He was overwhelmed by the terror these creatures must have experienced before they died. Dozens, perhaps hundreds, of brothers had been slaughtered here but remained undead, their lives unfulfilled. Like Tarl, they'd had no chance to complete their mortal missions. Their screams were his screams. Their pain was his pain. His mind was barraged by dozens of messages unsent to loved ones, and an untold number of emotions ranging from panic and terror to remorse and relief assaulted his psyche. Tarl lifted his holy symbol high. "Rest, brothers!" he shouted firmly. "As Tyr is my witness, we mean no harm!"

Again and again, he repeated the words as he turned slowly in a circle, letting the reflection from the holy symbol of Tyr shine in every direction, touching each undead warrior. One by one, the skeletons lowered their weapons to their sides. The three holding Ren and Shal released their grips. When the two of them held up their medallions as well, the rest of the skeletons closing in on the party halted their advance. They appeared to remain agitated and continued to move about, but it was obvious they were no longer interested in harming Tarl, Ren, or Shal.

"Whew!" Shal breathed quietly. "I've heard of clerics turning the undead, but I've never heard of anybody turning a whole army of them!"

Tarl heard Shal's words, but this was no time to celebrate. "Something or someone is keeping these men in motion, but I think we'll be able to explore in peace now," he said.

From where he lay on the ground, Ren did his best to quell a chill of revulsion at the word "men." He realized that Tarl was somehow seeing human characteristics in these rotting, maggot-covered creatures. "My legs and ankles feel as if they're frostbitten."

"I'm sorry, my friend," said Tarl, and he rushed quickly to the big man's side.

Shal beat him there by a step. Immediately she pulled Ren's leggings loose to reveal several white-yellow rings of nearly lifeless skin circling Ren's ankles. She didn't question Ren's self-diagnosis. Her own two arms had felt a biting, bone-chilling cold when the skeletons had grabbed her. When the cleric reached forward to lay hands on Ren, Shal stopped him. "No, Tarl, save your strength. I have just the thing." Shal pulled from her belt one of the healing potions she had helped Ranthor prepare. "We'll need your powers soon enough if one of us gets hurt badly. For frostbite, this should do nicely." Shal daubed the pasty liquid on the rings of whitened flesh. Within seconds, a healthy pink color began to return to the affected area.

Even after Ren was able to stand, the memory of the icy grip was still with him. He found walking among the skeletons unnerving, medallions or no, but he forced himself to lead the small group through the keep. Nothing but kindling remained of the first building on the left, probably once a storage shed. The roof of the second structure was totally burned off, but the base of the building was still intact. As they approached the building, the skeletons wandering in the courtyard converged from all directions. A number of the undead warriors followed the party of three, then assumed gruesome positions of death among what remained of the cots that lined the walls.

"What—what are they doing?" gasped Shal, sickened by the sight of the creatures.

"They are showing you . . . showing us . . . how they died," Tarl replied, once again feeling the men's anguish and frustration. "Many of them died here, in their beds. They never had a chance to prove themselves." Tarl tried to describe the myriad of sensations, from frustration to horror, that were somehow being communicated to him.

They moved on to the other end of the building, but found nothing new. As they passed the corner of the building, they noticed that they had gained a new entourage of earth- and fungus-covered companions. Without touching any of the three, the new group of skeletons seemed to be pushing them on to the next doorway in the complex. They entered the door cautiously and found themselves in a foyer. They peered through an open doorway off to the left, and as soon as they did, a dozen or so undead warriors brushed past them and began moaning and crying in an almost deafening dirge.

"The high clerics' quarters," said Tarl, as if his companions had requested an explanation. "The ghostly remains of these men suffer the most, because they were unable to protect the fledgling clerics they vowed to safeguard."

Ahead, still whole and beautiful, was an ornately carved double door that bore the hammer and balance of Tyr, the Even-Handed. Tarl felt compelled to enter the temple, but Ren was already stepping cautiously through an open doorway to the right.

Tarl and Shal followed. Just as the three companions entered, the tongue of a giant frog shot out, circled Ren's leg, and tripped the big man. Tarl rushed forward and slammed the man-sized creature's head hard with his hammer. The weapon merely glanced off the frog's wet, slippery skin. It took two more blows before Tarl's hammer connected solidly. When it did, the creature's flesh buckled and splattered under the force of his blow, and it fell to the wet floor, quivering. Ren hacked its encircling tongue off and leaped to his feet, just in time to face six more of the gigantic amphibians. He hurled a dagger at the frog closest to him. Like Tarl's hammer, the knife deflected off the tough, slimy hide of the frog.

Behind him, Shal was muttering something in the language of magic. As she finished her incantation, she tossed a handful of powder past Ren and extended her hand toward the lead frog. Immediately it shrank to normal size. Ren kicked it with his boot and sent it flying up at one of the waiting monster frogs. The creature shot its huge tongue out, and in an instant, it slurped the small frog down whole.

The remaining frogs, caught up in the prospect of a feeding frenzy, began to leap willy-nilly—up, sideways, backward—in a primitive, instinctive dance designed to freeze their victims in terror. In a frantic reaction to his own revulsion, Tarl lashed out again and again with his hammer, but it only slipped off the sides of the giant frogs. When one got too close, though, he bashed it with his shield with all his might and sent it slumping to the floor, where he finished it off with a blow from his hammer. A wave of nausea surged through him as he watched the frog's legs twitch wildly, independent of its pulverized head.

Shal, meanwhile, had called for her staff, and she was swinging it wildly at the huge slimy creatures. *Swoosh! Thwack!* The walls echoed with the sounds of her brutal attack, and the strength of her frenzied swings was so great that when one connected solidly, it was as if Shal had folded the center of the monster's body in two. Its flesh folded over the staff and stayed that way until Shal could pull the staff out. She must have broken the creature's spine, for when she removed the staff, the monster's body folded grotesquely in the opposite direction. Just as Shal freed her staff, another giant frog came leaping toward her. In an almost instinctive defensive measure, she pointed her staff straight up at the flying monster and then watched in horror as it skewered itself on the staff's sharp end and slid down over her arms. She screamed loud and long and immediately pulled back for all she was worth, extending her arms outward to get the disgusting animal away from her.

At that moment, Ren, who was fending off another frog, backed into the one Shal had just unskewered. The frog he was battling took advantage of the distraction to jump and land on top of him, squeezing his body against the body of the dead frog.

Ren became a human sandwich, folded deeply into the dead frog's soft, quivering belly, and covered by the mass of the live frog. He flailed out in panic, slashing up, down, sideways, pushing frantically at both of the creatures as their guts began to ooze over him. Soon both frogs lay jerking spasmodically on the floor on either side of Ren, who was shaking the slime and gore from his arms and retching. . . .

"Behind you!" Tarl yelled, but it was too late. The last of the frogs was leaping at Ren with a vengeance. It smacked into his back with a wet *thwack* and sent him sprawling into the back wall of the room. As he struck the wall, it collapsed, and Ren fell to the floor of the next room with the frog on top of him. Shal spoke the final words of a Magic Missile spell, and three projectiles shot from her fingertips and buried themselves in the cold flesh of the frog. It jerked to its death on top of Ren before Shal and Tarl could reach their friend and pull the creature off him.

When they finally got Ren out from under the giant amphibian, his complexion was a pasty white, and his black leathers and armor were dripping with blood and ocher-colored ooze.

"Are—are you okay?" Shal asked, anxiously releasing her tight hold on Ren's hand.

Ren lay silent for more than a minute, then rose slowly and shook himself head to foot. "God, I need a bath! I've fought some of the most disgusting creatures in the Realms, and I've never felt this filthy. . . ." He noticed their expressions of concern turning to relief. "Some valiant fighter, huh?" he asked, embarrassed.

"We should all stand up so well," Tarl said sincerely. "For a minute there, I thought I was—"

"Hey, you two, come and take a look at this." Shal was standing near the frog she had just killed, pointing at it. A grayish-green band encircled the creature's broad, damp neck. If it hadn't been for a triangle of silver that hung from it, the band would barely have been visible. The triangle, embossed with a small silver pyramid, glistened even in the dull light from the larger room. "It looks like a collar or something," said Shal, gingerly reaching for the medallion.

Ren grabbed her outstretched hand with startling speed. "Don't touch it!" he hissed. "Who knows what cursed master these god-awful animals served? That's not a symbol I'm familiar with, but these creatures sure weren't sent by anything friendly."

"Look here!" whispered Tarl. He had come around the frog from the other side and was holding up the far end of the stretch of canvas on which Ren and the frog had landed. Underneath was a veritable armory of weapons—ball and chains, throwing hammers, daggers, throwing stars, axes, shields, armor. Most were rusted or corroded, but two items stood out from the rest: a dagger and a hammer, both of which shone as though a metalsmith had polished them the day before. Each glowed with an eerie green light, and each was in mint condition and obviously of top quality.

"Those wouldn't glow like that unless there was some danger nearby," hissed Ren. "My own daggers do the same." He pulled Right from his boot, and sure enough, it was gleaming with a bluish light. "Listen . . ." whispered Ren. He pointed toward a gaping hole in the wall of the muddy room where the frogs lay dead. The sound of grating humanoid voices drifted through the air like the buzz of so many cicadas. Quickly Ren handed the hammer to Tarl, keeping the dagger for himself.

Together the three moved silently back into the larger room and worked their way along the wall to the opening. Ren crouched down and glanced cautiously through the hole, then quickly pulled back behind what remained of the wall. "There's a lot of them—orcs, hobgoblins, kobolds . . . a real mixed lot," he whispered. "Must be at least forty of them. We've got to get out of here—maybe back through the barracks and over the wall."

Tarl shook his head. "We haven't located what we came for," he whispered. "Our information is only partial, and the undead still walk."

"At least we know what kind of creatures are here," argued Shal, also in a hushed voice. "We can tell the council and they can send troops."

"No," insisted Tarl. "I think we should talk with them and try to get more information about their leader."

Ren tugged gently on Tarl's collar. "You're a nut case, my cleric friend. I speak orcish well enough to know that their idea of a pleasant conversation is to say, 'Die, human scum!' " He tugged lightly on Tarl's collar again and whispered with intensity, "Do you understand me? We've got to get out of here!"

"Get out of here?" The sharp, barking voice of a kobold sounded behind them. "Get out of here?" He let out a low chuckle, a perverted sound, like a dog growling.

Tarl and Shal turned to see a kobold strut through the doorway with an entourage of about two dozen orcs and goblins behind him. Ren watched as the troop of humanoids began to climb in through the hole in the wall.

"The party? The party? Is this the party?" snorted a fat orc, obviously, from his dress, a leader of the troop.

"Yes, master," barked the kobold. "The three of them . . . ours for the taking for the Lord of the Ruins."

The lead orc's yellow, piggy eyes gleamed brightly, and he snorted again in his excitement. "Torture the party . . . kill the party . . . get big praise from the Lord of the Ruins!"

"Power to the pool!" shouted the kobold.

"Power to the pool!" Orcs and hobgoblins alike took up the chant. "Power to the pool!" All jabbed cudgels, axes, or swords into the air in time with the chant as they began to circle round the companions, who were pressed together in a small cluster, back to back.

"What's that they're chanting?" Tarl asked, looking to Ren for a translation.

"They're getting ready to kill us, probably by torture, and they're saying something over and over again about 'Power to the pool,' " Ren replied.

Tarl tried to block out the jeering and chanting. He managed to concentrate long enough to cast a spell of Enthrallment. He had practiced the spell many times before, but he had never before tried it on a hostile group.

If the spell were successful, the group of creatures would understand and be receptive to anything he said, at least for a short while.

"Tell me, friends," he asked evenly, "to what pool do you refer?"

The kobold beamed, his tongue lolling over his yellow fangs like a panting canine. "Pool belongs to the Lord of the Ruins. He says to kill, we kill. Pool glows brighter. The Lord of the Ruins grows stronger. We grow stronger. We kill more. Nobody stops us . . . Power to the pool!" he shouted once more.

Others started to pick up the chant again, and Tarl could feel his control slipping. He waved his arms in a benevolent gesture. "Surely killing us can be of no value to your lord—or to the pool. Can't we do something else to add power to the pool?"

Ren signaled Shal to brace herself for a mad dash. The chances of them escaping from this mob seemed slim to none, but now, while they were still calmed by Tarl's spell, was the time to move if there was ever going to be any.

The pig-eyed leader suddenly stuck his dripping snout up close to Tarl's face. "You have power stone? Ioun stone? Give us stone, you live. No stone, we kill. Power to the pool!"

"Ioun stone?" Tarl repeated, puzzled.

"No ioun stone?" the leader started to snort. "Kill! Kill them!"

The spell was broken. Tarl smashed his shield hard into the orc's pig face and started swinging his hammer with a vengeance. Ren lunged forward, slashing and hacking madly with his short swords, parrying as he had never parried before to block cudgels and axes descending all around him.

Shal swung her staff high and brought it down hard, repeatedly, sending several humanoids within her range sprawling, but there were many more. She could not see, but could hear and sense, the flight of several daggers and arrows, weapons that all her swinging could not protect her against. Out of the corner of her eye, she saw Ren taken down by a vicious blow to his abdomen. Tarl was barely managing to keep the pressing masses of orcs and hobgoblins away from overwhelming him. She knew that she and the others would soon be beaten senseless.

An axe bit deep into her shoulder as she took her next swing. Her scream of pain and terror was voiceless . . . as was the cry of her familiar! *The staff! The Staff of Power! Use it now!*

"*Halcyon!*" shouted Shal, and she extended the staff toward the frenzied beasts around her. "*Harak!*" Brilliant electricity, nearly the color of amethyst, coursed up and down the staff's surface. Bolts of lightning arced out in all directions. She spoke another word, and small, purple balls of flame crackled from the tip, doubling in size with each inch they traveled. With yet another word, deafening thunder shook the building to its foundation. The screams of sizzling humanoids rose up everywhere. Shal turned, and more lightning bolts and fireballs flew from the staff. Doglike kobolds burned to charred stumps. The fatty flesh of orcs and goblins spattered and sizzled. Shal turned yet again, but this time there were no takers. The handful of unscathed humanoids that remained were bolting away as fast as they could go, barking, squealing, and screaming like wild animals fleeing a forest fire.

Shal slumped to the ground, her fists clenched white around the staff as blood spurted from the gash in her shoulder. She stared numbly at her two friends, each of whom was in turn staring open-mouthed at her.

All around them was wreckage. Shal's lightning bolts had blasted huge holes in the building's already damaged ceilings and walls, and the smoldering remains of dead humanoids lay everywhere. Shal slowly turned her head from side to side in disbelief, awed by the power she held within her grasp. She had never before killed, never been party to such wholesale destruction. She had also never been so consumed or driven by terror—fear for herself and fear for her companions—but she knew that she would react the same way again if confronted with the same situation. She looked at her friends, who were still staring at her in amazement.

When he could stir himself out of his shock, Tarl reached out and pressed his hands to Shal's bloodied shoulder. The power of Tyr flowed warm and strong, and he could feel the healing surge through his fingertips. Once again he experienced an overwhelming bond to the red-haired fighter-mage. As he healed her, he somehow felt the key to his own wholeness.

Shal reached up and pressed her hands over Tarl's. "Thank you. Please . . . please help Ren now."

Tarl snatched his hands away, ashamed that he could have forgotten his other companion for even a moment. He placed one hand on each of Ren's firm, muscular shoulders. Tarl could feel the pain of untold bruises, and he sensed internal damage where Ren had taken the blow to the stomach. Tarl waited for the healing warmth to flow through his hands. Once it did, he spoke. "You should feel better, but when we get back, you must rest. I can do little more."

"I can't think of a time when I've felt better," said Ren cheerily, shaking himself from his own stunned silence. "I mean, what more can a fellow ask? You carry on friendly conversations with orcs, she packs a weapon that even the gods must find frightening, and then you patch us up besides. We've even managed to fulfill our mission and collect some bonus information for the council."

"How's that?" Tarl asked.

"The old armory, the stuff about the shiny pool where the boss fellow, that 'Lord of the Ruins,' gets his power—that wasn't anything we agreed to dig up for Cadorna."

"That's true, but we still aren't done here," said Tarl.

"Not done!" exclaimed Shal. "I've had more than enough adventure for one day, thank you. Skeletons . . . oversized fly-slurpers . . . orcs and kobolds . . . You've got to understand, I used to get tired just dusting Ranthor's laboratory."

"But the skeletons . . . my brothers, the clerics of Tyr," Tarl insisted. "They still walk the keep."

"They seem pretty quiet, though," said Ren. "You calmed them down."

"Yes, but they're not at rest. I can feel it! They're still undead, tormented souls. I need to go to the temple and try to find out for myself what keeps them so agitated."

Ren stood and reached his hand down to help Shal to her feet. "I guess we can take a tour of the temple with him, don't you think? I mean, if it weren't for Tarl, you and I probably would have been killed by the skeletons—that is, if the cloud over this place hadn't killed us first."

Shal gave Ren's hand a squeeze, and then reached out and squeezed Tarl's. "Let's go, then," she said. "I really think we should get out of this place before dark."

Skeleton warriors were still milling in the entryway, but they did nothing to stop the three. Tarl lifted the latch on the ornately carved door to the temple and pushed. The altar inside was covered with dust, but it had not suffered from dragonfire. A lone specter flitted back and forth before the altar. Instead of moaning or screaming, it was shouting oath after oath, curse after curse.

Tarl felt his breathing speed at the sight of the ghostly visage. Its appearance reminded him of the vampire's minions. Tarl swallowed and struggled to get his breathing under control. With considerable effort, he spoke clearly and deliberately. "Who are you, brother, and what is troubling you?" Tarl asked.

The specter continued to flit up and down and back and forth among the tables and seats in the temple, but in between oaths, it spoke in a gravelly voice. "Ferran Martinez . . . I am Ferran Martinez, ruling cleric of the sacred order of Tyr. I am the high cleric who remained in the temple while each of my men died, then died of starvation myself because I could not bear to go outside and face them. The bloody dragons came. They burned and killed and left our mission's work undone."

"What keeps you undead, Brother Martinez? What work remains undone? Can I be of help?" Ren and Shal just looked on as Tarl coaxed and soothed the agitated apparition.

The creature swung its phantom arms straight through the altar repeatedly, as if to strike it, but managed only to knock over several dust-coated candlesticks from the flurry of wind it generated. "Devils to the Abyss! Blast them in the fiery furnace! Sleep, men! Rest." He ended in a piteous scream.

"Brother Martinez, can I help?" Tarl repeated.

"The city of Phlan is dead! Monsters! Nothing but monsters! And the temple . . . it was never used. We had just finished building it, but there were no worshipers, only the clerics who built it. No peace in the city! No peace! Nothing but walking dead and unending nightmares . . . and the Lord of the Ruins, Tyranthraxus, still lives! Cursed creature from the pit! Power-grabbing blasphemer! May his soul rot!"

"They've reconstructed part of the city, Brother Martinez. It's civilized again. In fact, they call the new part Civilized Phlan."

" 'Civilized Phlan'?" the specter repeated, then grew still and floated closer to Tarl.

Tarl flinched involuntarily but stood firm. "Yes, and we're building a new temple to Tyr. That's why I came, to aid others in the construction and startup of the new temple."

"A new temple to Tyr? Then you can use the holy scale?" The specter whisked to the altar and pulled back a cloth. A silver balance, the balance of Tyr, God of War and Justice, stood on the table. "You will see that this gets used in the new temple?"

Tarl dropped down on one knee, both awed and humbled at the prospect of being given a second chance to deliver a holy symbol of his god to the temple in Phlan. "I will see that the scale sits proudly on the altar of the temple in Phlan."

"Then I can at last rest," said Ferran Martinez, "and so can our brothers." He held the scale out to Tarl, and Tarl wrapped it carefully in the cloth that had covered it for five decades.

And the apparition of Ferran Martinez reclined at the foot of the altar, with its ethereal hands folded across its chest, and vanished in a puff of mist.

*　*　*　*　*

Outside the keep, the grounds stood empty. No skeletal warriors walked the courtyard. In fact, the most noticeable thing was the sunshine that filled the sky over Thorn Island. The brilliant orange of the setting sun glistened unimpeded off the walls of the temple and the tall grasses that covered the courtyard.

❧ 6 ❧

Restless Spirits

When he heard that the three tavern brawlers had actually returned from Thorn Island, Porphyrys Cadorna left his dinner and rushed to the council chambers. He had waited anxiously before for the return of other groups, but he had always been disappointed. This time he had intentionally gone about his normal business, not wanting to waste his energies only to be left disappointed. But the three were back, and according to Cadorna's attendant, they claimed to carry proof of their success. The councilman positioned himself at the dais and signaled for the attendant to let them enter. He would inform the rest of the council of his victory when he was sure of their achievements and not before.

The cleric, Tarl Desanea, entered first, followed by the big man who called himself Ren o' the Blade and the young mage, Shal Bal. They were covered with dirt and grime, and from the big man's movements, Cadorna could see he was struggling with some great pain. Still, they made an impressive trio. Cadorna felt a chill run through him at the thought of meeting any of these three under less than amicable circumstances.

"So . . . what have you learned that will help us recover Thorn Island?" Cadorna asked after thumping his gavel twice, as if to silence a nonexistent audience.

"We have certain useful information, and with the help of the mighty Tyr, the Even-Handed, we have also succeeded in quelling the undead forces that made Sokol

Keep uninhabitable," announced Tarl, bowing before Cadorna with as much formality as he could muster. "The resettling of Thorn Island may begin immediately."

This was splendid, more than Cadorna could have hoped for! He wanted to appear pleased, but he didn't want these three to think that their obligation to the court was so easily fulfilled. He gazed down from the dais, his eyes gleaming with avarice. "You say it is so, but how do I know it is so?" Cadorna waved his hand at the three in an encompassing gesture. "Even assuming you have been to the island, how can I be sure it is safe to send our citizens there to settle that blackened rock?"

Tarl proceeded to tell the story of their encounters at the keep, with Ren and Shal occasionally adding details. They described the odd triangular medallion they found on the frog and the humanoids' strange rantings about the Lord of the Ruins and "power to the pool." They deleted mention only of Shal's Staff of Power.

Cadorna could hardly contain his excitement. He had manipulated these pawns perfectly, gaining a foothold with the Lord of the Ruins by warning him of their mission and earning the trust of the three by alerting them to the likelihood of encountering orcs or hobgoblins. And they had even brought him new information about the Lord of the Ruins and the magical stones he was seeking! Perhaps, one day, these three might even be able to find such stones or the lair of the Lord of the Ruins for him. . . . But first things first. He still needed proof of their day's work—perhaps a little something to add to his own coffers. "What you have told me is good news indeed, but how do I know these things are true?" Cadorna prodded.

"We bear artifacts, magical artifacts, from the armory and from the Tyrian Temple at Sokol Keep." Tarl held out the scale. "This is a treasured holy artifact. I am sworn by the late Brother Martinez to donate it to the temple in

Phlan." Ren produced the dagger and Tarl the hammer they had found in the armory. "And these are the magical items. Even now you will notice a faint glow. . . ."

Cadorna pulled back as Tarl moved the hammer toward him for his examination. "Yes . . . yes, I see." Cadorna hated blunt objects. He had no interest in the hammer, but the dagger would be his to use or trade, a small token from the council for sensing the exact nature of the dangers at Sokol Keep and sending exactly the right party to tame the island. "You may keep the hammer for your efforts," he pronounced beneficently. "The dagger you will place on deposit with the court attendant before you leave. And, of course, the scale you will relay to your temple."

What a shame, thought Cadorna, that the solid silver balance cannot also be confiscated, but with the cleric's testimony a matter of council record, he dare not risk it. Cadorna eyed the throne intensely before going on. "And the island—has the shadow lifted?"

"Yes," answered Shal excitedly. "As we left, the afternoon sun was shining gloriously on the cliffs. The whole bay looks different—"

"You needn't babble on," Cadorna said sternly. "I'm satisfied that you've fulfilled the goals of this mission. In fact, you all deserve further reward, but I will not know the verdict of the full council with regard to such rewards as you may have coming for at least another day. In the meantime, I'd like you to think about the possibility of completing a small task for me one day soon. I happen to believe you are the perfect party for the assignment."

Ren bristled a little at what he read as a couched threat. The way Cadorna leaned over the dais, clasping and unclasping his hands and making fleeting eye contact with each of them, left Ren with no doubt that Cadorna could and would make life very difficult for the trio if they did not at least attempt to complete Cadorna's "small task."

"We'll be in town," said Ren matter-of-factly. "You can leave a message for us at the Laughing Goblin Inn."

"Count on it," Cadorna said crisply, sensing Ren's resistance. "You are free to go now—with the understanding that you are on call to me and this council until further notice."

*   *   *   *   *

On the side of the city opposite Civilized Phlan, the farthest corner of the uncivilized part, a great dragon was listening to the whimpering excuses of a liver-bellied kobold, two gutless orcs, and a recreant hobgoblin. The beast met their vacant, yellow-eyed stares with its gleaming eyes, and they saw their master, the Lord of the Ruins, for the first time.

"A party of three defeated an army of fifty?" The dragon clawed the ground and spewed a jet of flame from its nostrils. "You let them tame Sokol Keep? Idiots! Clods! Humans will flood into Phlan by the shipload and gain new footholds in my portion of the city! Incompetent slugs! Die as your companions did!" The dragon exhaled, and lightning flashed and crackled about them. Before they could finish their screams, the four were encompassed in flames. In moments, their bodies had melted and drained into the golden, crescent-shaped pool nearby.

Where the incinerated remains of the humanoids met the bright water of the pool, it bubbled and boiled, blazing with the intensity of polished gold in direct sunlight. The dragon turned and lumbered slowly into the pool. In the physical portion of its brain, which reflected raw instinct and reaction, the only part still controlled by the original persona of the dragon, the water registered as hot . . . very hot. The dragon flinched and tried to back out of the pool. It took the power of a trenchant will to force the physical body to scald itself in exchange for the pulsing energy the water would bestow. The will was that of Tyranthraxus, the Great Possessor.

It was the will of Tyranthraxus that commanded the dragon to submerge its entire body in the pool. When it did, power—undiluted power—flowed from the pool to the dragon, and the creature commanded a hundred more humanoid slaves into it presence.

Kobolds, orcs, gnolls, and other strange creatures of the ruins flocked to the heart of Valjevo Castle, the lair of the Lord of the Ruins. Their eyes glazed over with yellow, they never saw the creature that controlled them.

"Hear me, slaves! You will spread the word that there is a price on the heads of those three, more treasure than any of you can imagine . . . You will also procure for me two more ioun stones. When you do, I will complete the circle of power, and I will rule all of Phlan . . . and much more."

* * * * *

"I didn't realize you were still hurting so from that blow to your stomach," Shal said, touching Ren gently on the arm as they left the council room. "Here . . ." She took his arm and pulled it up over her shoulder, then slipped her own arm around his waist. "Let me help you."

Ren glanced over his shoulder at Tarl and grinned in delight. "Thanks. That's better. I'm sure by the time you walk me all the way to my room, I'll be feeling much better." He pulled Shal a little closer and spread his hand on her firm waist.

"As Tyr is my witness, don't you think you're a little big to be leaning on the lady for support?" asked Tarl.

"I'll be fine," said Shal, not waiting for Ren to answer. "All this size and strength has to be good for something besides climbing ropes and looking homely. I mean, you guys wouldn't even let me row the boat."

Ren glanced over his shoulder at Tarl and winked again. "She'll be fine. I won't lean too hard."

Tarl glowered and bared his teeth in a half-mocking, half-serious warning. When they reached the inn, Sot treated them to a huge feast. Later, Tarl made a point of accompanying Ren and Shal to Ren's room in the loft.

Ren moved swiftly from the door to the window, checking both, as was his habit, to see that they weren't followed and then securing them to make sure no one could enter. He unbuckled the fastenings on his leather breastplate and then tugged gingerly to remove the armor. Shal was about to reach over and help, but Tarl stepped between them and carefully removed the breastplate. "I can make a poultice for you. You won't be smelling too good while you wear it, but I think you'll find it soothing."

"And if I know you," said Ren, "it'll be about as pleasant-smelling as those orcs at Sokol Keep."

Shal was reminded of a question she'd been meaning to ask. "Do you two know what stones those creatures kept talking about?"

"Ioun stones," Tarl filled in the name.

"They're incredibly valuable, but I don't think most people understand why," Ren said as he sat on the mattress in the center of the room. "Tempest was killed over two ioun stones."

Shal sat down on the floor, and Tarl sat beside her.

Ren removed Right and Left from his boots. "These are ioun stones," he said, flipping the hilts open so they could plainly see the blue-black stone inside each handle. "If you hadn't started blasting everything in sight with your staff, Shal, I was going to pull one of these out and offer it to those goons. They probably would've killed us anyhow, but I might have been able to distract them long enough so you could get away."

"What's so special about—" Shal dropped her question

and gazed in wonderment as the two dark stones floated from the hilts of the daggers and began to circle Ren's head, glowing a deep, iridescent midnight blue.

"Wow!" Shal and Tarl breathed in unison.

"What—what else can they do?" asked Shal.

"I don't know very much, really. I think it takes strong magic to take full advantage of their powers. For me, the ioun stones make the blades return at my command, and I never miss my mark. I guess they must add a measure of talent or strength to whoever's in control of them." Ren held the knives up by the blades and said "Return." The two stones immediately dropped into the open handles, and Ren flipped the hilts shut. "Tempest died over those two little rocks, and today the three of us almost died for them. I don't know what the head of the Assassins' Guild wanted them for, or what the Lord of the Ruins wants them for, but I think we'll all be better off if they don't get them."

"You were right to not give them up without a fight," Tarl said. "Who can say what evil forces would do with such stones? I vow, as Tyr is my witness, to aid you to the best of my abilities should you be threatened again."

"And I, too," said Shal. "as Selune is *my* witness. But I have a mission of my own, and I'm anxious to get on with it."

"To avenge the death of your teacher?" Tarl asked.

Shal nodded. "And after a good night's rest, that is precisely what I plan to do."

"You know you can count on our help," said Tarl, speaking for Ren as well as himself.

Shal looked at Tarl and then at Ren. Before Tarl had even said anything, she knew they would stand behind her. At every encounter on Thorn Island, she had been aware that their first thought was always to protect her first, even though with her new strength she was probably as strong as Tarl, if not Ren. Since adolescence, Shal

JAMES M. WARD AND JANE COOPER HONG

had taken pride in her looks above all else. Now her appearance was the antithesis of what she had always believed attractive, yet two thoughtful, considerate, handsome men were quite obviously vying for her attention. They admired her magic abilities and praised her newfound fighting skills, they sought her opinion despite her inexperience in countless other areas, and they certainly did not seem to be put off by her muscular body. "Thank you," she said simply, reaching her hands out to hold each of theirs. "I've . . . I've never had such friends."

Shal related what she knew of the location of Denlor's tower and the murder of her master. She described the wretched helplessness she had felt watching his murder and being unable to communicate through the crystal. Tarl squeezed one of Shal's hands and Ren squeezed the other as each thought of the death he had witnessed and been unable to prevent.

Using water from Ren's canteen and a combination of herbs and tar from his pouches, Tarl made the poultice he had promised for Ren. It was effective, but offensively smelly as promised, and he and Shal made their way quickly from the room once it was applied, but not before the three of them had agreed to meet at noon, after a good night's rest, for the trip to Denlor's tower.

* * * * *

After seeing Shal to her room, Tarl returned to the temple. Before he could get to Anton's bedside, the brothers from the temple had flocked around him. Rumors of a sunlit Thorn Island had already reached the temple, and they were anxious to hear of Tarl's experiences there. Since all the brothers had arrived in Phlan only since the rebuilding of the new temple began, no one had known that the fortress contained a Tyrian temple. They were momentarily speechless when Tarl presented the sacred scale, and they actually clapped when he told them of the laying to rest of the tormented souls of their brothers at Sokol Keep. Tarl warmed at the praise; he had never felt so strong in his faith as he had when he faced the skeletons and convinced the spectral Brother Martinez that he could finally be at rest. Several of the brothers made plans to journey to the island the next day to pray for the peace of their brothers and to be sure that any artifacts that remained were put to good use.

Tarl finally took his leave as the others talked on into the night. He found Anton, writhing and calling out, awash in torment. Tarl no longer could feel any joy for having recovered the silver balance. As he stood there watching his friend suffer, he renewed his commitment to retrieve the Hammer of Tyr and restore it to its rightful place at the altar in the temple of Tyr.

He fought back the pain that surged through his own body as he laid his hands on Anton's shoulders. He held on until he dropped to the floor, overcome by his brother's agony, and there he slept.

* * * * *

Shal was surprised to find a package on her bed. It was a soft bundle, bound in white cotton by black string. She realized from the stamp on the cotton that the package was from the seamstress who had made her leathers. Curious, she slipped off the string and unfolded the cotton. Inside was a delicate silk nightgown. Shal laughed with unabashed delight. She was about to hold the garment up to herself to check the fit, but she stopped before touching it. She was filthy with blood, mud, dirt, and other stains she didn't even want to think about.

Quickly she pulled off the filthy black leathers, first the tunic and then the belt and leggings. Sot had left a sponge and a tub of water waiting for her, and the water was still warm. She left the leathers in a heap beside the bed, climbed into the tub, and scrubbed herself clean. After patting herself dry with a towel from the room's small bureau, she reached for the sensuous mulberry-colored garment and slipped it over her head. She turned apprehensively to face the long mirror on the door. The nightgown was as feminine a garment as any she had ever owned, carefully tailored to accentuate the curves of her ample form. Shal removed the clasp from her hair and shook her auburn tresses loose over her shoulders. Her gaze never left the mirror as she combed her long hair. The woman returning her stare in the mirror was at least an acquaintance now, no longer a complete stranger. She could use a whole new set of adjectives to describe herself now: powerful rather than petite, firm rather than willowy, buxom rather than diminutive—but she was every bit as much a woman. In fact, she realized with a shock, she was attractive in a way she had not previously appreciated.

Shal made a note to herself to send the seamstress flowers for her thoughtfulness. She had even remembered that Shal had mentioned purple was her favorite color. In the morning, Shal would brush the beautiful chimera leathers clean, but right now she wanted to luxuriate in the sensation of sleeping between clean sheets in a soft, feminine new nightgown. She bolted the door and secured the heavy wooden hatch that fit over the window opening, and then snuffed the flames of the room's two lanterns before climbing into bed.

Surprisingly, sleep did not come quickly. When it did, Shal was plagued by visions of Ranthor pawing and clawing to get out of the crystal ball. "You should have warned me he was coming!" he shouted.

"But I couldn't!" Shal shouted back. "I didn't know how!"

"You should have known. You should have figured it out! Now, I walk the night like the skeletons you faced today! Aaaauuuggghhh!"

Once more the shadowy figure loomed behind Ran-thor. He struggled even harder to escape the confines of the ball, but the dagger stabbed out again and again. With the coiled snake insignia on the attacker's armband, it gave the doubly frightening impression of a snake striking repeatedly. The pounding of Ranthor's fists against the crystal thundered in Shal's ears, until finally silence exploded around her as his body slumped and slid down the inside of the globe like a discarded piece of clothing.

She woke to the feel of her own body flopping back and forth through no force of its own. She could feel sweat streaming down her front and back.

It was Sot who was shaking her shoulders. "I don't make a habit of entering the rooms of my guests when they're inside 'em," he explained hurriedly, "but I heard you scream, and I ran up here to see what was wrong. I pounded on the door, but you just kept screamin'."

Shal shook herself to clear her head of the nightmare. It was bitterly real. She was sure her master was still suf-fering, tormented like those skeletons at Sokol Keep, and it was her fault. She wanted to leave immediately for Denlor's tower, but Sot managed to quiet her down enough to convince her that she should at least wait till first light. He insisted she take several large gulps of his own house liquor. It was a powerful brew that burned all the way down with each swallow. . . .

Shal slept till well after dawn, and there were no more nightmares. It was the grumblings of her familiar that fi-nally woke her. . . . *I might as well spend my time in a sta-ble. At least I'd have oats and hay to keep me company,* were the first words she actually comprehended. Each syllable seemed to echo in her brain like the clanging of a gong.

"Quiet!" Shal hissed, closing her eyes tighter.

I'm not making any noise, Mistress, retorted the familiar. To Shal, it sounded like the crash of thunder.

"Will you please shut up?" Shal shouted, then she clasped her hands to her ears to muffle the sound of her own voice.

Pardon me, but weren't you planning to go to Denlor's tower today to try to find our mast—uh, Ranthor's murderer?

Shal sat up slowly and tried through tightly squinted eyelids to see where she had left the belt with the indigo cloth. Maybe if she covered it with a pillow, the familiar's voice would be quieter inside her head. Better yet, maybe she wouldn't be able to hear it at all. But she saw neither the belt nor the cloth; instead, a horse was standing directly in her way.

Comprehension came slowly, and Shal did her best to ignore the monstrous animal as she got up to splash water on her face and prepare to face the sunshine she could see trying to sneak through the closed window hatch.

"Yes, I'm planning to go to Denlor's tower today," she finally answered. "And this will be your chance to show that you're good for something besides making wisecracks."

That's not fair! The horse stomped and whuffled agitatedly. *You would have been nothing but orc fodder yesterday if I hadn't reminded you about the Staff of Power.*

"*You'll* be orc fodder if you don't give me a chance to wake up in peace!"

Hmph! The very idea! . . .

"There's a deep, dark pocket just waiting for you, Cerulean."

Is that an order, Mistress?

"It will be if you don't get out of my brain—now!"

The horse hung its head and retreated to a corner of the room.

"And please, Cerulean, don't sulk! It doesn't become you at all."

The big horse lifted its head and switched its tail. Switch. Switch. Switch. He whickered quietly as he eyed the ceiling and pawed the floor gently. Not a whisper of mental communication jarred Shal's throbbing head as she carefully brushed her leathers and then took time to meditate and memorize her spells.

Much later, she ordered Cerulean into one of the pockets and took him out to the stable, where she let him out again and fed him apples and carrots. Finally she began to brush his coat to a high sheen. "How well did you know Ranthor, Cerulean?" Shal asked, electing to speak aloud as long as she was alone in the stable, except for a half dozen or so other horses.

How well do you know anyone? He summoned me when he was an apprentice—younger than you, even. I used to help him memorize his spells. I begged him to take me along to the tower of the red mage, but he could be a stubborn old goat. I'll bet now he wishes he had listened to me.

Shal laughed. "I'm sure if he wishes anything, he wishes he had taken you."

The horse stamped and shook its mane, obviously pleased by her apparently improving spirits.

"Cerulean, what do you know about the Wand of Wonder? Ranthor didn't tell me much. I suppose you know what he said."

He got the wand as a gift some time ago, Cerulean answered. *I don't keep track of years, but he was much younger then. Still danced regularly—*

"Danced? Ranthor?" Shal looked dubious, with one eyebrow raised in surprise.

He loved to dance. Never went anywhere in those days without a woman on each arm. But as I was saying, he got the wand as a gift. Used it three times, as I remember.

The first time, he was deep in the Deadwood Forest, hunting secil. It's a rare fungus he needed for a spell component. He was in quite a huff that day—swore I was stepping on every mushroom in sight—and he finally insisted I keep a good distance away from where he was working. Working—ha! Scrounging around on his hands and knees like some pauper, brushing dust into a bag. I, on the other hand, was exploring the area with dignity when I found the clump of secil. Did I step on it? No. I—

"The wand, Cerulean. What does this have to do with the Wand of Wonder?"

I was just getting to that, Mistress. Must you be so impatient? Anyhow, I didn't step on it. I quite understandably happened to miss seeing another clump of insignificant fungus. It was brown, and spores puffed up everywhere when I stepped on it. The air was thick with the stuff, and it didn't feel at all healthy. I could hardly breathe, and as far away as I was from Ranthor, he was still affected. He coughed and coughed, doubled over so bad he couldn't even catch his breath to cast one of his spells. Finally he just pulled out the wand and managed to mutter a word or two.

"And?"

And all of a sudden bubbles started floating up everywhere—sticky ones that splattered icy water when they burst. The spores didn't stand a chance. The ones that didn't stick to the bubbles were doused to the ground when they burst, and the magical cold killed the fungus.

Naturally, Ranthor got his secil in the end, and he was quite pleased with the wand.

"You said you remember three times. What about the other two?" Shal asked.

The second time was just as successful. He was trapped between an umber hulk and a dragon—horrible things, umber hulks; look like giant beetles that walk up-

right. Anyway, one of his hands was hurt—Ranthor's hands, I mean—so he couldn't cast a spell, and that was before he had the Staff of Power. When he used the Wand of Wonder, the dragon suddenly sprouted huge worms all over its body. Well, the umber hulk simply went wild, what with worms being its preferred diet. It tore right past Ranthor and me and started attacking the dragon with its big pincers. Needless to say, we beat a hasty retreat.

"So why did Ranthor worry so much about using the wand?"

As I said, there was a third time. I was galloping with godspeed, with a foul wizard, one of Ranthor's most powerful foes, chasing us on one of those flying carpets. Instead of just asking me to go faster, Ranthor whips out the wand, points it at the wizard and says, 'Turtle speed.' Before I could blink, I was the only thing going turtle speed, and the wizard was zooming by overhead. If there hadn't been a tree in her way, we'd have been dead.

"Huh?" Shal waited for an explanation.

I slowed down so fast she overshot us. She tried to turn, but the carpet was still going at full speed, and she slammed into a tree. Wonderful old tree. Burned to a crisp when her acid blood spilled all over it and ignited the thing. Of course, the wizard went up—poof!—right along with it.

"Then that was still a positive effect, wasn't it? So why should I worry about using the wand?"

As I said, Mistress, I was the one going turtle speed. Ranthor pitched over my head and flew almost as far as the other wizard. He swore that was when his rheumatism set in.

"Oh." Shal couldn't help but wonder if the wand wouldn't be less dangerous if Ranthor had a different familiar.

I resent that!

"Sorry." Shal hadn't meant for Cerulean to "hear" that. She tried to change the subject. "Are you ready to go?"

"You're asking the *horse?*" Ren had entered unnoticed and stood within a few feet of Shal. She almost fell into the feed trough at the sound of his voice.

"How did you get in here without my hearing you?" she demanded.

He reached for her hand and pulled her gently away from the feed trough and the dung gutter. "I didn't mean to startle you. I was just practicing my thieving skills. They've gotten a little rusty in the last year."

"It seems to me they work just fine," Shal said, a little defensively. "I guess I was concentrating on what I have to do today."

"It could be tougher than you think to get into Denlor's tower," Ren said. "I went there to scout it last night, and the place is a regular fortress of magical traps. Even most of the creatures that gather outside the walls at night seem to be kept at bay by some force."

"What do you mean, you went there last night?" Shal's green eyes blazed, and she pushed Ren's hand away. "You were supposed to get some rest so you'd be fresh for today."

"Could you have slept with that stinking poultice on? I laid there till the stars came out, and then I got up and scrubbed myself with salts and lye and anything I could think of until I finally got rid of that stench. I couldn't go anywhere undetected smelling like that. And I sure couldn't hope to get very close to you."

Shal blushed and turned to continue currying the horse. "Your girl friend . . . Tempest . . . must have been very special."

Ren cocked his head, surprised that Shal would bring up the subject of Tempest.

Shal answered his unspoken question. "I know you're

only attracted to me because I remind you of her."

Ren swallowed hard and was about to say something when Tarl entered the stable. He quickly took a step away from Shal.

"You're moving easier than you were last night," Tarl said to Ren.

"Yeah. That poultice helped, but I think the workout I got washing it off probably did almost as much good."

"Now, that's a fine thank-you," Tarl said with a smile. He turned to say good morning to Shal, but she spoke first.

"Look, I don't want to be rude, but I'd really like to get going." Shal related the events of her dream the previous night and her sense that Ranthor's soul was not at rest. "Are you sure you still want to come?" she asked when she was finished.

Ren's acknowledgement was simple. He led out a roan mare from three stalls down and began to prepare her tack.

Tarl just looked up at Shal and said, "Can I ride with you?"

The streets of Phlan were mostly straight, and Ren led the way. In the heart of town, where the Laughing Goblin Inn was located, the streets bustled with activity. At every corner, peddlers touted their wares. As was his custom, Ren took in everything, watching for anything out of the ordinary. The closer they came to the outer walls of the civilized portion of the city, the sparser the crowds grew and the more wary Ren became.

Tarl wasn't nearly so watchful, at least at the start. He gladly wrapped his arms around Shal's waist and leaned his head gently against hers as they cantered to the farthest end of Civilized Phlan. What made a woman smell so good? he wondered, able for the first time that day to focus on something besides Anton and his own failings. Tarl had spent every ounce of healing that remained in him yesterday on Anton, and he knew his brothers continued to do the same daily, but if Anton had made any progress, it was measured in mustard grains.

Denlor's tower and the high walls surrounding it were built of red brick, which stood out in bright contrast to the gray-black fortress at the edge of the city. From a distance, the tower appeared friendly and inviting, a testimony to the wizard's benevolent character. But as they came closer, they could see that whole sections had been hammered away or blackened from repeated fires.

Ren reined his horse into the midst of a small grove of annonwood trees that paralleled one dilapidated wall of the keep, motioning for Shal to follow. More bushes than trees, the orange-leafed annonwoods made up the thick border of a small park at the farthest corner of the city. "I found this place last night when I scouted the tower," Ren said in a hushed voice. "It has a sort of natural peace about it. It's the peace of living things, not death like so much of Phlan. We can leave the horses here in safety and move under cover to the outer gates—"

"You may leave your horse if you want," said Shal, interrupting, "but Cerulean is coming along with us. He was my master's magical familiar, and now he's mine. He can be of help to us while we're trying to get through the magical barriers that guard this place."

Ren's first inclination was to argue the difficulties of trying to move inconspicuously with a huge war-horse tagging along, but Shal's tone left no room for argument. Shrugging, Ren dismounted and led the way to the tower, working slowly and silently through the border of annonwoods until they reached the stretch of wall that marked the edge of Civilized Phlan. Again and again, he glanced behind him and off to both sides, as he had when they were riding, sure but not sure that they were being followed. He noticed nothing, not even a whisper or a misplaced scent. There was just an occasional shimmer of ocher light vanishing from the corner of his eye each time he turned. It could be the sun, it could be his own lack of sleep, it could be nothing at all. Ren glanced behind himself one final time before they dashed under the vine-covered arch that led to the grounds of the tower. Still he saw nothing.

Nothing alive, at any rate. All around the tower lay the charred and rotting bodies of dozens of kinds of monsters and other marauders. Shal sucked in her breath at the sight and smell of the carnage, remembering the panic Denlor had shown in the vision through the crystal as hordes upon hordes of creatures converged on his tower, many of them gaining entrance by the force of their sheer numbers. In a fashion atypical among such creatures, those that lay at the walls had sacrificed themselves by diminishing the tower's magical energies so that others could enter and invade it.

Tarl dropped to one knee and waved his hammer in the air to form the sign of the balances. He, too, wondered what manner of evil force could convince so many humanoids and monsters to go willingly to their deaths.

Shal wasted no time in contemplation. She picked her way around the corpses that lay on the faint path. To either side of the door, bodies were heaped like cordwood, many of them decapitated, some otherwise mutilated from battle. Most showed signs of burning. Some were rotting with age, while others may have died within the last few days.

An icy spur of fear pulsed through Shal as she approached the door to the tower. It was a great brass door, its surface marred by numerous scratches, exactly as she remembered it from the images Denlor had projected through the crystal. She shuddered involuntarily, knowing that Ranthor's death, too, must have been just as she had seen it in the large clear globe. She reached out a tremoring hand toward the gate.

"No!" Ren hissed, grabbing her arm. "That door has a

charge that will knock a person flat." He reached in front of her and touched the metal lock with a piece of dead-wood. Instantly the stick shot from his hand. Were it not for his gauntlets, his hand would have been badly cut by the sheer force of it. "This whole place is buzzing with magical energy. The side doors are also magically guarded, but I've brought my thieving tools along. I think that with time and care, I can get us in."

"Ren, your tools aren't needed here." Shal explained how in his message, Denlor, the red mage, had left her with the "keys" to passage into and within his tower. Shal held her hand out toward the door as she had started to a moment ago and uttered two magical words. The lock began to glow a cherry red, and the door swung open. Ren and Tarl exchanged surprised glances and were about to enter cautiously, but it was Shal's turn to hold up a hand in warning. She repeated Ren's earlier safety measure, picking up a twig that lay on the path and toss-ing it into the open doorway. A crimson arc of energy il-luminated the area immediately in front of the door. It wasn't clear whether the twig ever reached the floor. There was a loud crackling noise, and flame erupted where the small stick had struck the arc, incinerating it in an instant.

Shal stood silent, obviously concentrating, and in a few moments Cerulean stepped forward, past Tarl and past Ren, and entered the tower. Brilliant red sparks erupted all around the horse's hooves as each touched the floor. The others peered in as the big horse paraded in a circle before the doorway. In his movements, Cerulean showed no sign whatsoever of pain or discomfort, but his hide began to glow an iridescent blue, the deep, al-most purple blue of a grackle's head, and the glow inten-sified with each step.

Shal spoke softly. "He's absorbing the power of Denlor's red lightning with each step he takes. It should be safe for us to walk across the magically charged floor in a minute."

Ren and Tarl looked on in awe as the floor continued to crackle with sparks at Cerulean's footsteps. Ren looked to Shal, wondering if it was safe to enter yet, and when she nodded, he eased gingerly, silently into the room. By the time Tarl and Shal entered, Cerulean was glowing like a fiery beacon, but there were no more sparks.

So bright was the light from the horse's body that they didn't need to bother with a lantern. The door shut silently behind them before Tarl could reach back to close it. They stood inside a great rhombus-shaped room, obviously a meeting hall, with solid, heavy benches set three rows deep in a horseshoe shape. A broad, low, ornately carved rosewood lectern stood at the opening of the U. Bizarre trophies, heads of beasts not even Ren had ever seen alive, were mounted along the room's walls.

"I didn't know that Denlor was a teacher," said Shal. "Ranthor always spoke of him as—"

Suddenly, from all around the room, came whispers of the name "Denlor," as though each bench were occupied by a row of students, whispering their teacher's name. As the whispers began to die, a red robe whisked into the room from the doorway opposite the lectern. It, too, seemed to be whispering, but in an exaggerated, breathy whisper that made it distinct from and more chilling than the others. "Denlor . . . I am Denlor," it breathed. The tattered robe was draped over nothing but blackness, a blackness that defied the brilliant blue light from Cerulean that bathed the room. The robe fluttered menacingly toward them. Tarl's hammer shone like Cerulean, as did Ren's dagger.

"Don't touch it!" said Shal, her tone icy. "Denlor's spirit does not rest; he guards his tower even in death. As long as we do no damage here, he will do us no harm, but touch that robe and you're dead."

Tarl and Ren lowered their weapons so they were at the ready but not threatening. Both were already convinced that Shal possessed a mastery of the magicks of this place that was beyond their understanding.

"I think Ranthor was killed in a spell-casting chamber, upstairs somewhere. It's strange and frustrating—from Denlor's vision, I know where everything in this building is, but my only image from Ranthor is of his death."

"I don't mean to be gruesome, Shal, but we'll find the place of his death soon enough," Ren said. "For our own safety, we need to check out every room. There are signs of struggling and scuffling all over this place. Look at the way those benches are misaligned there, the broken door frame over there." Ren went on, pointing as he spoke. "See the bloodstains on the floor . . . there and there? We don't know who or what's been here, or when, for that matter."

Shal nodded. Her every instinct was to press up the stairs fearlessly and find the murderous beast still lurking near her master's body, as it would happen in some stilted morality play of the type traveling thespians used to perform in the streets when she was a child. But she knew that somewhere upstairs she would find Ranthor's days-old body and, only if she was lucky, some sign of the creature that killed him. "That doorway off to the left." She pointed. "We can look in there first."

Shal continued speaking but in a hushed tone, her words no longer addressed to Tarl or Ren. "What do you mean, you'd rather not go in there? . . . So what if they occasionally served horsemeat? It wasn't yours. Go on, scoot! We don't want to fry on these high-energy floors."

The horse stepped forward, somewhat indignantly, Tarl thought, if horses can be indignant, but the floor of the kitchen he entered was normal, and the horse's brilliant blue light started to fade almost as soon as it had passed through the doorway.

Tarl didn't notice, however. He was lost in a muttering conversation with himself over Shal's behavior with Cerulean. "Right. Familiars do talk to their masters, I suppose. And their masters must talk to their familiars and not to their friends." He followed almost aimlessly behind Ren, who was following Shal. It wasn't until he felt the gentlest hint of a chill brush his back that he realized that the red robe was fluttering along behind him like some misplaced shadow. "By my oath, I wish I didn't feel so powerless when I'm with this woman," Tarl muttered, then shook his fist at the ghostly cloth. "Get back a few feet, will you? You give me the creeps. I'd gladly try some clerical magic beyond my means if I thought it would make you flap away."

The phantom obediently backed off a few steps, and Tarl felt a little better when he turned to resume following the others. Ren was already scouting the huge mess-style kitchen, examining the implements and foodstuffs left out on the cutting block and beside the great baking oven, silently opening doors to a pantry, a storage room, and a root cellar.

"I think I've found the cook," called Ren from the root cellar. "I need some light."

Cerulean's glow was fading fast, and he wouldn't have fit down the tight staircase anyhow, so Shal pulled out her light rod, which immediately began to glow with a constant blue-amethyst light. She held it high at the top of the stairs, then started down herself. "Here . . . can you see?"

"I can see fine now," answered Ren. "She was murdered, all right, about three days ago, I'd say. That's a burn mark from a cord that was pulled taut around her neck. It's the work of someone proficient, if not a pro."

Ren came up the stairs carrying the dead woman, a small figure with the dark coloring found in the far southwest reaches of the Realms. He laid her already stiff body on a long counter in the kitchen. "From what I can see, she was pushed down the stairs after she was killed. There's still a ladle in her hand. My guess is she never even saw her murderer. We're talking about a really brave assassin here." Ren felt like spitting to clear the bile that rose in his mouth at the thought of the kind of vermin that would kill with so little cause.

"From the way things are laid out there," Ren went on, pointing to an assortment of dishes, cooking utensils, and foodstuffs, "I'd say she had already finished preparing a meal for her master and guests and was working on food for the servants, if that matters any."

Tarl spoke a prayer for the woman, soliciting Tyr's aid in helping ". . . another victim of the darkness that rules the outskirts of this city" to find her peace.

"The way those rope marks pull up on her neck doesn't look to me like the work of a kobold or anything else that short," Ren mused.

"Whoever or whatever killed her, may Tyr help her find the solace of her patron god."

They left the woman, agreeing to return and bury her when they left. The door across the hall led to what were apparently servants' quarters. There were two beds, and beside one they found a young man, dead. He'd obviously seen his attacker and struggled with him—or it. He had fallen victim to repeated stab wounds to the chest. Once again, Ren noted the nature of the wounds and suggested that the killer was tall, perhaps as tall as Tarl.

"I grieved only for my teacher," said Shal. "It never occurred to me that others died with him." She was near tears and stood clenching and unclenching her fists as she stared down at the bloody corpse. She spoke to no one in particular, pausing between words. "When Denlor sent his message in the crystal, he was completely overwhelmed by monsters and humanoids. But Ranthor and this poor young man and the cook . . . you're suggesting they were killed by another human being. I—I couldn't see the attacker, you know—only an arm, stabbing over and over. I just—just assumed it was a hobgoblin or one of the other beasts that were attacking the towers."

"Shal, I'm not saying for sure that it was a man," said Ren quietly. "I'm saying I think it was. But at any rate, they wouldn't be any less dead if it was a hobgoblin or a kobold that killed them."

"I know that!" Shal shouted. "Don't you see? Monsters and humanoids kill on whim alone. Men kill for reasons—however distorted. A kobold I could kill and be done with it, with no regrets. A man I'll hate . . ."

Tarl put an arm around Shal. "And you will probably be right in that feeling."

Shal gently removed Tarl's hand from her shoulder, squeezing it firmly before letting go. "I need to find Ranthor." She turned to leave the room.

"Wait!" called Ren, quickly reaching for Shal's arm. "Don't you think it would be better for Tarl and I to lead? We can't be sure that everything within these walls is dead."

"No, but we do know that almost everything within these walls is magical. Tarl was the right person to lead us at Sokol Keep. I'm the right person to lead us through the red mage's tower."

Once again Shal left no room for question. She turned again and went through the meeting hall to the door from which the red robe had emerged. The horse, the two men, and the red robe followed.

The door opened into a splendid, almost palatial landing at the foot of a great, broad soapstone staircase. The floor was inset with tourmaline, amber, amethyst, aventurine, and other semiprecious stones. A brilliant light beneath the stones shone through their translucent surface, creating a glorious speckling of many-hued rays that colored the walls in a dazzling display. The whole party stopped for a moment to admire it.

When Shal finally started up the stairs, a ruby-colored cloud, in the image of the red mage himself, formed on the staircase.

Tarl didn't recognize Denlor. The only contact he'd had with such cloudlike visages had been with the wraiths that had killed so many of his brothers in the graveyard. He charged past Shal and would have challenged the ghostly vapors had not Shal caught hold of his armor and used all her recently acquired strength to stop him.

"Poison! It's poison, Tarl!" shouted Shal, hauling him back. "It's a poison image of the master of this tower!" Tarl looked sheepish, and she softened her voice. "I'm sorry, but I must insist that you let me go first. I welcome your company, and I can use your help, but as I said to Ren, this is my mission."

Even as Shal spoke, the cloud expanded, spreading its deadly haze down the stairway. Both Shal and Tarl started to cough.

Shal held her breath and concentrated, then spoke the words she'd heard from Denlor. "*Lysiam calentatem*, Denlor."

The cloud dissipated immediately, and the wide soapstone stairway once more stood vacant. Shal started up again but stopped when she heard Cerulean's whimper inside her head.

She spun around, very nearly bumping into Ren and Tarl, who were following close behind her. "What is your problem?" she exclaimed, her eyes blazing.

Tarl and Ren, who were both feeling less and less comfortable about their roles in this venture, looked up at her and started stammering in unison.

"No!" Shal shook her head furiously and pointed down the stairs in disgust. "Not you—him! He's whimpering in my ear like some sick child!"

Surely you can see that I could slip and kill myself on this treacherous staircase, Mistress!

"Stairs don't come any broader or shallower than these, Cerulean," Shal answered in a tone that was decidedly lacking in patience.

The horse continued to stand at the bottom of the stairs, shaking its head and whickering and stamping one front hoof. Bathed in the colorful lights from the stone floorway, he looked like some child's giant stuffed toy.

Shal pulled the indigo cloth from her belt and started down the stairs, holding it out in front of her.

No, not that! Cerulean pleaded. *You may need me. Just make me small and carry me up.*

Shal's eyes glinted for a fleeting moment. "If I make you small, will your voice be small, too?" She didn't wait for a reply. She concentrated for a moment and said the words for a Reverse Enlargement spell. A cat-sized Cerulean instantly appeared, looking pathetic at the bottom of the stairs, overshadowed by the hovering robe. Shal strode down the stairs, slapped her hip a couple of times, and called, "Here, boy! Here, boy!" as if she were calling a dog.

That's low. That really hurts! came the first of the mental barrage Shal knew would follow. But at least the voice was small, an irritating buzz at best.

Shal picked up the flailing miniature horse and climbed to where Ren and Tarl were still standing, looking more than a little bewildered.

"Would you take him?" she asked Ren, holding out the kicking animal. "I need to keep my hands free to cast spells."

Ren's mouth was open, but no words came out. Shal immediately headed back up the stairway.

"I thought rangers liked horses," said Tarl, jabbing Ren with one elbow.

Ren leveled a gaze at Tarl that might have turned him to ashes, but the cleric only grinned more broadly.

Ren stuffed Cerulean up under his left arm and clamped him against his side in a near rib-breaking grip. Of course, he had no way of hearing the horse's hysterical complaints, and Shal wasn't paying any attention.

As Shal reached the top of the staircase, the red robe swished ahead of her and stood beyond the stairway, waiting. Shal looked back toward her friends and shrugged. "I think we have a new guide."

The robe remained still, flitting nervously, till everyone got to the top of the stairs, which ended in the foyer to a large dining room. Like the meeting hall downstairs, the dining room was rhombus-shaped and appeared to serve as the hub of the second level. Set in walls to the right and left were two shiny brass doorways, both of which showed signs of recent battering. Straight ahead was another doorway that they could only assume led to the third level. But the red robe did not leave the room; instead, it whisked to the mammoth walnut table at its center and stopped over the high-backed head chair.

"Look—ashes," Shal said as she reached the chair. "Denlor must have died here."

"At the table?" asked Tarl.

"While he was sitting down to a meal, apparently with two other people," said Ren, pointing to the haphazard place settings.

"Two? Who do you suppose—" Shal started to ask, but Tarl interrupted.

"What could possibly turn a man to ashes in his chair?" he asked, watching the robe hover over the remains of its owner.

Shal shrugged. "Denlor was terrified by the idea of having his body eaten by the creatures that swarmed around this place." Shal paused, remembering once again the horror and helplessness Denlor had communicated through the crystal. She told how he had used every magical resource at his disposal, and how the monsters must have climbed over their own dead to press through his defenses.

She went on. "When Ranthor reached Denlor, all kinds of snarling, slavering beasts had probably already entered the tower. Denlor and Ranthor must have stood side by side, casting spells till they had no more energy left, trying to purge this place of hundreds of monsters like we saw stacked outside the tower."

Tarl was moved by Shal's explanation, especially her description of Denlor's feelings as the beasts kept coming and coming, but he repeated his question. "But how was he turned to ashes? By what?"

"By himself," Shal answered. "I'm almost certain he set a spell into place to—" she hesitated to say the word—"to cremate himself at the instant of death so no beast would feed on his corpse." The thought of the venerable wizard dying at his own dinner table and then bursting into flames like a body on some sacrificial pyre brought tears to Shal's eyes. "The wizard locks and magical energies we encountered, the red gas on the stairway—those were probably all activated by Denlor's death, too."

"Wouldn't bursting into flames leave whatever killed Denlor in pretty rough shape?" Ren asked.

"Perhaps," Shal said. "I don't know for sure." She remembered that when the parchment Ranthor left for her burst into magical flames, no harm whatsoever came to the desk. "It would depend on Denlor's intent. If he wanted the flame to burn the things around it, I think the chair and table would have caught fire, or at least they'd show some sign of damage." She shook her head. "A wizard of his talents might be able to make the flame burn flesh and not objects. I just don't know."

Tarl was still looking at the robe. "What about the robe?"

JAMES M. WARD AND JANE COOPER HONG

"Like I said before, I suppose that his spell may have been designed to burn flesh only."

"No, I mean why does it stay there like that? What's it waiting for?" Tarl pressed.

"For us to finish our business and leave, I guess."

"Ouch!" Ren dropped Cerulean unceremoniously to the floor and shook his hand. "He bit me!"

The cat-sized horse let out a tiny whuffle, struggled to its feet, and immediately began to complain in a high, squeaky voice. *That giant ape nearly flattened me! Why, he would've crushed my ribs if I'd stayed under his arm one more second!* Cerulean clomped round and round the floor, like a child wearing new hard-soled shoes.

"I'm sorry, Cerulean, but I'm sure Ren didn't mean to hurt your ribs," Shal reassured him.

"I didn't mean to carry a horse around, either," Ren muttered.

Cerulean continued to charge around the big room, galloping in steadily widening circles until he was running next to the walls. Each time he approached either of the two brass doorways, the door would glow red and the tiny horse would turn a brilliant shade of blue.

"Wizard-locked, both of them!" exclaimed Shal, not waiting for the question she knew one of her friends would ask.

Shal knew the magical commands that would get her past the wizard locks, and she used them. Tarl and Ren followed, marveling once more at Shal's cool confidence and command of magic. They followed her first through Denlor's private chamber and the treasure room adjacent to it, and then the scroll chamber and the magical supply room adjacent to that. She instructed them not to touch anything.

"Eventually I'll have the skills to come back here and add part of Denlor's magic to my own, but for now, so that his spirit can rest, we have to leave everything the way we find it. And above all, we've got to find Ranthor."

Cerulean once again galloped around the circumference of the dining room, clip-clopping his way to the doorway that led to the stairs. As he started to pass through the door frame, his tiny body blazed the brilliant blue hue for which he was named, in startling contrast to the shimmering crimson curtain of energy that appeared in the doorway.

"The curtain will fight any negative energy you carry with you. To pass through it, you need to relax your thoughts and emotions," Shal explained, then walked effortlessly through it, causing the curtain to glow brightly once again. As soon as she stood on the other side, the curtain all but vanished, giving the appearance of a few stray rays of sunlight reflected through a ruby.

Ren turned one shoulder toward the barely visible curtain and tried to barge through, but he leaped back in pain as the curtain sizzled and crackled. Next he tried to run through, only to be jolted to the floor as if he had bounced off a piece of taut leather.

Tarl reached down to help his friend up, but Ren shook his head in stubborn refusal and stood on his own. "I'll lick this thing. Just give me a minute."

"Stay calm," Shal reminded him. "The key is to stay calm."

"Let me try it," said Tarl. "My clerical training might help me."

"Sure, be my guest," Ren replied, still rubbing his stinging shoulder.

Tarl began to speak the words of a traditional cleansing ritual intended to purify thoughts, "As Tyr controls the balances, may I measure the things that weigh upon my heart, and may they balance the sides of the scale equally that I may meet my god at peace." Tarl's words were correct, but he knew that the balances did not rest evenly within him. Thoughts of Anton, his dead brothers, and the missing hammer outweighed all else. When he tried to pass through the barrier, he was thrown to the ground with every bit as much force as Ren had been.

Tarl concentrated once more on the cleansing ritual, this time envisioning his successes at Sokol Keep and letting each small victory there offer balance against the horrors of the graveyard. When Tarl felt his inner being had reached a point of equilibrium, a point at which nothing could easily sway him off balance, he tried again . . . and passed easily through the shimmering curtain.

"If he can do it, I can do it," muttered Ren. The ranger-thief knew no cleansing ritual, no rite of concentration. But he did know how to steel his thoughts before trying to disarm a foe or to silently make his way down the length of a corridor unobserved. He imagined that the wall was a passage that he must slip through unnoticed. He thought of nothing but passing through, and that is what he did. The magical panel barely shimmered as he eased through the door.

"Well done!" exclaimed Shal.

Ren's first reaction was one of anger. Why should she praise him for finally doing something that she and Tarl had accomplished so easily? But when he looked into Shal's eyes, he saw that her words had been sincere. Shal dropped her gaze to where Cerulean stood beside her, picked up the miniature horse, and handed him to Ren once more. She caught the big man's attention again with her green eyes and smiled—a playful, teasing look that Ren had never seen before from Shal—and then she turned and started up the stairs.

Much steeper and narrower than the soapstone stairway, the staircase to the third floor was made of terrazzo, with sizable fragments of a deep burgundy-veined marble running through it. The stairwell was lit from above by some kind of arcane light. At the top of the stairway, they came to a bronze door, decorated with splendidly forged handiwork, obviously of dwarven design.

Shal touched the outer edges of the door with her fingertips, incanting a different syllable as she touched each of the door's four corners and the intricately embossed lion's head at the door's center. At her touch, each of the four corners shone a rich vermilion. When her fingers reached the lion's head, it blazed the color of molten metal, opened its mouth, and roared loudly. When the roaring ceased, the mouth remained open, forming an opening into the room. Shal reached through the lion's mouth and pulled on a latch, then removed her hand. Where no seam had shown before, the door parted vertically down the center, and the two halves disappeared into the pocket frame of the doorway.

"Neat trick," Ren commented, still nervous about watching Shal reach into the lion's mouth.

Shal felt relieved. She knew that if the words had been spoken incorrectly or if her concentration were broken, she could have lost her arm or worse. She knew from the cold knot wrenching ever tighter in her stomach that she was near the place of Ranthor's death. The room behind the bronze door was obviously an equipment chamber, not unlike the one she had been working in when Ranthor sent his message through the crystal. Shal didn't stop to look around the room but proceeded straight across it, knowing that Ren and Tarl would follow.

The door on the opposite side of the room, beyond the racks and shelves full of vials and beakers, was of plain wood. Shal knew it contained the most insidious death trap of all.

"Cerulean, I need your help on this one," Shal said, working a spell of enlargement to return the horse to his original size. Then she backed away from the door and took position behind a row of shelving, motioning for Tarl and Ren to follow suit.

Cerulean didn't need to be told what to do. He began to paw the floor and snort. Folding his ears tight against his head, his white coat began to glow, much as it had downstairs, but this time the glow radiated around him like a shield. Finally he moved up to the door, reared on his hind legs, and kicked the wooden door in with his front hooves.

Immediately the door burst into thousands of splinters, each tipped with red—poison, Shal knew. The splinters sparked crimson against the horse's blue shield, creating flare upon flare of purple fire so intense the three could hardly look on.

When the flames finally died down, Cerulean stood immobile, looking spent, in the open doorway. Shal emerged from her hiding place behind the shelf and went to him quickly. She patted the horse's withers gently, feeling an appreciation and affection for the big animal she had not felt before. "Well done, Cerulean! Ranthor would be proud of you."

Ranthor is gone, Mistress. Cerulean nodded toward the room with his head. *I hope you are proud of me.*

Shal patted the familiar again, then stepped past him into the spell-casting chamber.

Ranthor's body lay crumpled behind the casting stand. Crystal fragments littered the room, many glued to the floor in Ranthor's blood. As Shal knelt beside her former master, her shoulders and then her whole body began to shake as she felt the tears come. She had held on to the faintest, most minute hope that what she had seen in the globe was a vision only and not reality, that the chill she had experienced at her teacher's passing was only a reaction to a vivid nightmare. Now the truth lay before her. It was irreversible. And so she wept.

Tarl knelt behind Shal, encircling her in his arms, his head bowed. Silently he prayed, both for his friend and for the man he had not known. There were no words, he knew, to comfort Shal, any more than there were words that would make him feel better about Anton or Sontag or Donal or any of the others.

Ren didn't share Tarl's talent for offering comfort. His mind thought in terms of action. He walked silently past his two friends and leaned over the body, then turned the stiff corpse over and examined the wounds. What he found made him recoil. Ranthor had been stabbed in the back, over and over again, with a dagger that would have killed with the first scratch, for it was tipped with the same green acid poison that had killed Tempest. From the angle and the profusion of the wounds, Ren knew that Ranthor's murderer was taller and probably less skilled than the assassin who had killed Tempest, but unfortunately no less deadly.

Mistress . . . Cerulean's gentle call penetrated Shal's grief. *Mistress, I will bring Ranthor with me into the darkness of the cloth. Once you have sealed this tower, I will take Ranthor on one last ride to put his soul to rest. It will be my final duty as his familiar.*

But can he truly rest if his murderer remains unpunished? Shal communicated mentally.

In the back of her mind, Shal heard Ren relating his theories about what he had found in his examination of the body, but it was Cerulean's answer that Shal listened to. *Ranthor will be at rest, Mistress. It is you who will not.*

Shal stood and quietly explained the familiar's bidding to Ren and Tarl. They lifted the rigid mage's body onto the horse's back and watched as Cerulean reared up, then disappeared into a small pocket of the indigo cloth. After being witness to an entire day of magical wonders, they barely thought twice about the horse's unique method of departure.

Though near exhaustion, Shal moved through the tower hurriedly, sealing door after door, making sure all was as they found it. She spoke her assurances to the robe as they reached the second floor, but the ghostly garment continued to follow them as they removed the bodies of the cook and the servant. Finally it stood hovering inside the front door as Shal closed it and sealed it by reversing the same utterance she had used to open the great bronze door.

As they reached the park where Ren's mare was tethered, Tarl and Ren strapped the two bodies across the roan's broad back. Shal called Cerulean forth from the Cloth of Many Pockets. The horse leaped from the cloth and straight into the air with the grace of a unicorn and flew upward. Shal watched, misty-eyed, as it left a blue stardust trail behind it. She could just barely make out Cerulean's message: *See you soon, Mistress.*

❧ 7 ❧

Deceived

Porphyrys Cadorna held in his hands the official proclamation from the council making him Fourth Councilman. It praised him for "prudent judgment in the matter of assigning punitive tasks for the betterment of the community." It commended him for recognizing the caliber of the three barroom brawlers and for immediately acting on the information they provided by arranging to add new shipping lanes in and out of the harbor. Advisors to the council were suggesting that the resulting influx of newcomers to Phlan would double its present population and ensure further expansion into the uncivilized portions of the city.

Cadorna sat in his personal study, admiring the piece of parchment. It was written in the elegant script of the town's head scribe, a man known throughout the Moonsea area for the elegance of his calligraphy. Cadorna made a mental note to make the man his personal scribe when he became First Councilman.

"Finally, some credit for a Cadorna's talents." Porphyrys spoke aloud as he stared up at the portrait of his father that hung on the wall opposite his desk. "To think that simply because you had dealings with dragons they could assume that you were somehow responsible for the Dragon Run! That's like saying that because I send bits of useless information to the Lord of the Ruins, I must be in league with him. The fools just don't recognize the importance of maintaining connections . . . of fending first and foremost for yourself!"

Cadorna shook the parchment at the portrait. "But here, finally, is some credit. It's still not what we deserve . . . what I deserve. It was Second Councilman Silton whose incompetence was exposed by my proficiency. It is his seat I should have assumed, but the council in its "wisdom" opted to advance the Third and Fourth Councilmen ahead of me." Cadorna rattled the parchment once more, then set it on his desk. "However, I won't spend forever waiting for—"

A stiff rap on the door interrupted Cadorna in midsentence. "State your business," Cadorna called.

"Gensor reporting, Honorable Fourth Councilman."

Cadorna strolled to the door and lifted the bolt that secured it. "Enter, mage. What news do you have?"

"I followed them from the inn to—"

"I instructed you to follow them; of course you followed them! I asked you what news you've gathered."

"They—"

"Remove that hood in my presence. I like to look a man in the eyes when he speaks."

The mage's face was hidden deep within his black hood. "You think you control me because you are Fourth Councilman? You wish to look me in the eyes? So be it." Gensor reached up and pulled back his hood.

Cadorna blenched at the sight of the man's face. Gensor's skin was shriveled and ashen, an unnatural gray that gave him an almost corpselike appearance. His eyes were the color of a steel blade, and they seemed to bore straight into Cadorna as he spoke, his voice like ice. "I have no need of your reimbursements, Councilman. I work for you because, like you, I desire to know certain things."

Cadorna said nothing. There were ways of taking care of ingrates, even magic-users, when they got out of line. He returned Gensor's stare with a cold look of his own.

"They went to the tower of the red wizard—Denlor, to those of us who know him."

"Yes, I knew Denlor," said Cadorna.

"*Knew* him? I've no doubt," said Gensor. "The woman's mentor died there, as I gather did Denlor. I listened in on the party's conversations until they reached the tower itself, but I did not follow them in. My cloak of invisibility would not have functioned within those magicked walls."

"Spare me the details of your ineptitude, mage! What else did you learn?"

Gensor glowered at Cadorna until the councilman took a step backward, and then he proceeded. "Her master was murdered—by a beast, she believes."

"Her master? Who—"

"A wizard named Ranthor. She knew something of Denlor's death and of the siege on his tower by creatures from the outside." Gensor paused for a moment, looking inquisitively at Cadorna. "And her steed is magical, a familiar inherited from her dead master."

Cadorna stepped closer at this news. "A familiar? What are its powers? Can *anyone* control it?"

"A familiar is a mage's helpmate. A good one offers advice, warning, sometimes even protection from attack. Some are practically useless, but she insisted on taking the horse with her into the tower, so I expect the animal has some power to dispel magic."

"Are those powers someone else could harness?"

"A good familiar is loyal to the death and will serve another only at its master's bidding. Even I couldn't control the horse unless its master wished me to do so. You'd never be able to control it. Familiars communicate telepathically, by virtue of their spiritual tuning with their masters."

"Cursed magic-users! You intentionally exclude yourselves from the rest of us!"

"Yes, Councilman, that we do. And even though I don't

have any use for the Cormyrian woman's naivete or her righteous friends, I still recognize her as a growing force within my profession, a force to be worked with . . . or reckoned with."

"Or taken advantage of," said Cadorna, twisting his face into a smile.

At this, Gensor smiled, too—an equally corrupt smile—and then chuckled, a muted, synthetic sound. "What did you have in mind, Councilman?"

"You, of course, know my interest in those three, my belief that they may be able to help me recover the legacy due me from my family."

"Yes . . ."

"She seeks her mentor's murderer, does she not?" Cadorna asked, his narrowed eyes glinting.

"Yes. So?"

"It just seems to me that one of the gnolls that have overrun the Cadorna textile house may have had something to do with his murder. I mean, I'm sure I could make her *think* that was the case and get her to go there . . . don't you?" Cadorna was obviously calculating as he spoke. "My idea, of course, needs some refining, Gensor, but I'll certainly let you know when I can use your services again. In the meantime, since you don't need my monetary reimbursements, perhaps you'll take this for your efforts." Cadorna held out the magical dagger from Sokol Keep. It gleamed even in the daylight.

"How strange, Gensor. By its glow, this knife tells me that you are dangerous."

"Or that you are, Councilman." Gensor accepted the knife, turned, and left the study, closing the double doors firmly behind him.

* * * * *

"You remember how Cerulean used to have a bluish tint to his coat?" Shal asked, setting down her mug of ale.

"Yeah," answered Ren. "He does have a little bit of a blue tinge to him, even when he isn't collecting sparks from the floor."

"Well, since he returned this morning from putting Ranthor to rest, his coat has just the slightest hint of purple to it." Shal looked up with a grin of pure delight, obviously expecting Ren to comprehend her excitement. But he simply returned a puzzled stare.

"Don't you see?" asked Tarl, plunking down his own mug for emphasis. "Purple is Shal's color, not Ranthor's. The wizard has truly been put to rest, and the familiar is wholly Shal's."

"Purple is Shal's color? How would you know?" Ren appeared puzzled and looked to Tarl for some kind of explanation.

"I asked," Tarl said simply, and he locked eyes with Shal for just a moment before adding, "because I wanted to know."

"Well, thanks, Tarl. What a pal!" Ren said sarcastically. "Why don't you just come out and accuse me of being unobservant?"

"I wasn't suggesting—"

Tarl didn't have a chance to finish. The doors to the inn were flung open wide, and two trumpeters entered. They took position on either side of the double doors and began blasting their horns so loud that Sot's collection of rare glass liquor bottles rattled in their rack behind the bar. Sot grabbed his cudgel and seemed likely to throttle the two, but at that moment a herald entered the inn, stepped between them, unfurled a long scroll, and began reading:

"The Honorable Porphyrys Cadorna, Fourth Councilman of the City of Phlan, requires the presence of Tarl Desanea of Vaasa, Ren o' the Blade of Waterdeep, and Shal Bal of Cormyr directly in front of these premises immediately."

JAMES M. WARD AND JANE COOPER HONG

"Fourth Councilman now, eh?" Tarl noted. "I guess we'd better see what he wants."

"I don't get the impression we have much choice," said Ren, rising from the bench.

The herald exited, and the trumpeters stood holding the doors open until the three followed. Outside the inn, a gleaming white carriage, drawn by two white horses with braided tails and manes and feather plumes, pulled up in front of the inn just as the three came out. After calming the spirited horses, the herald opened the carriage door and dropped to his hands and knees before it. Cadorna stepped from the high carriage onto the man's back, then down to the street.

"Ah, I see you're all looking well." Cadorna waved his hand toward the three with a flourish. "Recovered from your mission to Thorn Island?"

"Recovered, and all ready to tend to our own unfinished business," said Ren, a slight edge in his voice.

"Not before assisting me with a small project, I hope," said Cadorna, his tone mirroring Ren's. "I believe my request will be of particular interest to the cleric, if not to the two of you. I assume that, in your concern for the cleric's best interests, you would consider accompanying him."

Shal wasn't anxious to enter into a discussion with any man who stepped on the flesh of others, but she did want Tarl to know he had her support. "Please state your request, Fourth Councilman," she said.

"I will . . . in the privacy of the inn," said Cadorna.

"The *privacy* of the inn?" Shal repeated. She and the others looked at him curiously until he instructed his herald and trumpeters to enter and clear the tavern.

Within a matter of minutes, the customers were emerging through the doorway. Sot's angry complaints coming from within could no doubt be heard for blocks.

Chuckling quietly, Ren suggested that Cadorna allow

the feisty innkeeper to stay, noting that he was a friend and, after all, the owner of the inn. To his surprise, Cadorna agreed.

In fact, as the newly appointed Fourth Councilman began to describe his family's demise at the time of the Dragon Run, he pointed out Sot as an example of the type of businessperson his parents and grandparents were—hardworking, indefatigable, and possessing a kind of street sense that kept their business alive when others failed. "That's why I'm sure the family fortune, or at least a portion of it, must still be intact," he said.

"As you can see," Cadorna continued with uncharacteristic humbleness, "I'm no fighter. I've recently received word from a half-orc spy I employ that the Cadorna textile house is now the dwelling place of a particularly disagreeable band of gnolls. Twice I have dispatched parties in the hope of recovering what is rightfully mine, but both times they failed to return." Cadorna paused for a moment, shaking his head. "Imagine being defeated by anything as lazy and unobservant as a gnoll!"

"Lazy and unobservant, perhaps, but big," Ren noted. "Not to mention completely amoral."

"Yes . . . well, be that as it may, they certainly don't compare to the likes of the beasts you defeated at Sokol Keep, though I have heard some rather ugly rumors about the gnoll leader. . . ." Cadorna paused a moment, watching them closely. "What I've heard is that he's a half-breed, the product of some poor woman's misfortune at the hands of a raiding band of gnolls. . . ." He gave the others time to express their revulsion, then took out a piece of yellowed parchment.

The map Cadorna produced was tattered from age and repeated folding. It showed the entire city, before it ever became separated into the civilized and uncivilized segments. Businesses were identified with notes about their ownership and their relative success. Cadorna didn't need to point out the location of his family's textile house; it dominated a large corner section of the city, and expansion plans had been sketched in on the map. When Cadorna was certain they knew the location of his family's business, he turned the map over. A crude sketch, obviously not the work of the cartographer who had drafted the city map, filled the other side.

"This is my father's drawing of the property, including the family living quarters," Cadorna explained. "I believe the treasure is here," he continued, pointing to a wall of an area labeled as a bedroom. "I don't know if the bulk of the family holdings will be in coins or bullion, but I do have notes from my mother describing several family heirlooms that I expect will be there . . . *if* the treasure is still intact."

"I don't understand, Councilman Cadorna," Tarl interrupted. "You implied earlier that I would have some special interest in this. . . ."

"It is my plan, should you recover the treasure, to give a generous portion—let's say fifteen percent—to the Tyrian temple."

Tarl leaned forward, his interest obviously piqued. "Why haven't you made this offer to the warrior clerics from the temple?"

"Simple. I consider the recovery of this treasure a personal matter. I'm not anxious to make this news public until such time as the treasure is actually in my hands," explained Cadorna.

"You'll forgive my straightforwardness here, Councilman," said Ren, "but if I understand you correctly, you aren't asking us to reclaim the textile house for human habitation."

"That's correct."

"Then if the venture were made in daytime, when most of the creatures outside the walls sleep, what's the difficulty? Is there something you aren't telling us?"

Cadorna cleared his throat, and his eyes darted from side to side. "Yes, well . . . the, uh, the gnoll leader I mentioned . . . They say he's as much a hyena in appearance—the mangy mane and yellowed teeth, you know—as any gnoll, but that he behaves like a man. Sometimes strangles his prey . . . even uses poisoned daggers. Highly ungnoll-like." Cadorna didn't wait for that to sink in, but instead plunged ahead. "A creature such as that might explain the, uh, difficulties experienced by the other two parties. With a superior intelligence leading them, the gnolls would indeed be formidable—even in daylight."

At Cadorna's words, Shal squeezed her mug of ale so hard that the pewter dented in her hands. Ale flowed over the top of the mug and onto the table. Almost in unison, Ren and Tarl reached over to calm her.

Cadorna pulled back, genuinely startled by her raw strength. When he was sure Ren and Tarl had calmed her down, he spoke to them as though she weren't there. "What ails the poor woman?"

Tarl answered. "A friend of hers was killed recently . . . by a poisoned dagger."

"And two people who were near him were killed by strangling," said Shal, regaining her composure.

"Really?" Cadorna widened his eyes and reached forward in his best effort at a consoling gesture. "I'm sorry. I didn't know. I was only relating rumors that I'd heard." He stopped speaking long enough to look Shal square in the eyes. "You don't think . . . ?"

Shal didn't respond. Instead, she turned to Ren, as if expecting him to offer some reason why Ranthor could or couldn't have been killed by the creature Cadorna had described.

"A half-gnoll . . ." Ren shivered visibly. "I've never seen one. Half-orcs are disgusting enough, but I suppose anything's possible."

Ren rose to his feet and moved behind Tarl and Shal to face Cadorna with them. He placed a hand on one shoulder of each of his companions. "There seems to be good reason for each of you to do this. You can count me in if you're of a mind to go."

"My purpose in coming to Phlan hasn't changed," said Shal. "I'll go."

Tarl stood and held his hand out to Cadorna. "We'll all go together, and if there's treasure within those walls, we'll bring it back to you."

Cadorna extended his clammy palm to Tarl, and then in turn to Ren and Shal. That done, he left the inn with as much pomp as when he had entered. As he stepped onto the herald's back and into the waiting carriage, he reminded himself to make arrangements that would guarantee receipt of the complete treasure upon their return.

*　*　*　*　*

It was nearly noon by the time the three of them were ready to leave Civilized Phlan. Ren was mounted atop the roan mare and Shal and Tarl on Cerulean.

" 'Tis advisable to leave the city by boat if you're inclined to be returnin'!" shouted one of the four guards from the wall as they approached.

"We have business in the uncivilized parts of the city," shouted Ren in return. "We'd be obliged if you'd open the gates."

The guard and one of his companions trudged down the stairway. "A mission for the council mayhaps?" asked the guard, eyeing the two well-armed men and the large young woman.

"A mission for a council member," Ren answered. "We'll be returning toward evening by the same gate."

"Ha! An optimist!" The guard slapped his thigh and chuckled for a moment. "Well, Tymora be with you," he said, reaching for the latch mechanism that barred the gate. "You just holler when ya come back, and we'll open the gate for ya. I won't be holdin' my breath a-waitin', though, if you don't mind."

"Charming fellow," Tarl whispered to Shal. "Just the sort you want guarding the city."

"My hearin's pretty good, cleric," said the guard, wagging a finger at Tarl. "If you're wantin' inside later, you'll show me some respect."

"No offense intended, Captain."

"None taken, cleric. Say an extra prayer to your god and be on your way. Daylight's a-wastin'. One word o' advice, though, before you go. If you don't go lookin' for trouble in the old city, you're less apt to find it."

Immediately beyond the gates stood some of the worst slums in the Realms—lean-tos, propped haphazardly against the new city's tall stone walls, shacks waiting for the wind to disperse their pieces like dandelion seeds, long-abandoned buildings in an advanced state of decrepitude. The inhabitants were physical misfits and half-breeds, the only creatures despised enough by both humans and monsters to serve as go-betweens for the civilized and uncivilized parts of the city.

Even the horses lifted their heads high in a hopeless attempt to avoid the stench, high-stepping to keep their feet clear of the refuse that littered the alleyways. Cerulean barraged Shal with comments about the smells picked up by his superior olfactory senses. Shal hushed him by reminding him that horsemeat was undoubtedly a delicacy in these parts.

Unscathed except for the loss of a few copper pieces to insistent beggars, they soon passed into the square that surrounded Kuto's Well. There was no sign of movement as they entered the ramshackle gateway, and they proceeded quietly past the buildings that lined the large square.

Shal mentally ran through the spells she had memorized that morning. She could feel the hairs on her neck bristle with the sense that they were being watched, and she could tell from Tarl's tightening grip on her waist that he felt it, too. Ren drew out one of his short swords, and Tarl pulled his hammer from his belt. Behind them rose a loud squeal, and Cerulean instinctively spun around to face the sound. From the other direction came the unmistakable snorts and squeals of orcs. Cerulean spun again, positioning himself and his riders halfway between the two sounds, then backed toward the center of the square. Ren jerked the mare's reins and followed.

Six orcs, all at least six feet tall where their mangy, manlike shoulders met their piglike heads, emerged from two shabby buildings, wielding clubs and axes and closing in on the three riders.

"Get 'em!" Ren hissed, shifting his weight in the saddle and extending his sword.

"No! Talk to them!" said Tarl firmly. "They must know they're no match for the three of us. We'll be able to find out more by talking."

The orcs pressed forward, shouting in their own crude language of grunts and snorts.

Ren glanced at Tarl as though his head were on backward, but when the orcs came closer, he started to speak first in broken orcish and then in thieves' cant, which they appeared to understand. "Stop right there," Ren threatened, "or we'll bash your heads in!"

The creatures stopped but continued to snort and snuffle and brandish their weapons.

"We're passing through this way. We don't want trouble," Ren continued.

"We kill! No trouble!" grunted the orc closest to Ren.

Ren pointed his short sword at the big orc and said, "I kill you, even less trouble." Ren bared his teeth and clicked his tongue, readying the mare for a charge.

"We no kill! We no kill!" the orc snorted in panic. "Others kill. You worth much gold."

Ren rushed the orc and grabbed it by the neck from behind. Then he pulled his blade high and tight under its neck. "Come again?"

"You same party open up Sokol Keep. Lord of the Ruins want you dead. Offer much gold for your heads. We not take. Others take!"

Ren glanced at Shal and Tarl, who were staring uncomprehendingly at the strange exchange. Ren repeated an abridged version of the conversation to them, then pushed the orc away with the flat of his blade. "Leave us alone and we don't kill you. Touch us or send an alarm, and you die. All of you!" Ren bluffed a charge toward one group, and Shal and Tarl took the cue and charged a short distance toward the other. The orcs fled like kicked dogs into the surrounding buildings.

"They'll alert every orc in the old city the minute we leave," said Ren. "And with a price on our heads, you can bet they'll find enough friends to come back and try again. The only reason they didn't fight now is that they were scared to death. You can imagine how it must've sounded to them when they heard we had handled fifty or so orcs, goblins, and kobolds at Sokol Keep. Even a reward wasn't tempting enough for just six of them to risk a fight."

"I'm not waiting around to be fodder for a bunch of orcs," Shal said. "Let's get to the Cadorna place and find what we came for." She spurred Cerulean ahead across the widest portion of the square, past the well site, and across to the opposite gateway.

Ren reined his mare up beside her and cautioned Shal as they reached the gateway. "We'll find that half-gnoll, if there is such a creature, and we'll find Cadorna's treasure, if it exists. In the meantime, we need to move quietly and keep our ears and eyes open."

"He's right, Shal," said Tarl. "Like it or not, the three of us are wanted by the Lord of the Ruins for what we did at Sokol Keep. We've got to be ready for anything from these creatures. There's no sense in announcing we're coming."

Shal nodded and made sure Cerulean, too, understood the need for stealth. They passed silently into a portion of the old city that had once served as quarters for scholars. Every city of any size had such a place, but the extent of this one made Shal and the others realize how great a city Phlan must once have been. Small tutorial houses lined one entire wall of the immense square. Students trying to keep up with their studies must have spent countless hours in this place, grilling with other aspiring scholars in an attempt to pass the tests that allowed them to enter their chosen professions. Large schools, colleges, and trade houses filled one whole side of the square. At the center stood a huge building, lined with shuttered windows, only its roof damaged from dragon fire. The design of the building reminded Shal of other libraries she had seen, and there was little doubt that the building was in fact a library, but it was much bigger than the ones in either Arabel or even Suzail, the capital city of Cormyr.

Shal halted for a moment, tempted to explore the tremendous archives that remained within the great building. She knew that Tarl shared her fascination with books and scrolls. Who could tell what secrets might lie within those dusty tomes?

When she mentioned it, Ren stared at her in exasperation. "You're the ones who have business in the textile house," he said in a hushed, taut voice. "I haven't had occasion to steal many books in my time, but I'd be willing to bet there's some creature lurking among the shelves who'd make mincemeat of you in a second."

Shal nodded reluctantly, and they continued on, their

horses' hooves barely a whisper on the dry, dusty earth of the streets. When they got closer to the wall that, according to the map, separated the scholars' square from the ruins of the Cadorna textile complex, Ren reined the mare in behind some sort of school building and signaled for Shal to follow. Ren dismounted and tethered the mare. Shal and Tarl followed suit. Then Shal ordered Cerulean into the Cloth of Many Pockets.

The wall around the textile house showed signs of gnoll habitation. It was fortified with a tall, makeshift log stockade, with jerry-built towers protruding above the logs here and there. Spikes were pounded into the top of the logs that made up the wooden gate, and an assortment of heads in various stages of decay were skewered onto the spikes. Ren pointed toward the guards manning the towers and then whispered to Shal and Tarl. "Gnolls guard everything, but they're terrible at it. When they aren't sleeping, they aren't paying attention, either. Remember, if we should have to fight them, they're incredibly stupid. They'll line up like toy soldiers before they attack. Just be careful not to get in the way of one of their clubs. They pack a mean swing." He pointed at the ghoulish display of heads. "It's surprising any of those heads are still in one piece."

"What about the half-gnoll leader?" Shal asked.

"If there is such a monster, he might have enough brains and influence to organize their attacks." Ren looked at Tarl. "I don't go for yacking with orcs to get out of a fight, but fighting with gnolls can normally be avoided just by working quietly."

Ren led them to a point between two guard stations. Then he tossed up his hook and rope, and climbed up for a look. The setup looked perfect. A rooftop sloped down from just below the wall, nearly to the ground. He motioned for Shal and Tarl to follow, then slipped silently over the top. Shal hoisted herself up with an ease that belied her size and for just a moment was thankful for the dignity of not being helpless.

Tarl followed, but halfway up the rope, he stopped and plastered himself tight against the wall. The gnolls in the tower to their right were stirring, and one was looking his way. He couldn't know that the uneven rooftop where Ren and Shal were concealed housed the mess where the next exchange of guards was finishing up their meal and getting ready for duty. Nor did Tarl know that, even if the gnolls had seen him pressed flat against the stockade, they would have been much more interested in lunch. Tarl clung to the rope, unmoving, till his arms ached. When finally the two tower guards lumbered down the ladder, not even waiting for their replacements, Tarl could barely haul himself up.

"What took you so long?" Ren hissed. Tarl just shook his head. "See that double chimney?" Ren whispered, pointing. He flared his nostrils and sniffed, a look of revulsion spreading over his face. "We're on top of their mess hall. There's bound to be gnolls inside, so move slowly and quietly. Taking his own advice, he slipped gently down from the roof to a small catwalk between two buildings. Like everything he was able to see from the rooftop, the catwalk was littered with rubbish. Ren helped Shal and Tarl ease their way down, and then he made his way carefully through the piles of refuse.

"If that map was accurate, one of those buildings over there should contain the bedroom we're looking for." Ren pointed across the littered courtyard, where three sentries were dozing with their backs against a timber frame complete with shackles and nails for holding and tormenting prisoners, of which there were none at the moment. "Gnoll justice," Ren whispered with a sneer.

And then he saw the garden. The map had it marked "cook's garden," but instead of herbs and vegetables, there was only corruption and despoilment. Twisted, cracked plants, identifiable as cabbage only because of the color and vaguely overlapping leaves, sapped the soil in one corner of the garden. A tangle of brown, contorted vines, abominable mockeries of thyme and spearmint and other herbs, blighted another. Raised and trained as a ranger, Ren admired natural beauty above all else. The sight of the gnolls' crude and intentionally vile parody of a garden caused something to snap inside of Ren. It was as though the defiled garden somehow signified the corruption that had led to Tempest's death. What was wrong with the assassin was the same thing that was wrong with this garden, was wrong with the gnolls that planted and neglected it. Ren was filled with rage of an intensity he hadn't known since Tempest's death.

"Look at that!" he said, pointing, fury contorting his face, and then louder, "It's sick! It's sick, like everything else in this parody of a world!"

Tarl could appreciate that the garden looked strange, ugly even, and Shal recognized that all of the plants were distorted, but when Ren stalked off toward the nearest open door, they had to assume that he had seen something they didn't. In his rage, he moved with a speed they couldn't match.

When they slipped through the doorway behind him, Ren had already crossed the room to the other side of an elaborate set of yellow curtains. He was in the process of strangling a robed gnoll in the crook of his big right arm. With his left hand, he clasped the creature's hyena jaws so tightly that it couldn't even scream. At the same time, he mashed the monster's body downward so it couldn't flail or struggle. They watched in awe as the body quivered one last time, and Ren silently lowered it to the floor.

Before they had time to react, Ren had passed between two incense stands and through a second yellow curtain and was slitting the throat of another one of the gangling hyena-men. As with the first, he muzzled it, then forced it to the floor so it made less sound in death than it had in life. Shal and Tarl stood dumbstruck. Having no idea what had caused such rage to possess their companion, they followed mutely and watched as he passed through yet another yellow curtain and dispatched a third robed gnoll in a similar fashion.

It wasn't until Ren had slipped through the fourth curtain that he finally stopped short, and so did Tarl and Shal when they entered the cavernous golden room. Four more robed gnollish priests were kneeling before the dais of a shrine. A fifth, more elaborately attired, stood behind the shrine grunting an incantation over and over, which Ren realized was the same he had heard at Sokol Keep: "Power to the pool! Power to the pool!"

When the fifth figure, who was apparently the head priest, first saw the three, he stood stock-still for a moment, uncomprehending. Then he let out a squeal of warning to the others. The four scrambled to their feet and turned with surprising alacrity for creatures of their awkward proportions. Each produced a short, contorted staff, almost like a cudgel. Their faces were strangely pinched and yellow, almost jaundiced-looking. But their yellow eyes gleamed with fervor, and they charged forward with the conviction of religious fanatics, snorting monosyllabic gnollish equivalents of words like "infidel" and "heretic."

The burst of crazed anger that had propelled Ren past the first three gnolls was spent as quickly as it had come, but as the snarling, slavering gnolls pressed closer, it returned. Ren rushed the nearest attacker, both short swords drawn. Confronted with a form of worship more corrupt than any he had imagined possible, Tarl responded with a pent-up rage of his own, meeting the swinging club of one gnoll with his shield and slamming another with the broad side of the hammer he had recovered from Sokol Keep.

Shal shared neither man's sense of purpose. She called for her staff out of fear and used it only when the fourth gnoll crashed through the melee and toward her. Hellbent on claiming the life of an infidel, the gangling creature charged forward, oblivious to Shal's extended staff. Even after it impaled itself, it continued to press forward, jaws snapping, club flailing, a yellow glaze burning in its eyes. It wasn't until the gnoll had pushed forward almost the length of the staff, its entrails pushing out behind it, that it finally jerked in the spasms of death. Shal had never once even moved. Slowly the gnoll's dead weight pulled the staff to the ground, and the monster started to slide back down the length of the staff. Shal dropped to her knees and covered her mouth to keep from gagging. Only when she heard Ren's voice saying something in the guttural language of the humanoids did she collect the wherewithal to pull her staff from the body of the dead gnoll.

The three other priests lay dead not far away. Tarl was holding the high priest in a hammerlock while Ren asked it questions. Shal stepped past the bodies and walked numbly toward the shrine. An upside-down **T** shape, the altar stood a little taller than waist-high. Its mahogany surface was polished to a sheen that struck Shal as highly unusual among the disgustingly dirty gnolls. At the crux of the **T** was a rounded gray mound. On either side of the altar stood embossed silver chalices, the work of dwarves, if Shal was any judge, but they were dark with rust and somehow corrupt in appearance. At first Shal couldn't grasp what made such carefully and ornately ornamented pieces seem repugnant, but as she came closer to one of them, she realized what was wrong. Its surface was covered with the contorted faces of the benevolent gods. The faces were those of the same gods

carved in relief on Shal's Staff of Power, but like everything else in the gnoll village, they represented a grotesque permutation of what was natural and beautiful.
In a subtly gruesome way, the chalice made a mockery of
the staff Shal carried and of everything that was good in
the Realms.

She started to reach forward to dash the hideous piece
and its companion to the floor, but then she stopped
short. The dreadful stink of rancid meat bit into her nostrils before she could lay a hand on the chalice. Mixed
with it was the sickening sweet smell of blood, and she
saw now, with shock, that the gray lump she had seen
earlier was actually the days-old head of a human being,
its skin livid and its eyes bulging as if from strangulation.
The body stretched out behind it, excoriated as if from
repeated blows with some heavy, abrasive object.

Shal slapped one hand to her mouth and drew the
other tight against her abdomen to stave off the new
wave of nausea that gripped her. Through clenched
teeth, she stifled what would otherwise have been an
earsplitting scream of horror and revulsion. Unconsciously she tipped her head back, as if that would clear
her nose of the fetid stench. When it didn't help, she
lurched forward wildly, slamming the gore-filled chalice
nearest to her with the back of her hand and coming
back deftly with her forehand to smash the other one.
Blood splattered everywhere as the two chalices rocketed end-over-end into the golden walls on either side of
the great room.

The captured priest shrieked hysterically and struggled in vain to free himself from Tarl's viselike grip. "No
blood, no power! No blood, no power!" Again and again
he repeated the pained cry, failing to stop even when Ren
backhanded him hard against his hyena jaws.

"Animal!" Shal screamed, her rage driving her voice to
a level loud enough to be heard over the shrieking gnoll.

"Animal!" she shouted once more, moving deliberately around the altar, her large hands outstretched toward the creature's throat.

"No! Stop!" Tarl pushed the gnoll to the floor with one hand and held out the other to stop Shal. "He's an abomination, and deserves to die, but we must not kill him."

Shal screamed through her teeth again, then dropped to her knees and pointed up at the altar. When Tarl saw what he had not seen before, he began to pummel the groveling gnoll with his fists. Despite his outrage, he shouted: "We must not kill him! Not yet!"

"That's right, Tarl . . . not yet," Ren said, getting a hold on the gnoll and pushing Tarl gently away. "Both of you, take a few minutes to compose yourselves. I'll take care of him."

Tarl dropped down beside Shal and slipped an arm around her. Together they knelt, sobbing tearlessly as they stared at the appalling wreckage of a human being that lay on the altar before them. Tarl uttered a prayer to Tyr to put the unknown soul to rest.

Just then a piercing voice penetrated Shal's consciousness. *A cloth would cover the poor soul's eyes, Mistress.*

Yes, it would. Thank you, Shal thought silently. She called forth a cloth from her Cloth of Many Pockets, then covered the head and body beneath its rich violet folds. Tarl murmured one last prayer and stood beside her.

"Look there," said Shal, pointing. Beyond the body, at the foot of the **T**-shaped altar, was a painstakingly detailed diorama of a scene so lifelike that Shal thought if she blinked she might become part of it. A sculpted wall of golden stone rose up like a backdrop for the scene, making it clear that the diorama's setting was a cave, a mammoth cave with an airy, vaulted ceiling. A perfectly crescent-shaped pool, with waters that reflected off polished surfaces, was the focal point of the miniature scene. Centered along the inside curve of the crescent was an elegantly simple, raised hexagon, with tiny blue gems glittering from four of its six points. The hexagon looked pitiful and incomplete, like a once-magnificent broach with only empty sockets where gemstones should be. Though no more than two fingers wide, the hexagon, with its two missing gems, detracted from the perfection of the entire scene. Perhaps it was Shal's imagination, but the glistening golden waters of the crescent even seemed at their darkest near the six-sided mounting.

Centered along the outside curve of the crescent was a tiny replica of the **T**-shaped altar. On it was a minute fountain that was spewing blood-red fluid into the pool. Where the dark fluid hit the golden waters, the pool should have been ocher or orange, but instead it radiated a staggeringly brilliant yellow gold. Like staring into the sun, it caused pain merely to look upon it.

"The focus of the shrine," said Tarl, explaining the diorama. "It's a replica of a sacred place—or at least a place sacred to the gnolls."

" 'The Pool of Radiance,' this guy calls it," said Ren, moving closer to the altar, the yellow-faced gnoll still in the crook of his elbow. "He says they have to keep up a steady supply of sacrifices to keep the pool yellow and the Lord of the Ruins happy."

"Sacrifices? This is worse than a sacrifice," said Shal, pointing at the body that lay under the purple cloth.

"I'm afraid that's probably the gnoll version of a pretty gruesome practice," said Ren. "I don't have any love for orcs or kobolds, but if they have similar altars, you'll find equally dead bodies but less gruesome."

Tarl's face paled visibly, and his hands clutched the edge of the wooden altar. His usually clear, deep voice tremored noticeably as he spoke. "You don't mean to suggest there are more altars like this? More of these sites of abomination?"

"I'm sorry," said Ren. "But this priest says it was all done for the Lord of the Ruins. As I understand it, all the creatures in the uncivilized parts of the city worship him."

"Worship?" Tarl spat and shook his hands as if to shake off some clinging coat of slime. "Worship a creature that is not of the gods? A creature that demands blood sacrifices? What powers does this abominable beast possess that it can demand such horrors?"

8

Half-Gnoll

"You're the priest. You tell us." Ren waved his free hand toward the altar, clamped the gnoll's neck a little tighter, and began to question the creature again. The gnoll was obviously responding to Ren's questions, but Shal and Tarl could only look on, uncomprehending.

"He says there's temples like this everywhere the Lord of the Ruins' power reigns. He says the pool makes him feel strong."

Ren paused as the gnoll grunted and continued with its explanation.

"What was that? Why you—!" Ren slammed the top of the gnoll's head with his free hand.

"What?" Tarl and Shal reacted in unison.

"The filthy piece of dog meat said we'd all become sacrifices to the pool."

"I can't stomach any more of this," Tarl said firmly. "As I serve Tyr, let this be the first of many such temples to be destroyed by my hand." Without waiting for the others to join him, Tarl raised his hammer up next to the diorama. The heavy end slammed powerfully into the crescent-shaped pool, sending a shower of gold droplets in all directions.

"Acid!" screamed Tarl, and he shook his hammer-hand where the flesh was searing from the contact with the drops.

Ren and Shal had leaped back instinctively as Tarl's hammer came down. Mere inches from where they stood, shimmering acid was burning through every piece of wood and cloth it hit. Where the acid landed on stone, it was sizzling and spattering like water in hot grease.

Shal quickly summoned forth a skin of water from the Cloth of Many Pockets and poured it generously over Tarl's right hand, which was already raw in two places, and then over his hair, which was smoking where a drop had landed.

Enraged, fury and agony blending in his screams, Tarl lashed out again and again at the blasphemous altar, hammering with all his might until the lower end splintered and collapsed. Still he wasn't satisfied. He dropped to his knees and pounded at the miniature fountain, the hexagon, and the rest of the diorama till only splinters and fragments remained.

By then, the gnoll was screaming steadily in reaction to the destruction of the altar. Ren chopped down hard on its head again. This time, its body slumped and its hyena head lolled loosely from side to side. Unwittingly, Ren had snapped the creature's neck. Remorseless, he pushed the dead gnoll to the ground beside him and moved to calm Tarl.

The cleric had not stopped hammering, even after the diorama was pulverized. Nor did he stop now in response to the coaxing of his friends. It was not until the cloth-covered corpse balancing on the crux of the altar slid down onto his arms that he finally dropped his head and stopped. Pulling his arms loose from underneath the body, Tarl turned and faced Ren and Shal. "I—I'm sorry. I couldn't help myself."

As one, they spoke to comfort him.

"I'm sorry," he repeated. "I've heard of altars to Bhaal and other gods whose worship I cannot fathom, but never have I seen anything so repugnant as this. I—" Tarl paused, distracted. "The priest—what happened?"

The gnoll's body was lying on the ground behind Ren and Shal. Its jaundiced face looked even more pinched and grotesque in death than it had in life, and the fervent yellow of its eyes had been replaced by a dull umber glaze. "He's dead," Ren said matter-of-factly. "I didn't mean to kill him, but I can't say I'll stay awake nights over it."

"No," said Tarl. "He would've killed us without a second thought."

"He probably would have skinned us alive with one of those meat tenderizers," added Shal, pointing to the row of torture implements that filled a wooden cabinet against the far wall of the big room.

"By Bane and Bhaal and all that's perverse . . ." Ren's curse came out almost in a whisper as he eyed the morbid array of tools. Despite his lifelong habit of quickly examining everything within eyeshot upon entry to a room, he had not seen what filled the cabinet. "Gnoll religion . . . You're right, Tarl. It goes against nature. It's an abomination."

"Are you okay?" Shal asked suddenly, reaching for Tarl's acid-marred hand. She didn't want to think about gnoll religion or gnoll justice anymore. She'd seen enough of both, and she was worried about her friend. She poured more water over the burned spots. "What about your head? Does it hurt?"

Though Tarl had not been conscious of it until Shal brought it up, the spot on his head continued to sting, as did the two raw wounds on his hand. "I have a salve that should help." Tarl met Shal's gaze and spoke earnestly. "I'll be all right. I'm sure I'd be worse off if you hadn't reacted so quickly."

Shal released Tarl's hand and reached up and ran her fingers through his thick, silvery hair till she found the spot where the acid had splashed. He flinched as she located the jagged, finger-length depression where the hair and flesh were burned off. She poured a little more water on that spot and then on his burned hand. She completely missed the smile Tarl flashed at Ren as she asked him to give her the salve so she could apply it for him.

"Not here," snapped Ren. "If your salve smells anything like that infernal poultice you put on me last night, the gnolls will pick up the scent in a minute."

"He's right," said Tarl, sobered by Ren's words. "In fact, we're lucky they haven't heard us. The walls here must be pretty thick—better insulated than the rest of this rat trap of a fort."

"Don't underestimate the gnolls." Ren pointed back to the curtained hallway from which they'd come. "They probably did hear us. The lazy, bloodthirsty bastards are probably just waiting for us to come out. Fact is, I was hoping we'd find another way out of here. Let's look behind those curtains."

Ren's instincts were good. There was a door behind the curtains, and it led to a covered crawlspace that apparently ran behind the temple, between it and the stockade. They remembered no such corridor from the map, but the temple hadn't been on the map, either. They were pleased to find that the passageway skirted the full length of the temple. When they finally reached its end, they found themselves well beyond the entrance they had used when Ren first stormed inside. No party of gnolls lay in wait at either doorway, but the three didn't feel any worse for having taken the precaution.

Ren whispered, "The gnolls are gonna be up and around just as soon as the midday heat has passed. We've got to find what we came for and get out of here before they discover the mess we left back there." He pointed to their left and whispered again. "The bedroom should be that way. Stay close to the walls like we did when we came in." The faintest hint of embarrassment showed in his expression when he added, "And don't go looking for trouble!"

Ren moved like a shadow among the cartons and rubble that cluttered the way along the makeshift square. Shal followed, aware as always that she was no match for Ren in terms of stealth. She watched and admired his careful movements, realizing she admired even more his presence of mind and worldliness, especially his knowledge of things like gnolls, which she had never before encountered.

Tarl followed close behind Shal, conscious that he was even more distracted than usual by her catlike elegance. He could almost picture her as a shape-shifter, a powerful panther one moment, muscles rippling; the next, a powerful, sensual woman he felt so drawn to. . . .

He paused just long enough to force his thoughts back to their mission. A single glance at the courtyard gate and the ghoulish display of heads posted there brought him quickly to the present. The guards that had been slumbering earlier were beginning to stir.

As they approached one building, they could hear the grunts and growls of several young gnolls roughhousing inside. The three blurred past the open doorway and continued on their way.

Ren whispered back to them that the next building appeared to be their destination. When they reached it, he peeked through a small window. If Ren were alone, he would have felt challenged, invigorated by what he saw. With others to worry about, he felt annoyance, disgust, and a twinge of fear.

Though defiled with refuse like everything else in the gnoll encampment, the chambers were still used as private sleeping quarters—and a huge gnoll, no doubt the chieftain, was sleeping inside, with a sleeping female gnoll naked beside him, her gangly body all the more vulgar for its revealing posture. Lamps left burning in the room exposed elaborate, though tasteless, decorations. Eye-jarring combinations of gold-leaf-framed paintings and chartreuse and magenta embroideries covered the walls. All around the foot of the huge, overstuffed bed were slumbering female gnolls, their long, knobby, fur-covered legs protruding awkwardly from garish print wraps. Ren could see no way to get to the back of the chamber except to go right through the door and past all those sleeping gnolls. He gestured at the window and gave Shal and Tarl a moment to take in the situation.

Ren moved silently up to the door and tried it carefully. It was locked. Before Shal could even think of a spell to help, Ren had it open with his picks. He slipped inside with the ease and stealth of a mink. Shal and Tarl followed, their movements as close to Ren's as they could make them, but Ren was already past the sleeping females and across the room when Shal was just beginning to tiptoe her way through and Tarl was still easing the door shut to avoid attracting attention.

The creatures snorted and grunted in their slumber. Occasionally one would stir, letting an arm slip to the floor or rolling over to a more comfortable position. One started pawing and writhing, apparently in the throes of a dream, and clipped Shal with a clawed foot as she tried to edge by. She sucked in a breath of air and then kept her teeth clamped shut to keep from crying out from the stinging pain. Behind her, Tarl dodged to one side to avoid the restless sleeper, and the two finished crossing the room without incident.

At the back of the sleeping quarters, behind a gaudily embroidered curtain, stood a door that, according to the map, should lead to the inner bedroom, where they would find the hidden treasure vault. The three filed in behind the curtain. Ren touched the door handle—and immediately jerked his hand back. Pain ripped through his body, and it took all of his years of training as a ranger and a thief to stifle the scream that threatened to burst through his tightly clenched teeth. When finally the jets of pain had eased their pulsing, he turned to Shal and mouthed the words "Wizard-locked."

Shal felt as if she had endured the tremendous jolt of pain Ren had just suffered right along with him. She marveled once again at the big man's endurance. Gently she touched his shoulder as she slipped cautiously, quietly in front of him. She was gratified to see that her touch had a quieting effect on Ren. Voicelessly she called for Cerulean, mentally shouting the thought *Silence is critical!* to the horse to avoid his clumping out of the cloth like a bumbling clown.

To her great relief, the horse emerged from the velvet square with no more than a whisper of sound. He nuzzled his mistress's shoulder and reminded her to cast a spell of Protection. Quickly she whispered the incantation and nodded. Cerulean touched the door with his nose. As at Denlor's tower, he immediately began to glow, but this time he glowed a brilliant amethyst, and there was no crackling sound to be heard. When the magical energy abated, the door swung open.

For one painful moment, all four held their breath, waiting for the door to crash against the inside wall. It did not. Shal held up the cloth, and Cerulean poured in without so much as a *Do I have to?* Shal thanked him mentally and entered the room.

When Tarl and Ren were both inside as well, Shal sealed the door with a little magic of her own. They found themselves in complete blackness, and Shal took out her light wand so they could see. "Cadorna said noth—" Shal stopped as she saw the look of horror on Ren and Tarl's faces. She realized immediately what was wrong and explained her boldness in speech. "Nobody's going to hear us now. This is a wizard's spell-casting chamber. It's soundproof. They all are."

Ren swallowed to avoid the temptation to whisper in contrast to Shal's brazenness. "What—what were you going to say?" he asked nervously.

She finished the thought. "Cadorna didn't say anything about a wizard, either in his family or among the gnolls."

"I think he would've said something if he knew," Ren reasoned out loud. "If I'd taken a tighter grip on that door, I'd be dead from the charge. If he could help it, I don't think Cadorna would've risked having us die before we could get the treasure."

"Cadorna knew from the map only that there was a treasure," said Shal, agreeing. "He probably didn't know the thing was wizard-locked." Shal gasped as she turned and faced the opposite wall for the first time. Painted on the wall were two coiled snake emblems identical to the one she had seen on the armband of Ranthor's murderer. Her eyes widened, and she started breathing with a rapidity that frightened both Ren and Tarl.

"What is it, Shal? What's wrong?" asked Tarl hurriedly.

Ren reached out and touched Shal on the shoulder, much as she had touched his a moment ago.

Shal pointed, but for a moment she couldn't say anything, and when she did speak, it was not in her recently acquired rich, husky voice, but in a breathless, almost childlike stammer. "The symbol—the s-snake . . . It's like the one . . . Ranthor's k-killer wore. It stabbed him again and again . . . Cadorna was right. The gnoll . . . the half-gnoll outside . . . He m-must be Ranthor's killer! He must be a magic-user. And that must be his sign!"

Ren rested his hands on both of Shal's shoulders and spoke calmly, firmly. "Shal, the gnoll leader could be Ranthor's killer, but that sign—the coiled snake—is common in these parts. I've seen it all over the place. And I doubt that any gnoll or even half-gnoll has ever been inside this room. Look around. There's not a scrap of trash anywhere, and other than the coiling snakes—which are admittedly pretty ugly—this place doesn't look too bad. Compared to the stuff outside—the bright green curtains and all—this just doesn't look like a place where gnolls have been."

Shal glanced from side to side, then turned her head and began to take slow, deep breaths. Ren was right. The room showed no sign of gnoll occupation. In fact, it was practically dust-free, an indication that the wizard lock had probably not been opened any time recently. Shal knew from experience that a wizard's chambers normally get dusty when they're in regular use, not when they're vacant. She didn't know immediately what to make of the signs before her. But she did know that she no longer cared if the killer was human, humanoid, or monster, a half-gnoll or the ruler of the land. She was going to find him regardless and avenge her master's death. Shal reached up, touched Ren's hands with her own, and lowered them from her shoulders. "Let's get what we came for," she said, composed once again.

The vault proved to be well hidden. It wasn't until Shal cast a Detect Magic spell that a sizable emerald-colored square began to glow on the wall. A simple cantrip opened the door, which apparently was not wizard-locked because it was so carefully hidden that it didn't seem necessary. When they entered the vault, it took only a glance to realize that the Cadorna family treasure was still intact. Several bricks of gold bullion shone brilliantly, even in the dull, unnatural light from the wand. Behind them were a forged gold brooch inlaid with coral and ivory, several gold and silver chains, and a superbly preserved, shatter-glaze vase, obviously an ancient piece from the Eastern Realms. There was also a chain-mail vest, a splendid example of the finest dwarven workmanship. Ren's eyes gleamed when he saw it, but Tarl cast Ren a withering look that spoiled his taste for the garment. On further examination, the vest proved to be of a size for a dwarf, anyhow, and would be of no use to Ren.

In one corner of the vault were two gold armbands and a locket, both embossed with the coiled snake design they had seen on the wall outside the vault. Shal looked questioningly at Ren as he picked up the three pieces. "Cadorna?"

"I'll only say what I did before. This is a common symbol in these parts. You'd probably do well to look it up in that library we passed by—some other day, of course."

Shal said no more. She slipped the vase and the armor into the Cloth of Many Pockets. The bullion and jewelry, Ren and Tarl divided up and placed in their packs.

The three left the wizard's chamber as quietly as they had entered. Outside, they were greeted by the reassuring snores of the gnoll leader and his mates. Just as they were about to step from behind the curtain, however, a deafening gong sounded in the courtyard, and squeals and screams resounded from one end of the compound to the other.

They could see nothing from where they stood, plastered tight against the wall behind the curtain, but they could hear the chaos in the room beyond when the gnoll leader leaped from his bed, kicking females out of his way as he scrambled to reach the courtyard. Then they heard scrambling noises as the dozen or so gnoll mates pushed and shoved their way out the door after him.

"Can you call that horse of yours out?" asked Ren.

Shal nodded.

"Good. Just as soon as we clear the door, you two mount up and get out of here while the camp is still in an uproar. I'll act as a decoy till you can get across the courtyard. You can count on the gnolls to fight in lines like fools. I'll manage somehow to dodge my way past them, but be ready to pick me up!"

Shal and Tarl followed Ren's instructions without hesi-

JAMES M. WARD AND JANE COOPER HONG

tation. In moments, they were mounted on Cerulean's broad back, plowing through the center of the courtyard in the midst of the chaos. Shal held the Staff of Power out at just the right height to clip the tall gnolls in the neck as they approached, sending them to the ground like so many ninepins. Others who managed to duck under the staff reached up, grabbing, trying to stop the big horse, but Cerulean was relentless. Tarl, in the meantime, was swinging his hammer with passion.

At that moment, the air was pierced by a loud war whoop, and Ren emerged into the courtyard, brandishing his twin daggers. Immediately several disorganized groups of gnolls began to advance toward him. Ren knew that the key to fighting gnolls was to avoid getting hit. The creatures were big and gangly and awkward in their movements, but when they connected, the person at the receiving end of a blow seldom got up. In a blur of motion, Ren began to dodge, duck, and knife his way through the lines. One gnoll got hold of his shoulder and shoved him down roughly, so that his elbow jammed hard into the rocky ground. It took all of Ren's presence of mind and willpower to ignore the pain and jump quickly back to his feet, but before he could get free, a gnoll's spiked cudgel slammed into his left hand, goring through flesh and bone and pulverizing the flat of his hand with its impact.

The pain was like a massive electrical charge that jolted through Ren's body. He felt as if his insides were going to burst, just as air would explode from a burst balloon. He could no longer react rationally, but fought on in a frantic, instinctive, uninhibited frenzy. Pain and fear drove him forward with a fury that was frightening. With his good hand, he drew out a short sword and wielded it with such a vengeance that he emasculated one gnoll with a swing, then gashed partway through the belly of another with his next. Even the bloodthirsty gnolls grew wary, and Ren sensed that he had to keep moving while he retained the advantage. As he started to dart across the courtyard, he came face to face with the huge gnoll chieftain.

Obviously Cadorna hadn't lied about the ancestry of the gnoll leader. Ren had never seen such a creature. The chieftain had the ungainly height of a gnoll, coupled with the bulk of a brawny human. Ren might well have mistaken him for a giant, were it not for his face. A man's nose protruded like a wart from a hyena snout, and pink human lips framed slavering canine teeth. But it was the eyes that were most terrible of all. They were unnaturally large, wide-rimmed and wide-set like a gnoll's, but they bore the searing intelligence of a human being—a sick, crazed human being. The creature bore a monstrous double-edged sword and a long, sharp dagger.

"Human slug! Don't think for one minute you can run from me!"

The creature's speech was thick and difficult to understand. Obviously its distorted mouth could barely produce the sounds of the human language. Ren stopped immediately, brandished his own short sword, and issued a challenge of his own.

"Half-breed vermin! Don't you think for one minute you can stop me!"

"So it's a fight you want, is it, worm?"

"Aye," said Ren. "A fight it is. One on one. To the death."

A ring of gnolls had started to close in around Ren, but the chieftain waved them back. From every building, gnolls swarmed to the center of the courtyard, and it was only the threatening glances of their leader that kept them from pressing in and crushing the duelers.

In moments, not a single gnoll remained to block Shal and Tarl's path, but instead of fleeing, they remained motionless, watching horror-struck as the strange duel unfolded. They watched as the huge gnoll-man landed a devastating blow square on Ren's head with the flat of its sword.

"Gods and demigods! I've seen enough!" Shal shouted in a voice that could be heard even over the tumult. With a piercing mental command, she spurred Cerulean into the midst of the mob. Without a moment's hesitation, she leveled her staff at the half-gnoll chieftain, intoned three syllables, and watched as a bolt of lightning blasted straight through the creature, sending it flying across the compound. When the horrified gnolls turned in unison toward her and Tarl and started to charge, she leveled the staff again and blasted away unmercifully. Fireballs and lightning ripped through the hordes of gangling hyena-faced creatures, and their squeals and shrieks of pain blotted out all other sound. Only the few who were fortunate enough to be near Ren were spared.

As soon as Ren recovered from the blow to his head and the shock of seeing his opponent jolted across the courtyard, he fled toward the compound gate, afraid of being consumed in the flames that were exploding everywhere. Quickly he mounted the terrified mare that stood waiting and spurred her away from the burning encampment at a gallop.

When she was sure Ren was safe, Shal spurred Cerulean around and charged out the gate after him. Tarl clasped her waist tightly, marveling at the uncharacteristic fury of his companion. In minutes, the huge magical steed had caught up with Ren.

When they reached his side, Shal reined to a stop. Behind them, there was no sign of any pursuit.

"What in the Abyss did you do that for?" Ren's face was crimson with rage.

Neither Shal nor Tarl had ever seen Ren so angry. Shal responded with an anger of her own. "That ugly thing was clobbering you back there! You would've been killed if I hadn't done something!"

"But it was a duel of honor!"

"Honor? What good is your honor if you're dead? Don't you understand?" she cried. "He would've killed you! I'd seen enough for one day. I suppose it was also honor when you went off on that rampage over the damn garden and killed those four innocent gnolls without batting an eye!"

"Innocent? You call them *innocent?* Don't you remember you nearly puked when you saw that corpse in the temple?"

"Okay, so they weren't innocent. But they hadn't done squat to us. And our goal was only to get the treasure and get out safely, not to see how many gnolls we could kill!"

Ren's face reddened as he blurted, "And who was it who wiped that place free of gnolls, anyhow? It sure as Tymora wasn't me!"

"Okay, so I got carried away. But I've never been so disgusted by anything in my whole life. All day it was building up in me—what with the trash, the stench, that poor soul in the temple, the blood in those chalices, the snake symbols, and that filthy creature fighting you in the courtyard. By the—"

The adrenaline that had carried Ren through the bloody battle in the courtyard suddenly gave out. Pain and loss of blood took over, and the big man dropped limply from his horse in a cold faint.

Shal and Tarl were at Ren's side in seconds. There was an ugly gash in his head, and his hand hung limp and useless. Shal immediately applied pressure to his wrist to slow the bleeding, and Tarl held his hand on Ren's head and prayed. In moments, severed capillaries fused shut and the bleeding stopped. Tissue stretched over crushed bone and melded with other tissue until the wound was no longer life-threatening, but the severity of Ren's wounds was such that Tarl could not hope to heal them completely. It would take a cleric with the acquired skills of Brother Sontag to fully mend such an injury. But Tarl could help. He could make him more comfortable and cure some of the worst of the damage. In a few minutes, Ren regained consciousness.

The argument of a few moments ago was completely forgotten as the three shared their concern for each other's physical well-being. Shal and Tarl insisted that Ren take time to soak his hand before they attempted to move on. It wasn't until the sun was low in the sky and darkness was creeping over Uncivilized Phlan that Ren convinced them that he was ready for the ride back.

All had had enough trouble for one day, and the gate to a city never looked so good as it did that evening. As they waited outside the gate, Tarl was the first to spot the cynical guard they had spoken to on the way out. He started to smile when he saw the guard ride out from behind the open gate accompanied by a young watchman. When they drew near, the guard raised his sword and pronounced, "You're under arrest."

Tarl stopped smiling as the guard jabbed the point of his sword into his ribs and ordered all three of them to come with him.

"What the—" Ren spluttered, his anger quick to surface again.

"Under arrest for what?" Shal blurted out. "By whose orders?"

"For unauthorized travel in the ruins," responded the other guard. "By authority of Fourth Councilman Cadorna."

"Fourth Councilman Cadorna!" It was Tarl's turn to be angry. "Our mission was under his auspices! It was he who sent us out here!"

"We're just followin' orders," said the first guard. "Frankly, if'n I were you, I'd be tickled to make it out of the uncivilized portion of the city alive. Matter of fact, I think we discussed that this mornin', didn't we? You were a might cocky, as I recall it. Seems that the Fourth Councilman suspects you might have borrowed some things that weren't yours."

Ren's face was crimson with anger. "That's ridic—"

The younger guard jabbed him hard with the point of his sword. "Enough! Come with us!"

When they reached the council building, the younger guard once again began barking orders. "Get off your horses. Move over against those tables there. Open your packs, your pouches; empty your pockets, your shoes. Everything on the table. Separate out the treasure that belongs to the Fourth Councilman."

With a word, Shal protected her magical items from tampering. She then discreetly removed the vase from the Cloth of Many Pockets and was waiting for an opportunity to remove the armor unseen when Ren caught her eye. He barely moved his head, but she knew what he meant: "Don't take it out."

At the same time, with the dexterity of a polished street magician, Ren slipped the two ioun stones from the hilts of Right and Left and into the chameleon gauntlet on his right hand. As Shal began unhitching the heavy belt she wore at her waist, Ren sidled up to her and said, "Here, sweetheart. Let me help you with that."

The older guard chortled at the big man's forwardness, and Shal blushed even as she realized that Ren was pressing something into her waistband.

With one hand, she made a point of pressing Ren away, while with the other, she appeared to be holding fast to the belt he had offered to help her remove. "I'll get it myself, thank you!" she said tartly. The paper-thin gauntlet Ren had slipped her remained unseen inside one of her big hands, and as she fumbled with the buckle, she was able to press the gauntlet—and the ioun stones inside it—into the Cloth of Many Pockets for safekeeping.

From the shadows of a doorway, Gensor watched the two companions. He suspected that something, physical or verbal, had passed between them, but he hadn't actually seen anything.

Tarl bridled at Ren, no more aware than the guard of what was really transpiring between the two. With angry deliberateness, not uttering a word, he slapped down his hammer, his shield, his armor, and the treasure of the textile house without so much as a word. But when the young guard insisted he remove his sacred medallion, he said coldly, "You'll have to kill me first."

"Come now, there'll be no need for that." Cadorna strolled into the courtyard. His gray eyes were glued to the gold bullion Ren had just removed from his pack.

"What do you mean by having us arrested for doing your bidding?" Shal turned on Cadorna with a look not unlike the one she'd given the gnolls at the textile house before blasting them to dust.

"No need to be so testy, young woman," Cadorna replied smoothly. "Obviously these fine guards misunderstood my intent. I wanted them only to escort you here safely so that no one would have the opportunity to rob you of your treasure."

" 'No one' meaning us?" Ren asked pointedly.

"Naturally I wanted to see everything you brought back with you."

"Are you reneging on your promise to give a percentage of the treasure to the Tyrian temple?" asked Tarl.

"Why, Brother Tarl! I'm offended that you would suggest such a thing. In fact, I just wanted to be sure your partners were honest in providing all the treasure so the temple would be sure to get its fair share."

"I trust my friends," said Tarl.

"I trust no one," retorted Cadorna, his face growing cold. After examining everything carefully, the councilman assembled the treasure into one pile. A crooked, toothy smile pasted on his face, he handed a single gold brick and the coral and ivory brooch to Tarl. "For the temple. Quite generous, don't you think?"

Tarl clenched his teeth but nodded reluctantly. The portion was nowhere near fifteen percent of the treasure, but he knew he would receive no more and that the temple could do worse than inherit a gold brick and an emerald brooch.

"You're free to go now," Cadorna said finally. "I do thank you all. You will help me out again if I need it, won't you?"

❦ 9 ❦

Assassination Weather

All of Phlan and the entire Moonsea was awash in the tumult of a terrific thunderstorm. Lightning ripped through the sky in every direction, and deafening thunder reverberated for tens of miles. A person versed in weather and the natural pattern of things might have noticed that the lightning was almost perverse in its configuration, bolting upward and outward from one point and shattering the sky in an unnatural purple brilliance, but most people were undoubtedly more than content to huddle in their homes, hoping they were out of reach of what the next day they surely would refer to as "a demon storm."

Not far from the heart of the storm, at the northeastern edge of the ruins of Phlan, stood Valjevo Castle, a structure that even in its present decrepit state dwarfed the ruins that abutted it. Awe-inspiring despite its fallen walls and toppled turrets, the castle must once have been one of the largest in the Realms. No doubt fantastic works of magic had been required to move the gargantuan slabs of marble and granite used in its construction. Those few who had seen the castle since the Dragon Run were amazed that the dragons had been able to raze even portions of its great walls, and in fact, much of the castle and the fortress around it was still intact.

Despite damage to parts of its structure, the castle stood several stories by any measurement and remained among the tallest buildings in the Realms. Its toppled turrets must once have reached one hundred feet or more. Now, almost that far beneath the castle, the great bronze dragon shifted in its resting place in the curve of the Pool of Radiance.

"Shall I have no peace?" The beast's voice boomed and echoed against the golden walls of the cave. "The ground shudders with magic that is not my own, power that is not mine! What say you, Quarrel? Where are my ioun stones?"

A curious figure, lying prostrate before the dragon, lifted its head. Shimmering black hair parted to reveal the face of a half-orc woman. But for her piglike snout, she could have passed for human. Her eyes, mouth, and facial contours were flawless. Were it not for the blight at the center of her face, she might have been called attractive, even pretty. She stood to speak, flipping a charcoal-colored cape over her shoulders to reveal body-contouring chain mail and leathers that accentuated her lean, muscular, human form. Her voice was throaty. It had long ago lost its timbre, sounding now as if she had tossed back too many shots of hard liquor. "They're not in Surd nor indeed in any part of Sembia. My assassin troops and I tortured and killed any who might have knowledge of the whereabouts of an ioun stone."

"And you found nothing? Two weeks gone from these parts, and you brought back nothing?"

"I didn't say that, master. I said I brought back no ioun stones. Blood ran freely for you and orc slaves carried it back to your temples." The black-haired assassin gestured to a shimmering mound in front of the dragon. "Treasure such as few have dreamed of lies at your feet. And, as I said, you can rest assured that there are no ioun stones in any corner of Sembia." She paused and let her cold, black eyes be mesmerized by the dragon's blazing gold ones. "I am ready for my next assignment."

The dragon switched its giant tail into the pool.

"Yesssss . . ." It hissed warmly as energy channeled from blood spilled in a dozen temples surged through the golden water, charging the beast with its power. "So you are, Quarrel." The dragon shifted once more, lowering itself deeper into the burbling waters. The great wyrm grunted its satisfaction as the water's powers continued to invigorate its lifeblood. "Three wretched humans have destroyed one of my temples, in the process slaughtering most of an entire gnoll encampment. Still another part of my city has been taken over by human scum because of their cursed interference. They are the same three I spoke to you of before."

Quarrel nodded, remembering her master's fury after the party recovered Sokol Keep for Civilized Phlan. When she returned, she had expected to hear of the party's demise at the hands of any of the thousands of creatures in the service of the Lord of the Ruins. Certainly none within range of his tremendous power had missed the message to kill the three on sight.

"Yes, they still live," the dragon snarled, as if reading Quarrel's mind. "Cowards faced them and died at their hands. Now I'm trusting you, Quarrel, to either convert them to our cause—my cause—or kill them like worms. Unlike most of the creatures I control, you can pass freely into the civilized part of the city. . . ."

Quarrel clenched and unclenched her hand around the hilt of her favorite dagger. The Lord of the Ruins would never know how many had died because they harassed her or made some unflattering reference to her nose.

"You have all of my resources at your disposal," the huge dragon went on. "With two more ioun stones, I will be able to complete the figure of power." Slowly the giant creature reached up and put a taloned appendage on the hexagon that already held an ioun stone in four of its six corners. "When these two last holes are filled, I will be able to control elves, dwarves, even humans. But in the meantime, you must learn what motivates those three. Promise them anything, but get them working for me—or bring me their miserable flesh and blood, and let it fill my pool. If you succeed, your reward will be—"

Quarrel's black eyes gleamed with a fresh intensity. "I already know the generosity of your rewards, master. And you also know the reward for which I work most anxiously."

"Yes . . . Yes, Quarrel, I know."

The moment she successfully completed the bidding of the Lord of the Ruins, Quarrel would receive the one thing murder and looting could never get her—a human nose, a small triangular-shaped nose that would not snuffle when she intended to be silent, that would not be an object of harassment and derision, that would not identify her as a half-breed . . . an object of contempt.

* * * * *

The great bronze dragon enjoyed the surging warmth of the energy-giving pool for a few more glorious minutes after Quarrel departed. The giant amphibious body of the dragon was an impressive one—strong, vital, and impervious to most attacks, an excellent choice for possession by Tyranthraxus, the Great Possessor.

For more than a millennium, the dark-minded entity of Tyranthraxus had dwelled on the material plane. For more than a thousand years, Tyranthraxus had been hampered by the nuisance of mortality, forced to control the weakest or the most corrupt mind he could find and then to function within the confines of that creature's physical resources, however limited. He had at times been forced to possess even creatures as mean as lizards and squirrels just to survive. Inevitably he drove their pathetic, inhibiting bodies to the breaking point as he searched frantically for a new vessel to contain his essence. He had possessed humans by the score, men and women overrun by such overwhelming greed that their minds had lost the capacity to reject his usurping presence. He preferred humans because they made his record-keeping so much easier. Since humans were themselves gifted with a capacity for language, maintaining accounts of his subversion and conquests was easier for Tyranthraxus when he inhabited a human body.

But the dragon had been a good choice. Its mind had been subverted by a powerful wizard's Mind Control spell at the time when Tyranthraxus had last been forced to leap to another host. The Great Possessor now found himself mental companion to a mind that, unlike most on this plain, had withstood centuries of life, a mind that had, over the years, acquired a tremendous capacity for magic. Tyranthraxus was, of course, obligated to keep pushing back the beast's lawful good tendencies, and he was forced to cope with physical features that made writing difficult. But the ability to intimidate with a dragon's body was a tremendous advantage. Then, too, the dragon had led him to the pool. . . .

What Tyranthraxus could never hope to achieve in his own plane, where he was merely a minor entity among giants, was finally within his grasp here on this plane of weak mortal minds. He already controlled the actions of a legion of creatures within his telepathic reach. By corrupting the Pool of Radiance, a magical body of water that had been created by the goddess Selune to purify her followers before arcane rites, and expanding its powers with the enhancing forces of a perfect hexagon of ioun stones, Tyranthraxus had found the means of becoming the supreme ruling being of an entire plane.

Each drop of blood added to the pool gave Tyranthraxus new life energy. Each ioun stone added a measure of power to his own. For years he had researched the magical gemstones' power, and he knew that the hexagon was the ultimate figure of control. With six stones, lined up perfectly, and his tremendous mental capacity, he would control the actions of every creature on this plane, and with the power of the pool, he would do it forever. . . .

* * * * *

" 'By proclamation of the Honorable First Councilman of the City of Phlan, Porphorys Cadorna is hereby declared Second Councilman.' "

Cadorna bowed graciously before the First Councilman, members of the council, and the audience of onlookers assembled in the public chambers. An encampment of gnolls had been ousted from the uncivilized portion of the city, freeing up the old Cadorna property. Cadorna had immediately acted in the council's name to employ the Black Watch, a band of exceptionally efficient mercenaries, to storm the adjacent library and slums and reclaim those properties for Civilized Phlan. At the same time, an unprecedented donation had been made to the Tyrian Temple in Cadorna's name. Finally, a large number of coins had changed hands to ensure Cadorna's ascension to the second most powerful position on the council. "Your honors, people of Phlan . . ." he began. "I thank you for entrusting me with this tremendous responsibility. I will, as before, work unrelentingly for the betterment and expansion of our fair city."

Cadorna descended from the dais, shook all the proper hands, smiled all the right smiles, spoke all the proper words—then slipped away to his private chambers, where Gensor was waiting.

The councilman whisked past the mage and turned around to face him as he spoke. "You believe the three have kept something from me?"

"Whether or not it is some part of your treasure they hide, I cannot say." The mage lowered his hood as he approached Cadorna and looked straight into the councilman's eyes. "But the bigger man, the one called Ren, no longer radiated the magic he once did, and I saw him make contact with the woman when they were unloading their goods on the table. I saw nothing pass between them, but he is very smooth, and her magic is strong. They may well have made an exchange, or he may have passed something to her for safekeeping."

"Scoundrels! Lying thieves! I'll—What are you laughing at?"

The mage snorted and then laughed again, a wheezing, hissing snicker. "Surely, Councilman, you've heard of the turtle calling the tortoise hard-shelled?"

"Ingrate! There'll be a day when you wish—"

"Wish what? That I'd treated you better? Councilman, you and I both know this relationship will end the day it doesn't serve one of us. In the meantime, let me remind you that I *did* contract the Black Watch as you requested, and they *have* completed their first assignment."

"Yes . . . the mercenaries did well with the recovery of the gnoll embattlement. But what of the second task?" Cadorna clenched and unclenched his hands, eager for the news that would confirm his ascension to the position of First Councilman.

Gensor grinned, his ashen lips pulling so thin they almost disappeared. "Everything is in place for them to take over as guards of the city. Per your instructions—" Gensor stopped when he saw a mix of fury and terror rise in Cadorna's eyes. "Per *my* instructions," Gensor corrected, "they have prepared an orcish arrow for the First Councilman. I saw it myself. Everyone will assume the murderer is an assassin from outside the walls. Your plan is a good one."

Cadorna nodded his acknowledgment. "I thought so. . . ." For a moment, his eyes gleamed in anticipation, and then they darkened. "But what of the treasure taken by those three? Can you recover it for me? Are you mage enough to acquire the stolen items from that hulking woman?"

"Brawn is not common to magic-users, I'll admit, but don't assume that our skill grows in proportion to our frailty. I wouldn't choose to go one-on-one against her. . . ."

"You mean you won't do it?" Cadorna fairly snarled the words.

"I will. I'll use my full resources to try to recover your treasure. I meant only that I wouldn't go looking for it while she was in her room. And, remember, there may not be any more treasure. I didn't actually see anything."

Cadorna scowled, then snapped at the mage: "You'll bring back *anything* that may be of use to me!"

"Of course." Gensor pulled up his hood and turned toward the door.

"Go, then, but bring back word this evening. Understand?"

"I think so. Oh, before I forget . . . what of the Lord of the Ruins?" asked Gensor.

"What do you mean?"

"What have you done to satisfy his inquiries about the gnoll encampment? He must be furious."

"As soon as I meet with his next messenger, I'll explain that I was forced to take action but that I'll see that those parts quickly fall back into his hands."

"Interesting." Gensor scrutinized Cadorna with a look. "Is that *really* your intent?"

"Is that *really* your affair, mage?"

"I suppose not. But I'll know soon enough, in any event." Gensor turned and slipped through the door. Cadorna just barely made out the mage's parting words: "See you too soon."

* * * * *

Slate-colored thunderheads billowed and churned in a circle directly over Shal's head. Lightning bolts raged out in every direction above her. Shal extended her well-muscled arms skyward and flexed her taut fingers at precisely the right moment as she incanted yet another Weather Control spell. The bit of moistened earth she'd been holding vanished into the gray sky, and the bottom of the nearest thunderhead immediately became like so many bowls of gray dust, swirling first in one direction and then another.

The largest of the bowls swelled and bulged as if the cloud's mists were fighting against themselves and the confines of the bowl. Moments later, a snake of curling, writhing vapor broke free from the thunderhead and spiraled down, bringing with it the dragon winds of a fierce tornado. In a triumphant gesture, Shal dispatched the descending cyclone out to sea, where it became a waterspout filled with fury, vacuuming the Moonsea's waters into its hungry vortex and spewing them high into the air.

When the twister did not dissipate as she had intended but continued to rage across the bay, Shal beat the air with her fists and exhaled through clenched teeth. "Damn!" She watched in despair as the waterspout changed direction and surged back toward the docks of Phlan, which were lined with boats whose captains had chosen not to risk travel during such a violent storm. Shal spoke the words of a simple cantrip, one she had tried only on much smaller, less volatile subjects, and did her level best to push the tornado away. It held and came no closer, but she had to channel all her energies and repeat the cantrip three times to finally get it to turn back to sea. For several minutes, the twister darkened the waters of the bay. Finally it slowed, began to dissipate, and spewed its last. Shal slumped down on the rooftop of the inn, exhausted.

Her nose and mouth buried in her steepled hands, her windblown red hair spilling down her back and arms, she spoke quietly to Cerulean, who stood, shimmering a rich amethyst color, beside her. "I did it, Cerulean. I mastered the weather."

You took a foolhardy risk, the familiar corrected her.

Shal lifted her head and rested her chin on her knuckles. "Perhaps. But it was a necessary step, a step I needed to take in order to see Ranthor's death avenged and make myself worthy of his legacy.

"When Ranthor was alive," she went on, "I merely toyed with magic. I failed to take advantage of the opportunity right in front of me."

Agreed, but—

"You don't need to agree with me."

I was only trying to be, uh . . .

"Agreeable? Thanks, but I think I prefer you to be ornery." Shal reached up and patted Cerulean on his flank, then gently stroked his fetlock, admiring the beauty of his color even as it faded. "I *do* prefer the purple," she said absently, still flushed by her success with the difficult weather spells. She had taken a naturally overcast and blustery day and added rain, lightning, a little hail—and a tornado!

I don't distinguish colors, Mistress, so the color of my aura makes no difference to me. But you're changing the subject. What you did—casting spell after spell at the limits of your experience and expertise—was terribly dangerous. I simply don't understand why you've suddenly become so obsessed with improving your skills so rapidly. Cerulean pawed the rooftop and turned quietly to let Shal stroke his opposite leg.

"I think you do, Cerulean. It's more than wanting to do my best for Ranthor. As much as I admired him and want to do right by him, it's myself I have to please now. I always thought of magic as a way of making a living, a pastime, a way to get by. It was never a profession for me, just an easy route to security. In fact, I hated to think about what it might do to my appearance if I performed too much magic. Long ago, I decided I'd use my limited skills for commercial purposes—to help someone move a little equipment around, to frighten lowlifes who didn't pay their bills on time. . . ."

I can see—

"No, wait, Cerulean. Let me finish. What I wanted to say is that I never took magic seriously. In Ranthor's absence, I've realized, first of all, that I have talent, and second of all, that I enjoy the power magic gives me. And—and—" Shal paused, groping for words—"I don't—I don't hate this new body anymore. There are some real advantages to being strong. And I don't feel so—so concerned about what magic may do to my looks. I know there is probably no reason to think this, but I feel . . . protected somehow from the effects of spell-casting. It's as if my body is no longer susceptible to damage."

"No longer susceptible to damage?" The voice came from behind Cerulean.

The big horse stamped and spun around to face the intruder.

Shal turned her head. Ren stood not more than ten feet from her, silhouetted against the brightening sky. He'd climbed the same creaky ladder Shal had climbed to reach the roof of the inn, and he had done it soundlessly. She shook her head, marveling. "You shouldn't sneak up on people."

"It gives me a chance to . . . see things," said Ren, and he came closer, holding a hand out toward Shal.

She tipped her head and laughed lightly as she let him pull her to her feet. "To see what? An exhausted, half-baked magic-user and a purple horse?"

Ren pulled Shal up close and reached for her other hand. "A beautiful woman who I—"

The ladder creaked behind Ren. In a single motion, he dropped Shal's hands, turned on his heels, and whisked Left from his boot.

Tarl's head poked out over the rooftop. "Sot said I might find you he—" On seeing Ren's stance and expression, Tarl glanced down at the ladder. "I'm sorry. I—"

"No. Tarl!" Shal pushed her way past Ren and extended her hand to Tarl. "Come up. Please."

"Sorry about the knife. I didn't mean to be so touchy." Ren spoke in a hushed voice. "Ever since we got arrested coming back into the city, I've been a little jumpy. Even at the temple, getting my hand healed . . . I've had this feeling as if I'm not safe anywhere. I mean, it's in my training to watch my back, and there's always seemed to be a person or two around who has it in for me, but now I feel shadows everywhere. I don't feel alone even after I've checked everything around me."

Tarl sensed that he had interrupted something between Ren and Shal, but he was not about to be the one to bring it up. He climbed up onto the rooftop and spoke of a concern of his own. "I don't share your eye or ear for movement, Ren, but I do know that I was followed here. The one who shadowed me didn't try very hard to be subtle. In fact, she's sitting downstairs in the common room right now."

Shal and Ren looked at Tarl with intense curiosity.

"Who?" they asked in unison.

"A half-orc. She'd pass for human except for her nose. It's as boarlike as they come. She carries an unusually small scimitar and several thief's daggers, and she cloaks herself in a dark gray cape. I don't know who she is or why she's following me, but I've got the feeling she's waiting for a chance to talk to me."

"Cadorna," said Shal firmly. "It's not enough that he has his thugs accost us like criminals at the city gates. Now he has us followed, too."

"You, too?" Ren asked.

"No, not that I'm aware of. But the two of you . . . and for what?"

Ren crouched down and spoke in a whisper. "The treasure? The part we kept?"

"Then let's return it," said Shal. "It's just sitting on the nightstand in my room. We've no need of it. I wasn't even sure why you wanted me to keep it in the first place."

"Two reasons," Ren responded. "I didn't figure there was any way you could yank that armor out of your cloth without somebody noticing . . ." Ren spoke even more softly. "And I needed to get those ioun stones where they wouldn't be found."

"But since the stones are safe now, shouldn't we do as Shal says and return the armor?"

Ren heaved a sigh and spoke resignedly. "If I thought Cadorna was to be trusted, I'd be the first to hand back the rest of his treasure. But he's a rat of the first order, and I don't want to meet the fellow he sends after me wearing that armor or wielding weapons that jewelry paid for."

"You think he did it, don't you?" Shal looked at Ren.

The big man arched one eyebrow, puzzled. "Did what?"

Tarl answered. "You think he killed Shal's teacher—and that he'd kill us if he thought we knew."

"Yeah, I think so. But I don't know for sure. I do feel pretty certain that even if that half-gnoll was involved in it, it was work-for-hire. He at least had a sense of honor."

Shal hissed her words. "My flesh creeps every time I get near the councilman, and my gut feeling is that he did it. But I've no proof, and I don't know what his motive is. I'm prepared to test him by magic."

Cerulean stamped and snorted as though sharing Shal's anger and indignation.

"While coming from the temple, I heard that Cadorna

has been made Second Councilman," Tarl pointed out. "That means we need physical proof before we do anything rash. Cadorna has tremendous resources at his disposal now. I heard he even hired a mercenary militia to guard the city."

"I've heard the same thing," agreed Ren. "We'll need to work together—carefully. When we know the why, we'll know if Cadorna is the murderer. For now, though, I'd settle for some supper."

"What about the woman in the gray cloak?" asked Tarl.

"If she's really following you, maybe we can learn why . . . or at least who sent her," Ren answered.

"I'll find out," said Shal, a strange fury in her eyes.

*   *   *   *   *

A sprinkling of guests sat at tables in the inn, one here, two or three there. There was someone at almost every table but not a full table in the house. Those who were with others were speaking self-consciously, the way people do when a room gets too quiet for comfortable conversation. Shal and Ren and Tarl made their way to a large oval table that had just emptied near the bar. Neither Ren nor Shal had to ask where the half-orc woman was. She was seated at the center of the common room, and while no one appeared to be looking directly at her, she seemed to be the focus of attention, her shining black hair and dark complexion contrasting boldly with the light walls of the inn.

She did not look over at the three, and made no move to approach them while they ate. It was not until they had finished eating and were talking quietly that she approached their table. She didn't wait for an invitation. As soon as she had made eye contact with all three, she sat down. She immediately leaned across the table and began speaking directly to Tarl in a treacherous, whiskey-hoarse voice. "I can make your brother well."

Tarl sat silent, compelled to look into her black eyes.

"I can make him whole again."

"How? What do you know about Anton? And who are you?" Tarl spoke coolly, showing no emotion.

"I am called Quarrel, and I've been sent as a messenger—" she hushed her voice to a whisper—"a messenger of the Lord of the Ruins."

"The Lord of the Ruins?" Like the others, Shal had not expected to encounter an emmisary of the Lord of the Ruins inside Civilized Phlan.

Ren flashed a dagger in each hand. "Speak your piece and make it quick, orc-meat," he hissed.

The look Quarrel returned would have sent needles of ice through a lesser man. "Hold your peace, thief! No fewer than five warriors gathered in this room are also in service to the Lord of the Ruins, and there isn't a one who couldn't slam a knife into your jugular before you could ever lay a hand on me."

"You and two more would die before I fell."

"Perhaps, but that's not what I'm here for, nor is it what they're here for," she said gesturing around the room.

The woman spread her hands flat on the big table in a calming gesture, then spoke in a still-throaty but less biting voice. "I'm here to make a deal with you—a very good deal."

"Speak," said Shal, her staff now raised.

"I've already made one offer . . . I'll see that the cleric's friend is healed. I'll also name your teacher's murderer. I'll even kill him for you, if you wish. . . ."

Shal started for a moment, wondering if the woman had heard any part of their conversation on the rooftop.

"And for you, thief, I'll get the name of the assassin who killed your red-haired lover. I'll let you kill him yourself, of course."

Ren fairly threw himself across the table and grabbed

the orc-woman roughly by the collar. "Orc vermin! What do you know about my Tempest?"

"Unhand me, you bastard, or I'll have that assassin kill you instead!" Six armed warriors had leaped from their tables and moved in closer.

Tarl pressed his hand firmly on Ren's shoulder, and Ren loosed his hold. "I want to know what she thinks she can do for Brother Anton."

"How do you know these things, and what's the rest of your 'deal,' Quarrel?" Ren fairly spit the words.

She spoke slowly, facing each of the three in turn. "I know who your master's murderer is, mage. . . . Cleric of Tyr, I know who can heal your friend. . . . And, yes, thief, I know who killed your lover. I know because I work for the one who controls all. Serve him, and each of you will be given the knowledge and the time to fulfill your quests."

"He can heal Anton?" Tarl asked hesitantly.

Ren wheeled to face his friend. "She'll see that he gets healed—in exchange for your soul! Think, Tarl!"

The woman's voice was like honey again. "Your friend exaggerates, Tarl. Service to the Lord of the Ruins is hardly the exchange of one's soul. The Lord of the Ruins is no god. He demands obedience, not worship. Look at me—I am a free woman."

"You are a free pig!" said Ren.

"That's enough!" Shal cried, standing to face Ren. "I've no more use for your bigotry than I do for her offer!" To Quarrel, she said, "I speak for the others. We've seen what obedience to the Lord of the Ruins means, and we want no part of your deal. Leave us!"

Fire blazed in Quarrel's black eyes for a moment. "The Lord of the Ruins gets what he wants," she said, "sooner or later." The half-orc stood, pivoted on her heel, and began to walk calmly toward the exit. The warriors rose as if to follow, but just as soon as she had opened the big door, Quarrel spun around and launched a tiny dagger from her hand.

"Down!" Ren shouted, and he leaped to try to deflect the dagger, but a big warrior rammed him from behind and sent him sprawling across the table.

Before Shal could duck or react with a spell, the dagger was buried deep in her collarbone, and green death began to spread through her body. She stood for a moment, a silent mental cry shrieking through her numbness, and then she flopped, twitching and jerking, to the ground.

In a lightninglike move, Ren rolled and disemboweled the man who had rammed him from behind. Tarl reacted with equal speed, bludgeoning the two warriors closest to him before they could pull their swords from their scabbards. But it was Cerulean who reacted with the greatest ferocity. Before Shal's silent cry was finished, he had burst forth from the cloth, trampling everything between his mistress and the assassin. The half-orc never stood a chance. The huge horse reared and stomped, reared and stomped, again and again, pulverizing her with his sharp hooves, smashing her piglike snout deep into her crushed face, so that not even the greatest mages of the Lord of the Ruins would stand a chance of fixing it.

But killing Quarrel did nothing for Shal, who continued to jerk and writhe from the spasms caused by the deadly green poison. Nor did it help Tarl with the last of the warriors, who had just sliced up under the cleric's ribs with his sword. It was Sot who finally clubbed the man to death with the cudgel he kept hidden behind the bar.

Ren ran immediately to Shal and cradled her head and shoulders in his arms. "No! No! Not again!"

"The temple . . ." Tarl clutched his side and spoke in desperation. "Get us to the temple!" He tried to work some healing on himself, but he passed out before he could finish the incantation.

Sot stuffed a bar rag against Tarl's wound and started shouting orders at the confused patrons still standing around in the inn. "What're ya gawkin' at? Get a wagon hitched up! Now! And, you, hand me a fresh cloth from behind the bar there! Move!"

Ren carved at Shal's wound and sucked and spit the poison as fast as he was able to, but he could see the vein of green pushing its way toward her heart, and he wept openly as he carried her to the waiting cart, where Sot had already laid Tarl. Cerulean whinnied and whickered and stamped furiously, and none but Ren dared to hitch him to the cart, but the moment the harnesses were secure and Ren had clambered aboard, the great horse bolted away and galloped with a speed no other horse could match.

"Make way! Make way!" Ren shouted at the top of his lungs as they reached the temple gates. "Wounded aboard!"

The clerics at the gates hurried to lift the latch as priests in their studies flocked outside to see what the commotion was about. Cerulean charged through the gates and straight toward the central temple. He didn't slow until he reached a circle of priests waiting at the temple stairs.

Ren spoke so rapidly that he jumbled his words, and it was only the clerics' experience in dealing with distraught people that helped them to catch the words "poison" and "bleeding." Two of the brothers held Ren as the others carried Tarl and Shal inside the temple.

"Our brothers will do everything they can for them. There is nothing more you can do, ranger. Go, find your peace where you can, and return in the morning."

Ren stared at them numbly, tears still welling in his eyes. "You can't let them die! If there's anything I can do . . . anything at all . . . I'll be . . . I'll be at the Laughing

Goblin Inn, or maybe . . . maybe at the park, the one by the wizard's tower on that end of town." Ren pointed absently and walked dejectedly toward the gates.

"Don't forget your horse!" one of the clerics called.

But Ren only muttered, "No. It's hers," and walked on.

* * * * *

Ren didn't remember passing anything between the temple and the park. He didn't even have any idea how much time had passed. He had been at one place, some time ago, and now he was at another. The storm had cleared before Shal left the rooftop of the Laughing Goblin, but the sky was still cloudy, and it was now pitch dark, the kind of night when only rangers and elves saw well. Ren walked without hesitation through the annonwoods and into the center of the park, where a huge evergreen towered into the darkness.

He gathered pinecones till his hands could hold no more and laid them gently before the tree. Then he piled needles on top of those. Finally, he picked violets that had folded their flowers for the night and laid them atop the pile. He faced the tree and spoke softly. "I want desperately for my new friends to live, and I need somehow, Tempest, to finally accept your death. . . . You know there's no one like you. Even Shal, as much as she looks like you, isn't really like you at all. I'm not . . . I'm not going to look for your replacement anymore, Tempest. There isn't one. But you're going to have to forgive me if I go on now with my life."

Ren clenched his teeth to hold back tears, then tossed the flowers and the needles and the pinecones, a handful at a time, around the tree. "What is it they say, Babe— 'from the earth to the earth'? You loved trees and the outdoors, like me, so this is my way of . . . of . ." Ren's voice cracked, and he stopped until he could speak again. Then he gazed skyward and continued. It seemed fitting that the nearly full moon had broken through the clouds and was shining down on the little park. "This is my way of leaving you where you'd like to be. Okay?"

There was nothing more to say, so Ren simply stood for a while, staring into the night. After several minutes, his melancholy was interrupted by an ear-piercing shriek.

Ren made his way stealthily to the edge of the park closest to the fortress wall. The sounds were coming from the opposite side of the wall. Ren launched his grappling hook high into the air. It caught, but when he tugged, it fell back to the ground. On his second try, the three-pronged hook held firm, and Ren hauled himself steadily to the top of the fortress wall.

Below, a lone warrior was lashing out furiously at an attacking troll. Two other warriors lay nearby, probably dead, the area around them a scrap heap of troll parts. From where he crouched atop the wall, Ren could see the hands, legs, even heads, and other miscellaneous bits of troll beginning to move together, regenerating.

Few creatures in the Realms were as hideous as trolls. Their bodies, even whole, were nightmarish—elongated parodies of giant, emaciated humans—and their faces were morbid caricatures from every child's worst dreams, with long, wart-covered noses and black, seemingly empty eye sockets. Worse yet, their mutilated bodies refused to die. Even if a fighter were lucky enough to slice a troll to ribbons, its detached hand might claw at his leg and pull him to the ground, or the rolling, moss-covered head might bite and gnaw at his exposed flesh. Given enough time, the pieces would actually scuttle together and eventually form a whole new troll.

But it was the troll's skin that bothered Ren most. He had seen trolls in daylight, and he knew that their skin was always decaying and rotting, even as the creatures lived—just so much slime, mold, and fungus troweled onto greenish, tarlike flesh. Relieved that the night's filtered moonlight prevented him from seeing more clearly, he wasted no time dropping his rope over to the other side and swinging down to aid the valiant fighter.

He started by slopping oil from his fire flask on all the troll parts he could see. Flames shot up instantly as the magical fluid made contact with the arms, hands, and legs, and Ren was nearly overcome by the putrid smoke from the burning of wet flesh. Hunched over, fighting a cough that would not stop, Ren pivoted just in time to face the knees of the troll, which was now directing its attention to him. He thrust his short sword out between the troll's knobby legs and pulled straight up with all the strength he could muster. He ripped through flesh he did not want to think about, then staggered back and fell to the ground, just out of immediate reach of the troll's gargantuan hands. The nearly bisected creature bellowed with rage and lurched forward toward Ren.

It would have killed him on the spot were it not for the quick action of the warrior, still behind the troll, who swung a huge broadsword, low and level with the creature's pelvis. Razor-sharp metal, powered by the strength born of terror, ripped through skin and bone, and the troll's upper body flopped back onto the warrior's extended arms. Four-fingered hands, tipped with vicious, aquiline claws, reached by instinct alone and began tearing into the fighter's upper arms. Ren crab-crawled to avoid the amputated legs that were still stalking his way, and then rolled, stood, and dodged beyond them. He leaped forward and immediately began hacking at the creature's upper body, which was clinging to the shoulders of the enraged warrior. The troll didn't loosen its grip until Ren severed its arms from its hands, and even then Ren had to yank the clawing hands from the fighter's shoulders. Again he threw oil, and again there was a terrible stench as the troll flesh burned and smoked.

The warrior collapsed, whether from the wounds or the smoke, Ren wasn't sure. It wasn't until Ren reached down to lift the prostrate form that he realized he knew the fighter. Her blonde hair was stuffed into a fighting helm, but he recognized the face as that of one of the women he had jested with just days before at the inn. Jen—what was it? Jensena? Yes, that was it. The other two fighters must be her two companions, he realized. As soon as he had moved Jensena away from the smoldering troll bits and patted the gouges on her shoulders with a blotting powder he carried, he checked the other two. They were both dead. He pulled their bodies up alongside the wall, along with their purses and light weapons. Guards could pick them up in the morning—if they were still intact.

Ren got a good hold on Jensena and started up the rope. While she didn't rival Tempest, much less Shal, for size, Jensena was still a big woman, and all muscle. Lugging her to the top of the wall was no mean feat, and Ren felt unanticipated relief when she started to rouse as they descended the other side. At first she just coughed and made pathetic squeaking noises as the coughing jarred her wounds. As soon as they reached the ground, Ren held her tight to keep the coughs from racking her body so hard, and when she seemed ready, he offered her some water. Still leaning against him, she tipped her head back and let him pour the water into her open mouth.

When she'd had her fill, she turned her head away. "Salen? . . . Gwen?"

"I'm sorry," said Ren softly. "Their bodies . . . are alongside the wall. In the morning—"

"Damn! Damn!"

Ren pulled the big woman closer and held her as she cried, gently at first, and then in hard, convulsive sobs. He said nothing. What was there to say when someone lost two friends? He surely didn't know.

Together they made their way slowly to the Laughing Goblin, Ren supporting Jensena. After a quick word with Sot, the two of them helped the woman up to a room, where they eased her onto the bed. To break the tension in the room while he readied a basin of fresh hot water, a sponge, and several strips of clean gauze, Sot joked quietly about the ineptness of Ren's replacement. Ren appreciated the older man's thoughtfulness and the room he let him keep above the stable, but he said nothing just then. As soon as Sot left, Ren gently sponged Jensena's face and hair and helped her remove her chain mail and armor.

In spite of his own numbness, Ren found himself unabashedly admiring Jensena's impressive figure and musculature as he worked. Apart from wincing as the garments brushed her shoulders, the big blonde woman made no move to stop his efforts. The cloth of her blouse was matted against the bloody skin of her shoulders. When he used a dagger to tear the cloth around the wounds, he ripped the blouse almost down to her waist. Still she continued to watch him in silence. When he began cleaning the gashes in her shoulder, she finally spoke. "In the pouch, under my belt, you'll find a healing potion."

Ren let his gaze pass slowly from her shoulders to her beltline, and then he glanced up and met her eyes. Ren's pulse speeded, and he could feel his face flush. Jensena nodded lightly, and Ren reached for the potion, pausing just long enough to let his fingertips brush her warm, smooth skin. He closed his eyes for a single moment before his hand closed around the small glass bottle.

It was an excellent healing potion. He used it sparingly, but it did the work of a cleric. She reached for Ren's hands and squeezed them hard. "Thank you. When my pain is less . . ."

"I'd like that, Jensena . . . Good night."

* * * * *

"We've slowed the poison, but we haven't stopped it. I'm sorry. I know she's a friend of yours."

Tarl tried to sit up, but he sucked in his breath in pain when the newly mended flesh under his ribs pulled tight. "No! I can't . . . I can't lose her, too. Brother . . . Brother Tern, you've got to keep trying! Surely there's some antidote for the assassin's poison!"

"Tarl, we've done everything we know. Our clerical spells have done some good, or she'd be dead already. But the poison still burns through her. Her body still twitches like a fish on a hook, . . ." Brother Tern pointed across the chamber. Two clerics held Shal gently to keep her from harming herself further by involuntary movement. "I . . . I don't believe she can last much longer."

Tarl looked briefly at Shal and then turned away. "I'll call on Tyr myself to heal her!" Tarl fought the pain that throbbed through his whole body as he tried to stand. "I'll go to the meditation chamber, to the innermost sanctuary. There can be no reason for her to suffer, too!"

"Few so young dare to attempt to enter the inner sanctuary, but like any of us, Brother Tarl, you're free to try. Cleanse yourself thoroughly first, though, and mind your attitude and your motives."

"Thank you, Brother Tern. I shall."

* * * * *

Tarl gratefully accepted his brother's help as he bathed his healing body and changed into full battle garb. But when he stood at the door of the meditation chamber, he stood alone.

Tarl knew from his earliest catechisms the nature of the meditation chamber. He would enter the first of four concentric squares clean of body, the second clean of extraneous thoughts, the third with a focus of purpose, and the final one with a focus on his god. While technically open to any worshiper of Tyr, few who were not grounded in the faith through years of clerichood and service bothered to enter, since a spiritual barrier prevented most from passing beyond the first or second square.

Tarl raised his hammer to the entrance of the first square. It glowed blue, and he passed through the curtain into the chamber. The space between the outer square and the inner one was only four cubits, and the ceiling was low and confining. Tarl could feel his breath constrict. He wondered for a moment if he was doing the right thing, but he proceeded as he had been taught. His hammer and shield bared, Tarl walked the inner perimeter of the square, speaking the words of a mantra designed to cleanse the mind of miscellaneous thoughts. After twice around the square, his breathing eased, and he could feel his head clearing. Another time around and he could feel a healing warmth, greater than that from the hands of his brothers, spreading through his body, mending even the soreness brought on by his wound.

After four more times around the square, his hammer glowed blue again, and Tarl entered the second square. This square was of course, smaller, and the distance between the walls of the squares was the same, but the ceiling was easily half again as tall as that of the previous chamber, which gave the second chamber an illusion of a greater size. Once more Tarl felt his breath constrict, and he experienced an intense pressure on all parts of his body, as though the walls of the room were closing in and the air had nowhere to go. Tarl found it impossible to think about the concerns he had planned to bring into the sanctuary. He remembered the advice Brother Tern had offered as he helped him with his robes and armor: "When you can go no further, fight. Find physical balance, and the rest will come. Tyr is God of War and Justice. He seeks focus of purpose and balance."

Tarl raised his shield and wielded his hammer, pushing and swinging, charging and parrying against imaginary foes that lined the narrow hallway. It was not until his body began to revel in the movement and Tarl found a familiar joy in the control of it that his focus returned. Unconsciously, almost as an afterthought to his physical action, he began to speak and respeak the concerns that plagued him: Shal, Anton, the Hammer of Tyr. Every time he brought his shield up or swung his hammer, it was for Shal, or Anton, or for the return of the hammer. His focus was so strong, he didn't even think about the fact that he was now moving without pain.

Soon his hammer began to blaze a brilliant blue, and Tarl stopped, relaxed his shield and hammer, and passed through the curtain to the third square. The square of the inner sanctuary stood before him. It radiated an intense, bright blue.

Faith had never been difficult for Tarl. Tyrians practiced a hands-on kind of worship that made sense to him, and Tyr seemed infinitely believable. Pictures of him were always the same, a burly but gnarled, bearded old fellow with a hammer as big as his arm. The irony of references to his evenhandedness was that, from all accounts, he was missing one hand, and somehow that made him all the more approachable. Tarl's strong faith had already been rewarded with exceptional healing powers for one so young.

Only now, when two people he valued, perhaps as much as his standing as a cleric, lay filled by evil, did Tarl ever question his god or his faith.

"My thoughts of Shal, Anton, and the Hammer of Tyr I give up to you, and thoughts of you, great Tyr, Grimjaws, the Even-Handed, God of War, God of Justice. I offer up my fate to your hammer and to the balances." Tarl waited, continuing to meditate on his god.

Moments later, his hammer began to glow once more, and Tarl entered the innermost sanctuary. Each of the four walls and the vaulted ceiling were mirrors of highly polished silver. At the center of the small room was a cushioned kneeling stool with a small, covered platform before it. Tarl knelt and rested his hammer on the platform. He was surrounded by his own image—a warrior, armed and ready for battle, but completely submissive and vulnerable.

He stared at the hammer and continued to focus his thoughts on Tyr. The hammer began to radiate an even brighter light, and then it began to rise slowly from the platform as Tarl watched, his mind filled with the wisdom and thoughts of his god. The sensation was not like hearing spoken words, nor was it like the occasional shared thought between intimates. It was a flooding, a purging wave of guidance.

Tarl had no idea how long he'd been in the inner sanctuary. He had no memory of coming out. He knew only that he must find Ren immediately.

*　*　*　*　*

"Your daggers! We have to get them to Shal! Now!" Tarl hammered on the door and shouted to Ren again and again, but the big man was rummaging his way out of a deep sleep that had come from exhaustion, and he wasn't comprehending what all the ruckus was about. In fact, Tarl was lucky he was pounding outside the door because Ren probably would have killed him on instinct as an intruder if he'd managed to get into the room. As it was, Ren launched both Right and Left at the closed door.

"Tyr and Tymora!" Tarl leaped back as the two dagger points pierced through to his side of the door. "Wake up, man, before you kill somebody!"

It was Ren's own movement that finally woke him, and he slowly comprehended the source of the clamor. "Be right with you," he muttered.

It took Tarl only a few minutes to explain that he needed to use one of the ioun stones to increase his clerical powers in an attempt to heal Shal, yet it seemed to Tarl more like hours, and longer still before they were finally back at the temple.

The clerics could not keep Shal on a cot or bed. Her body jerked with nightmares and spasms induced by the poison, so she lay on a thick cotton quilt, a soft cotton blanket that was constantly being replaced crumpled over the lower half of her body. Tarl sat on the cool stone floor beside Shal and pulled her twitching body up close to his own. He clenched a blue-black ioun stone in one hand and his hammer in the other. Tenderly he wrapped his arms tight around Shal, then began to pray as he had never prayed before. Blue light like that he had seen in the inner sanctuary blazed from the stone and the hammer. For a moment, Shal's body jerked even more violently, and then a vile green vapor filtered up from the pores around Shal's collarbone and dispersed into the clear morning air. Her body quieted immediately, and Shal went limp in Tarl's arms.

"Shal? Shal!" Tarl pulled her even closer, praying to sense warmth and a firm heartbeat rather than clammy, cooling skin and silence. Suddenly strong arms wrapped around him and pulled him closer still, and he immersed himself in the passion of her grateful embrace.

"Glad to have you back, Shal," said Ren, and he pulled her from Tarl for a hug of his own.

❧ 10 ❧

Yarash

"This is the rest of your treasure," said Gensor. He watched Cadorna's face darken as he laid out the dwarven armor and then the jewelry. He knew the councilman had killed for far less than the handful of expensive baubles before him, and Gensor had every intention of redirecting Cadorna's attention so he wouldn't take that route. "Not bad for a night's work, eh? But mark my words, there are far bigger prizes to be had."

"Oh?" Cadorna cocked his head and waited for the mage to go on.

"The woman . . . the mage. She took an assassin's poison dagger in the shoulder last night. I made my exit from the inn unseen just as the brouhaha started."

"She's dead? It serves her r—"

"No. She lives. The Tyrian cleric—" Gensor paused for emphasis—"he used an ioun stone to heal the woman."

"An ioun stone?" Cadorna stood up from his chair and came around in front of his desk. He had to check himself to keep from grabbing Gensor by his robes. "The cleric has an ioun stone?"

"Not his, I suspect, or I'm sure he would have left it with the temple. But, yes, he used an ioun stone. All the clerics and even some of the peasants who were worshiping in the temple early this morning saw it."

Cadorna stood mere inches from Gensor, his eyes blazing with avarice, his thoughts turning to the first reports he had heard from the trio after their venture to Sokol

Keep—about ioun stones, the Lord of the Ruins, and "power to the pool."

Gensor went on. "This is only conjecture on my part, but as I said, I don't think the gem could belong to the cleric."

"Yes? So?" Cadorna actually began to tap his foot in his impatience.

"Do you remember the strong magic I detected in the big man's boots? An ioun stone could explain that."

"You think the stone belongs to him?"

It was Gensor's impatience that showed now. He leaned almost nose to nose with Cadorna. "Yes . . . and he has *two* boots!"

Cadorna's eyes widened. "You mean—"

A cloud of ocher-colored smoke puffed into the room right alongside Cadorna and Gensor. Both moved away from it, but Cadorna moved twice as far and twice as fast as Gensor. A sulfurous smell burned the nostrils of both men, and then a faint hum sounded as a short, spry, almost elflike wizard appeared in the room, his yellow-gold cape billowing with the last puffs of smoke.

"A messenger from the Lord of the Ruins," said Gensor.

"Yes . . ." Cadorna acknowledged. "We've met."

The messenger wasted no time. "I am here concerning a certain party of three, Councilman. You warned the Lord of the Ruins before they went to Sokol Keep, and he's tried since to have them killed. In fact, only last night an assassin assigned to either gain their services or kill them was smashed to a pulp by the mage woman's horse. The Lord of the Ruins wants those three dead."

Gensor licked his thin, dry lips and swallowed. He'd had his own run-in with the horse shortly after he'd taken the jewelry and armor from the woman's room at the inn. He had been startled at the time to find the horse loose in the streets. He figured the familiar must have bolted from the building after trampling the assassin.

The messenger went on. "Rumor has already spread that one of the three made use of an ioun stone in public. The Lord of the Ruins wants that ioun stone. He offers any item in his immense treasury in exchange for it."

"Why so much fuss over a gemstone?" Cadorna asked coyly.

"The Pool of Radiance, of course," said the messenger. "He needs two more stones to complete the figure of power." The wizard hesitated a moment when he saw Cadorna's twisted expression, but not knowing what to make of it, he continued. "At any rate, Councilman, he knows you have worked with these three before, and he would pay dearly for their heads, particularly if they were accompanied by an ioun stone. Have I made myself clear?"

"Quite clear. My thanks for the message."

The wizard exited in the same manner as he had come, and Cadorna bit his lip in a twisted smile, his eyes gleaming with his calculations. After a moment, he let his eyes meet Gensor's and began to speak quietly and deliberately. "Gensor . . . I'm sure, quite sure, I know the answer to this, but I still need to ask. What . . . motivates you? You've made no secret of riding my coattails to some private end of your own. Just what is it that you're after?"

Gensor didn't pause for even a moment before responding. "I know you know the answer, Councilman. The nature of your rewards for my services demonstrates your understanding. To practice magic to its fullest requires a great deal of money, not to mention incredible resources of other kinds. Who has time to go running off to the desert every time he needs the juice from a euphorbia or a special cactus needle? There are also, of course, many people who have a certain distaste for the byproducts of magical experimentation. To create, a person must also be allowed to make occasional mistakes."

"Yes? So what are you saying?" Cadorna thrust his head a little closer to Gensor as he waited for him to continue.

"The ideal I seek is to practice my art—completely unfettered by monetary constraints, limits of materials, or government interference. In lieu of that, I take the increasing freedom you provide as you make your rise to power."

"Exactly! It's perfect!" Cadorna could barely contain himself, so impressed was he with his own brilliance. "Only a few more hours and a Black Watch mercenary's well-aimed arrow stand between me and the First Councilman's seat. But with your news of the ioun stones, you may just have provided me with the exact knowledge I need to go even beyond that position."

Gensor's scheming was way ahead of Cadorna's, but he contained his impatience and let the councilman think he was presenting ideas that were completely new.

"If that big oaf has the two ioun stones as you suggest, *I* can use them to complete the figure of power and control the Pool of Radiance and all that goes with it. As the legitimate First Councilman of Phlan *and* controller of the pool, I'll have authority and power over the living and the dead, humanoid and human alike! . . . And I'll be able to provide you with the precise environment you require to practice your art!

"Think of it!" Cadorna put on his best sales pitch. "You'll have first crack at any and all magical finds. That dagger I gave you and those spellbooks—they'll be only the beginning!" Cadorna drew up his hands like a young child seeing a present for the first time. "And . . . I'll be able to provide you with an unlimited supply of subjects for your experiments."

This last idea hadn't occurred to Gensor, and he beamed with genuine pleasure when Cadorna brought it up. "Yes! Truly outstanding. You *do* understand my needs, Councilman. But how do you expect to get the ioun stones, and how do you expect to defeat the Lord of the Ruins?" This was the part Gensor hadn't figured out yet, and he was looking for some of Cadorna's usual ingenuity to pull the whole thing off.

"The first part is simple . . . perfect, in fact." Cadorna strolled back to his desk, sat down, and motioned for Gensor to sit as well. "You haven't forgotten our old friend Yarash the sorcerer—the one whose magic pollutes the river?"

Gensor immediately knew the tack Cadorna's thoughts were taking. "What about him?" he asked eagerly.

"Well, there he is, an eccentric, obstinate wizard whose power and independence have been a thorn in the side of the Lord of the Ruins practically forever . . . I simply send word to the Lord of the Ruins that I've sent those three off on a death mission to deal with Yarash. Win or lose, the Lord of the Ruins is happy because he doesn't want Yarash alive any more than he wants the cleric, thief, and mage alive. You contact the sorcerer. Yarash, old fool that he is, won't care one whit about the ioun stones beyond their immediate monetary or exchange value. You can flatter him—tell him a partial truth—how we could think of no one else strong enough to defeat the mage woman. . . ."

There was truth to that, Gensor thought, and he nodded and gestured for Cadorna to go on.

"Promise him a virtually unlimited supply of guinea pigs for his 'experiments.' "

"Same thing you promised me, eh?"

Cadorna flushed. "No! I didn't mean—"

Gensor waved a hand to silence him. "Merely a joke, Councilman. I understand the difference." While Gensor didn't trust Cadorna to tell the truth about the time of day, he knew the councilman was serious about providing an unfettered environment for his magic—at least, as long as it was convenient to do so. And once Gensor was powerful enough, he really wouldn't need Cadorna anymore. . . .

"Uh, well, anyhow, as I was saying, I want you to enlist Yarash's aid. Meanwhile, I'll see that the three parties under discussion are arrested for something . . . maybe even the brawl last night." Cadorna sped ahead. "The council won't care about the details once I tell them that I propose to send the party upriver to find the source of its pollution and put a stop to it. Not even the First Councilman himself knows about Yarash. Can you believe it? But that won't stop me from telling the party something about the old wizard to pique their interest. Those three will bound off on this mission like lambs to slaughter when I tell them about the chance to stop the horrible devastation being done to the river . . . *and* when I mention that Yarash knew Denlor well. . . ."

Gensor nodded in deference to Cadorna's insight, and Cadorna continued.

"If Yarash defeats them, I get the ioun stones. By the time they return—*if* they return, and I can't imagine how they'd manage it—I'll be First Councilman. I'll simply have the Black Watch arrest them at the city gates."

"On what grounds?"

"I don't know—treason, perhaps. It won't matter. No one will question my authority. Under completely legal auspices, the Black Watch guards will strip them of their weapons and magical items, including the ioun stones! And the beauty of it is that that's merely my contingency plan. I fully expect Yarash to turn all three of those bunglers into sea slime."

"You have a great mind, Councilman."

"Thank you, Gensor." Cadorna wagged a finger in the air. "And now for the second part of the question—the Lord of the Ruins. I know that he's a dragon—oddly enough, a bronze dragon. I can't imagine what would possess a good dragon to go quite so far afield, but I guess it must simply have sensed greater room for power in the control of humanoids. . . ."

Gensor had heard other rumors, but he wasn't about to spoil Cadorna's fun. "Yes?"

"Well, any decently armed troop of warriors with a magic-user or two can defeat a dragon, and for whatever reason, the pool doesn't seem to give it control over humans. I'll lead a party there myself, confront the wyrm, kill it, and complete the figure of power for myself."

The mage literally clapped, his admiration genuine. How Cadorna managed to gather so much information eluded him. Perhaps one day he would make Cadorna tell him. . . .

* * * * *

"You've been before this council before," said Cadorna sternly, condescendingly, as he peered down at Shal, Ren, and Tarl from his dais. "And for the same offense, no less. I have no choice but to send you on an even more dangerous mission." Cadorna went on to tell the three what he wanted them to know about Yarash.

"How do you know this sorcerer is responsible for the pollution of the Barren River?" Ren demanded belligerently. "And if you know, why haven't you done anything about it before now?"

Cadorna sighed. "The council sent seven groups upriver before an orc spy told me of Yarash. None of the groups returned." Cadorna looked up at the big man, his gray eyes pleading for sympathy. "I allowed the tragedy to continue because I was afraid for the lives of any who might try to stop the sorcerer. You must understand, I am sending the three of you only because your reputation precedes you." Cadorna waved his hand to the south with a flourish. "Look at Sokol Keep! Untold numbers died there before you succeeded. And the gnoll encampment . . . I expected you to return with my treasure.

Imagine my surprise when others came back with news that the gnolls had been vanquished completely. The three of you have a formidable reputation. You are perhaps the only ones capable of defeating the sorcerer."

Tarl spoke next. "We all have personal obligations that go wanting as you send us on these tasks, Second Councilman. Do we have a choice in this matter?"

"You most certainly do. You were arrested for brawling. Naturally you may wait in our holding cells until midnight, at which time the Black Watch will toss you over the north wall, and you will be banished from Civilized Phlan . . . permanently."

The glint in Cadorna's eyes was noticeable even to Tarl. He spoke no more.

"Defeat the wizard," Cadorna went on, "and you will be hailed as heroes. I personally will see to it that the town council bothers you no more. The young mage"—Cadorna pointed toward Shal but addressed Ren and Tarl, as if she could not comprehend his words—"may be interested in speaking with Yarash. He was known to have consorted with the wizard Denlor."

Tarl turned his gaze from Cadorna to Shal, watching for her reactions. The town guards had arrived before he could tell her about his meeting with Tyr in the inner sanctuary of the temple. Tarl had learned three things there: that an ioun stone would greatly enhance his powers so he could heal Shal; that Anton would not recover until the one who spat the word into his forehead was defeated; and that his own immediate calling was to follow Shal. The message from his god was clear—Shal's mission would lead Tarl to his own. "As Tyr has directed me, I will follow Shal," he declared.

Shal didn't understand the full implication of Tarl's words. She thought only that her friend was assuring her of his loyalty to her cause of avenging Ranthor's death. Tarl had already done a great deal. Without his healing, she knew, she would be dead. Shal now felt a to-tal rejuvenation of spirit and physical health, and she was forced to recognize a very special feeling for Tarl that she had not acknowledged before. "I've made my de-cision," she announced. "For me, there is no choice but to go."

"I personally find bashing it out with sorcerers—especially very powerful ones—a real treat," said Ren sar-castically, and then he turned serious. "If you're right about what that wizard's doing to the river, he's dead meat."

"Good! Then it's settled," said Cadorna. "Be on your way by the tenth hour tomorrow morning. Godspeed and good luck." With a wave of his hand, he dismissed the three from the council chambers.

* * * * *

Ren, Shal, Tarl, and their two horses left Phlan from the docks, choosing to travel by a small single-masted ferry around the mouth of the Barren River, rather than risk trying to cross its foul waters where the river dou-bled back on itself north of Phlan. More than two hours after they debarked, they could see the high walls of Valhingen Graveyard off to the west.

"That's the place where my brothers died," said Tarl, pointing at the high timber fence. "In Vaasa, there is no city as large as Phlan. We believed at first that those wooden walls were the fortress around the city. We were already within the gates before we knew. . . ."

Shal and Ren said nothing. The pain of Tarl's recollec-tion was palpable.

"I will return here and, with Tyr's help, fight the vile creature that tricked me into parting with the Hammer of Tyr."

"*You* lost the hammer?" asked Shal, aware that Tarl had previously made oblique references only to the fact that the hammer was lost in the graveyard.

Tarl made no response at first, then began haltingly to describe the full horrors of his first day in Phlan. The time since that day had weighed heavily on Tarl, and he felt a rush of cleansing energy just from speaking truthfully about his encounter in Valhingen Graveyard. He described each moment he had omitted from his earlier descriptions—his terror when the skeleton hands had reached up and gutted the horses, how he had forgotten the words to clerical spells he had known for a year or longer, the fight—enchanted word cast against cursed word—between Anton and the vampire, and finally how he had foolishly given up the hammer in exchange for freedom instead of using it to fight the vampire.

By the time he finished, he realized they had ridden past miles of countryside, and he had seen none of it. The others had remained silent throughout his tale. It was only after they stopped for the night, when Tarl told them his plan for retrieving the hammer, that Ren spoke.

"You'll never get through that place alone," Ren said as he unpacked the mare. "As soon as we get this river cleaned up, I'll go with you."

Tarl turned from where he stood unpacking Cerulean and faced Ren. "No, friend. This is my fight. The ruler of Valhingen Graveyard holds in his hands my heritage and my pride. I must seek vengeance for my lost brothers, and I must take back that which belongs in the most holy place in the Temple of Tyr."

"I'm not saying you don't have an appointment to meet up with that vampire," said Ren. "I'm saying you won't make it to his lair without help. How many of your brothers—men strong in their faith—died before you even saw the vampire? What do you think—you're going to say, 'Take me to your leader,' and the skeletons and wraiths are going to bow and let you walk by?"

"With Tyr's strength—"

"With Tyr's strength, you'll face the vampire *after* you've let me help you get past the riffraff."

"And me," said Shal. "I'll help, too."

Tarl simply shook his head. He would not endanger the others. He would challenge the vampire on his own, but there was no point in arguing the fact. He would make his move when they returned.

For now, he sat down across from Shal and thanked Tyr once again for sparing her. His assignment from his god was too much of a pleasure to be a burden: Shal's mission would lead to his own. In her, he would find strength. He watched for a time as she diligently studied her spellbooks. Then he looked to his own books and began to think about what he must do in the days ahead.

Shal, too, was thinking—about facing Yarash. She didn't think she had mistaken the combination of awe and animosity Cadorna felt toward the wizard. She felt this challenge would possibly be for her what facing the vampire would be for Tarl—surely not a personal challenge such as his, but a test of newfound strengths and skills against an experienced sorcerer. Shal had grown much in her magic in the short time since Ranthor's death, but Yarash was, from Cadorna's accounts, a wizard with talents that perhaps rivaled even Ranthor's. Cadorna insisted the wizard was not evil but crazy, and that he would attack on a whim, in keeping with his own chaotic nature. Spell against spell, Shal knew she could not hold up against so formidable a wizard. She could only hope that with the help of her friends, the Staff of Power, and her sheer physical strength, she would stand at least a chance.

* * * * *

By the time Shal woke up the next morning, nightmare dreams of violent lightning bolt feuds still fresh in her memory, Ren had already taken care of the horses and packed up everything except her bedroll and Tarl's, which she noticed was teasingly close to her own. Ren held up his finger to his lips to shush Shal so she wouldn't bother Tarl, then he reached out his hand to help her up. He continued to hold her hand even after she was standing and led her toward a clear brook that fed its pristine waters into the black bile of the Barren River.

"I've tried before to tell you . . ." Ren began awkwardly. "That is, before, I wanted . . ." Ren stopped again, groping for words. "You remind me so much . . ."

"Of Tempest. I know." Shal looked down into the clear water. Every stone was visible, even in the deepest parts of the stream. The morning sunlight sparkled off the clear water and shone off the submerged leaves of the silverweed that lined the stream's banks.

"I've wanted so many times to tell you how much I . . . But the other night, I finally put Tempest to rest, Shal. I said good-bye to her once and for all. I know that a part of what I've felt for you has been tied up with my feelings for her. . . ."

Shal reached for Ren's other hand and searched his sapphire-blue eyes with her own. "And now we can be friends and see where that takes us? Is that what you want to say?" Shal smiled and held Ren's hands tightly in her own.

Ren had noticed Shal watching him a dozen times or more. He knew she was attracted to him. How could she so easily understand and accept that he was asking only to be friends? He had not wanted her to be hurt, but he had expected her to show at least a glimmer of regret. Yet here she was, smiling, her green eyes twinkling as though she were delighted with the news.

"I'm no fool, Ren. You should realize that by now. I know your stares and attention were really directed at a memory."

Ren let his hands drop to his sides as Shal relaxed her

grip on them.

"I'm happy to have the chance to be a friend to you on my own, without the help of your love for Tempest. I've appreciated your attention, really, but I always knew it wasn't directed at me. Now, if there's still some attraction between us, it should be genuine. . . . Besides, Sot introduced me to Jensena and tried to warn me I had some competition. I tried to tell him she's more your type, but—"

"You . . . you sure have a way of putting a fellow in his place."

"Ren, how do you expect me to react?" Shal tossed her red hair back over her shoulders and extended her hand toward the big man. "Friends . . . again?"

Ren clasped her hand firmly. "Friends . . . still . . . always."

"A good enough friend to help against a crazy old wizard whose actions are no concern of yours?" Shal asked.

Ren didn't answer right away. He waited till they were back at the camp near Tarl, who was just waking. "I don't know just how Yarash is polluting the Stojanow River, but his actions are my concern, too. I can't stand to see that river like that. There's no reason why the Stojanow shouldn't be as pure as that brook over there. Instead, it's as black as night and reeks like some festering wound. It's bothered me since the day I first saw it. My first thought was of a black snake surrounded by dead and dying plants and animals. . . .

"As a thief, I could say it isn't my affair, but I'm beginning to discover that rangering is a deeper part of me than I realized. I can't ignore the state of this river any more than I could ignore that ruined garden back at the gnoll camp. I'm more committed to this mission than I have been to anything we've done so far." Ren offered Tarl some water from his pouch and several strips of jerky, and then he helped Shal roll up her bedding.

Finally he mounted his horse and waited for Shal and Tarl to mount Cerulean. "I've decided to return to rangering," Ren said softly.

Both Tarl and Shal turned in the saddle to face him.

"It's a more difficult lifestyle, but it puts me closer to nature . . . and to myself. If I had followed my instincts, I probably would have made this trip weeks ago, when I first arrived in Phlan. Just look at that river! It doesn't only look and smell dirty; it's actually toxic. Somewhere upstream, it has to be pure, because dead fish float ashore, and you know nothing can possibly live in that water. It even permeates the land. Look at those gray tree trunks lining the riverbanks—a fire would do less damage."

"Rangering is an honorable profession," said Tarl. "I know not everyone chooses to be like a cleric in their spirituality, but I'd think you'd find comfort in the added fulfillment of being a ranger."

"Yeah. It's kind of a calling, I guess. I mean, I have a natural knack with animals, and once I learned how to trail, I never forgot it. Besides, there's something that drives me to see nature set right."

Ren patted his horse as they rode. "This mare was abused, and her owner said she was worthless. I won her in a dagger toss. I never did anything special—just talked to her and treated her right—and she's been the finest horse I've ever had."

She sleeps around, interjected Cerulean. The mare whinnied, and Shal chuckled.

"How would you know?" Shal asked aloud.

Ren bridled at her words, thinking they were meant for him. "What's wrong with my horse?"

"No, it's . . . nothing," Shal said quickly. "It's Cerulean. He said . . ." Shal grinned weakly and then pointed at the mare. "He said your horse sleeps around."

Ren pulled the mare around eyeball to eyeball with Cerulean and said in a loud falsetto, as if he were speaking for the mare. "Oh, yeah? How would you know, big fella? You got—" Ren stopped suddenly in midsentence and motioned for the others to keep quiet. In the stillness that followed, Shal and Tarl could make out what Ren had heard. From not far off came the sounds of something crashing and thrashing through the brush—and the unmistakable snorts and grunts of a party of orcs!

Shal didn't wait for any word from Ren or Tarl. She spurred Cerulean around and headed for a nearby thicket. As the big horse charged, Shal let out an ear-splitting war whoop. Tarl added a bloodcurdling cry of his own and leaned back away from Shal to swing his hammer through the air with a vengeance that made it hum. Five orcs burst from the thicket near where Ren waited. He caught the first of the orcs in his huge, bare hands, stuffed its head under one huge arm, and held tight. "Move and he dies!" Ren hissed to the other four.

Ignoring their companion's plight, the orcs charged forward. Ren slit the creature's thick, meaty neck with Left. As its body slumped to the ground, Ren drew one of his short swords with his free right hand and hacked straight down between the neck and shoulderblade of the nearest orc. Blood from the creature's severed jugular spouted high into the air, and the beast danced crazily in its death spasms. By this time, Cerulean had come full around, and the remaining three orcs were hemmed in between the horses and the thicket.

"I know, Tarl. I know," said Ren, spotting the cleric's staying hand. "You want to talk to them, to parley, to find out what a couple of nice orcs like these would be doing in a place like this. Go right ahead. Ask 'em anything you want." To the orcs, he grunted a threat.

"Thanks. I will." Tarl did not miss the fact that the orcs' eyes were glazed yellow, like those of the gnoll priests. "Ask them about Yarash. See if they know anything.

Then ask them about the pool—where it is, what they know about the Lord of the Ruins."

Ren snuffled, snorted, and clicked his tongue in the crude language of the pig-men, and they sniffed and snorted their responses. Ren interpreted. "They claim they don't know anything about the river—they say it's always been this way. Said they like the smell—what's the problem, anyway? . . . They're building some kind of tower—a templelike thing that will stretch the domain of the Lord of the Ruins from . . .

"From where, you big slug?" Ren slammed Left to the ground less than two inches from the nearest orc's foot, then immediately called for the knife to return. The orc's eyes widened as the knife floated through the air, and it blurted out its words in barely coherent clusters. Ren translated, trying to fill in the holes where the creature spoke nonsense. "The castle—the big one at the edge of old Phlan. Castle Valjevo, I think they call it. The oinker says the Lord of the Ruins lives there."

"Tell them to tear down the tower," said Tarl. "Threaten them with Shal's magic . . . and the wrath of Tyr. And then let's get out of here."

As if on cue, the three orcs suddenly charged Cerulean with their pikes extended. Shal uttered the words of a spell so fast that she hardly had time to extend her arms. Bolts of energy shot from her fingertips, and orc screams filled the air. To the one that lived, Ren repeated Tarl's demand that they tear down the tower. "And don't even think about following us!" he added menacingly.

*   *   *   *   *

It was nearly noon on their fourth day of travel when they dismounted at a spot where the poisonous river widened into what looked almost like a broad, boggy lake. Equidistant from both shores stood an island, featureless except for a huge silver pyramid that protruded abruptly from the blackened sand. The three looked on in awe at one of the largest and most unusual structures any of them had ever seen.

To Shal, there was something oddly familiar about the silver pyramid. She scanned it once, twice, then a third time, trying to take in the total image. And then she knew. "The frogs!" she said. "Remember the frogs at Sokol Keep?"

How could I forget?" Ren asked, shuddering at the thought of the slimy encounter. "But what—"

It was Tarl who answered Ren's unfinished question. "The medallion. The medallion the frog wore—it was a picture of this very structure."

The pyramid's perfectly matched, windowless sides shone as the medallion had, as though they were gilded in silver, though none could imagine how such a project could have been completed on an isolated island in the middle of a desolate wilderness. More striking than the building itself, though, was the fact that it was obviously the source of the black corruption that flooded the Stojanow River. From where they stood, Shal, Ren, and Tarl could see plainly that the water to the north of the island was clean and pure. Healthy, verdant trees towered up from the banks upriver from the structure, in jarring contrast to the gray and black stumps that littered the banks downstream to the Moonsea. Thick black sludge was spewing from a great pipe that ran from the southern base of the pyramid into the river. For days, they had ridden within smelling range of the river's abominable stench. Now they were at its source, and the odor was even worse.

They had barely had time to take in the full scene, when suddenly the water to the north of the conduit began to stir. Before their eyes, a column of water rose from the river's surface and began to spout high into the air like a fountain. As Shal, Ren, and Tarl watched, the tower of water took on almost solid form, gushing even higher and then collapsing in on itself to create the shape of a chair, the illusion of a glittering, translucent throne of water. Waves crested along the front, back, and sides of the water throne, gently pushing it, water atop water, toward the three. Though neither Shal, Tarl, nor Ren blinked, none could identify the moment when a grandiose figure, looking like a white wizard out of children's lore, appeared on the eerie magical throne. His pure-white robes flapped in the breeze. His face was warm, benevolent even, and he made a gesture and shifted the wind so that the stench was no longer carried to their nostrils. "Ho, travelers and friends! Few find their way to my keep. I am Yarash, and I bid you welcome!"

Shal wanted to believe the fairy tale, but the lie was too obvious, the contradictions too many. "Back!" shouted Shal, extending her staff and gesturing toward the conduit. "No wizard of good intentions would allow such corruption to continue!"

Yarash showed no sign of being either offended or flustered by Shal's words. Instead, he responded in the same cheery, lilting voice with which he had first greeted the three. "A product of simple experiments, my dear. My life's goal is to create the ultimate sea creature, an intelligent being to communicate man's messages to the myriad life forms of the ocean depths. Alas, surely you must realize that the biproducts of magic are sometimes not pretty," said the wizard, shaking his head. His chair of water surged and receded, but continued to hover in one place.

"Experiments? Biproducts of magic? Are giant frogs perchance part of your experiments, or are they some of the 'not pretty' biproducts?" Shal challenged.

"Giant frogs?" With the suddenness of a flipped switch, the wizard's voice completely lost its warmth. "You mean, you're the ones? You're the ones who murdered my beautiful creations on Thorn Island?" The wizard's eyes blazed with crazed fury, and his face became contorted in anger. The watery throne splashed back to the surface of the river, and Yarash stood right on top of the now frothing and boiling water. He swept his arms high above his head and brought them down again. His robes instantly turned dark green, and in his hands he clutched an algae-covered rope. "You killed my frogs!" he shouted, and his voice thundered and reverberated across the river.

Suddenly the water began to rise, and the wizard along with it, as if some great tidal wave were about to swell from the depths. But the water parted to reveal the fishlike head, fins, and gaping maw of a huge, kelp-covered sea animal. Yarash was standing atop the flat of the creature's massive brown-speckled head, pulling up on the slick green rope.

The monster reared high, its flagellating tail holding its body suspended above the water like a dolphin. With a sweeping gesture that reminded Shal of a circus showman, Yarash dropped the rope and waved his hands with a flourish. Again he shouted, this time in arcane words, unfamiliar even to Shal, and again his voice boomed across the water and back. A deafening hum filled the air, and all around where the wizard stood mounted on the dancing sea monster, torrents and eddies appeared in the river water, a dozen or more highly exaggerated versions of the rippling a bystander would notice as a trout came to the surface to gulp a fly. Carplike heads the size of men's bobbed and poked out of the water, their wide brown lips gaping and closing. Yarash's words continued to reverberate in the river valley, and the giant fish plunged forward across the river toward Shal, Ren, and Tarl.

"Halt!" shouted Shal, but the water near the shoreline churned and the fish heads appeared again, much closer.

This time, though, they rose straight up from the water. Mage, ranger-thief, and cleric took a frightened step backward as the fish heads' bodies came into view. The creatures were neither fish, amphibian, nor humanoid, but a sick crossing of the biological classes. Awkward, overly long fins beat the air where arms should have been, and thick, scaly torsos ended in stunted, barely separated legs. As the creatures lifted themselves from the water, their breathing became a labored sucking through the gills, but Yarash kept up his conjuring, and the misfit fish-men slogged closer. The wind changed directions, and the stench from the creatures was staggering, like the stink from the Stojanow multiplied and remultiplied.

Ren gulped for air and charged forward, lunging at the first of the grotesque beasts to emerge from the water. He stabbed deep into its gut with one of his short swords and pulled straight up through the torso. By rights, the thing should have died, but no blood poured from the body. Instead, a dark, tarry ooze seeped from the wound like dirty pus. Worse, the creature showed no sign whatsoever of pain, and before Ren could distance himself for another attack, it began flailing his head and shoulders with its fins and ramming him with its putrid, scaly body. Ren swung for all he was worth, even as he fell backward, and his sword sliced a deep gash across the fish-man's pelvis.

By this time, more fish-men were closing in. Tarl charged with his shield and slammed with his hammer, but the creatures were impervious to his attacks. Not wanting to waste the Staff of Power's charges on such mundane beasts, Shal put all of her strength behind her staff and jabbed and stabbed at the hideous creatures with its sharpened point, but it didn't slow them, and now their gaping mouths were spewing a dark green fluid that seared and burned wherever it spattered against flesh. When she felt the scalding, searing acid eating through the skin of her neck and hand, Shal changed her mind about the degree of danger presented by the fish-men. She scrambled to gain enough distance from her foes to wield the staff.

Ren did his best, meanwhile, to recover his balance and continue his attack against the first of the fish-men, but others started circling. He wielded both short swords as furiously as he was able. He chopped a wedge out of the torso of one, and it bent on top of itself, but the creature still lived, still fought on. Chop and hack as he might, Ren could not stop the creatures from flailing and spewing forth their deadly poison.

"Get back!" Shal shouted to her companions, afraid that using the staff would threaten Ren or Tarl, who were nearly surrounded by the fish-men. But they could not retreat, and it was all Shal could do to keep the fish-men away from herself.

Tarl discovered he was able to push the fish-men off balance, and he was doing his best to do that in hope that either Ren or Shal would somehow be able to finish off the creatures. Push, swing. Push, swing. Again and again, Tarl slammed into their rubbery, scaly bodies with blows that would have pulverized a humanoid. Finally Tarl released his hammer with the smooth spring action Brother Anton had taught him. It caught one of the fish-men square in the eye. For the first time, fishy flesh and bone splattered and shattered. The carplike head caved in, and the fish-man flopped to the ground, twitching and jerking in the throes of death. "Aim for their heads, their eyes!" yelled Tarl. "That's where they're vulnerable!" Even as he shouted, he wheeled to face another of the ghastly beasts.

Shal and Ren heard Tarl's cry and acted immediately. Ren swung high and viciously with his swords. With the efficiency born of her impressive strength, Shal used the staff to skewer eyeballs. Fish heads rolled, and within a few moments, an unnatural calm reigned where chaos had been supreme just moments before.

From his vantage point high atop the giant sea monster, Yarash let out an anguished moan, a soul-piercing, pitiful cry, and began another incantation. At his command, more vaguely humanoid amphibians, frog-men gone awry, slogged through the water toward the three. Each creature seemed more horrible than the last, and all struggled under the burden of cruel deformities—distorted body parts, missing eyes and limbs, hideous appendages that appeared to have been added as an afterthought.

Shal commanded her own most powerful conjuring voice to speak to Yarash. "What manner of abominations do you send our way? If these tortured creatures are your creations, how dare you call yourself a wizard?"

"How dare you speak to me in such a tone, apprentice!" Yarash raised his hands skyward, and lightning crackled in the air. He spoke a sharp word of command and pointed at the three companions. With the movements of defective zombies, the river creatures closed in to attack.

"Don't do it!" shouted Shal to the wizard.

Ren and Tarl raised their weapons, prepared to fight the approaching monsters, but Shal motioned them back, at the same time uttering four arcane syllables to the Staff of Power. Balls of flame rolled from the end of the staff, and Yarash's creations ignited like so many giant torches. Their miserable existences ended in even more miserable screams, but it was Yarash's scream that would stay forever etched in Shal's memory. Every hair on her body bristled as he shrieked in a combination of rage, horror, and devastation that would have been no more terrible had it come from a mother watching her firstborn put to a slow and painful death.

"Bitch! Bitch, be prepared to die!" the wizard shouted

in a voice tainted with panic and frenzy. Magic missiles, spheres of flame, acid-tipped arrows, and lightning bolts burst from Yarash's fingers in rapid succession as he called on all his resources to destroy the intruders. The deformed brush all along the shoreline immediately burst into flames, and a bolt of lightning struck Ren's mare in the chest, killing her on the spot. Cerulean blazed a vivid purple from the profusion of magical energies all around him, but as he remained vulnerable to attack. Shal and Tarl acted at once to dispel what magic they could, while Ren dodged for his life.

As soon as Shal found a spare moment, she leveled the Staff of Power at the huge fish-beast beneath Yarash, then at Yarash himself, and pronounced the arcane words to call forth its full power. Lightning ripped through the air, jagged and blinding. The bloated sea monster exploded as if it were under pressure. Green, acidlike goo sprayed everywhere, and Yarash was blasted into the air. He managed to halt his descent with a hastily summoned spell, but he was still vulnerable to Shal's attack. A bolt of lightning slammed his body back against the pyramid. Electricity crackled all about him as his energies clashed with Shal's, arcing off the metal sides of the pyramid in a violent display of green and purple.

The wizard bellowed in rage and pain and raised his hands skyward to draw new energy from the churning gray clouds above. Shal recognized the gesticulations of a Weather Control spell and fought with all her new-found skills to turn the ferocious winds Yarash was creating back in his direction. Daylight disappeared as tornado fought cyclone for space in the sky and wizard strove against wizard. Shal seemed to thrive on the raw power that surged through her body in the exchange. With Cerulean's mental aid, she fought to maintain the precious concentration needed to hold back the magical winds. At the same time, Shal brandished the Staff of Power once again. Yarash released the winds and leveled his hands toward Shal. With one word, even as Shal spoke the command to activate the staff once more, he let loose a force of energy that ripped the Staff of Power from her hands. In the same instant that the staff's second lightning bolt exploded against Yarash's chest, silhouetting the wizard's bones through his robes and skin in its brilliance, the staff burst like a piece of crystal, sending wood fragments flying in all directions.

"The staff!" Shal shouted, reaching out desperately toward where she had last seen it. Before she could think to try the Wand of Wonder or a magical spell, Yarash vanished, leaving what was left of his tornado to be devoured by Shal's. Within moments, the unnatural winds collided, lost most of their magical force, and drifted off to the north. The quiet that ensued was uncanny. Ren and Tarl still stood nearby, their mouths agape with awe over the display of power they had just witnessed.

Shal remained tense and her muscles taut as spent energy dissipated through her body. Cerulean's color faded rapidly, an inadvertent barometer of the forces dispelling through the air all around them. Time passed unreckoned before Shal finally broke the eerie peace. "He lives yet. He teleported himself to safety."

Shal's words jarred the two men from their stunned silence. Tarl rushed to Shal and wrapped his arms around her. The big woman's muscular body went completely limp, and Tarl could only slow her collapse to the ground.

"I've—I've never seen anything quite like that," Ren said simply. "Will she be okay?" Ren looked to Tarl, and in his eyes he could see the fear that blanketed his friend's face. "Can you help her?"

"I—I don't know," Tarl responded numbly, and he shook his head. "My god, she's powerful! . . . But even as strong as she is, her body wasn't ready for that kind of expenditure of energy."

He closed his hands around both of hers and uttered a prayer of restoration and rejuvenation. In moments, he could feel a pulse of warmth and renewed strength building in Shal's exhausted body. As with the other times he had healed Shal, he was nearly overwhelmed by the bond that flowed between them. He felt as though he were only a whisper away from sensing all of her emotions, and for the first time, he was certain that she shared the bond. When she opened her eyes and stared directly at him, he knew she did.

"Are you okay?" asked Ren, stooping down beside Shal. She nodded, and he cuffed her gently on the shoulder. "I don't ever want to be on the other side of a fight with you, woman. I never felt so helpless in all my life. My swords and daggers could've been butter knives for all the good they would've done me against you or Yarash."

Shal sat bolt upright. "We've got to find him! He won't stop making those creatures, those abominations. He's obsessed. It's the generation of those perverse creatures that pollutes the river, and he thrives on their creation. I'm no mind reader, but during the battle, I could feel his presence, his essence. He's crazy—completely chaotic. And his obsession doesn't end with the Stojanow River."

"Can you get us out to the island?" Ren asked. "I know you've probably already used your quota of magic for at least the next week, but—"

"For a month or more, I think," interrupted Shal. "I don't think I can do it."

Tarl reached out and gently helped her to her feet. "Take your time," he said.

Still shaky, Shal slowly walked over and patted Cerulean. "I don't think I'd have come through that without you, big fella. Thanks."

Cerulean stamped one hoof but kept his thoughts to himself until Shal held out the Cloth of Many Pockets.

I'll stay right here, thank you! Cerulean sniffed.

"No, please. I have an idea. I know I don't have the strength to teleport all of us to the island, but I believe I can teleport myself."

"You can't go out there alone!" Ren and Tarl spoke as one.

"Shush." Shal waved her hand at the two. "Cerulean, you have to tell me something. Are you able to go in the cloth because you're magical, or can anybody do it?"

It has nothing to do with me, Mistress, though it does take a certain amount of concentration.

"How's that?"

I could walk right up to that cloth and bump into it. Unless I was planning to go inside, I wouldn't. I have to kind of get myself prepared for it—mentally, I mean. I dislike going in there, so I always pretend I'm going to land so hard in there that I'll rip the pocket, and then I won't have to do it anymore. Do you follow me?

"Yes . . . and I think it'll work," Shal said aloud.

"What?" the two men exclaimed together.

"I don't have the energy to transport all three of us across the river, but if the two of you can get inside the cloth with Cerulean, I think I can fly myself over."

Cerulean folded his ears down against his head and pawed the ground thoughtfully. *Since you put it that way . . . Tell the two gentlemen to observe me closely. Be sure to explain what I just told you about getting prepared mentally.*

Without a sound, Cerulean leaped forward and poured into the cloth, where he immediately proceeded to expound on the virtues of a well-lit environment.

Tarl and Ren both looked at Shal skeptically as she repeated Cerulean's advice. Ren paused to collect his thoughts, then jumped toward Shal, but he stopped short before crashing into her, unconvinced that he could really pour himself into such a tiny space. Even

Tarl, with his clerical skills, could not keep doubt from hindering his attempts to enter the cloth.

"Enough!" said Shal. "I don't know what I'll have left when I face Yarash, but I'm going to cast a Shrink spell."

Neither Ren nor Tarl had any opportunity to object. A moment later, they were mere fractions of their former size. A gigantic Shal stooped over, picked them up, and deposited them in the cloth. Another moment later, they were all on their way to the sorcerer's island with the aid of a Fly spell.

On the shore of the island, Shal pulled Tarl out. The Shrink spell wore off moments later, and he was back to original size and standing beside her. "Boy, it sure is black in there!" he exclaimed.

"So I've heard." Shal said Ren's name and reached for him, but nothing came within her grasp.

"Ren? Can you hear me?" Shal said excitedly. "Cerulean, is he in there with you?"

Suddenly the big man popped out of the cloth as if he had been shot from a gun. "By the gods, I've been to the Abyss and back! It's blacker than the Pit in there, and it's not all that easy to get out."

"Okay, okay! So it's dark in there. Can we get on with this?" Shal vowed silently to get Cerulean a lantern to take with him for future stays in the dark folds of the cloth.

To Ren's keen senses, the smells of lightning and charred cloth were still recognizable. Set flush with the pyramid and barely discernible even up close was a teleport platform. A smudged footprint was the only telltale sign that made the surface of the platform visible. Ren pointed the teleport surface out to Shal and Tarl, then explained, "This should take us to him."

They took position on the platform together, and immediately found themselves inside what they had to assume was the dark interior of the pyramid. An empty hallway stretched before them, but Yarash was nowhere in sight. "He's been here," said Ren, sniffing, his keen eyes darting from side to side. They walked the length of the long corridor, Ren as alert as a fox to any sight, smell, or sound. They passed doorway after doorway, but Ren didn't even pause. "There!" He pointed suddenly. "Another teleport platform!"

Ren led the way, and three teleports and a walk upstairs later, they came upon Yarash, sitting against the corner of a room filled with books and ledgers, obviously his personal study. His robes were seared to his body, and his flesh was horribly burned, but he was still able to summon another contingent of fish-men. With no water, the strange creatures gasped for air, their malformed gills heaving and collapsing with such effort it seemed they would drop, but instead they crowded forward as their counterparts had, threatening the adventurers with their bulk and poison spittle. This time, there were no surprises. Shal, Tarl, and Ren went straight for the creatures' oversized heads and gawking eyes. In moments, their flopping, twitching bodies and decapitated heads littered the floor. Shal knew the wizard's paltry effort signaled his defeat, but she did not anticipate his next move.

As the last of the creatures flopped and twitched on the floor in death, Yarash began to rant. "Killing my creations! All my research, gone! You can't carve my brain! You won't get my secrets! You'll never get my secrets!" And before they could reach him, he had disemboweled himself with his own dagger.

"Tyr and Tymorah!" Tarl pressed his hands against the spasming body to stop its grotesque twitching. "What do you suppose the sick fellow was thinking of?"

"It looks to me like the answer might be in those ledgers," said Ren. He wasted no time getting started on a search of the sorcerer's belongings. "Bloody divination!"

he shouted as he rifled through one of the larger ledgers. "Look at these maps! He was going to try to contaminate the entire Moonsea and use those freaks of his to control things! He was sicker than—"

"Cadorna," said Shal, who had also started poring over the ledgers. "Yarash's notes are thorough. Cadorna knew everything. Look at this! The councilman didn't send us to check out a rumor or even to stop the pollution. He knew exactly where he was sending us. He did it to get the ioun stones."

Ren moved behind Shal and started reading over her shoulder. "Would you look at that? Yarash wasn't even going to give the stones to Cadorna. The Lord of the Ruins had offered a higher price!" Ren stopped cold and then began reading aloud. " '. . . I can't imagine what all the fuss is over a couple of rocks. The dragon has dispatched assassins to Waterdeep and beyond, looking for the stones, and now the councilman wants *me* to give them to *him*. . . .' "

Ren's eyes were wide. "The Lord of the Ruins—he sent the assassin to kill Tempest!"

Shal reached out and patted Ren's arm soothingly. Then she pointed to an entry in another ledger and started reading it aloud. " 'Thank goodness Porphyrys has followed the instructions of the Lord of the Ruins this time and had those two interfering windbags killed. Between the red mage and that blue fellow, they were seriously depleting my supply of experimental stock. . . .' " Shal could read no further.

"I've seen enough!" she said. "I wanted vengeance. Now I can get it. I want Cadorna to pay for this. Between these writings and what the three of us know already, I think we can convince the First Councilman of his guilt."

"If we can't," said Tarl, helping Shal load the ledgers into the Cloth of Many Pockets, "there's more than one bad apple on the council."

Outside, the pyramid still looked like a giant bauble protruding from the landscape, but Yarash's abominable creations had ceased forever. The conduit that had pumped the vile byproduct of his unnatural magical creations into the Stojanow was still, and the last of the black sludge had begun its slow journey downriver to the wide expanses of the Moonsea.

❧ 11 ❧

Valhingen Graveyard

The trip back, without the mare, was slow, in places arduous. Even with Cerulean carrying all their equipment, it was taking the three nearly twice as long to return to the city as it had to travel to the sorcerer's island. No one was complaining, though. In fact, all three of the companions were lost in thoughts of their own.

Ren was thoroughly enjoying what was proving to be a quiet return journey. He realized that the victory against Yarash had been Shal's, but as he watched the Stojanow's waters begin to wash away the black poison from the sorcerer's pyramid, he felt an unrivaled sense of achievement. He looked at the brown riverbanks and imagined what they would look like in another year, with healthy new grasses spreading across the now-barren earth and the first saplings poking their leaves above the ground. The recovery would be far from instantaneous, and the gray stumps would remain for years, ugly reminders of one man's gross abuse against nature, but the healing growth would be a signature of hope.

Ren realized that an entire lifetime of thieving in the city wouldn't give him half the sense of purpose he'd felt on the missions to Thorn Island and the gnoll stronghold, and contributing to the purge of the Stojanow had done more for his spirit than any loot he had ever stolen as a thief.

Ren was as ready as he would ever be to accompany Shal as she sought Cadorna's punishment for the slaying of her mentor, and he had already made up his mind to ignore Tarl's insistence that the young cleric face the vampire alone. But most of all, Ren was ready to face the Lord of the Ruins himself, whoever he was—the real murderer of Tempest.

In this quiet interlude as the cleric and his companions hiked the length of the rejuvenating Stojanow, Tarl meditated on the messages he had received from his god when he met him in the innermost sanctuary of the temple. In the same moment in which he comprehended that his healing powers would be greatly enhanced by the ioun stone, Tarl had also learned that Anton could not possibly recover until the master of the word embedded in his forehead was banished from this plane. The tremendous joy he'd felt when he healed Shal was nearly overshadowed by the fact that, try as he might, he could not heal Anton. Neither would Tarl recover the Hammer of Tyr and avenge the deaths of his brothers until he saw the destruction of the beast that ruled over the graveyard.

Tarl's faith had carried him through Sokol Keep, and it had driven him through the gnoll encampment. He wanted very much to believe that Tyr would see fit to aid him against the vampire, but the memories of the sounds—the soul-rending shrieks of the horses and the agonized screams of his dying brothers—challenged his faith over and over again. Tarl had never known such fear, and as much as he wanted to destroy the vampire and its minions, he was also terrified of facing them.

Shal was still thinking about her confrontation with Yarash. The terror she had felt initially at confronting the powerful sorcerer had turned to exhilaration as her mastery of the weather challenged his and she was able to match him spell for spell in magical combat. She understood now that she had failed at her Weather spells earlier simply because it had not been important enough for her to succeed. She had learned the invaluable lesson that a spell's intensity could be magnified many times over by the attitude of the caster. It had not been until she was able to channel her own raw fear and use it against Yarash that her power over the cyclone had become complete and she was able to cast spell after spell in rapid succession.

The fact that the Staff of Power was gone was just beginning to sink in. Without the staff for protection, Shal could no longer think of spell memorization as routine or idle. If she had faced Yarash without the staff, she would have been forced to cast a Lightning Bolt spell of her own. Her life and the lives of her friends would have depended on the spell's success. She could never again afford to look at her magical studies as mere academic exercises. Every time she committed a new spell to memory, it would be in preparation—preparation to do whatever necessary to see to the conviction of Porphyrys Cadorna, preparation to aid Tarl in his quest at Valhingen Graveyard, and preparation to help Ren as he sought the beast responsible for the murder of Tempest.

They waited near the mouth of the Stojanow for a full day before the ferry finally arrived. All three of them felt relief when, two hours later, the small sailing vessel finally approached the docks of Phlan. Though Shal, Ren, and Tarl each called another place home, Civilized Phlan had become a home between homes for all of them, and the sight of the sturdy walls surrounding the civilized city was comforting. None of the three particularly sought fame or recognition, but they knew that they would soon receive the accolades of the city and the town council for their success in halting the pollution of the Stojanow River. The proof of their deed would be evident within a matter of days as fresh, untainted water would wash the last of the sorcerer's black sludge into the Moonsea, where it would be diluted millions of times over, and finally come to rest deep in the great body of water.

As the ship's captain maneuvered his vessel closer to the docks, Ren nudged Tarl and Shal and pointed toward the shore. A row of soldiers stood at ten-pace intervals the length of the shoreline and the docks. All were identically outfitted in black, with chain mail vests depicting an archetypal demon's eye on a red crest. "The Black Watch," observed Ren. "Cadorna must've convinced the council to replace the town guards with them."

"Why such heavy protection along the docks?" asked Shal.

Ren shrugged. "There's probably been quite an influx of riffraff since word got around that two new sections of Civilized Phlan have been opened up recently."

The captain, who also served as crew, hurried back and forth as he first prepared the moorings on the port bow and stern, then expertly guided the ferry in toward the longest of the harbor's piers. The four soldiers closest to the ferry approached hurriedly and made motions as if to help with the moorings, but just as the small ferry eased in alongside the dock, one of the four heavily armed soldiers shouted, "By order of Porphyrys Cadorna, First Councilman of the City of Phlan, prepare to boarded!"

Shal looked wide-eyed at Ren and Tarl. "First Councilman?"

Ren's reaction was instant. "We've got to get this ship turned around."

"But we have evidence against Cadorna," argued Tarl in a low voice. "When we present it to the rest of the council, they'll—"

Tarl stopped in midsentence as he saw Shal and Ren both shaking their heads. They knew there would be no council meeting, no hearing that would result in Cadorna's conviction. In fact, with Cadorna now in the First

Councilman's seat, they knew that the only conviction would be their own. "Didn't you read the sorcerer's notes?" Ren hissed. "Cadorna knows about the ioun stones. He's behind all of this!"

Ren didn't wait for Tarl to agree. Quickly he turned away from Shal and Tarl, hurried to where the captain stood at the stern, and placed a knife tight against the man's neck. "I don't want any trouble. I don't want to hurt you." Ren spoke softly and smoothly. "I just want you to turn this boat around. Now!"

Tarl needed no more convincing. He loped to the bow and grabbed for the mooring rope the captain had tossed out. One of the soldiers of the Black Watch had hold of it, and the other three were approaching to help him haul it in. A fifth had joined the original four and was reaching for a gangplank.

"Ahoy on shore!" Shal shouted, facing the mercenaries and waving her arms in a circle to draw their attention. As soon as they all looked up, she tossed a handful of dust and hurriedly incanted the words of a Sleep spell.

The closest man was overcome immediately. He blinked, nodded, swayed forward and back, dropped his hold on the rope, and slumped forward off the pier and into the water. Two nearby mercenaries shouted an alarm to shore, and one of them bellyflopped onto the dock to grab for the mooring rope, which had been pulled into the water. The rope was still barely within reach, but just as he caught hold of it, he too was overcome by sleep. His eyes fluttered for a moment, and then his head drooped over the side of the pier.

Tarl continued to haul in the line, but the boat hadn't turned yet. The captain wasn't cooperating with Ren. Instead, the feisty sailor jerked his head down and away from the knife, jabbed his elbow hard into Ren's ribs, and staggered forward. Ren lunged to gain a fresh hold on him, but as quick as a flash, the captain pulled a dagger from his belt. Ren quickly drew his own knives and was beginning to circle cautiously, when suddenly the captain spun and hurled his dagger toward the front of the boat.

Ren turned and watched the blade's rapid flight. Poised on the end of the dock, a mercenary stood with a knife upraised, about to launch it at Ren. The captain's blade lodged itself deep in his chest. Desperately he dropped his own knife and yanked the dagger from his chest. Blood gushed from the wound with each beat of his punctured heart, and he clutched his chest in a futile attempt to quell the flow of blood.

"You're—you're with us?" Ren asked wide-eyed.

"Aye. And if ye'd stopped to ask, ye'd have known a good deal sooner. Now get outta my way and keep those devils offa my ship so I can turn her around."

Ren reached Tarl's side at the bow just as the fourth and fifth soldiers began to charge up the gangplank. "Hold it right there!" Tarl shouted threateningly, his hammer raised.

But the soldiers ignored the warning. When they reached the end of the gangplank, they vaulted over Ren and Tarl, then pivoted immediately to face their adversaries. One wielded two short swords, as Ren did, and he and the ranger immediately faced off against each other, one mirroring the movements of the other. The other soldier faced Tarl. In his left hand, he wielded a dagger. In his right, he brandished a vicious-looking whip. Quickly he cracked the whip at Tarl. It smacked with the sharpness of close thunder a mere hairbreadth from Tarl's shoulder, and Tarl instinctively jumped back. Once again the whip snaked out, this time at Shal, who was busy incanting a spell. She never finished it. She tried to dodge, but she wasn't nearly as fast as the uncoiling weapon. The black leather cord of the whip whisked round and round her wrist. Its metal-tipped ends bit cruelly into the flesh of her hand. With one hard jerk, the mercenary yanked Shal off balance. She staggered to one side, and before she could recover, he retracted the whip and brought it down again. It ripped through the chimera leather of her sleeve, and the tips flayed the flesh of her shoulder.

At Shal's cry of pain, Cerulean burst onto the deck, his nostrils flared wide, his ears pressed back flat against his head. The mercenary turned quickly to face the new threat and snapped his whip viciously at the big animal. But Cerulean was oblivious to the danger. He pawed the air with his great, sharp hooves. His muscles rippled as he reared to an awesome height above the man, and his hooves came down like hammers on the mercenary's shoulders.

The man slashed up at the horse with his dagger, even as he toppled backward. His eyes bulged as he saw the huge horse rise up above him once more, and he scrambled and crab-crawled backward, terrified, searching desperately for any nook or cranny that would offer safety from the pummeling hooves. Again the horse's hooves came down, this time on the man's bent legs. They buckled under him, and he rolled to get away.

"Enough!" shouted Tarl, and he braved Cerulean's wrath to try to help the soldier to his feet.

"Don't . . . need . . . your . . . help!" The man's eyes flared in rage as he screamed each word, slashing wildly with his knife. Tarl leaped back out of reach.

Cerulean reared and stomped on the soldier again, but his hooves did not stop the slashing motion of the soldier's hand, and the big horse took a wicked cut that stretched from his cannon to his fetlock.

Before Cerulean could rear again, Tarl darted in once more. He slammed the knife from the man's hands with one swing of his hammer, then cracked the man's skull with his next swing.

Tarl glanced up to see six more soldiers storming the gangplank, headed straight for Shal, who had scrambled to her feet to face them. Tarl reached her side just as the first leaped toward her. The warrior-cleric released his hammer with a snap, and it slammed into the soldier's forehead with explosive force that drove his head and neck backward. At exactly the same moment, Shal completed a Phantasmal Force spell, and the soldier and his companions were driven back as if by a tremendous gale. Two landed in the water, while the other four fell to the dock. At the same time, the captain was finally able to bring the ship around hard to starboard to catch the wind he needed to pull the vessel away from the pier.

Ren was within handshaking distance of his adversary, with sword pressed against sword. Suddenly the soldier gained the advantage, forcing Ren back against the cargo hold. Now the mercenary's swords flashed with the speed of adders' heads—in and out, in and out—jab, thrust, parry. It was all Ren could do to fend them off. At that moment, Cerulean, head down, with all the fury of the pain he shared with his mistress, charged. The horse thudded into the soldier's side with enough force to send him staggering sideways, and Tarl hit him from the other side with his shield. Ren finished him off with a hard thrust through the ribs.

Tarl, Ren, and Cerulean stood still for a moment, and then they heard Shal, hissing the rapid breaths of a mantra for pain control. Sitting awkwardly, she was pressing a rag to the gashes on her shoulder, but blood was seeping through. Her wrist was already purpling where the tips of the whip had wrapped tight around it. Ren and Tarl rushed to her aid. Cerulean limped to her side, whinnying plaintively, blood welling the length of the slash on his lower leg.

"Look!" shouted Ren, pointing back at the pier. "More soldiers are coming!"

The captain had gotten the small ferry scudding along at a fair clip in the brisk breeze, but a small group of the Black Watch had commandeered a small schooner, and they were preparing to cast off the line.

"Can you outrun them?" Tarl hollered back to the captain. "I need time to heal these two!"

"I can try!" the captain shouted back. "How far are ye goin'?"

"The other side of the river," Ren called back quickly.

Tarl looked to Ren for some sort of explanation.

"No matter where we go, they're going to come after us, but they'll think twice about following us into the graveyard." Ren paused. "That's where we were planning to go next, isn't it?"

For a moment, Tarl didn't say anything. Then he nodded quickly and said, "Go help the captain. I'll take care of Shal." Tarl felt trapped. He was fleeing a boatload of pursuing soldiers to return to a place where he knew he would have to face an army of undead. He did his best to quell thoughts of Valhingen Graveyard and focus on what he must do right this minute for Shal.

He started to work on her shoulder first, cleansing her wounds with a wet cloth. Shal sucked in air through clenched teeth each time he dabbed at the stinging wounds. When he had cleansed her wounds, Tarl put his hands on her shoulder. The lacerations were inflamed and painful-looking, but they weren't especially deep. The energy that flowed through Tarl's fingertips was strong, and he could feel the skin beginning to heal at his touch. Then suddenly the smooth tingle of the healing force was interrupted. Tarl realized that one of the whip's tips had bared an earlier wound of Shal's. Tarl remembered it well: Sokol Keep . . . the axe wound. Tarl's faith had not been so strong at that time, and neither were his skills. He had given his best effort, but he realized now that the wound had not healed completely.

Tarl withdrew his hands from Shal's shoulder for a moment as he called for special power from Tyr. Then he placed his hands on her shoulder once more and held tight. Tingling energy surged between him and her as he focused on the deeper, older wound. He could feel the energy purging, expunging the decay, and then he could sense the mending, that wonderful warmth of regenerating tissue. As always, he felt a very special exchange of spirit with Shal. When he was done, the only sign of either the old wound or the new one was the rent leather of her tunic. He said a silent thank-you to Tyr for granting him the ability to heal Shal.

Because of the swelling and bruises, Shal's hand and wrist looked bad, but the cuts appeared to be shallow, abrasions really. It was not until Tarl squatted beside Shal and clasped her wrist in his hands to heal it that he realized that the tails of the whip had buried grime and dirt beneath the skin for the length of the cuts. He said nothing to Shal. She smiled up at him as he worked. Tarl felt the exhilaration of healing one more time, but he also felt a slight drain from using his clerical powers twice in rapid succession.

What about me? Cerulean's question jogged Shal's awareness.

"Tarl, look!" Aghast, Shal pointed at the horse's leg. A pool of blood had formed beside one hoof, and blood was matted the length of Cerulean's foreleg. "Can you help him?" She stood up and put one arm around the big stallion's neck, marveling at the speed and totality of her own recovery.

Without hesitation, Tarl cleansed the gash in the horse's leg. Blood that had started to clot freed up, and fresh blood pulsed down the foreleg, adding to the puddle by Cerulean's foot. Tarl pressed his hands over as much of the wound as he could. As healing energy left him for the third time, Tarl started to sway, and as the wound began to close over, he had to catch his balance with one hand to keep himself from slumping down onto the deck in a faint.

"Tarl!" Shal scrambled to his side. "What's—what's wrong?" she asked, anxiously steadying him with her strong arms before he swooned.

"Just . . . tired," he said in a puff of breath. "Need rest . . . no time . . ."

"Shhhh." Shal pulled Tarl close and whispered the words of a cantrip that would double the intensity of Tarl's rest. Then she turned back to the horse. *Are you okay?* she probed.

It still hurts. He didn't quite finish, but it's stopped bleeding—

"The schooner's getting closer!" Ren's shout carried from the other end of the boat. "Tarl! Shal! Can you help with that sail?"

"In a minute!" Shal shouted back. She laid Tarl down gently on the deck and removed her own healing potion from the Cloth of Many Pockets. Quickly she applied a drop to each of his temples in hopes that its powers extended to rejuvenation as well as physical healing.

In the meantime, Cerulean had made his way to the flapping sail Ren had pointed to and was trying to get hold of it by grasping the untied end with his teeth. He had probably pulled the stay loose when he tried to trample the mercenary, and now he was doing his best to make up for his clumsiness.

Not waiting for Tarl to respond to her treatment, Shal went to Cerulean's aid. She was no whiz at knot-tying, but she did her best to secure the sail. Just as soon as she got it pulled taut into place, the whole sail filled with a gust of wind, and the small ship shot forward. Looking back, Shal could see that the Black Watch's schooner had indeed gotten closer. In fact, it was rapidly approaching arrow range despite the ferry's increased pace.

Shal glanced quickly at Tarl. He hadn't moved. By the gods, she hoped he'd be all right—and soon. For the moment, she did her best to focus her thoughts on the approaching vessel and the magic she would need to stop it. The Weather spells were still the freshest in her mind. She let her body sway gently with the slight rocking motion of the boat. Then she let herself feel the uneven surging and gusting of the southern crosswind. Finally, with a gesture and the mouthing of a spell, she caught the unexpelled force within the gentle wind in the space between her two hands, expanding the force and channeling it away from herself. She directed it to push at the waters surrounding the approaching schooner. Restless waves rolled up from the calm surface of the water, and the entire expanse of sea between the schooner and the ferry began to roil and churn.

Shal pushed with her left hand and pulled with her right, pushed with her left hand and pulled back with her right, over and over again. She watched as the schooner began to spin involuntarily, in the beginnings of a whirlpool. A feeling not unlike electricity tingled up and down Shal's spine, and she relished the sensation of power. Magical power, her magical power, was controlling the very wind and the waves, causing a whole boat to turn round and round. She continued to push with one hand and pull back with the other, push and pull back, faster and faster. She started to repeat the words of the spell, saying them even louder so she could hear herself over the whining wind and the distant screams of the men on the schooner.

Then she felt strong hands grab her from behind, and Tarl's shout broke her concentration. "No! Stop!" He pulled her around to face him. "Don't kill my brothers! There's no need to kill them!"

Shal stared at him, taken aback by his regained strength, but not comprehending his message at all.

Cerulean nosed in and blocked the cleric, pushing him back with his body. Shal took up the spell where she had left off. The waters hadn't stopped swirling. A few movements of her hands and the water was churning with renewed ferocity. The schooner swirled crazily and within minutes disappeared nose-first into the growing spiral. The whirlpool swallowed the boat like a giant maw gulping down an insect. Then the swirling stopped, but the water continued to froth and boil.

Shal spun around and quickly ran to Tarl, who was sitting on the deck behind Cerulean. She squatted beside him and held his face in her hands and made him look at her. "Are—are you okay, Tarl? Do you know where you are?"

"I'm . . . sorry," said Tarl, rubbing his head with both hands. "I was dreaming . . . about the graveyard. It was so real. . . . The vampire was standing right there." Tarl pointed at the rail along the stern, where Shal had been standing only moments before. He killed them . . . my brothers, one after another. He wouldn't stop killing! I'm . . . sorry."

"Hey, it's all right, Tarl. Are you sure you're okay now? Really okay?"

"I . . . I guess I am." Tarl held his hand out to Shal and started to stand. "I feel completely rested, as if I hadn't used my clerical powers in days. I'm just jittery from the nightmare. Is your shoulder all right?"

Shal didn't get a chance to answer because both she and Tarl turned as one when the captain shouted, "Sail's loose again!" and they leaped like a team for the wayward piece of cloth. Unfortunately the winds were wilder than they had been, stirred even at this distance from the whirlwind force Shal had generated, and the sail flapped high, slapping loudly against itself. It slipped teasingly down and then flapped up again before they could catch it.

It took several tries before Shal caught hold of the sail. Tarl retied the knot, and they went to the bow of the boat, where Ren was securing another guy wire at the captain's direction. As before, once the sail was secured, it filled gloriously, and the small ship scudded forward at a brisk pace.

The captain had steered wide to avoid the still-blackened waters at the mouth of the Stojanow River, and now the ferry was finally approaching the opposite shore.

"You'll be wantin' to debark in a hurry," said the captain, addressing Ren. "You can be certain if a ship of the Black Watch goes down, there'll be more followin'. There's no way I can anchor. I'm afraid that horse is gonna break a leg tryin' to make it down to the water. How'd it get on here, anyhow?"

"The same way he'll get off," answered Shal, pointing to the cloth at her belt.

I'll try the gangplank, the horse argued.

And what? Dive off it? Shal pursed her lips, stared him down, and pointed once more. With no further complaints, Cerulean dove in.

"Well, I'll be!" The captain looked in awe at Shal. "I thought that little storm ye whipped up was pretty fancy, but makin' a horse disappear into your belt—well, that's some magic!" He wagged a finger at the three of them and said, "Now, get offa my boat while the gettin's good. The water here should be about ten foot deep, so its safe to dive."

Shal quickly added some of their gear to the Cloth of Many Pockets, then she, Ren, and Tarl dived overboard and swam for shore.

The captain had already turned the ferry away and was well out in the water before the three even made it to the rocky beach.

"So what now?" Shal pulled off her soaked leather

boots and stood in a sandy section of the boulder-strewn beach. "We got out of the city, but the captain was right. The Black Watch will be after us again. And you can be sure they'll let Cadorna know we're alive. We're not accomplishing anything sitting on this beach."

"You're right. We need to get away from the beach," said Ren. "We'll go north and west, toward the graveyard. We'll rest for the night, and then we'll help Tarl get his hammer back."

"No," said Tarl softly.

"I understand," said Ren. "If you aren't ready, I have my own sights set on Valjevo Castle and that gutless monster that sends out assassins to murder women." Ren wiped his salt-caked lips on his sleeve.

"No," Tarl said again. "I'm ready. What I mean is that you won't go with me. I'm the one who lost the hammer, and I'm the one who's going to go get it."

"Be realistic, Tarl," Shal protested. "Just because you're a cleric doesn't mean you have to be a martyr!"

Ren walked around in front of Tarl, put his big hands on his friend's shoulders, and gently pushed him back until he could sit him down on one of the boulders on the beach. "Shal's right. Anyhow, we've been through all this before."

The three argued heatedly until finally Tarl agreed to let Ren and Shal go with him. Since none of them wanted to sit in wet clothes with dusk setting in, waiting for soldiers to follow, they hiked inland, wide of the river, until they were a short distance from the graveyard, in a place with sufficient brush and cover to set up camp. Shal made a smokeless, arcane fire, but unfortunately it was heatless, too.

Ren volunteered to collect some wood. As he saw it, nobody from Phlan would attempt to come this way before morning, if at all. The creatures they had to worry about would more likely be repelled by a fire than drawn to it.

Alone together as they laid out their bedding and prepared a meager meal of dried fruits and meat, Shal and Tarl shared a brief few minutes of awkward silence.

Tarl cleared his throat and spoke hesitantly. "Shal, I really don't know how to say this. I—I know you care for Ren—"

"It's not the same," Shal said softly.

Tarl looked straight into Shal's green eyes. "Meaning?"

Shal held out her hands for Tarl's. She had been so unsure of herself when they first met on the docks of Phlan that she was aware only of his tremendous kindness. Ren's attraction to her had seemed justified somehow by her resemblance to Tempest, but Tarl's she had not fully accepted. Even after he healed her in the temple, she'd felt he might simply be caught in the overwhelming emotion of the moment. But right now, as he grasped her hands and pulled her close and wrapped his arms around her, she knew that Tarl's affection was both strong and genuine. "Meaning I love you, Tarl."

As warm and wonderful as she had felt every time Tarl had healed her, she felt twice as good now. A special electricity, an uncanny awareness of his touch, coursed through her as she felt his fingertips ever so gentle on her neck and back, his soft kiss on her forehead, and then the warmth of his breath in her ear as he whispered, "I love you, too, Shal."

There was a considerable thrashing in the brush nearby, and the two pulled apart instantly and drew their weapons just in time to see Ren returning to their makeshift campsite.

"You're not very graceful for a ranger!" Shal jested, fighting her own embarrassment.

"Every bit as graceful as I want to be," said Ren, smiling wistfully.

Tarl rushed over to help prepare the fire.

"There's no sign that there's been anything more fierce

than skunks or snakes traveling through this stretch of woods any time recently," said Ren. "I think we can sleep without worrying too much."

Tarl still kept a late-night vigil, watching and listening for signs of anything, living or undead, nearby. It was as Ren said, quiet and still except for the lively dancing of shadows from their flickering fire. Tarl sat beside Shal and watched her as she slept, the red cascades of her hair aglow in the firelight. When all remained quiet, he silently pulled his bedroll next to hers and lay down. While the stars rose and fell in the sky, he prayed and communed with his god until he fell into a peaceful, dreamless sleep.

Ren feigned sleep the entire time Tarl kept watch. His mind was churning with thoughts of the morning. Tarl and Shal had both proved themselves as fighters, but Ren was convinced that neither would make it through the graveyard tomorrow. It was too easy to wake the undead, to make a move that would bring them springing up by the dozens as had happened at Sokol Keep. And the undead of Valhingen Graveyard weren't former Tyrian clerics. His mind made up, he allowed himself a brief, restless sleep.

When Tarl and Shal awoke, Ren was gone. Shal's first thought was that he somehow felt alienated because of what he had seen when he returned with the firewood, but Tarl shook his head firmly. "No. He's told me more than once that I didn't stand a chance of getting the hammer back. He believes that, with his rangering and thieving skills, he can get it. I think he went into the graveyard alone."

Shal felt a chill was over her. She had heard Ren say as much yesterday—how the key to passing through a place filled with undead was stealth, and that Tarl's presence, his aura, his medallion, everything about him offended the undead because he was a servant of a benevolent god.

They wasted no time and broke camp quickly. The sun wasn't even completely over the horizon when they reached the gate to the cemetery. A huge lump caught in Tarl's throat when Shal called for Cerulean, remembering the deaths of his brothers' horses. Shal seemed to sense his thoughts and raised a hand to remind him that Cerulean was no ordinary horse.

Looking at the fence now, Tarl wondered how he and the others could ever have thought it was part of the city fortress. "We were country clerics from Vaasa," he whispered. "Just a dozen country clerics from Vaasa."

Shal looked at him questioningly, but Tarl didn't explain. Instead, he squeezed her hand once and then lifted his hammer and shield high before they walked tentatively through the gate. His hammer glowed, and he could feel his holy symbol heavy and cool against his chest as they entered. To look at Valhingen Graveyard today, it could be a park. Asters and black-eyed Susans waved their brightly colored blooms above the tall grasses that grew untended over the gravestones. Purple bougainvillea and other less showy vines covered the handful of mausoleums interspersed here and there within the confines of the walls. Though less than three weeks had passed since Tarl had last stood on these grounds, he saw no sign of his brothers. He said a silent prayer for each of them, hoping that their spirits had managed to escape this place before their bodies were savaged by crude flesh-eaters.

Ren was nowhere in sight, but Shal and Tarl didn't have to go far before they realized that Ren's stealth did not get him across the graveyard unnoticed. Through a swath of parted grasses, they could see scattered skeleton bones forming a veritable pathway along the fence-line of the graveyard.

They followed the fragments, each hoping secretly that Ren had dealt successfully with all the skeletal war-

JAMES M. WARD AND JANE COOPER HONG

riors remaining in that portion of the graveyard. The path of bones was replaced at one point by a path of decayed body parts, the gruesome fragments of several zombies. The pall over the place was palpable, and despite their silent mantras and meditations, both Tarl and Shal were strung taut as catgut on a fiddle, waiting for something to happen.

Tarl took each step as though it meant his life, striving for silence even though he was sure his medallion and magical hammer couldn't go unnoticed in this place of death. Shal followed suit, her Wand of Wonder raised before her. Cerulean was equally tense, stepping with the fluid, silent movements of a cat.

Tarl couldn't help but think the vampire was taunting him with his silence, luring him and Shal ever closer to the heart of the graveyard before he unleashed every miserable creature under his control. One more step, he was sure, and the place would be alive with zombies, wraiths, and specters. The joke would be on him. He could picture the naked vampire, his bloodless skin draped over his emaciated frame. He could hear his skin-prickling voice, coaxing him closer. His sick, hateful laughter pounded against Tarl's ears. No! Tarl raised one hand for Shal and Cerulean to stop. He could not let his fears or the silent persuasion of his foe get to him. He needed to pause a moment before going forward. Inhale the power of Tyr. Exhale the fear of Valhingen Graveyard. Inhale. Exhale. He touched his holy symbol and took another silent step, then another.

The tension shattered as a mutilated zombie bolted from the grass, sending clods of sod flying toward them. Instantly, responding completely on instinct, Tarl whipped his hammer hand forward with the full tension of a tightly wound spring packed behind it, decapitating the pitiful creature with the sheer force of his swing. A faint squeak came from Shal as she started at the sudden movement, and Cerulean's entire coat jiggled for an instant as a jolt of fear charged through his body.

All three hesitated for a moment before going on. Tarl was once again caught up in the sensation that the horrors of the graveyard were being held back, stored up until he, Shal, Cerulean, and Ren, wherever he was, reached the point of no return—literally. Tarl prayed once more to Tyr and pushed ahead as before, moving with painstaking caution. Tarl approached the remnants of a wall that had long since turned to rubble. There were no more bones and no more dismembered body parts to follow. He could only assume that Ren had kept going in the same direction. He stepped gingerly onto the rubble and climbed over the wall as deftly and as quietly as he was able.

Shal and Cerulean were right behind him. *It'll be difficult for me to do this without slipping.* Cerulean warned. Shal reached back to lead the big horse across, but it was she who slipped on the loose limestone fragments, sliding from the top of the rubble pile to the bottom, where her foot collided with the side of a granite mausoleum. Immediately the wooden door was flung open, slamming against the wall, and three horrible apparitions burst from the doorway.

"Wights!" yelled Tarl, charging forward to come to Shal's defense.

Shal had never seen such creatures. Their long hair bristled with filth. Their faces were wild, like men turned beasts, with gaping canine mouths and glaring nocturnal eyes. Their arms were elongated, like an ape's, and their gnarled hands bore claws long enough to inflict lethal damage. The wights separated right away, forcing Tarl and Shal and Cerulean to fight them one on one.

Tarl raised his shield against the wight nearest him. Talonlike claws flailed over and under his shield, and he found it all but impossible to get in a clean swing with his hammer. As fast as he was able to, he returned his hammer to his belt, smashed ahead with his shield, and did his best to splash holy water over the creature. It shrieked in pain and backed away, its flesh burning, but Tarl had not managed to hit any vital area, and much of the precious water went to waste. The creature charged again, and Tarl hurriedly uttered the words of a spell to raise the dead, the only thing he knew of that would stop a wight.

Shal backed up hurriedly, trying to keep enough distance between herself and the nearest wight so that she could utter an arcane command to activate the Wand of Wonder. As awkward as the creature appeared to be in the daylight, its big nocturnal eyes obviously pained by the sunlight, it charged forward, snarling and slavering and lashing out constantly with its yellow-taloned hands.

Just as the wight came near striking distance, Shal finished the incantation for the wand. Instantly flowers sprouted where the wight's claws had been—clean, white daisies with buttery yellow centers.

The wight swiped at Shal with its hands, fully expecting to rake her eyes from her face with one stroke and her bowels from her abdomen with the next. Instead daisies lightly brushed Shal's face and stomach, and the creature recoiled in horror. Shal might actually have laughed if it were not for the wight's furious response. Without wasting another second, it rushed at Shal with its great maw open like a mad dog. Shal couldn't move out of its way fast enough. She just barely had time to blurt a command to activate the Wand of Wonder again. Immediately, so fast that Shal didn't even see it happen, the wight's flesh vanished, and its skeleton crashed against her body. The impact sent her sprawling backward, and she scrambled frantically to get out from under the pile of bones, but the skeleton wasn't animated; the wight was no longer.

Cerulean was glowing purple with fury and magic. Three times he reared and stomped on the grotesque creature in front of him, and three times it managed to claw the flesh of his forelegs as his hooves came down. The magical nature of his attack protected Cerulean from the wight's life-sapping force but not from the pain of the wounds.

Each time the wight's claws combed Cerulean's flesh, blood ran freely, and at the same time, brilliant violet sparks flew, singeing the wight and causing it to cry out in a ghastly screech. It wasn't until Cerulean reared for the fourth time that he caught the wight square on the head and smashed the creature's brains into the ground.

Tarl's spell worked instantly. The spirit of the dead, trapped in the wight, burst from the creature's chest like a great puff of steam. The spirit was free at last, and the wight's hideous body crumpled in front of Tarl like a discarded shirt.

The three would have preferred to take a minute or two to recover. Tarl might even have had the opportunity to notice the blood trickling down Cerulean's legs and do something about it. But the moment of silence following their small victory was broken by the muffled sound of shouts and chants. The voices were eerie, distant, and inhuman, painful and chilling to listen to. They also seemed to have no source. There were no people, no humanoids, no undead visible. Cerulean's ears pricked up, and the horse whinnied and stepped forward past the vault that had concealed the wights. He stopped in front of a small wooden stake that marked a fairly large open area, when his coat began to glow again, this time a soft amethyst.

A trapdoor, Cerulean advised Shal, *marked by Ren's blood. I can smell it.*

"No!" Shal gasped the word.

It's fresh, Cerulean assured her. *Very fresh. He may yet be alive.*

"What is it?" whispered Tarl.

Shal could see the blood herself as she got closer, and she pointed it out to Tarl. "Ren's down there, underground."

There was no more to say. Carefully they removed the sod and canvas, which hid a narrow wooden stairway. The stairs were steep, almost ladderlike, and they led down into darkness. With no coaxing from Shal, Cerulean entered the Cloth of Many Pockets. Tarl clasped his holy symbol and started down the stairs. He whispered a prayer as he descended, a selfish wish that the bottom of the stairs would be unguarded. He met no guards. Yet, even had any been present, he wouldn't have been able to see them, for he was in total darkness. He reached up to help Shal through the entry, and then they stood together in the blackness. Shal didn't want to reveal their presence by using her light wand if she didn't have to, so they waited for their eyes to adjust and find some source of light, however small.

They were guided only by the sound of voices, the same strange chanting and shouting they had heard from above, but it was much closer now. A door, the only one they came upon in the dark, opened to a huge underground cavern. There seemed to be precious little light there, as well, but Tarl and Shal could make out figures—scores of them—in the dim, blue, twilightlike rays of light that barely illuminated the room.

The rays were fractured as they were blocked by zombies, absorbed by the blackness of the wraiths, captured and held in the eerie cloudlike presences of the specters, or fragmented by the bones of skeletons. The effect was the surreal look of a nightmare of the kind in which the haunted dreamer runs and runs through bluish mists and suddenly plummets to terrified wakefulness. Smells of mildew, dust, decay, and death made the dank underground air almost unbreathable, and the devilish chanting of the scores of undead set Shal's and Tarl's teeth on edge.

Suddenly a murmur started rippling from the back of the room, quickly spreading to the front. Creatures began to stir and then turned around in waves, causing the bizarre cold, blue light to fracture in new directions, revealing the undead in the cavern in even more horrible detail. Nausea clutched Tarl's stomach, and he was overwhelmed by unadulterated terror. He knew that Shal's presence, let alone his own, could not be a secret to these creatures.

Suddenly the light shifted again as the roomful of graveyard horrors shifted and parted, leaving an aisle between the two human intruders and the front of the room. At the far end of the aisle stood the vampire. Tarl sensed as much as saw him. "Very goooood," Tarl heard the creature say, and its spooky, condescending voice made his flesh crawl. The vampire lifted the source of the blue light high into the air. Tarl knew before he ever saw it that it was the holy Hammer of Tyr, but its power and its light had been subverted. Half the hammer radiated blackness, while the blue light that remained was barely a reminder of what it once had been. Tarl shuddered as another wave of nausea and fear passed through his body.

The vampire turned toward Tarl and Shal but didn't acknowledge them in any way. He merely twisted the hammer so its dim light shone on the space directly in front of himself. Shal's gut twisted with the hammer when she saw the figure illuminated by the light.

"Ren!" The name choked in Shal's throat as she saw her friend, prostrate before the gruesome creature of Tarl's nightmares. Even from where she and Tarl stood at the opposite end of the room, they could tell that Ren's clothing and armor were in tatters and that his blood was spilling on the ground.

"Welcoooome, huuumans," said the vampire, and then he laughed the sick, uncontrolled cackle of a maniac amused by his own unthinkable deeds. An uncountable number of bony fingers suddenly began prodding Tarl and Shal, nudging and pushing them forward. Tarl fought the gut-wrenching sensation that there was no way out of this pit now that they were inside. He tried desperately to concentrate on the sacred hammer, tried to visualize how and when he could snatch it from the hands of the blasphemous creature at the front of the room.

When more skeletal fingers touched Shal, she incanted the words to a spell and began touching every bony hand, wrist, or arm with which she could make contact. Electricity surged from her hands, splintering and shattering every skeletal arm she grabbed, and she charged forward, trying to reach Ren. Before the skeletons could regroup, she cast another spell, and frigid wind blasted through the room as sheet upon sheet of sleet showered down on almost half of the room. The undead caught in the storm were blinded by it, and Shal could hear the age-old elbows and hips of countless skeletons shattering as they lost their footing and slipped on the ice-coated limestone. Zombies and wraiths shrieked and swore as well, as they, too, slipped and fell on the treacherous coating of ice.

Shal plunged forward through a break in the bodies and was almost to Ren when dozens more undead stepped over their fallen counterparts and pressed closer to her and to Tarl, who had followed close behind. The skeletons were no longer prodding and poking gently. Now swords and other weapons glimmered in the dull light.

Tarl lashed out with his hammer, slamming at every creature within his reach, trying to create an opening so he and Shal could get through. When he managed to find some room to spare, he raised his holy symbol. "Leave us, undead vermin!" he shouted. "In the name of Tyr, leave us!" A blue light flashed. Creatures that looked at it dropped to the ground, screaming.

Shal lifted her hands and began the incantation to another spell.

"Enough!" The vampire's devil voice echoed in the room. "I will have no more of this!"

Shal extended her fingers in his direction and cast a Lightning Bolt spell. A brilliant bolt of electricity X-rayed the room, blinding many of the undead and forcing even the vampire to raise one arm over his eyes as a shield from the awful light. But the bolt never reached its target, the vampire's chest. Instead, the energy of the lightning bolt was deflected by the subverted hammer. Shal never knew what hit her. In the same fraction of a second it took for the bolt to reach the hammer, it also returned and caught her solid. Her body jolted into the air like a tossed sack of flour and came down with the same sick *thwack*.

"No!" Tarl screamed. "No!" He was horrified. He would gladly have died ten times to save Shal.

The vampire roared in delight. "It's just you and me now, *booooy!*" He gloated over the words. "I'm going to have your blood—and theirs—for dinner!"

Tarl could barely see. Tears of rage, fear, and pain burned in his eyes. He ripped his holy symbol from his neck and held it up while he charged toward the vampire like a man possessed. The medallion's blue light shimmered rich and strong—until Tarl flashed it at the vampire. Then, with one turn of the defiled Hammer of Tyr, the light from the holy symbol was extinguished, absorbed by the black light of the hammer. The vampire drew his icy lips in a pucker, as if to spit, and puffed one noxious breath of air from the putrid depths of his lungs.

Tarl was forced to stagger backward.

"Now, now. There is noooo reasonnnnnn to be soooo testy. Deny that foooolish god of yours. Jooooin my army, and I'll see that your friends are given safe passage oooout of here."

"So they can be living vegetables like Anton? No way, devil spawn!" Tarl took a precious few seconds to collect his thoughts so he could attempt to turn the undead vampire. He spoke a hurried prayer, calling for the force of Tyr to rise up against the creature. But Tarl's effort was strangled, stifled by the hammer, just as the light from the medallion had been.

The vampire tipped his head back and laughed, a grating, wicked laugh. "Fooool! I grow tired of these games. Jooooin my army, *now*, or die!"

"Never!" shouted Tarl.

"Kill . . . him!" The vampire said the two words separately, distinctly, and each reverberated the length, breadth, and height of the cavern.

Before Tarl could lift his holy symbol or cast another spell, a dozen wraiths and twice that many specters circled him. Just one touched him, and he felt his body freeze up as though he'd spent hours naked on the great glacier. He tried desperately to lash out with his hammer, to run, to move, anything, but his body had lost its ability to react. All around him, the wraiths' deadly nonmaterial fingers were reaching toward him. If he could force himself to move, he could stop one, two, maybe more before they killed him, but he could never hope to stop them all.

The vampire's laughter rang out again, and Tarl did the only thing he could do. In one stiff movement, he dropped to his knees and called on the full power of Tyr. In less than the time required for a simple prayer, he had to accomplish what had taken him hours at the temple— a complete cleansing and baring of his innermost self to his god, the purging of all fear in exchange for total confidence. In one mental picture, he had to devote his entire being to selfless concern for Shal, Anton, Ren, and the Hammer of Tyr.

On bended knee, Tarl did not even see the workings of his faith. The Hammer of Tyr erupted with the light of the sun. One horrible, bloodcurdling scream escaped the blue lips of the vampire before he and his light-hating minions turned to dust. And then the brilliant light from the hammer bathed the room, shedding the pure, healing power of Tyr on Tarl, Ren, and Shal.

❧ 12 ❧

The Pool of Radiance

"Incompetent clods!" Cadorna shouted. "What does the city pay you for?"

The fifteen assembled soldiers of the Black Watch stood mute before Cadorna in the council chambers.

"Didn't any of you at least see where they went?"

Finally one of the men responded. "I did. Eight of our soldiers pursued them in a small schooner. I was the only one to make it to shore after the wizard-woman sank our boat in a maelstrom—"

"Congratulations, soldier," said Cadorna, his tone dripping with sarcasm. "So you live! I'd expect that from a child. But what exactly do you *know?*"

"They didn't go straight south into the Moonsea. They skirted the mouth of the Barren River and made their way along the shoreline beyond the eastern edge of the city."

"How far beyond? Where exactly did they get off?"

"I didn't see, sir."

Cadorna threw up his hands, then turned to where Gensor stood beside him. "What do you think, Gensor? Do we have any way of tracking them?"

"Not that I know of," answered the mage, shaking his head. Then he lowered his voice and whispered, for Cadorna's ears alone, "Dismiss the others. Have them wait out in the hallway. We need to talk."

Cadorna looked at Gensor curiously for a moment, then did as the mage suggested.

When the two men were alone in the council chambers, Gensor began to speak, enunciating slowly and deliberately for emphasis. "You have no way of knowing where the three are—or where they are going."

"Correct." Cadorna's eyes widened and his voice raised agitatedly as he spoke. "And who knows what Yarash may have told them? It's absolutely imperative to catch all three of them. But how? You yourself said that there's no way to track them."

"Councilman, I hate to be so blunt, but you're missing the point. It's not what they know that you need to worry about. It's what the Lord of the Ruins might get from them. Think about it. . . . Remember your plan to get their two stones and complete the figure of power yourself? If the Lord of the Ruins should catch up to those three and get the two ioun stones they carry, you will lose your chance to usurp power. You will never have the opportunity to rule all of Phlan, civilized and uncivilized alike." Gensor leaned in close to Cadorna and spoke emphatically to make his point. "Honorable First Councilman Cadorna, as your advisor, I urge you to make your move against the Lord of the Ruins now, or you may never have another chance."

"You mean attack the Lord of the Ruins to get his ioun stones and then find the thief, cleric, and mage to get their two?" asked Cadorna.

"Exactly," Gensor said. "Even if you don't get their stones immediately, you should still have as much power as the dragon has now, which is considerable."

"Right you are," Cadorna answered slowly. His eyes gleamed brightly, and he clenched his hands in excitement. He didn't need to wait for Gensor to go on. Immediately he commanded the soldiers of the Black Watch back into the chamber. With Gensor's help, Cadorna explained to them that there was a certain bronze dragon he wanted killed, a very powerful bronze dragon that made its lair at the heart of Valjevo Castle, in the northernmost part of Phlan. "I'm giving you a chance to redeem yourselves," he said to the soldiers. "You stand to earn an unprecedented reward, but be forewarned, I won't tolerate cowardice or stupidity!"

"I'm sure I speak for the others, First Councilman," one of the soldiers at the side of the room called out. "You can count on us."

The mercenaries made hasty preparations for their mission, and just two hours after dawn, under Cadorna's direction, they arrived at the gates to Valjevo Castle.

* * * * *

Silence hung thick in the cavern, like spiderwebs. The stone floor was covered with thick dust. Shal opened her eyes and saw the gentle blue light that filled the room. She did not know what had happened. She was not even sure at first that she was alive. She pressed the heels of her hands into the dust and slowly pushed herself up into a sitting position. Tarl was nearby, kneeling, his hands lifted skyward, an expression of awe and innocence on his face. His silvery hair glowed almost blue in the soft light. The Hammer of Tyr hung suspended in the air just above him, its steel head shining with the vibrancy of molten metal. Shal could also see Ren, still lying facedown near the front of the cavern. Quickly she pushed herself to her feet to run to his side, but before she got there, he was already rousing himself up from the floor.

"Hell of a party," Ren said thickly, rising slowly to his feet. "What happened to our hosts?"

Tarl rose to his feet and joined the others, his face still bathed in light from the Hammer of Tyr. "Gone," he said simply. "Vanquished by the power of Tyr, the same power that saved and healed the three of us." He reached out his arms and pulled his friend and his beloved close.

Tears of relief welled in his eyes and in Shal's and Ren's. Though thoroughly shaken, all three felt strangely rejuvenated and infinitely grateful for their own survival.

They stood together silently, arm in arm, for several minutes. It was Tarl who finally broke the silence. "I feel an incredible sense of relief. Now that the vampire is vanquished, Anton can be healed and I can return the Hammer of Tyr to the temple in Civilized Phlan. I'm not even worried about the guards around the city. It's Tyr's will that the hammer be returned, and nothing's going to stop me from doing it."

Tarl reached out for the floating hammer, but the holy symbol quickly scooted away from his outstretched hand, the way one magnet moves away from another. He reached for the hammer again, and again it moved just out of reach.

Tarl wondered for a moment if perhaps somehow his motives were not right and so the hammer would not come to him. But when the hammer started to float away, he was gripped by a sense of dread, fearing the hammer's power was somehow being subverted again. Maybe the vampire wasn't really gone. Once more Tarl tried to catch the holy artifact. It floated to the front wall of the cavern, precisely above the spot where the vampire had hovered just a short time before. For one terrible moment, Tarl thought the hammer's light was darkening, turning black, but then its blue glow surged strongly and a blinding ray of light flooded the cavern.

Suddenly a blue oval was outlined against the wall behind the hammer. The stone surface within the oval began to shimmer like water under moonlight. As if wielded by some unseen but steady hand, the hammer cocked back and then forward, striking the calm, fluid center, sending out ripples as would a stone tossed into a quiet pool. Concentric rings of water spread from the center to the edge of the oval outline for several seconds.

As the ripples dissipated, so did the shimmering surface, and they could now see that the oval framed a doorway.

The hammer's light illuminated a small interior room beyond the oval doorway. Tarl quickly made for the door, with Shal and Ren right behind. When they could see inside the small room, Ren said, "Teleporter, just like the one Yarash used."

"And obviously I'm supposed to use it," said Tarl, the magical Hammer of Tyr finally settling into his outstretched hand.

"Obviously *we're* supposed to use it," Shal corrected him.

Tarl nodded, and together the three entered the small chamber. Once again the hammer blazed blue in Tarl's hand, for a moment blinding all three, and when its light diminished, they found themselves standing under an archway of strange-looking, sharply spiked shrubbery.

"Careful," Ren cautioned, pointing to the archway. "I've seen this kind of bush before. The thorns are tipped with a natural poison, and the serrated leaves can make some pretty wicked slashes. Don't even try to push aside any loose branches. Step around instead. Some bushes of this variety actually send feelers out, like vines do. They can move as fast as a man's hand, and their touch is deadly. There's plenty of snake venom in the world that's tame by comparison."

Beyond the archway were three narrow paths, one to the right, one to the left, and one straight ahead. All were lined with the same variety of poisonous hedge. Tarl looked to the hammer, hoping to receive some kind of sign or direction, but none was forthcoming.

"Where are we, anyway?" asked Shal.

Ren pointed to a tall, white turret, some distance ahead, the only thing that could be seen above the vicious shrubbery. "Valjevo Castle," he breathed, his voice hushed. "Probably one of the tallest buildings in the

Realms, and according to that party of orcs we ran into on the way to Yarash's, the home of the Lord of the Ruins. This must have been a teleport the vampire used when he needed to see his master."

"It's no coincidence the three of us are here," Tarl pronounced firmly.

"Nope," Ren agreed. "Fate and the gods." He looked to Shal. "If you're ready to meet the bastard who sent Cadorna to kill Ranthor, I'm ready to meet him, too—and to take a chunk out of his hide for murdering Tempest."

"I'm ready," said Shal. "But do we even know what we're looking for or which way to go?" A glance in any direction along the pathways through the tall hedges showed a series of turns. They were obviously inside a topiary maze, and an elaborate one at that.

Tarl spoke confidently. "We'll recognize the evil of the Lord of the Ruins when we find him."

"He's right. I think we should try going straight ahead," Ren said. "I have a hunch that if the vampire visited often enough to have a private passageway here, he probably wasn't forced to go through the whole maze every time he dropped in."

Ren led the way. The path immediately took a jog to the right, then left, where there were two archways leading off from it. They proceeded on straight ahead, then stopped when it came to a **T**. "Wait," Ren said. He sniffed the air, then very carefully touched one finger to the flat of one of the hedge's thick, serrated leaves. "There've been other humans here—recently. They sliced their way through. These bushes are screaming in agony."

"Bushes screaming?" Shal asked in astonishment.

"There's a pain scent from the fluids lost when any woody plant is cut. This hedge has been hurt bad, and in lots of places." Ren looked for a moment like a shaman searching for an aura, his hands outstretched, his nose uplifted to catch scents.

"This way," he said finally, leading them off to the left. Suddenly he stopped and raised his hand to stop Shal and Tarl. "Blood . . ." he whispered. "I smell blood."

Moving even more cautiously, they turned the next corner in the maze. The emblem of the Black Watch greeted them from the chest of a man suspended grotesquely in the hedge. His machete was still in his hand, but it hadn't done him any good once he'd come in contact with the bush's thorns. His skin had already taken on an unnatural color from the poison that had worked its way through his system as fast as the blood circulated in his body. His eyes were bulging, but when his mouth began to move, they realized that he was still alive—barely. With incredible difficulty, he gasped, "Cadorna . . . the bastard . . . didn't care . . . how many of us . . . died . . ."

Tarl reached out to try to heal the man, but he was too late. The soldier's last breath rattled in his throat, and his body hung limp in the thorny hedge. Beyond him lay a companion, another soldier of the Black Watch, also dead, lying facedown with his hand caught up high behind him in the hedge. Across from the two men, the hedge walls had been chopped wide open, wide enough for three or four men to pass through.

"Do you think he meant that Cadorna brought the Black Watch here?" Shal whispered.

Ren nodded. "I can't think of anybody else paranoid enough to let men die just to get through a hedge. I'm sure he's here somewhere. In fact, we might have a chance to get the Lord of the Ruins *and* Cadorna, because I don't see any sign that anybody's come back out through these bushes."

There was no question now which route would lead to the heart of the castle grounds. A nearly straight swath had been cut through at least a half dozen walls of shrubbery, and the two soldiers had died cutting through the final one. Ren wondered how many others had died hacking their way through the hedges. From where he stood, he could see a boot protruding near one hedge wall and a hand sticking out near another.

"Follow me," Ren declared. "Keep low and to the center of the path, as far away from the branches as possible."

Once they emerged on the other side of the maze, they found themselves staring up at the central tower. Its lofty walls were of rarest white marble. At another time, Shal thought, the tower must have been beautiful and pristine-looking, a giant monument to all that was good in the land, but now its every feature reflected the same kind of corruption and defilement Shal and the others had been fighting since their first mission for the town council. Runes of the type often used by black mages marred much of the marble surface of the building's exterior. Despite its light color, the tower appeared to be shrouded in shadow.

Part of the tower had tumbled in on itself. A scaffold had been erected halfway up the damaged portion of the tower, and two ogres lay dead beside it. "That's one fight we missed," whispered Tarl. Shal and Ren smiled. They were all feeling excited and obsessed with a growing sense of purpose, but at the same time, all three were as tense as stretched slingshot bands, so the levity, however brief, brought relief.

Tarl pointed to a huge doorway to the left of the scaffolding. Its monstrous wooden door stood wide open.

"I suspect Cadorna and any men he has left went in that way," Ren said. "Let's see if there's another door."

* * * * *

Cadorna was fit to be tied. The kill fee he would have to pay the Black Watch and the mercenaries' guild was astronomical. Five soldiers of the Black Watch had been poisoned by the bushes, and four more had died facing a wizard who kept trying to pass himself off as the Lord of

the Ruins. When Cadorna finally came face to face with
the dragon, he didn't have enough men left. The six remaining soldiers of the Black Watch had managed to
weaken the dragon considerably before getting themselves killed, and Gensor had managed to make a couple
of magical attacks, but in the end, Cadorna was forced to
flee with Gensor to a nearby room to plan what to do
next.

* * * * *

Shal and Tarl followed Ren cautiously as they circled
the tower. There was a second door of more conven-
tional size on the building's opposite side. It was an ebony
door with an elaborate carving of a dragon on it, but this
door was shut. Shal cast a spell to detect magical traps.
When a yellow aura glowed along the door's perimeter,
Shal summoned Cerulean from the Cloth of Many Pockets. As soon as the great horse touched the door with a
hoof, a yellow mist puffed from the dragon's mouth.
"No!" Shal bit back a scream as Cerulean bolted backward, snorting loudly. Immediately Shal murmured a
cantrip to disperse the poison gas, but the puff of wind
did not come soon enough to keep the first of the poison
from penetrating the big horse's nostrils and lungs. Shal
tried to calm Cerulean, but he was shaking his head furiously and snorting violently in an effort to get the toxic
gas from his lungs.

Tarl pulled a pouch from his belt and tossed some dust
at Cerulean's nose. Immediately the horse began to
sneeze, and he kept it up for several seconds. By the time
the sneezing finally slowed, Cerulean's eyes were bleary
with water and his nose was running thick and yellow.
He snorted once more, but then the fit was over. Shal
wiped his nose and eyes with a cloth and patted his neck.

You okay, big fella? she asked silently.

Cerulean nodded. His breathing was still a little uneven, mixed with sniffles, but the poison was obviously no longer a danger.

Meanwhile, Ren had checked the ebony door for mechanical traps. Finding none, he eased it open. Peering inside the door, Ren could see that the chamber inside was completely open, from the full height of the tower to the depths of the subterranean cavern below. The door opened onto a roomy landing, fenced by an iron guardrail. A black grillwork stairway led down. The walls inside the tower and the cavern below all glowed a brilliant golden color.

"I've seen this somewhere before," Ren whispered.

Behind him, Tarl answered softly, "In the gnoll temple . . . The model looked just like this. He'll be here, all right. This must be the lair of the Lord of the Ruins."

"Do come down," called a warm, avuncular voice from somewhere below. "I enjoy company."

The three exchanged surprised glances, but it was Ren who creeped out onto the landing and peered down into the great golden vault. He saw no sign of Cadorna or the soldiers of the Black Watch, but from the top of the stairway, he could see a crescent-shaped pool, a full-sized version of the model they had seen in the gnoll temple. It glistened with an unnatural intensity, as if it created its own light source. "The pool!" whispered Ren. " 'Power to the pool.' That's it! The blood from the temples is channeled into that pool!"

Beside the pool, partially hidden from view by the landing, stood a great bronze dragon, identifiable by its metallic color as one of the good dragons of the Realms.

"Please come down," the dragon repeated. Again the voice, which echoed through the golden chamber, seemed friendly and had a genuine warmth to it.

Ren had seen three dragons close up before. Each had seemed bigger than the one before, but this one was easily half again the size of any of them. Electricity crackled along the beast's gums and teeth each time it exhaled, and its tail switched behind it nervously.

"A bronze dragon," whispered Ren to Shal and Tarl, behind him. To the dragon, he said, "We seek the Lord of the Ruins."

"Dead," breathed the dragon, puffing a wisp of smoke into the air. "A puny man, but with tremendous magical powers of possession. As evil as anything I've seen in millennia."

"Do you live here?" Ren questioned. He had never heard of a bronze dragon choosing a subterranean lair.

"Yes, honorable Ren o' the Blade. This has been my lair for several of your lifetimes. Greetings to you and your companions, Shal Bal and Tarl Desanea."

All three were startled that the dragon knew their names. Tyranthraxus, the evil possessor of the dragon's mind, recognized their concern and immediately spoke to assuage their fears. "Now, now, there's nothing to fear. You see, your reputation precedes you, and I must say that the length and breadth of Phlan is safer for your presence. In fact, it is your weakening of the power of the Lord of the Ruins that has allowed me to finally free myself of his control. For years, he held me captive here by means of mind control and a form of possession the likes of which I hope died with him. But his rotting body remains here in my lair. I would be indebted to you if you would remove it."

Ren motioned for Shal and Tarl to follow him, and he started down the stairs. Shal called Cerulean back into the Cloth of Many Pockets, and she and Tarl followed.

As the three stood facing the dragon, they were awed all over again by its size. Shal had never been in close proximity to a dragon, and she felt an unreasonable terror creeping through her body as she stared up at the gigantic beast. She realized as she looked on that her fear was not from the creature's presence but rather from the thread of a memory that was slowly being drawn across her mind. ". . . *Beware of the dragon of bronze*." It took her a moment to recall the context in which she had heard the words, but then suddenly she remembered. Ranthor had spoken of the dragon! As he fought with Denlor to defeat the masses of monsters and humanoids that scrabbled at the tower's walls, he had warned her about the dragon of bronze!

At almost the same moment as Shal realized there might be good reason for her fear, Tarl became aware that the Hammer of Tyr, which he was holding at his side, was glowing bright blue in his hand. He could feel more than see the pulsing energy within the hammer, and he caught a glimpse of the dragon blinking as the hammer's rays reflected in its eyes.

"That thing you're carrying . . ." the dragon said innocently. "It's hurting my eyes. Can you cover it, please?"

Tarl lifted the hammer toward the dragon. "The light of the Hammer of Tyr should be soothing to you or any other good creature of the Realms."

Ren interrupted before the dragon could reply. "Where's the body you want disposed of?" he asked.

"Oh, yes, the body," said the dragon, turning its head away from the light. "It's here behind me. The Lord of the Ruins died along with several of his minions. Only two escaped." The dragon shifted its bulk to one side. Behind it were several charred bodies, piled together in a heap like sacks of flour. "I was finally able to break his—"

"The Black Watch!" Ren exclaimed suddenly. Despite the damage done by the dragon's lightning breath, the chain mail on the bodies remained intact, and those Ren could see bore the sign of the mercenary guild employed by Cadorna. "Those are soldiers of the Black Watch, not—"

"And the dragon is the Lord of the Ruins," whispered Shal, starting to back away.

Ren shook his head.

"Try to get one of the ioun stones," Shal whispered. "A good dragon wouldn't care."

Ren nodded his head imperceptibly, then turned back to face the dragon. "Which one of the bodies belongs to the Lord of the Ruins?" he asked as he walked to the inner curve of the crescent, the side of the pool opposite the dragon, as if to examine the bodies from that angle.

"He's at the bottom of the heap," answered the dragon. "He was the first to die."

Ren knew at that moment that the dragon was lying. Mercenaries such as those of the Black Watch would go to their deaths in hopes of treasure, but the minute their employer was killed, they had no reason to stick around. Ren also saw, as he came closer, that the necks of the soldiers had been sliced, and their blood was draining into the brilliant waters of the pool. Ren stepped up to the hexagon at the crux of the crescent, noticing that it was just like the one in the diorama on the gnoll altar. Ioun stones were set in place at four of its six corners, while two empty sockets stood gaping, waiting to be filled. "That's quite a collection of ioun stones," he said, reaching his hand out toward the hexagon.

In a move of exceptional dexterity for so large a creature, the dragon swiveled its entire body to face the ranger. "Yes . . . remarkable, aren't they?"

Ren pulled Right from his boot. "I expect you've heard that I have an ioun stone," said Ren softly.

Avarice spread over the dragon's previously composed features. "Yes . . . so I've heard." The change in its manner was not even subtle. There was a definite edge in its voice, a demanding quality. Suddenly the dragon snaked its tongue out at Ren and hissed, "Give it to me . . . or die!"

The dragon thrust its huge head and neck across the pool toward Ren, its jaws wide open. Ren hurled Right at the creature, diving and rolling before his release was even complete. At that moment, a thundering bolt of electricity shot from the creature's gaping mouth and exploded against the wall behind where Ren had just stood. At the same time, the dragon bellowed in pain and anger as the dagger buried itself to the hilt in its right eye. Quickly Ren scrambled to his feet and sprinted around the pool to the dragon's flank, the only place where he might be safe from the creature's flailing tail.

The dragon spun back toward Ren, pivoting its giant mass of flesh as though it were weightless. Ren hurried to keep close to the creature's flanks, all the while attacking mercilessly with his short swords, jabbing and chopping at the tenderest flesh on the dragon's scaly body. Somehow he managed to keep close enough to the dragon that the creature could not use its breath weapons on him for fear of hurting itself.

Shal had not expected the dragon's reaction to be nearly so quick or so violent, and she was terrified for Ren, who kept scrabbling to keep himself just barely out of the dragon's reach. Shal had never fought a dragon before, but she knew the lore: Creatures of lightning could not be hurt by lightning. She extended her hands toward the dragon and rushed through the words to a spell she had memorized but never tried before. Instantly a grayblue cone of bitter cold extended from the palm of her hand to the exposed side of the dragon. Within the radius of the cone's circle, the dragon's scales immediately began to turn white, popping and snapping with the extreme cold. The dragon let out a roar and spun to attack the new offender.

Tarl leaped in front of Shal, the Hammer of Tyr extended before him. The dragon's lightning bolt ricocheted from the hammer to the pool and back again for several deafening, blinding seconds. The dragon roared in frustration as the lightning grew in intensity, still trapped between the hammer and the pool. So strong was its energy that it was all Tarl could do to maintain his grip on the magical artifact.

Suddenly the dragon turned its lightning to the stairway and landing. The timbers immediately burst into flame. Flames shot up and smoke billowed as the exit was destroyed. Then the dragon roared and charged Shal and Tarl, forcing Ren to scramble to keep out of the way of its vicious tail. It was small consolation that the dragon's lightning wouldn't work against the hammer. The beast was huge. Its size alone could kill, and it was lumbering right toward them. Tarl hurled the Hammer of Tyr at the beast with all his strength as Shal hurriedly conjured up an ice storm. The dragon was nearly upon them when the hammer slammed into its chest. Blue energy crackled and arced from the point of impact, and the dragon reeled back, shrieking with the pain of the blow. A moment later, sheets of ice plastered over its chest, neck, and the exposed parts of its haunches. It scrabbled awkwardly on the ice, its movements hindered by the energy-sapping cold. It shook like a wet dog to rid itself of the bone-chilling cold and the nuisance pricking at its side, but it got rid of neither, and the glow from the blue hammer, now returned to Tarl's hand, was piercing its remaining good eye.

The possessor, Tyranthraxus, struggled to keep the dragon reacting with intellect rather than instinct. Intimidation was critical. The attackers must not know the weakness of the body. Under his impetus, the great beast puffed itself up, roared, and launched itself forward again toward the source of its greatest pain. Tyranthraxus could feel and smell the terror of the two as he closed in with the dragon's body. One more time, he thought—do it one more time, and then this fight will be fair.

Unwittingly, Tarl obliged. He launched the Hammer of Tyr at the dragon again. No sooner had the hammer left

Tarl's fingertips than the dragon thrust its great head forward. Brilliant yellow lightning and the hammer's blue light shattered the stale air in the dragon's lair. Even as the dragon staggered back from the hammer blow, Tarl was at the receiving end of a blazing yellow lightning bolt. The cleric's body slammed backward as though hit by a giant hammer and was driven flat against the wall. The smell of his flesh smoking and burning filled the air, and the Hammer of Tyr fell to the ground as his body slumped limply against the wall.

Shal felt something snap inside her. She screamed loudly, but she did not look back at Tarl. She aimed her fingers straight for the creature's mouth. Instantly flames jetted from her fingertips. The dragon's head jerked back as the fire whooshed around its face, its lower jaw fried clear through. Shal cast a special Magical Shield spell and called for the Wand of Wonder even as the dragon shrieked and brought its head back down to launch more lightning.

Ren had never ceased in his attack with his short swords. Again and again, he stabbed deep into the dragon's tough hide. When he saw Tarl hurled against the wall, his already frenzied attack became even more furious. Working his swords like a mountain climber's picks, Ren scaled the dragon's back. The gigantic tail slapped and flailed nearby, and when Shal's flames sent the dragon's head snapping back, it was all he could do to hang on and drag himself to the base of the dragon's neck, where the tail was no longer a threat. His legs clinging to the beast's broad neck, he used all his strength to plunge the two short swords deep into the tendons between the dragon's shoulder blades.

The dragon shrieked and roared in agony and rage. Yellow lightning shot from its mouth, only to be reflected off Shal's magical shield. An instant later, the dragon threw its head back as its own lightning returned and sizzled the flesh of its underbelly. It shrieked once more, flailing its tail and shaking its shoulders violently to try to rid itself of Ren, who had called for Right and was now stabbing with his two magical daggers.

Pain dictating its movements, the creature wagged its head, gulped a mouthful of fluid from the pool, and sprayed a jet of yellow acid breath at Shal through its drooping jaw. "Protect from poison!" Shal screamed, and she raised the Wand of Wonder. A million and more yellow droplets of poison hung suspended in the air for a fraction of a second, and then the cavern exploded with a riot of beating wings, as each droplet became a brilliantly colored butterfly. Under other circumstances, the sight would have been breathtakingly delightful, but now the thousands upon thousands of butterflies served only to reduce visibility to zero.

Ren continued to battle by feel alone, his magical daggers slicing through the dragon's thick scaly hide as if it were butter. He stabbed and sliced as fast and hard as his arms would move, scooting ever higher up onto the dragon's neck, hoping to find its jugular. Shal lowered her magical shield and cast another Burning Hands spell, aiming by memory for the dragon's abdomen, below where she had last seen Ren. Jets of flame shot from her fingers, and thousands of butterflies popped and burst, caught in the magical inferno. The dragon screamed, an almost inhuman scream, as the flames struck and spread across its chest. Just then one of Ren's daggers ripped through tendon and sliced through an artery in the creature's neck. It reared high on its hind feet, then pitched itself over in its agony, slamming Ren to the ground beside it. It clambered tentatively to its feet, flailing wildly with its tail at the smell and presence of the ranger. With all the force left within its pain-racked body, the dragon tail-slammed Ren against the nearest wall of its lair.

Shal could feel, could hear, the big man's bones shatter

as his body thwacked hard against the stone wall, and she could see, even through the haze of the remaining butterflies, that he was not moving. She leveled her hands at the dragon again, even as it turned its head to attack her, and let loose with a fireball. Fueled by her fury, the fireball was huge and white. It burst square against the dragon's already injured face and neck, and flames raged from its snout down its torso.

The creature spun wildly, crazy and blinded from the pain. By instinct or luck, it caught Shal with the tip of its tail as it spun, and she was hurled back against Tarl's charred body. For a moment, Shal saw only blackness, and she couldn't catch her breath. She knew she needed to finish the dragon off now, before it finished her, but pain and fear froze her body even after her vision cleared. She remained paralyzed, literally waiting to die, but to her surprise, the hulking creature failed to take advantage of her helplessness. Instead, it scrabbled backward and slid into the crescent-shaped pool. Her heart leaped as she realized the dragon must be retreating, perhaps even dying.

But her revelry was short-lived as she saw the snout come up from the golden water, and the neck after it. The dragon's jaw was no longer dangling. There were no frostbitten or charred scales, no gaping bloody wounds high on its neck. The dragon was whole once more, perfectly healed, and it was coming up out of the pool toward her. Shal screamed soundlessly. She had no spell, no words. But she heard Cerulean's cry loud and clear: *The ring! Wish it dead!*

Shal closed her eyes and wished with everything in her. She wished the damnable creature dead.

With its next lumbering step, the dragon toppled to the ground. It was in the best of health, but its heart stopped cold, and the body was dead in the fraction of a second that it had taken Shal to wish.

When they saw the dragon fall, Cadorna and Gensor came out of their hiding place in the next room. They didn't know what had killed the dragon, nor did they care. Cadorna would assume power over all of Phlan and more, and Gensor would practice magic to his heart's content. "Be sure all three are dead," Cadorna instructed quickly, and he walked up to the dragon to touch it and pay a moment's respect to its legacy of power.

Before his fingers ever touched the creature's cold hide, Cadorna screamed. It was the scream Tyranthraxus had heard through the millennia each time he entered a new body. The scream of a being possessed.

To Tyranthraxus, it was a glorious sound. He relished it for a brief moment as he pushed Cadorna's thoughts of power from his mind and replaced them with his own, which were subtler, infinitely more interesting, and grounded in thousands of years of experience. Tyranthraxus's immediate desire was to get himself out of range of the mage-woman who had just killed his previous body. If she could kill a dragon, she could undoubtedly kill a man, and Tyranthraxus could not afford to risk another possession so soon. As much as he hated to leave the power he had gathered here behind him, he knew the secret now of the Pool of Radiance and the ioun stones, and it would only be a matter of time before he could possess them again. Without so much as a nod to Gensor, who meant nothing to Tyranthraxus, the possessed Cadorna leaped into the golden waters of the Pool of Radiance, calling on its magical energies to teleport himself and his possessor to a place far away.

"No!" Gensor shouted. Gensor and Cadorna had both seen the power of the magical hammer. They had both watched as the dragon emerged from the waters completely healed, and Gensor was not about to let Cadorna take all the pool's energy for himself. The mage threw back his hood and dived in after Cadorna. But where golden fluid had boiled with incalculable energy only seconds ago, there was only plain water . . . deep, icy water. Tyranthraxus had absorbed all of the pool's magical energies.

Gensor knew nothing of Tyranthraxus. He didn't even know what had happened to Cadorna. But he did know what was hidden from sight at the bottom of the pool. The mage came quietly to the surface of the pool and uttered a spell to make himself invisible before climbing out of the cold water.

Gensor watched silently as Shal slowly recovered enough to begin to function again.

She turned first to the charred body of the cleric. Tears streaming down her face, she poured the contents of two healing potions on the priest. Much of his flesh mended, but still he did not move. She retrieved his hammer and lifted it in her hands. She screamed her words: "You healed your servant at Valhingen Graveyard so he could die here? You told him to follow me so he could be killed by my enemy?" Shal pointed the hammer at Tarl and cried, "Heal him! Please, heal him!" She dropped her head, lowered her arms, and wept unashamedly. She didn't even notice as the hammer began to glow. Instead, she felt her arms raise with its power, and then she saw the blue aura. It was a warm, almost turquoise shade, and it bathed the cleric in its gentle light.

Tarl's first view was of Shal, tears running down her face, the dragon stretched out behind her, and the Hammer of Tyr glowing in her hands, and he knew she had won. He reached up, pulled her close, and held her tight. He closed his eyes to hold back his own tears as healing energy pulsed through him to her bruised body. The exhaustion from having pressed her spell-casting abilities to their limit slowly left Shal as she and Tarl shared a tremendous warming of flesh and spirit. It was several minutes before Tarl opened his eyes again. His eyes fell on

Ren, still slumped against the wall behind the pool.

Tarl rushed to his friend. Ren's body was twisted. There were bends in his legs and arms where there were no joints. No simple laying on of hands would heal the big ranger. The cleric pointed to the hexagon with the ioun stones, and Shal rushed around the pool to get them. With two stones in each hand and the Hammer of Tyr before him, Tarl set out to heal his friend. Each and every healing was a miracle, but Tarl felt an overpowering sense of awe this time as bone melded to bone, tissue mended itself, and flesh and spirit healed, wholly, completely, flawlessly.

The three sat together silently in the cavern until Tarl finally asked what happened. Ren told the story as he had seen it, and then Shal took over, describing the dragon's final moments and Cadorna and Gensor's insane plunges into the pool. "I looked for them when I brought you the ioun stones. There's nothing there. The pool's energy must have turned against them somehow. They're gone, and the pool is filled with ordinary water."

Tarl and Ren went to the side of the pool and looked for themselves. The water was a quiet gray-blue. The surface was completely calm, except for an occasional ripple where a butterfly was struggling to lift itself out of the water. For a moment, Ren thought he felt something, a whisper of movement nearby, but he turned and saw only a whirl of butterflies rising from the cavern floor, as though disturbed by a gentle wind.

"Well," said Ren, returning to Shal's side along with Tarl, "are we ready to celebrate? I mean, the Lord of the Ruins is dead. You did it. You killed the real murderer of Ranthor and Tempest. Cadorna's gone. Tarl has the Hammer of Tyr. What do you say we find a way out of this place?"

"Cadorna and Gensor came from there." Shal pointed to a doorway that blended into the cavern wall so inconspicuously that a person had to look hard to see it. "But what about returning to Phlan? Aren't there going to be more Black Watch soldiers guarding the city?"

"Probably." Ren nodded. "But this time it will be different. Cadorna won't be there to keep our testimony from being heard. And remember, we still have all those documents from Yarash."

"Plus the fact that one of my brothers, an elder from the temple, was promoted to Third Councilman when Cadorna became Second. When Cadorna rose to First Councilman, he probably rose to Second," Tarl added.

"And now, with Cadorna gone, he must be First!" Shal concluded happily.

Tarl kept the four ioun stones from the hexagon for the temple. The hexagon itself was of pure gold, and Tarl and Shal agreed that Ren should take it, since he was no longer thieving for a living, but they found nothing else of value in the dragon's lair. When they left, the three discovered the body of the wizard Cadorna had killed, and Shal gathered up his spellbooks and notes as she had Yarash's. A handful of butterflies followed them out, then disappeared into the brightly lit afternoon.

On a whim, Ren went past the two dead ogres they had seen earlier and made sure the door with the dragon head was open. A brigade of butterflies—orange, yellow, blue, and green—flew out through the open door and followed the others into the light of a warm afternoon.

As they passed through the castle and then through the ruins of Phlan, they found signs everywhere of kobolds, orcs, gnolls, and other creatures, but left to their own devices, without the dominating influence of the Lord of the Ruins, the humanoids and monsters were not unified in their efforts, and even the few that did see the three passing had enough memory to know that they didn't want to mess with the party that even now they still called simply "those three."

As cleric, mage, and ranger made their return, they talked of the expansion the city would see with the artifacts of Tyr in their rightful place, the Lord of the Ruins vanquished, and the river flowing clean and pure into the bay. Shal hoped to return to Cormyr, to Ranthor's keep, for things she had left behind. Tarl promised to accompany her on the journey if she would just wait until he was sure Anton was healed, and she spoke earnestly of the possibility of returning to Denlor's tower and starting up his school again. After all, there was that huge library in the ruins that she had yet to explore. . . .

Shal and Tarl walked hand in hand, and Ren spoke wistfully of Jensena. Ren had asked Sot to keep an eye on her while she continued to recover and to be sure to find out where she was headed if she left. The innkeeper had agreed and even threatened to make Ren stay and scrub tables forever if he didn't hook up with her. "The woman needs your company," Sot had reasoned, "what with her friends gone and all." Ren hadn't disagreed. And, he felt certain, neither would Jensena. . . .

* * * * *

Back at the pool, Gensor had materialized quickly after the three departed, and his thin, pink lips were turned up in the biggest smile of his lifetime. In the depths of the pool he had found the dragon's hoard—gold and jewels that would fund his magical endeavors for a lifetime, magical items beyond his wildest imaginings, and spellbooks enough to keep him studying forever—and all magically protected from damage by the water. Who needed Cadorna?

♣ ♣

EPILOGUE

"You realize your name doesn't fit you anymore, don't you?" asked Shal.

Why? Because I no longer glow blue? I told you, I don't distinguish colors, so it doesn't matter.

"Well, it matters to me. I think Mulberry would be an appropriate name."

Mulberry? Cerulean hunkered his head down and plastered his ears tight beside his forelock. *Mulberry?*

"It's a little less pretentious, don't you think?" Shal pursued.

A lot less pretentious. Milbert or Herbert would put me in the same arena.

"Now, now. Mulberry's a beautiful color, and a splendid name. And if you're good, I won't even call you Mully for short."

Mully? Gads! Ugh! Kill me first. That's a cheap and dirty way of getting me to agree to the name Mulberry. . . .

"Oh, good, you like it! Then it's settled."

Shal reined "Mulberry" up to the hitching post before the seamstress's shop and dismounted. Before she was up the stairs, the spry woman was at the doorway.

"Your leathers could stand a little mendin', miss," she said critically.

Shal looked down at the velvety chimera-skin garments. They were so comfortable, she hardly remembered she had them on. "I guess they could at that, but actually I'm here about something else. I've been meaning to bring you something—a gift—ever since you sent me that beautiful nightgown. You can't imagine what it did to lift my spirits."

The woman cocked her head back almost to her back and broke out in unrestrained laughter. "Lass, you're more naive than I took you for! Sure as I'd love to give each and every customer a free garment, I'd not be in business long if I did that, now, would I?"

"You mean you didn't—?"

"No. 'Twas the lad that brought you, that young cleric fellow who had to be reminded to keep his eyes in his head. Truth is, he's got me makin' somethin' else for you right now. I asked him to get you here for a fitting, but he said it'd have to wait until you were ready. Well, as far as I'm concerned, this'd be as good a time as any. What do you think?"

Shal stood in open-mouthed astonishment. She might never have answered if her familiar hadn't nudged her from behind. *What are you waiting for, Mistress?*

"Tarl? Tarl had you make that nightgown? I never . . . I never . . ."

"Never suspected? Now you're puttin' on a show, miss! Get in here and try on this wedding gown before the price of lace goes up. I daresay it'll take a few yards to do you."

Shal stood motionless for a minute, and then waltzed up the stairs. "Take as many yards as you need! I'm not getting any smaller, you know!"

ABOUT THE AUTHORS

JANE COOPER HONG resides in Burlington, Wisconsin, with her husband Tsong-Ming, whom she met in a laundry in Taiwan, and her daughter, Aleta, whom she wishes she'd met the same way. For the last several years, Jane has made a living doing publicity and writing promotional copy, so her editor was advised to watch out for excessive words like "new" and "exciting" in this novel. Jane has edited books in the DRAGONLANCE series, among others, and written two short game pieces for TSR. *Pool of Radiance* is her first novel.

JAMES M. WARD was born on May 23, 1951. He started out reading Hardy Boys and Tom Swift books and has since become a huge fan of science fiction and fantasy. When asked about becoming a writer, he always replies, "If you aren't witty, brilliant, and insightful, you have to be persistent, dogged, and not shy. I will leave it to the world to figure out which one I am."

Jim has three genetically perfect male children—9, 18, and 19—and a charming wife. They live in a perfect two-story red brick home in a pleasant rural community.

Jim got his start in role-playing with the design of METAMORPHOSIS ALPHA, the first science-fiction role-playing game. He has been designing games and helping others to design them ever since.

Jim credits his start in gaming to learning to play poker with his dad and brothers. It wasn't long before he learned not to try for inside straights or to try bluffing his dad, he states rather ruefully.

When asked what he would like to do when he grows up, Jim always replies, "Commanding the starship *Enterprise* would be nice."

Jim has written, or collaborated in writing, numerous books for TSR.

DRAGONLANCE® *Preludes*

Darkness and Light
Paul Thompson and Tonya Carter

Darkness and Light tells of the time
Sturm and Kitiara spent traveling
together before the fated meeting at the
Inn of the Last Home. Accepting a ride
on a gnomish flying vessel, they end up
on Lunitari during a war. Eventually
escaping, the two separate over ethics.

Kendermore
Mary L. Kirchoff

A bounty hunter charges Tasslehoff
Burrfoot with violating the kender laws of
prearranged marriage. To ensure his
return, Kendermore's council has his
Uncle Trapspringer prisoner. Tas meets
the last woolly mammoth and an alche-
mist who pickles one of everything,
including kender!

Brothers Majere
Kevin Stein

Much to Raistlin's irritation, Caramon
accepts a job for both of them: they
must solve the mystery of a village's
missing cats. The search leads to
murder, a thief who is not all that he
appears, and a foe who is not what
Caramon and Raistlin expect.